ANGEL OF BROOKLYN

In January 1914, Jonathan Crane returns home to his village in the north of England with a rare thing—a beautiful, glamorous American bride.

Beatrice struggles to adapt to this cold, gray place and tries to befriend the young women who are her new neighbours. They are in awe of her—her foreignness, her blond hair, her smart clothes. Beatrice, born in Illinois, is a woman with a past. She has told them stories of her father, an amateur taxidermist, of her brother, a preacher, and of her friends back home in Brooklyn, but she will take the story of how she became the Angel of Brooklyn to her grave.

When the men leave to fight in the Great War, the women are left alone, the differences between them grow, and their fear and loneliness feed the jealousy they harbour for this mysterious newcomer. The years pass, the men are still not home and Beatrice finds her old life catches up with her—and, in a dramatic climax, proves to be her undoing.

ANGEL OF BROOKLYN

Janette Jenkins

WINDSOR

PARAGON

First published 2008
by Chatto & Windus
This Large Print edition published 2008
by BBC Audiobooks Ltd
by arrangement with
The Random House Group Ltd

Hardcover ISBN: 978 1 405 64999 5
Softcover ISBN: 978 1 408 41308 1

British Library Cataloguing in Publication Data available

Printed and bound in Great Britain by
CPI Antony Rowe, Chippenham, Wiltshire

For Simon

Be not forgetful
to entertain strangers:
for thereby some have
entertained angels unawares.

Hebrews 13:2

Anglezarke, Lancashire, England
December, 1916

A week before they killed her, Beatrice told them about the dead birds, the guillemot, the glass-eyed buzzards, the sparrowhawks in clusters on the mantelpiece. They were knitting scarves and balaclavas for the boys. Lizzie Blackstock was crying. She dropped twenty stitches.

'All those birds,' said Madge. 'I can't imagine such a thing.'

'Do you think it's snowing in France?' Lizzie asked. 'I can't remember. Does it snow a lot in France?'

Beatrice smiled, a thick grey scarf was trailing down her skirt. 'For sure it does, it's winter. But it'll be warmer in France. It's further south than here. It's always warmer in the south.'

'But they have mountains in France,' said Ada. 'They have the Pyrenees. People go skiing in the bloody Pyrenees.'

'Language.' Madge pretended to frown at her.

'My Tom doesn't like the cold,' said Lizzie. 'It goes straight to his bones.'

'You'd better keep knitting then,' said Ada. 'That looks more like a dishcloth than anything.'

They were quiet for a moment. Outside, the snow was falling fast, and the women were mesmerised by the fat dancing flakes, and the slow shutting out of the light.

'It muffles things,' said Lizzie. 'Have you ever

noticed how it muffles things?'

'It's pretty all right, until it freezes over,' said Madge. 'And I'm cold enough without it.'

'Aren't we all?' said Ada, rubbing at her fingers.

'I'm sorry,' said Beatrice. 'I tried.'

It was a draughty room, but she'd managed to light something of a fire. The women had arrived an hour earlier, with their needles and loose balls of wool. They were thinking of giving themselves a name, like The Anglezarke Army, The Warrior Ladies, or The Rescuers, but nobody could decide on one.

'We don't need a name,' Madge had said. 'Why do we need a name? It's just us, doing our bit for the boys.'

'It doesn't seem the same without Jonathan,' said Ada. 'This house. Does it feel too big without him?'

'I'm used to it now, though it still feels empty in the mornings,' Beatrice told them. 'No hustle and bustle, and all that English tea.'

'China,' said Madge. 'The tea comes from China.'

'Or Ceylon,' frowned Lizzie. 'It sometimes comes from there.'

'Don't you drink tea in America?' said Madge. 'What do you drink if you don't drink tea?'

'I like coffee,' said Beatrice. 'Good, strong coffee.'

'Well,' said Ada, slowly shaking her head. 'You might speak English and have the same coloured skin and everything, but it's the little things that turn you into a foreigner.'

Beatrice shrugged and wound the gramophone. The music made them smile, until it made them feel worse.

'Poor Butterfly,' said Lizzie. 'We used to dance to this.'

For a while, their fingers moved faster, the clock chimed the half-hour, and they listened to the fire, the way it popped and snapped inside the grate.

'Keep the home fires burning?' said Ada, rolling her scarf around the needles. 'What do they know?'

It was almost dark when they left. The snow had stopped, but the air was heavy, and Anglezarke reservoir was shrouded in fog as the women made their way across the snowy lane, slowly, arm in arm, stopping now and then, taking long, hard looks at the sky. The water made a licking sound.

MIGRATION

Anglezarke, Lancashire, England
January, 1914

In Anglezarke and Rivington, birds with beating hearts dived from the trees, startling her, the way they swooped so close, brushing over her shoulder. Jonathan laughed. He was leaning against the wall, lighting a cigarette.

'So what do you think? This is it. Anglezarke.'

She stood for a moment, her small gloved hands on the cold stone wall, watching the water as the breeze sent ripples through it. She shielded her eyes. In the distance, the trees were fine black bones.

'Well?'

'Yes,' she turned. 'I guess you were right, it is just like a picture, and so very, very quiet.'

'That's what you get for marrying an Englishman from the North,' he grinned. 'You get to live in that part of England where nothing ever happens.'

As they crossed into the lane, a horse and cart appeared around the bend, and the driver slowed down, clicking his tongue behind his teeth, pulling at the reins.

'Back then?'

'I told you I'd be back.'

'So, what's that place got that we haven't?' The man tutted as Beatrice went to pat the horse's sweaty muzzle. 'Oh, I wouldn't be doing that, miss. He's hungry. He'll have all your fingers off.'

'I'm used to horses. We have horses twice the size of him in New York.'

'We have horses twice the size of him right here, but they eat too much for my liking.'

'Jed, this is Beatrice, my wife.'

'We'd heard you'd wed a foreigner,' he said, flicking up the reins. 'Brown, black, yellow, we didn't know what to expect.' And as the horse stepped away, Jed looked over his shoulder. 'Well I never,' he winked. 'You're some souvenir. All I ever bring home from Blackpool is a stick of peppermint rock.'

* * *

That night in bed, he turned his face towards her, leaned on one elbow, and said, 'I think we should rehearse.'

'Now? Really? But I'm beat.'

'It'll only take five minutes.'

'All right, all right . . .'

He sat a little higher. 'So, Mrs Crane,' he smiled, 'tell me about yourself.'

She yawned. 'Once upon a time, my name was Beatrice Lyle.'

'Make it sound natural.'

'How's this? I was born in Normal, Illinois. My mother died in childbirth.'

'Having you?'

'Having me.'

'Go on.'

'My father was a teacher and an amateur taxidermist. My brother Elijah went to Chicago, where he became a preacher. I haven't seen him since.'

'And . . . ?'

'And when my father was killed in a house fire, I moved to New York.'

'Sounds terrible. How did it start?'

'A lamp. They say it could have been a lamp. Either that, or there was something wrong with the chimney. It sometimes made a whooshing sound. In New York I worked for a man called Mr Cooper. He had a booth on Coney Island selling picture postcards. Of course, I had no real experience, but he could see that I was honest. And that's where I met Jonathan. He was with Freddy, looking at the postcards. They were very popular cards.'

'I think I brought some back. The Steeplechase. The Boardwalk. You could put them into a scrapbook?'

'OK, I could do that.'

'And then we fell in love?'

'In Franny's Oyster Bar.'

'I couldn't help myself.'

'Neither could I. It was hopeless.'

They grinned at each other, pleased with the story, and lay back in the bed exhausted. Beatrice looked at Jonathan in the half-light; with his sweep of dark hair, his straight nose and teeth, he made her think of the man in the Arrow collar advertisements. She closed her eyes, resting her head on his shoulder. The bed had been made with fresh cotton sheets, and the dusky blue eiderdown smelled of English roses. She dreamed. After more than ten days at sea, she could feel the world tipping, but it was a comfortable kind of rocking, and the dreams were pleasant enough. Elijah was playing on the lawn whistling hymns through a fat blade of grass. The outhouse was there, with its pickling solutions and tubs of papier mâché. Her father was around, somewhere in the distance, waving his right arm, talking to a shadow. Then, just before she woke, she was back on the Island, laughing with Celina and Nancy, biting a chunk out of Marnie's giant hot dog.

'Grease!' Nancy yelped. 'You can't be smelling of grease!'

'Say, this whole place stinks of grease and onions.'

'Not in here it don't! Here, take this napkin, quick!'

The dream felt like real life, and when she opened her eyes, she put her fingers to her nose, but all she could smell was her sweaty morning skin, and the underlying hint of Pears' soap.

* * *

The next morning, finding herself outside a closed blue door, Beatrice rested her hand on the small brass knocker before giving it a tap; the door shuddered. Nothing. She tapped it again a little louder, and again, until eventually she heard footsteps and the door was opened by a surprised-looking woman wiping her hands on a dirty white towel.

'Yes?'

Beatrice swallowed nervously. 'My husband tells me this house is the store.'

'Store?'

'Shop?'

'What husband's that then?'

'Mr Crane.'

'Jonathan? Really? I'd heard he was back from his travels. They said he'd gone and got himself married, but I didn't believe them. He wouldn't do that, I said, but now it looks like he has done. And you must be her? The foreigner?'

'I'm Beatrice.'

'Ada. Pleased to meet you. I won't shake your hand, I've been gutting mackerel.'

Ada must have still been a young woman, but her scraped back mousy hair already had some grey in it; tall and angular, she had a long thin face and enormous pale green eyes.

'You can come in the front way today,' she said, 'but usually, you'd have to knock round the back. This front part, you see, is our own private abode.'

Private abode? Beatrice thought. *Did young Englishwomen really talk like that?*

Dipping her head, she followed Ada inside. The room was fuggy and, although the curtains were open, the windows were so small that the light had to struggle against the glass and the tightly leaded diamonds; she could just make out the embers in the grate, and the outline of the furniture. Ada watched her taking it in.

'The shop is at the back. Through here.'

The other room was light and airy. There were scales and well-stocked shelves. An advertisement for HP Sauce had been pinned onto the wall, and on a scrubbed pine table was the row of headless mackerel and a plate of oily guts.

'My husband does the meat down in the cellar. He's not exactly a butcher. The butcher comes with his cart on a Friday. Eleven o'clock sharp. My husband can do you a rabbit, and the odd bit of game. But he leaves the bacon and such to the experts. He couldn't kill a pig. He doesn't have the know-how, or the equipment.'

Beatrice shook her head, not quite knowing what to say.

'Whatever must you think of me?' said Ada. 'I must smell awful.' She went to rinse her hands. 'Anyway, what can I get you?'

Beatrice couldn't think, then suddenly she remembered. 'Eggs?' she asked. 'Eggs and orange marmalade?'

'Hen eggs? How many? Half a dozen?'

'A half-dozen would be good.'

As Ada busied herself with the eggs, two women appeared at the top of the cellar steps. They were giggling and talking, but as soon as they saw Beatrice, they abruptly stopped, looking flushed and embarrassed.

'Got everything you wanted?' Ada asked them.

'Yes thanks,' said the one in the grey tweed coat. 'I'll settle up on Thursday.'

'Right you are then, Madge.'

'Oh,' said Beatrice, with a tremble in her voice. 'You're Madge? My husband's mentioned you.'

Madge pressed her basket tight against her plump waist, looking worried. 'And why would that be?'

'Your Frank might owe him something,' said the other woman, swallowing a smile.

'Oh no,' rushed in Beatrice, 'it's just that I only arrived here a few days ago, and he's been telling me about the people here, the ladies in particular, and he happened to mention there was a Madge, and an Ada.'

'What about a Lizzie?' The other woman smiled shyly, pushing her hand through her springy brown hair.

'Yes, Lizzie too.'

'Lizzie might look like a baby,' said Ada, 'but she's five years older than me.'

'Well, I'm Beatrice. Beatrice Crane.'

'You married Jonathan?' said Madge. 'You're the foreigner?'

'I'm an American.'

'I can't believe it,' said Lizzie. 'I really can't believe it.' Both women stared at her, their mouths slightly open in awe.

'I don't suppose you'll be putting the kettle on, Ada?' said Madge. 'We should do something. We should celebrate.'

Ada Richards took down a packet of tea and scooped some into a pot. 'The tea's on the house. That means free in English, Mrs Crane.'

'American,' said Lizzie, chewing over the word. 'Do Americans marry in churches?'

'As opposed to wigwams,' said Ada, pulling out the chairs. The women laughed as Beatrice looked at them and smiled, her heart pounding, her face a little warm.

'It's just that we thought he'd marry at St Barnabas, like we all did,' said Lizzie, quickly sitting down. 'And his ma and pa are buried in its yard.'

'We married in the town hall, in Brooklyn, New York.'

'The town hall?' said Madge, scratching her head.

'It's a fine town hall. Very grand and churchlike.'

Ada poured the tea. 'Churchlike is better than no church at all,' she said, pushing a cup towards Lizzie, who seemed most in need of refreshment.

'And town halls are very important.'

'Oh, I can just picture it.' Lizzie spooned in some sugar and began to stir vigorously.

'Bolton has a nice town hall,' said Madge. 'It looks like a palace.'

They drank their tea in silence for a while. The tap dripped slowly into the basin until it seemed that Ada could no longer stand the noise and went to turn it off. Beatrice felt hemmed in, her elbows nudging Madge at one side and Lizzie at the other; she could feel her cup rattling in its saucer.

'Your hair is very light,' said Madge suddenly. 'Have you used a rinse?'

'No,' said Beatrice, pulling at a strand. 'This is how it grows.'

'Well,' said Madge, 'it's lovely.'

'Didn't you mind?' said Lizzie. 'Didn't you mind, coming all this way, and leaving your family behind?'

'My mother's dead. And my father too.'

'So you're an orphan?' Lizzie's hand flew up to her mouth. 'I'm sorry.'

'You can't be an orphan at her age,' said Ada, not looking at Beatrice, but at the shelves behind her; she straightened a couple of tins. 'The thing is,' she went on, 'if Jonathan's father hadn't passed away like that, he never would have got itchy feet.'

'Still, it seems he's always wanted to travel,' said Beatrice. 'He collects guidebooks, and you should see them all, it's crazy, really, he has dozens of the things.'

'He's twenty-five years old,' said Ada. 'He went all the way to America. He came back. He's scratched his itchy feet.'

'Guidebooks?' said Madge. 'What do you mean,

guidebooks? He never goes anywhere. He won't even come on our annual outing to Morecambe.'

'And he loves potted shrimp,' sighed Lizzie. 'We always bring some back for him. Morecambe's famous for its potted shrimp. They make it for the King. Do they have it in New York?'

'We have all kinds of seafood.'

'But potted shrimp? Made with real butter?'

'Not that I remember.'

'Thought not. You see, it's a real English delicacy,' said Ada. 'So, what else have you got on that shopping list of yours?'

* * *

In the cellar, Jim Richards stood smoking a cigarette, his fingernails jammy with blood. Above his head, rabbit pelts hung like shapeless stoles, and across the scored table, the shiny limbs glistened in the swinging yellow lamplight.

'I know who you are, Mrs Crane,' he said. 'I've been listening in.' He sniffed, wiping his hands across his messy front, cigarette sticking to his dry bottom lip. 'Hope all this gore doesn't offend you?'

'Not at all. In fact, I'm kind of used to it, my father was fond of taxidermy. It's not for the faint-hearted.'

'You're not squeamish then?' He raised his narrow eyebrows. 'Rabbit only today. Mind you, there's a lot you can do with a bunny. Have it on the house as a welcome-to-England present. And here's a foot for luck.'

She nodded her thanks quickly, as he slammed down the knife. The foot felt warm and bony in her hand.

Back upstairs, Madge and Lizzie had gone.

'Didn't you want an onion?' said Ada. 'You can't make a good rabbit stew without an onion.'

* * *

Later, sorting through her wardrobe, Beatrice stopped to press her cheeks against the collars of her dresses. She put her shoes and boots in pairs, slipping her hand inside, feeling the ridges her toes had made, examining the soles, wondering if a little piece of Coney might have made it over here. She found the menu from Franny's Oyster Bar and, lying across the bed, she started reading it out to the wall.

' "Open all year round! Walk right in and get yourself a real fresh taste of the ocean! We have the biggest juiciest clams. We have oysters with pepper sauce, oysters with lemon zest, West Coast octopus, sea urchin eggs, blowfish tails, crawfish, winkles, ink squid, barn-door skates, salmon cheeks, cod cheeks, cod tongues, sturgeon liver, blue-shark steak, squid stew, clam chowder, lobster tails." ' She threw the menu down. 'Franny Nolan was my friend and she'd have done potted shrimp if I'd asked her.'

* * *

Anglezarke stretched out into moorland, scrubby hills, grey, violet, black-brown in the distance. Its water sat brooding, waiting for the light to start bouncing off those small choppy waves, bringing it to life.

Liverpool felt as far away as America, with its docks, and the movement, that thick bitter brine, and the fumes that settled in the air, hanging like a stained piece of cloth, in yards where she'd seen couples kissing behind Costa Rican crates and off-duty sailors queuing for new tattoos. Of course, she'd heard all the screaming, the belly-laughing, two boys fighting, then four, crashing, dark faces, men snapping braces, and women with too much rouge and feathers in their hair, weaving arm in arm, like showgirls after the show.

'I thought that was England,' she told Jonathan, who'd finally arrived home in the car, his face burning red from the cold.

'Liverpool? What do you mean? Of course that was England.'

'It looked interesting.'

'What, that filthy place? No one goes to Liverpool, unless they're on their way to somewhere else.'

'We could travel? You have all those little guidebooks just sitting on your shelf.'

'But we've only just got here, my darling. You'll get used to Anglezarke eventually. Come now, hop in and I'll show you some of the countryside in this beautiful motor car—my father gave it to me, you know, said I should enjoy it. '

Beatrice stepped into the passenger side, slamming the door behind her.

'Forget the damn countryside. I want to see some buildings.'

'Fuel isn't cheap. We can't go too far.'

'All right, OK, any building will do, just so long as it's not in a field.'

*　　*　　*

The thin gravel road circled the reservoir, winding into town, where the buildings were small, crouching against the road with all their shutters closed.

'Look at them,' she sighed. 'They hardly scratch the sky.'

He showed her his office, above the printing shop, with its thick frosted glass and the painted gold scroll saying *Bonds*. A shop selling neckties promised credit, value for money and real silk linings. A closed cafeteria had its board still up, with a chalked *High Teas, Bean Soup and Freshly Cut Sandwiches*.

At the edge of the pavement, boys folded their arms and squealed at the sight of the motor.

'Are they loons?' she asked.

'Just boys.'

'Could have fooled me.'

'Boys in New York are the same.'

'In New York,' she told him, 'it takes more than an automobile to get them so excited.'

*　　*　　*

She wrote a letter home. She didn't like the paper she found in Jonathan's desk, it was far too thick and yellow; the ink smudged.

January 18, 1914

Dear Nancy,

England is empty. I am always hungry. I miss the little things, like saltines, muscatel, and music. We have a whole house to ourselves and no one either side. Imagine that. It sure is a one-horse kind of town. The noise comes from the animals. Sheep, cows, and birds. Lots and lots of birds. I do miss Clancy's ponies. I even miss the elephants. I never thought I'd miss the elephants.

The people here are strange. The young women talk and act so old. Oh you should hear them. They are wrapped up in each other and walk like the nuns at St Xavier's. But I am trying, Nancy.

We are having a party here Saturday night, and I have promised J that it will be nothing like the night at the Alabama Hotel, but that was a good night, wasn't it? The night when all the stars came out.

Well, Nancy, I must go heat more water. Washday here is a little like slavery, and I have the red arms to prove it.

Write soon like you promised.

Your best friend,

Your Bea x

*   *   *

Jonathan had six gramophone records.

'Caruso? Say, have you nothing lighter than this?'

'He's really very popular.'

'Sure he is, but he hardly starts the dancing.'

'There won't be any dancing,' said Jonathan. 'Remember? It's not that kind of party.'

Beatrice was trembling as she paced up and down, moving things. She'd chosen a plain blue dress and matching kid leather shoes. She was wearing a bracelet of freshwater pearls, drop pearl earrings, jasmine scent.

'Just keep things simple,' Jonathan told her, fussing with his cufflinks. 'No need for a neck full of clanking beads and whatnot.'

The kitchen was brimming with food, and she busied herself arranging it in the dining room.

'The girl could do this,' said Beatrice, straightening the plates.

'What girl?'

'The girl we need to help us run this house.'

'We said we wouldn't have a girl. We agreed.'

Sighing, Beatrice plumped up the watercress. She pushed the small veal pies into a circle, checking her fingertips for grease. 'It's hard for me,' she told him. 'I'm really not used to this way of life. Not any more. I lived in boarding houses, I bought all my food ready-made. We had radiators. Electricity.'

'Well, that's the New World for you,' he said.

'I have calluses.'

'You have hand cream.'

'Rose-scented calluses? Is that what I came to England for?'

By twenty past seven they were sitting side by side, hypnotised by the clock's loud tick and the pendulum.

'They'll come,' said Jonathan.

'Still, they sure like to keep us waiting.'

'They'll be here.'

'Does everything look all right?' she asked, screwing up her forehead.

'Everything looks perfect, my darling, and have you seen what I've put on the mantelpiece? I found those postcards. All of them. The Steeplechase. The Boardwalk. Luna Park by night.'

'Luna Park by night?'

'You sold me those postcards. That's how we met. I thought they'd like to hear about it.'

The doorbell rang and Beatrice stood up before quickly sitting down. Jonathan went to open the door.

'You stand when they come into the room.'

'Oh, I know that,' she said, standing up again.

* * *

They all came, as Jonathan knew they would. Before they'd had Beatrice to gawp at, they'd had his father, and, with their limp bunches of grapes and bottles of milk stout—'to put some flesh on your bones'—they'd brought their curious eyes, weighing up the ornaments, the paintings, the red Persian rug that sat in the room like a thick flying carpet.

Beatrice smiled meekly at all the congratulations, and the talk about foreigners.

'We thought you'd have skin like a gypsy, and look, you're whiter than me!'

'Have you always spoken English?' a man asked, narrowing his eyes.

'Oh, I'm afraid I can only speak American,' she smiled, but the joke fell flat, and the man backed away.

She tried to remember their names. Lizzie and Tom Blackstock. Madge and Frank Temple. Elsie Ward. Ada and Jim Richards (his bloody nails now scrubbed and full of carbolic, which he picked out all night). Lionel Bailey. Jed and Cora Matthews. The man in the corner was Jeffrey something. Then Mr Foxton from the quarry. Emily and Nathaniel. The man with the walking stick. Charlie.

Jonathan poured the ladies another glass of wine.

'Oh, we never usually,' said Madge, holding out her glass. 'My cousin's just joined the Temperance Society. What he'd make of all this, I don't know.'

'Ada makes a lovely lilac wine,' said Lizzie. 'It gives you such nice dreams.'

Candles filled the house with a buttery kind of light. Close to the fireplace, a man had all the attention. It was Lionel, with his small hunched shoulders and flat grey hair.

'All this electricity,' he was saying, 'we don't want it. It will make the birds fall out of the trees. Make fires. Create blizzards. And, you mark my words, it will hurt the innocent.'

'You really believe that?' said Frank.

'Believe it?' said Lionel. 'I know.'

'But electric light is just wonderful,' exclaimed Beatrice. 'It's everywhere. In Luna Park alone there are a quarter of a million light bulbs. It's a magical sight. Really it is. People stand gasping every night.'

'It's an amusement park,' Jonathan explained.

'An American amusement park?' said Frank.

'Yes. They call it the electric Eden.'

'Good heavens.' Lionel screwed up his eyes, as if all those lights had reached him.

'It's a marvellous place all right,' said Jonathan.

'Really? But what's so wonderful about an amusement park?'

'I don't know. They make you feel alive.'

Frank rolled his eyes. 'I like Blackpool. It tastes different.'

'Another drink?'

'Not for me,' said Lionel, putting down his glass. 'I have to be getting along. Being out at such a late hour only upsets my routine.'

Beatrice glanced at the clock. 'But it's only just gone nine.'

'Ah.' He tapped at his pocket watch. 'I've things to do. The dogs don't know what a party is. They'll want walking. And I have to read a certain amount of my good friend Sir Arthur Conan Doyle, before my brain will tell me that I'm tired enough for sleeping.'

'You really know Conan Doyle?' said Beatrice.

'We correspond from time to time but we haven't met, so to speak, in the flesh. Well, I'll take my overcoat from you now, and bid you all goodnight. Another Mrs Crane in the house, eh? I'll have to get used to it. I dare say that I will. You are indeed a pleasant-looking woman, I can't deny you that. Goodnight to you, goodnight.'

Beatrice could feel the draught from the door, making the candles flutter like gigantic yellow moths, before grabbing the back of her neck.

'Are people helping themselves to food?' she shivered.

'Oh, yes,' Ada told her, 'they've been nibbling all evening. The pies look very tempting. Pork?'

'Veal.'

'Well,' she smiled, 'they almost look too perfect.'

Beatrice found the men in a huddle drinking port and puffing at their cigars. Jonathan smiled as she walked into the small clouds of smoke.

'Now here she is again. My wife. She's quite the conversationalist. She'll certainly tell you what's what.'

'Are ladies allowed inside the smoking room?'

'Of course,' said Jeffrey, offering her a chair. Pale and blond, with wide grey eyes, he moved between the furniture like a dancer with oil on his shoes.

'What we'd all really like to know,' said Tom, 'is how did you find him? Was he somewhere making a daft silly fool out of himself?'

'A what silly fool? What was that word?' Beatrice laughed, scratching the side of her head. 'Another strange English word?'

'Well, it means thick in the head, of course. Acting silly.'

'Oh, I get you,' she smiled. 'No, he wasn't "acting daft" as you say. Not then anyway.'

The men laughed and sucked on their cigars.

'So how did you meet?' asked Jeffrey.

'I sold him some postcards.'

'You don't look like a shop girl,' said Frank.

'I worked in a booth, on the boardwalk, at Coney Island.'

'The what?'

'Promenade. She means promenade.'

'I had to work. You see, my mother died when I was born, and my father was killed in a house fire. My brother Elijah went to Chicago to preach. He was drawn in by the church and I haven't seen him since. After that, I just had to get away. And I chose New York.'

'Why New York?' Jeffrey pulled a strand of tobacco from his pale top lip.

'I read plenty of magazines and people in

magazines talk a lot about New York. And you know something, they're right. It's a wonderful tall place, full of opportunity. I was lucky. A man called Mr Cooper let me work in his booth. I hadn't much experience, but he could see that I was honest.'

'Aye,' they nodded.

'You look honest all right,' Frank winked.

'And that's how we met. Jonathan bought some postcards.'

'These,' he said, fanning them out. 'These are the very cards I bought from her.'

'So, you sold him these postcards,' said Jeffrey, 'and that was it? Did Cupid shoot you right in the heart there and then?'

'More or less,' said Jonathan, looking at his wife.

'Mary Pickford's American,' said Frank.

As they handed round the cards, they glanced at her, feeling the swell of the ocean, the taste of the exotic pouring through the ink.

'It does wear you out after a while,' said Jonathan, swirling his glass of port, throwing the last thick bite of his cigar onto the fire. 'You never saw so many people at one time.'

'Not like here,' said Jeffrey with a frown. 'I do hope you'll like it here, Mrs Crane.'

'Why shouldn't she?' said Frank. 'Life's just grand, and the air's clean. There's plenty of work for us and all the Irish. We've just bought ourselves a fancy new gramophone. Wonderful thing it is. We dance all night, me and Madge, and it sends the kiddies to sleep.'

'I met your little boy,' said Beatrice. 'He gave me a daffodil.'

'I'm sure he couldn't help himself,' said Jeffrey.

'Aye,' said Tom. 'A flower, for a flower.'

By eleven, there was a lull in the house. Glasses stained with lines of red and amber had been pushed across the table. Ashtrays held pyramids of warm grey powder. There was a stain on the tablecloth, a tattered port wine daisy. Eyes were being rubbed. Lizzie had taken off her sister's borrowed shoes.

Madge was in the kitchen. 'I wonder,' she said, licking pastry from her lips. 'Could I make up a plate for Mary? It seems a shame she missed out. I don't suppose you've met her? She's ill. Never leaves her room.'

'She doesn't? Well, of course, go right ahead, take whatever you think she'll like,' Beatrice told her. 'What's wrong with her?'

'No one really knows.' Madge forked up some ham. 'But she's as pale as a sheet all right, and her legs are thinner than cotton. We all look in from time to time.'

'Maybe I could too?'

'Good idea. She needs entertaining.'

Beatrice watched Madge making up the plate with cold meats, Lancashire cheese and a broken slice of pie.

'Have you got a tea cloth I can borrow?' she asked. 'To keep the food from spoiling?'

Ada appeared, grinning triumphantly. 'Here, use this,' she said, handing her a large paper bag, printed with the words *Swift & Son, Fine Bakers and Confectioners*.

'Thanks,' said Madge. 'That's very handy, that is.'

* * *

* * *

'They were all mixed up,' said Beatrice, looking hard into the fire. 'Mr Cooper told me about the rich and poor in England, and those in between, and how they all lead very separate lives. Tonight they were all mixed up.'

'It's like that here. I admit that it's strange, it isn't at all usual, but everyone knows everyone.'

'Apart from me.'

'Apart from you,' he said.

Jonathan yawned. He could feel his head crackling. The cigars had made his throat ache.

'Congratulations, my darling,' he said, stretching out his arms to her. 'It was a success. You pulled it off all right. I'm going up. What about you?' His shoulders made a clicking sound.

'I think I'll stay down here.'

He kissed her on the forehead. 'Well, goodnight for now, my darling.'

As soon as he'd gone, she closed her eyes and pictured her America. She folded her hands in her lap and willed herself to relax, until eventually the images came floating, and she was standing outside the Galilee Hotel, 16 July 1911, wearing a cheap grey suit, her coat all creased, and a sign in the window (cardboard, handwritten) said 'Be Good or Begone'. She didn't go inside. She was just too tired for that.

Yawning, she thought of other, smaller things. Ice, spaghetti vongole, the sound of the breeze as it flicked at the awning, and those long afternoons sipping lemon-flavoured tea through little lumps of sugar held underneath her tongue.

She looked at the sky through the window and shivered. The wind was whistling through the trees. The party was still in her head, the women laughing behind their hands, the men clasping their fingers in knots behind their backs, rocking on their heels, faces twitching. Cold fish. That's what Nancy called Englishmen. Tight lips. Insipid. Voices stuck somewhere deep inside their throats. And Nancy knew about these things, because she'd kissed at least half a dozen, behind McCauley's Tavern, though a couple of those were Irish, with hair like wet coal, and eyes the colour of water.

* * *

Jonathan couldn't sleep. His skin felt tight with whisky and tobacco, and the starch in the sheets made the cotton creak. Before America he'd slept in this room. From here, through the walls, he'd heard the nurse padding up and down, his father's chest wheezing, then coughing, retching, and crying out for Eliza, his long-dead wife, and sometimes a woman called Margaret. Was the nurse called Margaret? She was known as Miss Hopkins. He'd asked her once. 'No,' she'd said, 'I'm Catherine.'

Now all he could hear was the wind outside, pushing at the glass. He could see his old bear with its broken leather nose sitting on the washstand. A gift from his father the week his mother died. It was a stiff old thing, with a bony woollen spine and chipped glass eyes. He was seven years old, and of course, the bear hadn't made it any better.

'Still awake?' said Beatrice, suddenly standing in the doorway.

'Hmm.'

'Well, I'm here now,' she smiled.

'I can see that.'

'Are you glad?' she said. 'Glad I came to England?'

'Of course I'm glad. England's always needed a Mrs Beatrice Crane.'

'Is America missing me?'

'America?' he said, loosening the sheets. 'I'm sure all the men on the Island are wearing black armbands and weeping into their whiskey.'

*   *   *

St Barnabas Church, in nearby Heapy, sat cold and grey in the drizzling Sunday morning.

'Where's the steeple?' said Beatrice, tipping back her head. 'I thought all English churches had a steeple? It looks more like a schoolhouse to me.'

'It doesn't matter what it looks like, darling,' said Jonathan, carefully avoiding the puddles. 'It's what goes on inside that really counts.'

They walked side by side up the path, Beatrice folding her hands deep inside her sleeves as the rain fell like a web.

'My family's grave.' He suddenly pointed to a tall white slab beside a bent lilac bush. 'My mother, father and my baby brother Thomas are buried there, though today is certainly not the day to be standing mourning beside it, we'd only catch our death of cold and be joining them too soon.'

Inside, people shuffled and coughed. Women rattled through their handbags, rooting for lozenges. Men's hands ticked and trembled wishing they held cigarettes. Of course heads turned, Beatrice was the striking foreigner, the talk of the village; they'd been waiting to catch a glimpse of her, and now she was right here in front of them. She recognised Jeffrey and he waved with his fingers. Ada and Jim pretended they hadn't seen them arrive, but of course they had, and Beatrice could see Ada nudging Jim's elbow, his neck flushing into his collar.

As the Reverend Peter McNally stepped behind the lectern he lost his footing and dropped his sermon sheet. He had oiled black hair, a narrow white face, and Beatrice wasn't impressed with his voice, a droning monotone, but she went along with him, singing the hymns, the numbers chalked up on a board, religious arithmetic, screwing her eyes at all the tiny grey print in the prayer book.

'Let us pray for all the lost souls in the world. Those poor damned natives who have never heard the name of Jesus Christ Our Lord.'

After the final hymn, an out-of-key 'He Who Would Valiant Be', the reverend shook hands with his congregation, sheltering from the rain inside the vestry.

'Oh, I've heard all about you,' he said, taking Beatrice's hand with a playful kind of squeeze.

'Word travels fast.'

'Like a telegraph. You are the American? The new Mrs Crane?'

'You make it sound like I come from the moon,' she smiled.

'But, Mrs Crane, I have seen the moon. I have never seen America.'

'Well, it does exist. Really. First port of call after Ireland.'

'Her brother is a preacher,' Jonathan added a

little too brightly. 'And although he's a lay preacher, he trained for many years with the Church.'

'The Church of the United States of America?' the reverend winked. 'A most inventive branch.'

* * *

February 18, 1914

Dearest Bea,

I have never been much of a letter writer, but here goes. The last real letter I wrote was to Stanley, telling him it was over. You remember that? I was too much of a coward to tell him face to face. I was in love with that fiddle player. The Russian. That lasted all of five minutes.

We are all fine here. I'm still with Cooper and Co. A girl called Jessie has your old job. She's pretty enough, and fair, but she's the argumentative type. She used to work the trapeze at Eli's Circus, but then she put on weight. Don't get me wrong, she isn't even plump, but you have to be as skinny as a six-year-old to go up on the wire.

Marnie says hello. She's been busy these last few months and has just got herself married, so she sits all day in the beauty parlor, preening, drinking hock, and buffing up her nails. She went and married Lenny the barber. You know the one? He has a scar on his face like a sickle? She's already wife number three, and him not yet forty. I've told her to be careful. Well, we all have.

Lottie has landed herself a job. We had to laugh. Come April, our perfect Miss Lottie will be the microscope girl at the Minsky flea circus. How glamorous is that? We've worn out all the flea jokes, and the scratching.

I hope you are well and happy, being a good English lady. Jonathan's one of the good guys, and you know I think that.

I'm writing this outside Franny's. It's a fine and blowy day. Smell the paper, Bea. It's flapping on the table, and the table's none too clean, and you know the smell of mussels never goes away.

Better go and see if Sally's opened up (Irish girl, Marnie's replacement). How come you're all getting married? Poor little me, left high and dry on the shelf.

Take good care of yourself, princess.

Love and luck to you both,

Nancy x

* * *

Spring arrived slowly, then suddenly it was the first weekend in May, and in Rivington girls were dressed in white and disgruntled boys had flowers in their hats. A brass band was playing underneath the chestnut tree, as the children danced around the maypole, making complicated tapestries. Around the field, families sat on blankets and deckchairs, with full wicker hampers, or knapsacks, and glasses of fresh lemonade, a penny a glass, proceeds going to the church roof fund.

'We've been lucky with the weather,' said Jonathan, stretching out his legs and circling his ankles. 'Real sunshine. We usually have the maypole in June, just to be on the safe side, but this year, the vicar put his foot down.'

Jeffrey had sidled over to Ada and Madge. He was wearing a daisy in his lapel. Pulling up his deckchair, he made sure he had a good clear view of Beatrice, who was fanning her face, and laughing.

'It's like her hands are dancing,' said Jeffrey. 'Don't you think that she's refined?'

'Refined?' said Ada. 'She's an American.'

Jeffrey turned to look at her, surprised by the sharp note in her voice. 'So what do you know about America?'

'They have natives,' she told him. 'And Mormons.'

'They also have salons, libraries, cities to rival our own. I once met a man from Boston. A professor. He'd written a journal about nervous diseases. He was most distinguished.'

'Nervous diseases?' Madge shuddered. 'What an awful thing to write about.'

'Not at all. He's lectured all over Europe. I met him in Glasgow when I was attending a design conference. We met in the connecting hall. I was admiring a painting; he was admiring something similar, on the other side of the room. We collided. He was most charming. He took me out for supper at his club.'

'Charming you say?' said Madge.

'Utterly.'

'It isn't the same as refined,' said Ada, narrowing her eyes.

Jeffrey moved his thumb across the daisy on his jacket. 'Well, I think she's lovely.'

The air was heavy with small talk and laughter, and voices caught in the breeze, drifting over the trees, and into the field beyond, where the farmer sat brooding over his best shire horse. The band members were wiping their foreheads and gulping lemonade, as applause came bursting from the coconut shy, where Tom had hit three in a row and won himself a ginger cake.

Lizzie, in a rush of good humour, pulled her blanket over to Beatrice and Jonathan.

'Shall we go and join them?' said Jeffrey. 'Would Frank and Jim mind? Perhaps we could all sit together?'

Madge said nothing, but gave a little shrug. Frank was on the other side of the wall, drinking beer with his pals from the quarry. Resigned, she and Ada gathered up their things, as Jeffrey went striding on ahead, with a neatly folded deckchair and his picnic.

'Last year we held it in June,' Lizzie was saying, 'but it drizzled all the same. Do you have a lot of rain where you come from?'

'We have all kinds of weather,' said Beatrice. 'You name it, we have it.'

'You must excuse us. In England, we talk a lot about the weather,' said Jeffrey, opening out his chair. 'I think it's because it changes all the time.'

They began pulling out their lunches. The children appeared. Billy and Bert for Madge. Harry and Martha for Lizzie.

'We'll eat ours by the trees,' said Harry.

'All right,' said Lizzie. 'Just don't throw it all to the birds.'

'Oh, I'm sure it's far too tasty for that,' said Beatrice. 'As you all know, I'm not much of a cook.

We have the baker to thank for most things that we eat.'

'Didn't your mother teach you how to cook?' asked Madge. 'Before she passed away?'

'I never knew her, she died the minute I was born,' Beatrice told them as she handed Jonathan a plate of bread and ham. 'My father never remarried. I did some cooking as a child, but of course it was nothing very special, and in New York it was easy, because I didn't cook at all.'

'You ate out all the time?' said Lizzie.

'Yes.'

'Wasn't that expensive?' Madge licked her lips. 'For a postcard seller?'

'Not at all. Thing is, you can get a little meal very cheaply. Anything from a bag of hot nuts, to a plate of steak and salad.'

'Like Morecambe?' said Lizzie. 'I expect it's just like Morecambe. You can get shrimps in paper cones, whelks and fried potatoes, and you can eat them outside. Food tastes better outside, don't you think?'

'I'm not keen on outside eating,' said Ada, polishing an apple on her sleeve.

For a few long seconds, the sun was eaten by clouds, and Beatrice felt the goosebumps springing up along her arms. Looking at the sky, she smiled at the warmth that suddenly reappeared, when a breeze sent all the clouds scuttling.

'A lotus,' she said. 'That cloud is shaped like a lotus.'

Madge looked puzzled. She couldn't see a thing.

'So where are all its legs?' said Billy.

'A lotus is a flower,' said Jeffrey. 'You're thinking of a locust.'

'I've never heard of a lotus,' said Tom.

'It's a blossom from the Orient,' said Jeffrey. 'Like the ones on Mrs Crane's fan. Have you been there?' he asked. 'It sounds like a fascinating part of the world. I hear everyone's very small.'

'Gosh, no,' said Beatrice, opening out the fan. The lotus blossoms were pretty, but a couple of them had smudged. 'This is just a cheap trinket, from Mr Wong's emporium in Brooklyn. He sells hundreds of these every day.'

'I think it's charming,' said Jeffrey.

'It is very pretty,' said Tom.

'I used to have a fan,' said Lizzie. 'Real silk.'

'I don't remember that,' said Tom.

'It was a twenty-first birthday present. I hardly ever used it. Then it broke.'

'You always were clumsy,' said Ada.

Across the field, the vicar stretched his bony legs, while women offered him cake, and hovered with the teapot.

'I hear your brother's a vicar?' said Madge.

'Not exactly. Elijah is what you'd call a preacher. He travels with his sermons. In Normal, Illinois, almost every other son wants to go into the Church. It's either that, or the cannery.'

'I can certainly see the attraction,' said Jeffrey. 'Have you ever been inside the vicarage? It's huge and full of silver. He has a housemaid, and a secretary, not to mention the gardener, who doesn't charge a penny, and who cuts the vicar a fresh buttonhole every morning. I could do with some of that.'

'You're doing all right, old chap,' said Jonathan. 'You're hardly in the workhouse.'

'But look at all that fawning. They just won't

leave him alone.'

'You'd soon get tired of it.'

'Try me. I could get very fond of sycophants.'

Beatrice leaned back on her hands as a ladybird tripped across her fingers. She closed her eyes. Somewhere over her head there were birds that sounded like seagulls. The afternoon wore on. Boys full of pie and warm lemonade threw down their hats, and girls tripped over their new spring dresses, scraping their knees. Madge left early, pulling Frank home, with the promise of cold beef and pickle, and a hidden bottle of stout. The vicar had long since disappeared inside the sanctuary of the vicarage, and with the shades pulled down, his trousers loosened, he dreamed of a chubby girl called Iris, skinny-dipping in the reservoir.

'I'd like to walk home,' said Beatrice.

'But you have the motor car,' said Lizzie. 'You could be back in ten minutes.'

'I'd really rather walk.'

'Would you mind if I walked with you?' Jeffrey asked.

'I wouldn't mind at all.'

'You have a deckchair and a basket,' said Lizzie. 'However will you manage?'

'I'll take them in the car,' said Jonathan. 'And I'll trust Jeffrey with my wife.'

* * *

They walked slowly, making their way around families rolling up their blankets, brushing grass from their clothes, pressing at their faces. The sun had made them tender.

The lane was overgrown in parts. A woman in a

red skirt was letting out her chickens.

'These hens don't lay in the same place two days running,' she said, rolling up her sleeves.

Smiling, they walked in silence for a while. Beatrice liked looking at the hedgerow, the cow parsley, wild garlic, and the small, almost hidden tufts of lily of the valley with their tiny scented flowers and glassy emerald leaves. Behind them, they could hear the faint shouts and screams of the children in the field, the farmer whistling for his dog.

'This must be quite a change for you,' said Jeffrey.

'Well, there sure is a lot of green around here, hardly any buildings to speak of, and the people seem so . . .' She bit her lip carefully, and glanced at Jeffrey, wondering if she should continue. 'Well, they seem awful uptight,' she added, looking at her feet.

'Yes, yes, you're right, of course. Are you unhappy here? Are they making you unhappy?'

'Oh no,' she said. 'It isn't that at all. It's just that I'm used to a different way of life altogether, and I'm used to crowds, to watching people enjoying themselves, though of course there were plenty of times when it would just grate on my nerves.'

'What was it like?'

'Chaotic. Crazy. A constant battle of noise.'

'How on earth did you put up with it?'

'There are quiet places everywhere, if you know where to find them.' Smiling, she picked some grass from her sleeve. 'And what about you? You don't look or talk like a farmer's son, or a quarryman. So?'

'I'm an artist,' he told her. 'Well, I illustrate

advertisements.'

'Sounds interesting.'

He smiled. 'It can be.'

'What about your family?'

'Like you, my parents are dead. Long dead. Influenza. My sister Agnes is married and living in Hampshire. Husband's a wealthy banker.' He pulled his face and shuddered. 'Has two delightful children.'

Beatrice laughed. 'And you live alone?'

'Quite alone. In Fox Cottage.'

'Ah,' she said, 'I know it.'

They could see the water in the distance. There were cottages to their right. By an open gate, three grey kittens were curled on a hessian sack, quivering in their sleep. The sky was softening as Jeffrey tapped her arm.

'Lionel,' he mouthed. And through the window, they could see him, hunched over the kitchen table, blowing eggs, holding them gently; he sent the soft insides dripping into a bowl. He couldn't see the two of them. He was concentrating, his hands trembling as he placed the hollow robin's egg delicately onto the cotton.

'My father didn't bother with the eggs,' she said, walking on. 'He went straight for the bird.'

'Really? My grandmother had a stuffed bird on one of her favourite bonnets. A tiny thing. It looked like it had just landed there, resting for a moment. I quite expected to see it taking off again.'

'Oh, they never do that.'

They walked towards the reservoir, past the cottage where Mary lived in bed.

'The water changes,' said Beatrice. 'Today it

looks like glass.'

'Would you like a closer look?'

They climbed over the stile, Jeffrey catching tight hold of her hand as she lifted her skirt a little. The trees were rustling, the water breaking gently over the small brown stones.

They walked up the bank of tufted grass with its sprinkling of daisies. Beatrice could just make out Jonathan unloading the empty hamper. She waved, and he raised up his arm.

'Just think,' said Jeffrey. 'The people of Liverpool will soon be filling their bathtubs with these little grey waves.'

'I like the look of Liverpool.'

'Well, I expect that after all those days at sea, any town or city would appear more inviting than great chunks of water and the walls of your cabin.'

'It had a feel to it,' she said, rubbing the back of her neck. 'Things were going on.'

'Oh, it's a lively place all right, and one that I shouldn't like to visit after dark, though I am told that one of my better known designs is currently plastered all over its walls.'

'How exciting,' she said, sitting on the grass. 'It must be a wonderful feeling. Like seeing your name in lights?'

'Hardly.' He hesitated, wondering whether to join her, worrying about the light-coloured cloth of his trousers. 'It's an advertisement for anti-bilious pills.'

She laughed. 'I'm sure they will change people's lives, or at least give some relief. Yes,' she said determinedly, 'your design will do a very great service to the people of Liverpool.'

'The bilious people of Liverpool,' he smiled.

'Whatever that might mean.' He sat down gingerly, though the grass felt dry enough. There was something of a breeze.

'You must miss home,' he said. Beatrice looked away. She could see Jonathan walking towards them.

'I miss people more than anything.'

'I miss people too. They go away. Move on.'

'Have you always been friends with Jonathan?'

'Yes. Mind you, I think we once fell out for at least a fortnight, over not being picked for the rugby team.'

'Who wasn't picked?'

'Me,' said Jeffrey. 'And of course, it was him doing all the picking, standing at the front, like he owned all the world.'

'You don't look the rugby type.'

'I'm not. I just wanted to be picked. Doesn't everyone?'

Jonathan came leaping over the stile. 'You're not still talking about the rugby team? At least you avoided the mudbath. And you know how much you hate getting dirty.'

Jeffrey suddenly remembered his trousers. Jonathan threw him a blanket. 'I came fully equipped. Blanket. Bottle of whisky. Three little glasses.'

They sat looking at the water, the sky streaked with clouds, a pale orange light.

'Whoever would have thought it?' said Jeffrey. 'Jonathan Crane, coming home from abroad, with a wife.'

'I didn't go looking. Beatrice just appeared.'

'Like a vision,' she laughed, taking another sip of her drink and exchanging a look with her husband.

The whisky felt warm and smooth on her tongue, but it burned at the back of her throat. 'What about you?' She turned to Jeffrey. 'Might you fall in love? Be married?'

'Love's one thing,' he said. 'But I really don't think that I'll marry.'

Jonathan threw a fistful of pebbles into the water. They skimmed and broke the surface like a necklace.

'Never say never.'

'I think I just did, didn't I?'

'More?' Jonathan held out the whisky bottle.

'It's May Day,' said Jeffrey. 'Means nothing to me, but we have to celebrate something.'

The air was getting cold, but they didn't want to leave. Jeffrey, throwing caution to the wind, removed himself from the blanket, so they could wrap it round their shoulders, and the three of them sat with the world looking fuzzy, lights appearing at windows, the slow spitting out of the stars.

'It's almost perfect,' said Beatrice, 'but if I close my eyes, there are some things that are missing.'

'Like what?'

'Like music, faint and in the distance. Faraway screams. The good kind. The smell of grease, burnt sugar and spicy chop suey.'

Jonathan slumped hard into the blanket. 'So, might I suggest that you don't close your eyes?' he slurred. 'That's the solution, wouldn't you say? Easy. Just keep the bloody things open.'

* * *

The room was so colourless that Mary's dark

brown hair looked startling where it lay on the white cotton shoulders of her nightdress.

'I'm sorry I didn't come sooner,' said Beatrice. 'It must be difficult, staying in bed all the time?'

'Not really,' said Mary. 'I'm used to it. I've become quite the typical invalid. I daydream. I lie looking at the sky, which I can just about see through the window, and I read. I especially like the works of Charles Dickens. *The Old Curiosity Shop* is a favourite of mine. Do you know it?'

'No, I'm not a great reader. I prefer magazines.'

'But you don't need to read. You have a proper life. And yes, I do get lots of visitors.'

Her mother appeared, huffing with a tea tray, putting it down on a small painted table. Beatrice could see only one cup and saucer.

'Tea doesn't suit Mary. She gets very overheated. I'll leave you to pour. I've brought milk and sugar. I don't know how you Americans drink it,' she shrugged as she left the room. 'Same as us, I suppose.'

Beatrice poured herself some tea. It was already well brewed and it made her lips curl.

'I prefer coffee,' she whispered conspiratorially.

Mary smiled. 'I've never tasted coffee. I haven't done a lot of things. Tell me something about yourself. About your life before Mr Crane. Take me away from the village.'

'I'm not much of a storyteller.'

'It isn't telling stories, it's remembering. Where were you born?' she asked. 'I have read about America. I've read all of Mark Twain.'

Beatrice put down her teacup. 'I don't know . . .'

'Please?' Mary looked pained and Beatrice knew

she was going to have to say something.

'All right,' she began carefully. 'I was born in Normal, in a state called Illinois. My mother died just a few moments later.'

'Oh, I'm sorry.'

Beatrice shook her head, looking at the rain as she began to tell Mary the story she'd heard from her father so often, it didn't seem real. About the woman who came to help with the birth, how she'd laid her mother out, made her brother Elijah some lunch, before pouring her father a drink from the emergency bottle of brandy, and then helping herself to a large one. When he went back upstairs to say goodbye forever to his twenty-one-year-old wife, the woman broke into the cabinet, taking a gold pocket watch, several dollar bills and a copy of *American Duck Shooting,* by George Bird Grinnell. It was a well-worn copy and not at all valuable.

For the first few years of their lives, the children were passed around their grandparents and a few well-meaning citizens of Normal. Their father was a teacher, but sometimes he stayed at home, and by the time Beatrice was six he had stopped teaching at the school altogether.

From then on, he was a very different man. He hired a woman called Joanna Brown. She looked after the children, encouraging them to pick the wild flowers that grew by the roadside to take to the cemetery, where Beatrice would look at the words Grace Elizabeth Lyle, and think, 'That name was my mother.'

Their father was angry. He took his anger out on the furniture. He would thump the tables. Break chairs. He would spend most of his time in the outhouse. His new hobby was taxidermy, making dead things seem alive.

Over time, he filled all the rooms in the house with these stuffed and mounted creatures. Eating breakfast, there were birds looking over their shoulders. Glass eyes followed them. There were feathers in the bathtub. Feathers everywhere. They would sit and watch them, floating through the air.

'My brother became very pious when he was eight or nine years old,' said Beatrice, 'and he said these feathers were from the angels, that they'd fallen from their wings. He really believed it. I didn't. I'd seen how my father would bring them inside, caught up in his clothes, or sticking to his boots.'

She stopped, her hands were clammy, she'd had enough of talking and the birds were making her queasy.

Mary opened her eyes. 'Will you come another day?'

Beatrice nodded.

'Normal,' said Mary. 'That's a very strange name for a town.'

'And Anglezarke isn't?'

*　　*　　*

'All the girls are talking about it.'

'I'm sure they are.'

'Will you think about it?'

'Let me see . . . No.'

'Please?' Beatrice rolled over on the bed, naked. It was sunset, July, and her skin was drenched in a pale orange light.

'I never go to Morecambe.'

'Please?'

He traced her neck with his finger, down to her breasts, then further down, in zigzags, circling the tiny heart-shaped freckles that sat across her hips. Her hair, spread out in the light, making him shiver.

'Your halo. Well, it used to be.'

'Morecambe?' she teased, opening her legs a little wider. 'I think it sounds like a very interesting place.'

'It isn't.'

'Hmm.'

He watched her breathing. He kissed her lips, opening them up with his tongue. She tasted sweet, and flavoured with peppermint, as she guided him between her legs with her small cold hand.

'Morecambe?'

'You can't buy me with that,' he said, reaching for his cigarettes, shaking one out of the pack, Gold Flake, and she lit it for him, taking a couple of deep heady drags.

'The trip would help,' she said, blowing a line of perfect smoke rings, 'with Anglo-American relations.'

'You don't need help.'

'Oh, but I do,' she pouted, handing him the cigarette.

'Look, darling, I never go to Morecambe. They're a nice enough bunch, and I love them all dearly, but it's really not my thing.'

'You'll have me.'

'True.'

'And Jeffrey?'

'He wouldn't be seen dead on that promenade.'

'I could persuade him, and we'd have a ball. Think about it? We don't have to stick with the crowd. I want to see more of England. The sea. I've never seen your sea.'

'Yes, you have. We came in on the Irish. Gallons of the stuff.'

'That was Liverpool,' she said. 'And Liverpool doesn't count.'

'And Morecambe does? You'd be very disappointed, believe me.'

'At least let me look?'

He watched her, slipping her arms into her dressing gown, standing at the foot of the bed, hair dishevelled, her body almost hidden by the rippled cream silk, and the beginning of the shadows that made the room feel cold. His heart quickened. He could taste her.

'Morecambe,' he said, rubbing his eyes. 'Maybe it isn't much to ask.'

* * *

'I won't want to hear about Morecambe,' said Mary. 'Spare me. I hear it every year. Someone will get lost. Someone will get sick. Someone, Frank probably, will drink too much light ale, and his antics will make Madge hide her face for a fortnight.'

'OK. No Morecambe then.'

Beatrice was kneeling by the window, watching the smoke curling from the back of a cottage where the farmer stood chewing on his pipe, talking to his daughter, her hair tucked under a red chequered headscarf.

'I've been thinking,' said Mary. 'What happened

to Joanna Brown?'

'Joanna Brown fell in love,' said Beatrice, turning back into the room. Mary looked thinner and a cup of chicken soup sat untouched on the side.

'How?' she said. 'Tell me about it.'

'All right. It was in the fall. Autumn. The yard was ankle-deep in leaves. We were throwing them up into the air, laughing. Joanna was sweeping, tutting and shaking her head, and sweeping. Then a boy appeared. A man, I suppose. "You should be helping your mama," he said. Suddenly, we stopped. "She isn't our mama," said Elijah, stamping his foot. "Our mama is already with the Lord." '

Beatrice smiled, explaining how the man had suddenly looked sheepish. He said he was sorry, and could he help with the sweeping. Joanna walked over to him. She was patting up her hair, and straightening out her clothes. She said something, handing him a broom. Then the man took off his cap and rolled it into his pocket. He had sandy-coloured hair, freckles the size of beans, and the kind of face that just kept smiling. They liked him. He was nothing like their father. He swooped Elijah up onto his shoulders, then it was Beatrice's turn, and the man started whooping and hollering, running up and down, neighing like a pony. Joanna looked nervous. She knew their father was in the outhouse. She whispered something, and the man set Beatrice down, then he swept out the yard without another word, until there were four piles of leaves and the bare grey stones beneath them. He looked serious. He didn't want to play pony any more. He went over to Joanna. The children understood they were no longer wanted, so they went back inside, Elijah to the Story of Job, and Beatrice to her cut-out paper dolls. Joanna came in later, her face all flushed. She poured glasses of milk. Her hands were trembling. 'His name is Cormac Fitzgerald,' she said. 'Please don't tell your papa.'

'And did you?' said Mary.

'No, but he found out just the same. Cormac was a nurseryman. He'd bring Joanna gifts of plants, and bags of runner beans. One day, my father caught them holding hands and dirty bunches of carrots. He paled and said nothing, but that night Joanna was packing her case. She had four red lines on her cheek and she didn't say goodbye.'

'What happened next?'

'Nothing. We had to take care of ourselves. There were no more Joannas, no one came to replace her.'

'Did she marry Cormac?'

'No.' Beatrice shook her head. 'Cormac Fitzgerald was killed by a wild horse. The poor man didn't stand a chance. We read all about it in the *Chronicle*. My father, ever the taxidermist, enquired after the horse.'

'Did he get it?'

'No. It was too late; they'd fed it to the dogs. He was very disappointed.'

'What happened to Joanna?'

'She went back to her family. Last we heard, she was scrubbing floors in the orphanage.'

'Poor Joanna.'

'But I hated her for going because now we had nothing, and I missed her. Elijah would pray for the soul of Cormac Fitzgerald. I didn't. I simply cursed him for taking her away, and then for getting himself killed, so we'd lost Joanna for nothing. I'm sorry now of course. My life was much harder after that.'

'What about your father?'

'He was much the same. He kept himself to himself, spending his time in the outhouse, muttering to all those dead animals. He'd talk to us when he had to. He'd talk about skulls, and mounting glue. The skeletal structure of birds.'

'My father ran off with a barmaid,' said Mary.

Beatrice looked up. Her head felt fuzzy. She was still in Illinois.

'I beg your pardon?'

'My father,' said Mary. 'He left my mother and went to live with a barmaid. The day he walked out, he brought me a present. It was a stamp album, with six Fijian stamps.'

'Stamps?'

'I threw them away. I haven't seen him since.'

*　　*　　*

The charabanc was full. A thin slice of sunshine fell across their shoulders as the pot-bellied driver told them that his name was Coleman, and there was nothing he liked better than a run out to the coast.

'I can't believe I'm here,' said Jonathan, settling in his seat.

Beatrice turned her head. 'So what else would you rather be doing on this glorious day in July?'

Jeffrey looked hard at the sky, and frowned. 'It isn't glorious yet,' he said, 'though I'm sure things will warm up later on.'

As the charabanc moved away, Beatrice could

see Lionel standing by his gate, slowly polishing his spectacles.

'I should have asked Lionel,' she frowned.

'But it's Lionel's favourite day of the year,' said Jonathan. 'Didn't you know? It's the day he can have the whole empty village to himself.'

The sun brightened as they passed other charabancs, the passengers lifting their hats and hollering.

'Things are bad in Europe,' said Jeffrey.

'I've read the paper,' said Jonathan. 'It'll blow over. They're very hot-headed over there.'

After a couple of hours they stopped at the Holly Tree Inn, buying jugs of weak frothy ale and bottles of sarsaparilla. The driver sat on the steps with a slice of pork pie and a glass of ginger beer.

'Look at that sky,' he said to no one in particular. 'It's like a jewel, that is.'

Jonathan and Jeffrey joined in a quick game of cards while Beatrice sat with Lizzie and Madge on one of the thin wooden benches set against the wall. The children ran around on the grass, glad to be free of the bus.

'We stop here every year,' said Lizzie. 'Last year it was raining, and we had to go inside.'

'It was gloomy,' said Madge, settling back against the wall, her hands folded over her stomach, 'and everything smelled of motor oil and tobacco. This is much nicer.'

Twenty minutes later, Jonathan reappeared. 'Come on, ladies, drink up your sherry, the driver wants to be moving along.'

'It isn't sherry,' Lizzie blushed. 'It's only sarsaparilla.'

'He's just having you on,' said Madge. 'That

means he's teasing, Beatrice, and never mind being an American, we'll soon have you talking like us.'

'Aye,' said Beatrice, affecting their accent. 'And that'll be right grand, that will.'

'Get away with you! We don't talk daft like that,' said Lizzie. 'Do we?'

They arrived in Morecambe an hour later, pulling in beside Happy Mount Park. Beatrice stepped from the bus, shook out her skirt and listened to the low familiar shushing that could only be the sea, while above their heads seagulls moaned and voices drifted down the wide promenade reminding her of home.

'The boardwalk,' said Jonathan. 'Morecambe style.'

'It isn't all that different.'

'Surely everything's smaller?' Jeffrey took an advertisement from a girl in a badly fitting tutu. 'Especially the costumes,' he whispered.

Beatrice blushed and looked at Jonathan, who was looking somewhere else, but the girl in the tutu had already vanished, as had most of their crowd. Beatrice could see Ada and Jim, arm in arm, looking through the window of a rock shop. Madge and Frank were being pulled towards the beach, their boys jumping up and down at the sight of the waves and the small bobbing fishing boats.

'Isn't this wonderful?' said Beatrice. 'All this life?'

'What can I say? It's teeming.' Jeffrey brushed past a man with a cone of fried fish. 'Is it lunchtime?'

'It's just gone one o'clock,' said Jonathan. 'Shall we find an hotel?'

They made their way through the straggling lines of people, their cheeks already red from the sun. Beatrice smiled at a boy in a paper hat. She hovered outside a gypsy caravan, a large wooden hand propped against the steps said: FORTUNES.

'I can see into the future,' said Jeffrey. 'It says, three-course set lunch and half a bottle of wine.'

'Do you believe in all that?' Jonathan had caught a glimpse of the gypsy through a gap in the curtained door. She was wearing a gold-coloured headscarf and scowling.

'Sure I do,' said Beatrice. 'All those little lines etched into your hand must mean something, and those gypsies have been reading palms forever.'

Jonathan shivered. 'I don't want to know the future, not a bit of it, I want to be surprised.'

* * *

The Crest Hotel was bright, with light white walls and shiny blue floor tiles, and its 'world-famous' orchestra played dance tunes in the Palm Room. Beatrice liked the restaurant. It felt very English to her, with its potted ferns, lazy wooden fans and the low murmuring voices of the other diners. A waiter appeared, and after showing them to a table by the window, he offered them a menu.

'The set lunch,' said Jeffrey, ordering for them all. 'Oxtail soup, roast chicken, fruit tart and a reasonable bottle of claret.'

The waiter nodded and moved away. In the far corner, a woman in a lace-trimmed dress was sending back her fish.

'She looks the fussy type,' said Jeffrey, lighting a cigarette.

Through the window Beatrice watched couples strolling in the sunshine, their hands full of sticky buns, melting ice-cream cones and gaudy souvenirs. The wine was brought and Jeffrey started telling them about a friend who had mistakenly left his wife in Florence.

'He only realised when he arrived back in London and her parents were there to meet them off the boat train.'

'I don't believe you,' said Beatrice. 'How could he just forget her? Were they on vacation?'

'They'd been travelling,' Jeffrey told her, taking another sip of his wine. 'Venice, Florence, the usual little tour.'

'And he just left her?'

'He always was forgetful,' said Jeffrey with a smile. 'Probably had his head stuck inside a guidebook or something.'

The waiter arrived with three plates of soup.

'Gravy,' Beatrice said. 'This tastes exactly like gravy.'

'Don't you have soup in New York?'

'Of course they have soup,' said Jonathan.

'Oxtail?'

'Probably. They have everything in America.'

'Apart from potted shrimp,' said Beatrice.

All through the meal, Jeffrey regaled them with stories about his family.

'My sister Agnes kept a very large hatpin by her bed in case Burglar Bill ever paid us a visit. She planned to jab him with it. We were never burgled, thank God, but the pin made her feel better, and she dreamed of sending him running in a great deal of pain.'

He spoke of his great-uncle Titus who had a glass

eye and a fondness for maps; his grandmother and all her extravagant bonnets.

'What a great cast you have there.' Beatrice smiled into her coffee cup. 'Really, Jeffrey, you should turn them into a play.'

'Oh, I couldn't do that,' he frowned. 'You see, I might hurt someone's feelings.'

* * *

Outside, the crowds were still pushing their way down the promenade and they were swept along briefly until Jonathan stopped at a rifle range, persuading Jeffrey to shoot alongside him. Their shoulders jerked in unison as they shot at apples and dented tin cans. Jeffrey won a whistle on a piece of red string.

'I'm extremely jealous,' said Jonathan. 'I only missed because I was thinking about my wife, and how bored she must be, watching grown men shooting apples.'

They strolled towards the pier, where the Salvation Army band pounded their tambourines, singing songs of hope, swaying in the heat. A man appeared with a camera. He had a sign around his neck. *I Am Deaf and Dumb. Holiday Pictures. 2s.* He gestured with his fingers. He smiled at Beatrice and held up his camera. The photographer was young and nervous-looking as he handed her a card advertising his studio on Bare Promenade.

'I don't know . . .' said Jonathan.

'Oh, I think we should have one,' said Jeffrey. 'An official souvenir.'

So they grouped themselves together, Beatrice in the middle, Jonathan and Jeffrey with an arm each draped across her shoulders. They smiled. The sun was in their eyes, then the flash; it made them look surprised.

'Ticket,' said the man.

'I thought he couldn't speak,' whispered Jonathan.

Leaning against the railings they could see the end-of-pier show, the low-slung heads of people in deckchairs, laughing, clapping and joining in some of the songs. Beatrice looked towards the sea and shivered at the size and cheek of the seagulls; they looked dangerous, the way they came swooping. Bonaparte's Gull, she remembered from one of her father's large textbooks. *Larus philadelphia.* Length 11 inches. Wingspan 32 inches. Black head. Adult plumage reached in second year.

'Oh, do let's watch the show,' said Jeffrey. 'I think they have Pierrots.'

'All right,' said Jonathan. 'I like a good show, and the wine has made me sleepy. If they do a few quiet numbers, I might even get a snooze in.'

'I'm going for a walk,' said Beatrice suddenly.

'In this heat?' Jeffrey loosened his collar.

'I'll survive.'

'But what about the Pierrots?'

'I don't want to sit still. I want to keep moving.'

One hour of freedom. She bounced. She disappeared between the crowds, weaving her way across the road and heading for the fairground where Union Jacks fluttered and a man played a barrel organ. Beatrice stood by the Ferris wheel, neck cricked, looking up at the chairs tipping in the sky. The boy helped her on with his warm greasy hand, calling her Goldie, rubbing her penny between his fingers and sucking on his lips. From her creaking chair she could see the dance hall, a fried fish cart, boys running around with catapults. Her eyes drifted towards the horizon and the world felt very small; and when the ride stopped her legs felt like giving way as she stepped onto the ground. The boy held her hand for a second, blushing, before she moved away to the Magic of Italy, where the water had been coloured with a bright blue dye and the boats were made like gondolas. The man pushing the boats into the tunnel with his boot was dressed like a shabby gondolier.

'My name is Antonio,' he said to a bunch of giggling ladies, in a thick Italian accent. 'And I'm sure my ride will please you.'

He was handsome and olive-skinned and all the girls fell for it, though they half remembered him from last year as Tony, ripping tickets at the skating rink. From the mouth of the dark tunnel, a scratched gramophone record played Verdi.

'*Si?*' he said to Beatrice, holding out his hand. 'Is very beautiful Italy.'

'Oh, sure it is.'

'I will take you there myself.'

Throwing his money bag into the booth, where the other operator was sleeping, he took hold of her elbow, guiding her into the boat, before jumping in beside her.

'Hey, get yourself out of here,' she told him. 'I don't need you sitting beside me, I'm perfectly fine on my own.'

'I give you a tour,' he said, as they were swallowed by the darkness. 'We will see lemon trees, Pisa, the Colosseum in Rome.'

'OK, but no hanky-panky. One straying hand and

I'll swing for you.'

'No hands,' he said, sitting on them. 'I promise.'

The tunnel was filled with a strange pinkish light. Badly painted murals showed gladiators, men drinking wine, an opera house.

'See. We have much culture. We have fighting, drinking and many loud singing on very high notes.'

'So whereabouts in Italy do you come from?'

'The part that looks like a heel.'

'Oh, a heel,' she smiled. 'Interesting.'

'And you are not English?' he said. 'Look at Venice now. The man in the stripes, he looks a little like me, no?'

'No,' she said. 'I'm an American.'

'Do you know the Ziegfeld Follies?'

'Gee, let me think . . . Only one or two.'

The boat stopped. She could hear the chains creaking.

'Look at the lovely lady, eating her spaghetti.'

The woman in the picture had silver-coloured eyes and two pink circles for cheeks. She was flaking. Her large red mouth was wide, waiting for the spaghetti that was dripping from her fork.

'Are we stranded?' Beatrice asked. She could hear the girls in the first boat laughing like ghosts.

'Not really. Jimmy needs to crank up the chains.'

'He was snoring back there.'

'Let me assure you, signorina, that if I am allowed to remove my hands from underneath my persons, I can push us on to the next tableaux.'

'Just get us moving,' she said.

The boat jerked forwards and she could see the way out. There was a half-moon of sunlight as strands of coloured paper brushed across their faces.

'The seaweed,' he said. 'Is very wonderful? No?'

By the time they emerged, she was laughing, her head bent to her knees, as he told her all in one breath that his real name was Anthony, he was really from Silverdale, though spending the summer in Morecambe, and could he take her dancing later on.

'Sorry,' she told him. 'I'm married. My husband would never approve.'

'I'm heartbroken. But what the heck? It was worth a try.'

She smiled as he leaped onto the side, helping her out, taking her hand and kissing it. Madge walked by with a red-faced Frank and they waved.

* * *

The Pierrots were taking a long final curtain call. Jeffrey and Jonathan were whistling and stamping their feet. Beatrice couldn't help but smile at the sight of them.

'Look at you two,' she said. 'You're like a couple of kids.'

'I'll have you know,' said Jonathan, 'they were the best bunch of Pierrots that Morecambe's ever seen. You should have stayed, my darling. You missed Mamie Adams the soubrette, Juggling Jimmy Jest, and Smoky Joe, song-and-dance man, who'll be snapped up by the West End before the season's out.'

'So where've you been?' Jeffrey asked.

'Italy.'

'I thought you'd one glass too many at lunchtime,' said Jonathan.

They walked slowly now, pausing outside a confectioners while Jeffrey went inside to buy some sticks of rock. Jonathan squeezed her hand tight, saying, 'You were right to want to come.'

Outside a tattoo parlour, Beatrice stood for a moment, as the green-tailed mermaids combed out their hair and snakes curled around initials and sharp-looking daggers. *I could be back there,* she thought with a pang. *This place smells like Coney.*

Determined to snap out of this sudden feeling of homesickness, she grabbed hold of Jeffrey. 'Remember the fortune teller? Let's go find her.'

'But she'll hate me. She'll know that I'm a sceptic.'

'Of course she won't hate you, you'll be giving her a sixpence.'

'Sixpence?' said Jonathan. 'She'll charge you more than that.'

Jeffrey went in first. 'Here, hold my rock,' he said. 'I'll let you know if she's any good before you cross her palm with silver.'

Five minutes later he reappeared through the curtains looking slightly perplexed.

'Well . . . ?'

'The great gypsy Iva knew I had a sister, said I was artistic, then said all these things about bonfires, on and on, she went.' He shrugged. 'Bonfires? I don't know what to think.'

As Beatrice went through the curtain, she could feel her heart racing. The caravan was small, the curtains pulled, a small oil lamp was lit on the table. It was like stepping into night-time.

'You may sit,' the woman smiled as she took Beatrice's money and slipped it into a small velvet pouch. The lamp cast shadows on the walls; the room smelled of coffee and jasmine oil. 'Now, please uncurl your hand.'

Beatrice did as she was told and the woman looked at it for a long time, before she closed it up again.

'You have lived a wonderful life,' she said.

'Is that all?' said Beatrice. 'For a shilling?'

'You want your money back?' The woman shrugged and began undoing the pouch. 'Here. I don't mind. Take it.'

'But what about the future?'

The woman smiled carefully and pushed the shilling towards her. 'I read palms, but I don't have all the answers. I'm honest. If I can't see, then I won't charge for it. The lines on your hand make no sense to me.'

Beatrice left the shilling on the table. It was a bad-luck coin. She felt troubled as she went outside, blinking in the sunshine.

'So, what's going to happen to you?' said Jonathan. 'Am I going to make a fortune? Are you going to have half a dozen children?'

'Oh, I don't think so,' she said, looking over her shoulder. 'She talked to me in riddles.'

'Bonfires,' Jeffrey mused. 'Now, I'm not saying I don't like them . . .'

* * *

'We're having salmon,' said Ada. 'I hope you all like salmon.'

They'd met up again as planned, in the back room of the Sand Pilot, where the landlord laid on supper. The men were drinking beer, leaning against the bar, joking with the barmaid, a lively-looking redhead who had heard it all before.

'Just look at them,' said Madge, tutting.

The girls pushed their chairs together, giggling, secretly watching their husbands through compact mirrors, sipping light ale and comparing souvenirs.

'Look at my Frank,' said Madge. 'His face is as red as her hair. He's smitten.'

'He's drunk,' giggled Lizzie. 'They all are. Remember last year? Tom nearly broke his leg falling from the bus.'

Ada leaned back and looked towards Beatrice. She took a long slow sip of ale, wiping her mouth with the back of her hand. 'And last year,' she said, 'you were still in your America.'

'Yes, I was there selling postcards and cheap souvenirs.'

'And now you're buying them,' said Madge, laughing.

The supper had been set across a table at the back of the room. The children had been taken into the parlour. People stood around clutching their plates and talking about their day. *We played the amusements. Won a bat and ball. Lost a small fortune. Lost my stomach on the roller coaster. Found a beetle in a pie. Fully stewed it was.* More beer was poured, and then there was a lull until Jim started singing, in a good baritone voice, 'Lily of Laguna'. *She's my lady love, She is my dove, my baby love.* Slowly, other voices joined in. They sang the song again. Beatrice was swaying, Jonathan's hand on her shoulder. *I know she likes me. I know she likes me, Because she says so.*

It was a clear night as Coleman drove them home. He was happy. He'd had a good day. A woman called Nelly had complimented him on his very fine moustache, and so he'd smiled back, and bought her a few drinks. And now her address was tucked safely inside his pocket. They were making good time. The bus was in one piece, no one was fighting, and the one or two who might be the worse for wear had their wives to clean them up.

The singing continued as the moonlight fell across their faces, and the world around them was white; it was shining.

TEN (OR MORE) TRUE THINGS

1. Soap

When Beatrice Lyle was eight years old, a representative from Godfrey Beauty Products of Chicago knocked on the door with thin sweaty hands and a contract in his valise. Pulling at his collar, he looked at the sky, which was just beginning to cloud over. He looked at his brand-new shoes which were already starting to pinch. He had his fingers crossed. A well-rehearsed smile.

'A very good afternoon to you, sir! Might I introduce myself?'

Godfrey Beauty Products of Chicago wanted little Beatrice Lyle, with her butter-blonde ringlets (courtesy of Joanna), to be painted by a reputable artist, and used to advertise their Purest Honeysuckle Soap.

'Beatrice on a soapbox?' Her father was sceptical, but he couldn't help feeling flattered. He invited the man inside. 'Come on into the parlour,' he said. 'Take the weight off your feet. Soap you say?'

The man followed him inside. 'That's right,' he said, grateful for the chair. 'Our prize-winning soap is transported throughout the USA.'

'And you've come from Chicago?'

'Yes, sir, indeed I have, I arrived here this morning, fresh from the train.'

'So when did you see my daughter?'

'Sir, we have scouts all over the state of Illinois, looking for the right faces for our products.'

'And what's in it for me?'

'You?' The man sat back in his seat and rubbed his forehead. He scratched at the side of his chin, which after being on the road was just beginning to prickle. 'A small monetary remuneration. You also get to keep the painting. How about that? Something money can't buy. Not exactly. Not an everyday kind of thing. An image of your girl. Think about it. It would look terrific on your parlour wall. It might brighten the place up a little?' He swallowed, suddenly noticing all the beady eyes. Did the bird in the corner just blink? He loosened up his collar. 'Yes, sir,' he coughed. 'We'll have it professionally framed, at no cost to yourself. And of course, your daughter will be seen all over the States. It could be the start of something big.'

Mr Lyle shook his head. 'I don't think so.'

'Honeysuckle soap,' said the man. 'It's a pure and innocent product.'

'I'm not interested in soap.'

The man looked him in the eye. There were small black feathers sitting in his hair. Another one was flickering, just above his eyebrow.

'I could up the price a little. How about a year's free supply of our finest shampoo?'

'No.'

'Hand cream? Dusting powder? Hair balm?'

'I said no.' Her father drummed down his fist on the table, which the man noticed was covered in what appeared to be streaks of dried blood. In the opposite corner, a buzzard (one of his earlier, least successful attempts) glared down at him with what appeared to be menace, but which was, in fact, a very crooked eye.

'Well, thanks very much for your time,' said the man, quickly pushing back his chair and groping for his hat. 'Yes, sir, time's a precious thing and I appreciate it. I really, really do.'

Godfrey Beauty Products of Chicago didn't get Beatrice Lyle. After seeing three other little girls from their scout's list (one had a very pushy mother, one on closer inspection had bags under her eyes, and the other was dying of diphtheria), they decided to use a dog. For the next fifteen years, the face of Purest Honeysuckle Soap was a sloppy doe-eyed golden retriever called Rex.

2. Birthday

Beatrice Lyle was born on 19 April 1891 at 11.25 a.m. Every year her father would give her a card illustrated by the natural-history artist George Edwards. It would usually contain a small amount of money. This card would be handed to her with a smile that often looked more like an accusation than anything well meant. Beatrice kept the cards inside a shoebox. Her favourite was the Blue Flycatcher from Suriname. Her least favourite was the Brazilian Jacupema of Marggrave. It reminded her of a very strict aunt. She usually spent the money on notebooks and candy, which she shared with Elijah. She never had a party, or a birthday cake.

3. Be Careful

'You talk in your sleep.'

A lightning storm had sent her scurrying into her brother's room, which was in fact more frightening than her own, with its stark white walls, and its picture of Christ and the Devil, which lit up with every flash. But at least she wasn't alone.

'I do not.'

'You do.'

'So what is it that I say?'

'Mumblings,' he told her. 'A whole series of mumblings. *I can't. It's somewhere. But I really don't like it.*'

'Am I loud?' she asked, pulling on her lips.

'Not loud, but it's annoying all the same. Last night I covered my head with my pillow, and when that didn't work, I stuffed handkerchiefs into my ears, but they kept on falling out, so I just prayed to the Lord for guidance.'

'And what did He say?'

'He told me to sleep in another room, but I couldn't be bothered to move.'

4. Gold Buttons

On her tenth birthday, just after her father had given her the card (of Kin to the Wheat) and the very thin smile, Beatrice Lyle decided that she'd had enough of the birds and the stares, and she wanted to live in a house like her best friend Bethan Carter, who lived right next to the main road, had four noisy brothers, a dog, a Dutch rabbit, and a mother who had a sweet tooth, waddled when she walked and, best of all, always looked happy. Even when she was cross, she was very nearly smiling. Scolding, her mouth would be set tight, but her eyes would be saying something else. *I'm your mama, I have to shout, I'm shouting because I love you all to bits, and I want you to grow into good decent citizens, so forgive me.*

Their father was a quiet man, who chuckled at the funnies in the paper. He ran a small grocery store, and he'd come home exhausted, smelling of bacon, his pockets full of stale but edible candy.

There was nothing like this for Beatrice. What did she have at home? Joanna was busy planning her future with Cormac, her father slept in the outhouse most nights, and Elijah had taken to wearing dog collars made out of cardboard cut from a cracker box.

Is it any wonder that I want to get away? she wrote in her small, five-cent notebook. *Is there anything less normal, in Normal, than these Lyles?*

Inside the birthday card was a more than generous dollar bill. (Her father had run out of small change, and was in the middle of a delicate piece of neck wiring.) That afternoon, while Joanna was swooning over Cormac and his runner beans, Beatrice packed a small bag and stepped out of the gate and onto the sidewalk, heading for the sunshine.

She walked for (what felt like) at least half an hour. She smiled at passers-by, her head held high, as if she knew exactly where she was going. Outside Bethan Carter's house, she hesitated. It had always been something of a dream of hers to be invited in for supper, then a sleepover, a good wholesome breakfast, then what the heck, you might as well move in here, and we're sure your pa won't mind, he'll be happy, knowing you'll be happy, and hey, we're only down the road, you can see him all the time. We'll get a spare mattress, and you can squeeze in next to Bethan. On Wednesdays it will be your turn to clean out Trix the rabbit. Do you like chocolate pudding? We always have chocolate pudding on a Saturday.

The house looked empty. There was an old toy rabbit on the swing in the yard. It had an ear missing. It made her think about the birds. The gate was banging in the breeze, and suddenly, the house looked different. It looked small and dark. Frightening. Some of the shutters were broken. She took a long breath and carried on walking. Something would turn up.

On Beaufort Street, builders working on the new houses shouted down at her and waved. Beatrice looked straight ahead, wondering what the time was. She read notices in store windows. Perhaps she could find herself a job? She could sweep out yards and doorways, she made a good neat bed, she was sure that somebody, somewhere in town could use her for something, but most of these notices were old, the jobs long gone ('maid wanted', 'gardener required'), or they advertised beetle drives, and thrift-store sales, the proceeds going to charity. By this time she was hungry. The stores were closing. Martin Hoffmann the baker had run out of bread.

'Are you lost?' said a voice. She looked round. She certainly felt lost. She'd never been in this part of town before. Here, the streets were narrow, and the stores sold things with names that looked foreign.

'I'm not exactly sure,' she said, reading a sign for freshly pickled sauerkraut. The man appeared friendly. He had a large white smile. He had gold buttons on his coat. Bushy grey hair.

'You looking at my buttons?' he grinned. 'Twenty-four of them. Two on each collar. Pretty, ain't they?'

'Yes, sir,' said Beatrice, who'd always been told to address gentlemen as 'sir', especially those she didn't know at all.

'How old are you, and what is your name?'

'I'm Beatrice Lyle and I'm ten years old today.'

'Congratulations. Have you lost your party?' he asked, looking over her shoulder. He had a round flabby face, and Beatrice could see his jowls flapping when he moved his head quickly. His eyes were blue and icy, and pink around the edges, but they looked kind enough.

'Oh, I never have a party,' she told him, suddenly feeling a little sorry for herself. Didn't Bethan Carter have a party every year, with jugs of lemonade, boisterous games and coffee cake?

'That's too bad,' he said. 'So where are you going with that little bag and purse, looking all lost and sorry, and far too forlorn for a very pretty girl who's only just turned ten?'

'Somewhere else?' she said, because, of course, she had no idea where she would really end up that night, though she did think that her luck might be changing, because perhaps this gentleman might give her some employment? He certainly looked rich enough, with all his gold buttons, so he might own a store, or a place that made things, or have a large house she could clean?

'Aha, you're running away from home,' he said, as if he knew all about it, because perhaps he'd done it himself a few times?

'Yes, sir, I am.'

'Hungry?'

'A little,' she admitted. 'I do have a whole dollar, but everywhere seems to be closed.'

'Not to worry. I live around the corner. I could help you out.'

'You could?'

'Absolutely. Follow me.'

And so she did. Now, how many times had Joanna drummed it into her head, never to go off with strangers? Yet now she'd left home, she supposed it didn't count, because if you never went off with strangers, how could you meet new people? And what was it Elijah was always saying? Strangers are just friends I haven't yet met. Perhaps this time he was right.

The man walked with a shuffle, slowly dragging his left leg. Beatrice wondered if he'd been injured in a war, like her uncle Sonny who now had to keep his right arm strapped tightly to his chest, like a large broken wing.

'It's a small place,' the man said, 'but it's

comfortable.'

They walked down streets where the buildings looked empty. But the man was whistling and the sun was still shining, so Beatrice didn't feel afraid. She could hear some children laughing; the light whirring bell from a bicycle.

At a dark green door (paint peeling, numbers hanging crooked, like a warning), the man started rooting for his keys. Beatrice took a step backwards, suddenly wondering if this was such a good idea after all. What did she know about him? Perhaps he was fond of taxidermy too. His rooms might be stuffed with even more animals than the rooms she'd left at home.

'Are you coming inside?' he asked, his voice a little gruff, his cheeks a little pinker. 'You can't walk the streets for the rest of your life with nothing but a dollar.'

'I suppose not,' she admitted, looking at her boots.

It was dark inside the lobby, and it took a little while for her eyes to start adjusting to the light that came flickering from a small hissing gas jet just above their heads. There was a staircase in front of them. Torn burgundy carpet. The stale air carried the scent of raw onions, dead flowers and the smell that often sits inside your shoes.

'I think I'll be heading back now,' swallowed Beatrice.

The man clicked the door shut. 'No,' he said, shaking his head. 'I won't hear of it. You're here now. You might as well stay for five minutes. I'll get you a drink. A little bite to eat.'

'I'm not very hungry after all.'

'But I won't take no for an answer,' he said,

sounding like her father, pressing his hand into the small of her back, and pushing her forwards. 'I have macaroons. I have Danish sultana cake and muffins.'

'They'll wonder where I am.'

'Let them,' he said, waving his chubby hand. 'Isn't that why you ran away from home in the first place, to make them fret a little?'

He guided her into a room on the right-hand side of the staircase. She could feel all his fingers, tapping on her ribcage.

'Home sweet home,' he puffed, throwing his keys onto a table. Beatrice stood stock-still and stared. The room was crumbling. The walls were so full of cracks they looked like complicated wallpaper patterns. A table was covered in dirty crockery, cigar butts and an assortment of dirty drinking vessels. Holding her breath, she squeezed her purse tight.

'No woman's touch,' he said, batting away a bluebottle. 'Don't let the debris spoil your appetite. The food I am offering you is fresh; it's still in paper bags and smelling of the bakery.'

'No thank you,' she said. 'I'm not hungry. I don't think I ever really was. The thing is, when someone mentions food, you just think that you're hungry, but I know now for a fact that I'm not, and my brother, he's told me that fasting is good for the soul, and it does you no harm in moderation, and when I think about it, I've probably eaten far too much food in my life already, and I—'

'Enough!' the man shouted. Then he smiled, his dentures, though a little loose, were a brilliant shade of white. 'Now I think we need to wash before we eat anything, don't you? I propose that you take off all your dusty clothes and shake them out, and I've some lovely buttermilk soap that will take away all those fetid smells of the day. Do you like buttermilk soap?'

She nodded. Her lips were so glued together, and her teeth were clenched so tight they were almost in danger of crumbling.

'Whilst you are removing your things, I will go and run the faucet,' he said, lips twitching, shrugging off his jacket with the twenty-four gold buttons, two on each collar. 'It's nice to feel refreshed, especially after such a long walk as you've had. The dust can get everywhere. It can find its way into every crack and cranny.'

As soon as he'd gone into the other room, Beatrice tried the sitting-room door. Of course it was locked. She could hear him whistling again, running the water and moving around. She tried the handle both ways. She pushed and pulled it. Nothing. Then the water stopped.

'Are you ready?' he called, in a high-pitched sing-song voice.

'Not quite,' she managed. 'Just a few more minutes.'

'All right, slowcoach. Then I will start without you.'

Quickly, she scanned the table. Ashtrays. Coffee cups. A saucer full of fingernails. There were ketchup bottles. Spent matches. Trails of loose tobacco. And there, beside a leaflet headed 'Great New Inventions', were the keys.

She took them. Fumbling, she pushed the first into the lock, but it was too big. The second key turned, but he'd heard her.

'Where are you going?' he shouted, half lurching

out to her, but by this time, she was out of the door, her legs like jelly, but they could sprint, and the front door was now unlocked, and he was too big, and old, and his trousers were caught around his ankles.

She ran. The sidewalk bounced beneath her feet. Down the narrow streets, past houses with boys sitting on window frames, churches, closed stores, the cannery. Finally, she slowed, bent at the waist, retching into the gutter. Had he followed her? All she could see was a man with his horse, and a dog sniffing hard at some railings.

She was in Fennel Street. It was close to home. She wanted to cry, but she couldn't. The clock was chiming six. She'd only been gone an hour.

'Where've you been?' said Joanna. 'I made you some cookies. Your father has gone to see a man about a dead squirrel but Elijah's been waiting. Are you all right?'

'I'm fine.'

'Cormac brought you some flowers. I've put them in your room.'

It was only when she saw the flowers, pink and white, standing in the jug that she began to cry. Her whole body ached with it. She'd had a lucky escape. Running away was dangerous. Especially on your birthday. She'd be careful next time. Plan it all out. That night she dreamed about the buttons.

5. Allergy

Beatrice Lyle was allergic to goat's cheese.

6. Amethyst Rings

One of Beatrice's favourite relations was Aunt Jess Simpson, her mother's younger sister. Aunt Jess lived with her friend Alicia Wellaby in Springfield, Illinois. She had never married. The first time that Beatrice met her, she wanted to ask a whole lot of questions about her mother. She'd written a list and memorised it. Had she liked dancing? Was she a naughty child, or a good one? Had she been a skilled seamstress, or just as bad at sewing as Beatrice? Had she liked children? Would she have liked her? Did she fervently believe in God? How did she find and fall in love with her father? Was she allergic to goat's cheese? In the end, Beatrice, who had been given coffee to drink for the very first time, was too jumpy with caffeine to mention her mother at all. And Jess didn't either. So Beatrice spent the afternoon with her aunt, and her friend Alicia Wellaby, playing old maid, wondering how the two women were connected, why they wore identical amethyst rings, and called each other 'My lovely'.

7. Scar

'It wasn't my fault, the knife just slipped.'

'Onto your sister?' said Joanna.

'She was standing too close. She was nudging into my arm.'

'It was deep. It needed three stitches. Dr Jarman's coat was covered in her blood.'

'It did look messy.'

'You've scarred her for life.'

'The bottom of her thumb? Who will see that?'
'People look at hands all the time.'
'I'll save up. I'll buy her some gloves.'
'She has three pairs already.'
'I'll pray for it to heal quickly. I'll ask Him for forgiveness.'
'Never mind Him. What about her?'
'She can pray too. Two prayers are always better than one,' said Elijah. 'And I'm sure He won't mind, if she doesn't put her hands together. At least not for a while. Not in the circumstances.'

8. School

Beatrice and Elijah attended Bloomington School, on South Street. Beatrice would turn left into the entrance marked GIRLS, leaving Elijah to Mr Harland and the large rowdy classroom their father had once been so familiar with. (His framed picture of Jesse Fell, 'founding father' of Normal, still hung beside a map of North America and an illustrated account of the assassination of Abraham Lincoln.)

Beatrice sat beside Bethan Carter and in front of Norah Billings who was the niece of Miss Billings the teacher and who could get away with murder. Norah Billings liked dipping Beatrice's braids into her pot of black ink. Beatrice pretended to like it.

'It's an unusual shade and it makes them look distinguished, don't you think?' she'd say to Bethan, when Norah was close by. 'And I have heard that ink is as good as almond oil for giving it a shine.'

Soon after, Beatrice was summoned to the

headmaster's office, where Mrs Billings and a red-eyed snivelling Norah were already waiting. Norah's head was covered in her mother's Sunday shawl.

'Show her!' Mrs Billings said. 'Go on!'

'Do I have to?' Norah cried.

'Yes!'

Slowly, Norah pulled off the shawl. Her once dirty-blonde hair was streaked with blue and green. Beatrice covered her mouth with her hand and allowed herself a smile.

'Ink,' said the headmaster. 'Is this your doing?'

'No, sir,' Beatrice told him, honestly.

'But you said!' Norah squealed. 'You said!'

Beatrice tried to compose herself. She focused on the large globe of the world, fading on the window ledge; that pale Atlantic Sea.

'I just happened to mention,' Beatrice said carefully, 'that I had heard that ink might be good for the hair.'

'Then you were obviously misinformed,' said the headmaster.

'What are you going to do about it?' said Mrs Billings, rising to her feet. 'My daughter looks . . . hideous!'

Norah began to cry again.

'I'm sorry,' said Beatrice. 'I had no idea that you would want to wash your hair in ink. I know I wouldn't.'

'The impudence!' said Mrs Billings.

The headmaster, who was very fond of Beatrice, punished her reluctantly. He could not face using the cane, so he told her that she must copy out Psalm 119, not because it was particularly relevant to the so-called crime, but because it was the longest.

'And don't go praying for my forgiveness,' she told her brother that night, her hand already aching. 'Because I'm entirely innocent. And anyway,' she added, 'it was worth it.'

9. Housekeeping

From the age of six, when her father had left teaching and the neighbours left him to it, Beatrice's life had been full of fly-by-night housemaids who had baulked at the dust, the birds and her father's unpredictable temper. Joanna had appeared soon after her eighth birthday and had stubbornly refused to let the dirt and feathers get the better of her. When she went away two years later, her cheeks blazing, prematurely forced into the arms of her nurseryman (they had five blissful weeks before the horse got him), she left a rambling three-storey house that was cluttered and in need of a top-to-tail clean at least once a fortnight, what with two messy children, a man living in his own feathery fog, sixty-five dead birds, forty-four small stuffed mammals, and various ornaments that practically begged the dust to land on them. It was a difficult job for anyone.

At first, no one noticed the mess, though in any case, her father barely noticed anything, apart from his creatures and solutions, the *Journal of Native American Wildlife*, and *How to Mount*, by J. A. Flindermann, which he always brought to the table, flicking between 'Arsenic as a Preserve' and 'Skinning Small Mammals'.

These meals were now haphazard affairs.

Joanna, though not much of a cook, had usually managed to assemble something that passed as wholesome—a broth, vegetables in abundance (courtesy of Cormac), a piece of grilled meat or fish, and all at set times. These times rarely altered, and even the erratic Mr Lyle seemed to have an inbuilt alarm, perhaps his very own cuckoo clock, that told him when his plate was on the table. Now that Joanna had gone, meals were cold, or lukewarm by default. They came from inside packets and cardboard boxes. Saltines, lumps of cheese in wax paper, jars of compote, German ham, occasionally a loaf. These things were ripped apart, and often never left the table, from where the family were able to graze. Mealtimes were now any time you felt a rumble, an ache, a feeling of emptiness, when cracker boxes would be reopened, the crackers spread with jelly, peanut butter, chicken paste, shrimp mousse, in fact anything that happened to be left over from Joanna's last big foray to the grocers, the bill still tacked above the groaning kitchen sink.

Then one day Beatrice saw it, all at once, like her eyes had been washed. Hacking at a square of pressed beef, she suddenly saw the clutter, the crumbs, the dust hanging in the air like a curtain, silverfish, grease, the grey smeary tint on the windows.

'I can't stand this any longer,' she said, putting down her knife, suddenly feeling queasy.

'What?' Elijah looked up. He was flicking almonds into his mouth.

'This filth. Can't you see it? This whole house is filthy.'

Elijah shrugged. He could see their father

passing the kitchen window, carrying a barrel. He flicked another nut and it landed at the back of his tongue, making him choke it into his hand.

'Just look at us,' she said. 'Aren't you ashamed? I don't know how you of all people can stand it.'

'Me of all people?'

'Isn't cleanliness next to godliness?'

'Well,' he said, contemplating another almond, and then going for the beef, 'I think we're talking about purity of the soul here, rather than anything physical.'

She swooped on the crumbs. 'Are you going to help me?' she asked, rubbing them into the sink, a sink that was already clogged with bowls and plates, globs of fat, shrunken cherries, a shrimp.

'I don't know, it's a very big job.'

'Think of it as a mission.'

'By the time we finish, the house will be all messed up again. It will be a complete waste of time.'

It took nine days and a pile of fresh rat droppings to persuade him. They pumped water into pails, and found some disinfectant. They scooped debris into sacks. Beatrice mopped the floors until her elbows numbed. Then she washed the windows. Upstairs, Elijah changed the blankets and the greasy crumpled sheets that had been nibbled by moths. Somehow, he felt good about it. He even cleaned the bathtub, the solid black rim, the plug caught up with those wet angelic feathers. It was a big job. Huge. It took them ten days. Then Beatrice asked her father for some housekeeping money.

'Money? What on earth for?' He was studying a catalogue from a firm in Minneapolis, specialising in realistic glass eyes and reproduction beaks.

'Food?'

He looked up, as if he didn't know what the word meant, and then suddenly it dawned on him.

'You can cook? A real cooked meal, all set out on a plate, and everything?'

She didn't know what to say. She'd imagined plate chicken pies from Hoffmann's, and maybe fried potatoes and a tub of creamy coleslaw from the stand on Wilton Avenue.

'Joanna always said I was too young to cook, what with all the sharp knives and the heat.'

'Nonsense! When I was a boy our kitchen maid was nothing more than a slip of a girl. Anyway, you're older now,' he said. 'You must be.' He was getting a headache. He'd been soaking rabbit pelts and the solution had got behind his eyes. 'How old are you exactly?'

'I'm ten.'

'Elijah? Is ten old enough to cook?'

'I don't think so.' He looked worried. Beatrice was small for her age. He'd seen how the stove flamed orange, spitting out its fiery coals. It had burnt Joanna's apron. It had scarred her chubby hands. 'I could try?' he ventured. He didn't want to, but, as a Christian, he thought it was the right thing to say.

'Boys don't cook, end of story,' their father said to his catalogue. 'I'll leave some money on the fireplace every Monday. See what you can do with it.'

And so, at the age of ten years and nine months, Beatrice Lyle became their housekeeper. She did most things, though she let Elijah do the bathroom and the bedding because she didn't like the moths, or the feathers in the tub. A woman called Mrs Oh took in all their laundry.

10. Snow

One February morning, Beatrice woke early and the world sounded different. True, her clock was still ticking by her bedside, there was the faint grunt and wheeze of Elijah through the wall, and the bell of St Bede's was ringing the half-hour over on Morton Street. These sounds were the same, but something had changed.

It was half past five and the room looked blue. Rubbing her crusty eyes she got out of bed and slumped against the window, where she opened them properly, before rolling them into a squint. The yard had vanished. The world outside was white, clean and perfect. Creeping downstairs, Beatrice pulled her thick winter coat from the hook, jammed her bare feet into her boots, and stepped into the stillness, breathing it in, blinking, as her eyes became used to this new kind of light. She moved, and the world began to creak. Above her head she could hear a steady dripping and the fading full moon sparked across the rooftops. Beatrice shivered, but she didn't feel the cold because she was somewhere else entirely, stamping her initials in the Arctic, avoiding polar bears, jumping carefully from B to L, then falling down on the soft sweet square that used to be a lawn, where her thick sleeved coat made fat angel wings.

Behind her, the windows were blank dark rectangles. The house was tightly closed and Elijah would be sleeping, unaware, dreaming of a ministry and a large open-mouthed congregation. This white world was her secret, and it felt good to have it first, and to herself, but now her hands were starting to freeze, and her back was feeling wet. Scrambling to her feet, she shook out her sleeves, telling herself that she'd circle the garden before going back inside. A cat began to wail. Beatrice looked behind her, and suddenly the snow wasn't a good thing any more, it was a thief, a ghost, the sheet they'd wrapped her mother in. How many times had Elijah told her about that sheet? Her heart was racing, jumping into her throat, as she slipped, arms outstretched, and the snow felt like glass on the open palms of her hands. Then she saw the blood. Two red spots spreading over the white. She was next to the outhouse. Frozen. At the window there was a bright unsteady glow from the kerosene lamp and she could hear her father moving things, working already. He sounded happy. He was singing 'Yankee Doodle Dandy', tapping out the tune with something that might have been a hammer.

PATRIOTIC

'You know, I feel like a soldier,' said Jonathan. 'Do I look like a soldier?'

Beatrice laughed. 'You only signed up an hour ago.'

'Thanks to good old Vesta Tilley.'

'Never mind Vesta Tilley, I'm worried.'

'Look, darling,' he smiled, pouring them both a large slug of brandy, 'with all these new recruits, we'll soon have the Boche on their knees.'

It was the song that made them do it; every single one of them had signed up that night, hesitant at first, shuffling in their worn velvet seats and looking at the line down the aisle, those millhands, the office workers, quarrymen, men who suddenly looked young and haughty, and brave. How could they stay in their seats after that?

Vesta Tilley had finished her last number. At least they thought she had. They were applauding, the ladies were reaching for their bags, and then the curtain went back with a jerk, dust motes flying into the footlights, and there she was again, stamping her little boots and pointing with a baton, singing, 'We don't want to lose you but we think you ought to go!' It had made their spines tingle, making them feel they should be doing something better, because what on earth were they doing, sitting in a theatre enjoying themselves, when they could be out there, doing their bit, a bit that could make all the difference?

'When will you have to go?' Beatrice asked.

'First thing in the morning for the medical, then off somewhere for training.'

'So soon?'

'They need us. Aren't you proud of me, darling?'

'Oh for sure I'm proud, but it feels like I only just got here, and you're leaving me already.'

'An Englishman's duty and all that.' Jonathan smiled and tried to ignore her red eyes. The brandy was warming through his nerves. Yawning, he put his feet up on the ottoman. His head was buzzing; he could see himself in khaki, on a sleek chestnut gelding. There were rolling green hills and lines of rearing horses, like a painting he'd seen of the Napoleonic War. He was shouting crucial orders to men in smart lines.

'There's only Lionel left,' Beatrice mused. 'Lionel and the farmer.'

'What?' He'd been dreaming about France. He'd always wanted to go to France. He would take his guidebook up to bed. 'Lionel?' he said. 'Lionel Bailey must be at least seventy and no bloody use to anyone at the front.'

'It's not his fault,' she shrugged. 'We can't help when we're born.'

On his way upstairs, Jonathan plucked the guidebook from the shelf; though he was swaying slightly, and his eyes were prickling, he wanted to read something about the place, to see the names of those foreign French towns, and the folded tissue maps. Beatrice let him go, she was wide awake, and she sat for a while at the kitchen table, drinking a glass of milk.

It was January 1915, and Britain had already been at war for nearly six months. Jonathan had followed all the action in *The Times*, positive that things would end before long, and Beatrice had believed him. Across the top of the window, icicles dripped like small jagged teeth as she pulled up her feet, covering them with the hem of her cold pleated skirt. Sipping the milk, circling her finger over the rim of the glass, she thought about her uncle Sonny, a navy man who'd been in Cuba in 1898, and the stories he'd told with a wince in his face. 'They made me come home,' he'd said. 'But I felt like I'd abandoned them, and the men who were killed still talk to me in my sleep every night. They tell me that they're lost. That they're not really dead at all.'

She rinsed her glass slowly and looked through the window. The sky was a cold pitch black. She walked through the sitting room, with the remains of the fire, the clock ticking, next to the photograph of them smiling on Morecambe beach. She touched their faces with her fingertip. Jeffrey was the only one with his eyes open.

In the bedroom the lamplight jumped across the ceiling. Jonathan was asleep, mouth open, one arm out of the sheets, his finger tucked inside the pages of his guidebook, just about pointing to Amiens.

Beatrice slept fitfully for half an hour, her hand on his shoulder blade, and then she woke to the sound of someone banging hard on the front door. Jonathan turned over, mumbling something through the shadow of his lips, but didn't wake.

'The door,' she said, finding her dressing gown. It was an urgent kind of banging, and she suddenly felt afraid, almost sailing down the stairs, struggling with the bolts, and the key that had been pushed behind the curtain, the blast of cold air, fumbling, and then Jeffrey, his face white, his hair blowing back in the wind.

'I need to see you. I know it's a hell of a time, I'm sorry.'

She ushered him into the kitchen, where he sat at the table. Beatrice lit the lamp, and he looked at her.

'I didn't know what to do, you see, I've been thinking all night, and they didn't mention the procedure, and I've been wondering and thinking, and I needed to speak to you about it, because maybe they said something to Jonathan? Another booklet? A paper of some kind?'

'A paper?'

'Yes, a paper, you know, a get-out clause? You see, now that I've thought it all through properly, I don't think I'd be any real use in a war. I mean, look at me.'

'You'll be all right.'

She uncorked the brandy bottle and poured him a drink. He stretched his fingers around it.

'I really can't face it, Beatrice.'

'So tell them. They won't make you go. Volunteers are supposed to be willing.'

'I've been going out of my mind. What on earth was I doing there in the first place? I don't even like Vesta Tilley.'

He sat breathing hard. Beatrice folded her arms, rocking slightly in the cold. She had no idea how to calm him.

'Where's Jonathan?' he asked suddenly.

'In bed.'

'In bed? Yes, what am I thinking? Look at the time, of course he's in bed.'

'He's sleeping but raring to go.'

'He's the type who'll do well in a war, anyone can see that. Me? I'm easily broken.'

'Should I wake him?'

'Good God, no.' He lit a cigarette. His hands were trembling. 'He'll tear me to pieces for this.'

'I doubt it.'

'He will.' He downed the brandy and poured himself another one. He looked at her. 'I've heard such stories,' he whispered.

'People tell stories. They have to. It's what keeps them going.'

He rubbed at his face. 'Make me feel better?' he whimpered. 'Say something that will make me feel better?'

'Jeffrey, this war will be over before you even get there. Nothing will happen to you. And if you don't want to fight, you can do other things.'

'Like what?'

'I don't know.' She smiled. 'Hold flags? Draw maps? And of course you'll look dashing in the uniform.'

'You think so?'

'Absolutely.'

He smiled with her. 'What a start to the year this is. I don't want to be alone,' he said. 'Not tonight.'

'Then stay, have coffee. You'll feel better in the morning. Believe me.'

* * *

'Three weeks' training doesn't seem long enough,' said Beatrice.

'It's plenty. And I've seen more than enough of Queen's Park in the rain to last me a lifetime. I just want to get there. Get the whole thing over and done with.'

Jonathan talked as if he were going to save Europe single-handedly, though she supposed they'd drummed it into him.

'Well, let's hope it's over soon,' she said, 'for everyone.'

She'd made a special going-away meal, shrimp salad, brisket, syrup tart, and she was wearing her best blue dress, the one that matched her eyes, or so he'd told her. He was in khaki. A soldier now. She kept touching his sleeve.

'Is it comfortable?' she asked. It looked thick, and scratchy. 'Does it soak up all the rain?'

He speared a small shrimp. 'I'm not going on

holiday.'

'Sorry, I was thinking about the weather, I want you to be comfortable, whatever it is you're doing. Be careful not to drop sauce on your jacket.'

They ate, not saying anything for a while.

'This really is delicious,' said Jonathan, making an effort to smile.

'I'm getting better. I never thought I'd be a housewife.'

'So, what did you think you'd be doing?'

'I don't know. The same as before. Getting by.'

'And now you're stuck here in England without me, and I'm off to fight the Hun. It wasn't in the plan.' He put down his fork, but his eyes refused to meet hers. 'I didn't think for a minute that I would have to be a soldier.'

Afterwards, they sat looking at the fire, her legs draped over his knees, Jonathan tracing his finger over her face and squeezing her warm hand.

'I will be back, you know,' he said. 'I won't leave you here forever.'

'Of course you'll be back.'

'And I want you to know, I didn't go to America looking for a wife. You aren't my souvenir. I fell in love,' he said. 'Real love, and I mean it.'

They went to bed early, their heads swimming, as Jonathan carefully hung up his uniform, smoothing out the collar, and he looked more naked than naked, if that were really possible, as he stood at the foot of the bed, pushing his hand through his hair.

They made love, but it didn't feel right. It was too significant, their heads full of other things, the danger, the loneliness, the early-morning train.

He looked closely into her face, remembering

the first time he'd seen her, in that warm pale sunshine. A man was playing the violin. A sad song. He'd seen her hair first, and then she'd turned to him and smiled, the postcards fanned like tickets in her hands.

*   *   *

If it hadn't been for the rain, it would have felt like a holiday. The women looked for shelter, with a good view of the train. The children waved their handkerchiefs, still smelling of tobacco from their father's pockets, thrilled when the khaki men waved back, though most of them were busy with last kisses, or relighting cigarettes. Somewhere along the platform, a woman had lost her earring, and a man with arms like a prizefighter wiped a lick of soot from his mother's ashen face. A chestnut seller appeared, sparks flying from his brazier. Pennies were found. Hands quickly warmed. And then, suddenly, there was the cheering, as the train belched, with its windows pushed down, and card games already in full swing were interrupted by this first big goodbye, followed by laughter, slapped thighs and the relief. *Did you see that woman in the dress that showed everything? Off at long last. No more nagging from the missus. None of the other either, though my mate Sid tells me there are plenty of women over there up for it, French, but never mind, I wouldn't mind trying out a foreigner.*

The crowds were left with a gap where the train had been. Some waved at nothing. Beatrice rubbed her wet sleeves, her arms aching and her teeth chattering, wondering if he'd even seen her at the end, through the crowds, and the rain. His head was just an outline through the steamy carriage window.

'They seemed happy enough,' said Madge. 'Like they were going on a trip out to the races.'

'Some trip,' said Ada.

'They'll be all right, won't they?' said Madge, still looking at the track.

'They've had training,' said Ada. 'They're not completely green.'

They walked in silence to the bus that had been laid on for the villagers, a gesture of goodwill from the motor company. The driver looked old and arthritic, chewing on a short clay pipe, his overcoat steaming.

'Chin up, ladies,' he said. 'Best thing a man could ever do is fight for his country.'

Beatrice closed her eyes. The bus smelled of wet dog and stale cigarettes. She had a headache. She'd had a letter that morning, from Jeffrey.

Dear Mrs Crane,

Forgive me. I am a changed man, and the army suits me after all. Unlike the others I was sent to Aldershot, and by the time this letter reaches you, I'll be somewhere in the thick of it. I'm with a good bunch of lads. The CO, a man called Cragg from Preston, knew my father, and it's helped.

Please forget that night and all that I said. I don't know what I was thinking. Do write to me every now and then if you can manage it. Let me know how you are. They say all this will be over soon enough. The morale here is high, and we are ready for it. Give my very best to

Jonathan when you are next in touch.
Regards and all that,
Jeffrey Woodhouse

She thought about him. She couldn't really imagine him carrying his heavy pack, or charging with a bayonet as if he really meant it. But there were other roles in a war, and Jeffrey was an artist. Perhaps by now he was sitting in an office somewhere, behind a desk, designing propaganda leaflets in the warmth?

She took off her rain-sodden clothes. Her goodbye dress was a wet lump on the floor. The dye had stained her camisole, and her shoulders were smudged with small indigo bruises. At the foot of the bed her trunk was empty and full of stale air. It had been bought especially for the trip to England, and her new initials had been burned into the leather.

'B.C.,' they'd said at the store. 'Your trunk will look ancient.'

She opened it up; it was deep, like a miniature cardboard room, and she quickly, instinctively, stepped inside, pulling the lid over her head, like the girl called Eva had done twice nightly (three times on weekends) outside the Dragon's Gorge, and her lover, Solomon Finkle, dressed in a starry purple cape, would lock her inside and throw away the key, showing the crowd that there were no holes whatsoever, no escape routes, not even a pinhole for breathing. And then he'd dance and play the clarinet, while the crowd stared hard at the very small trunk, until suddenly, after what seemed like forever, the lid would fly open, and lo and behold, there she was, smiling and pretty, and not out of breath, the red feather in her hair all springy and perfect, and the crowds would clap and clap and clap, they were so relieved to see her.

Beatrice felt safe inside the trunk. The dark was thick, like a blanket, and she liked the smell of leather, mothballs and the fading scented soap flakes, but her legs were longer than Eva's, and so, with her teeth chattering, she pushed her way out, groping for a towel.

* * *

'I hope you don't mind me calling on you like this,' said Lionel. 'I wanted to pay my respects. Have you heard from Jonathan?'

'Not yet.'

'It's a sad time for the village; for the country as a whole.'

'Yes,' she said slowly, 'the children will miss their fathers, wives will miss their husbands, and the mills will have no one to work the machinery. The world's a dark and different place. The blacksmith's gone from the farm. He's gone to shoe horses in France. It looks to me like the women will have to take over.'

'You know how to shoe a horse, Mrs Crane?'

'I could learn.'

'I'm sure it won't come to that,' he told her. 'Anyway, there won't be any horses. The army are taking them away.'

'All of them?' she said.

'Every last one.'

She looked towards the window. The clock chimed two. Suddenly, she wondered where Jonathan might be.

'He'll be back before you know it.'

She gave a small smile. 'I know,' she said. 'And I have to think about the others. Those who have children, they must be suffering the most.'

'Now that's something to look forward to,' he smiled, lifting his cup from its saucer. 'Having children of your own. A family.'

He'd left soon after, looking strangely uncomfortable, suddenly remembering something else he had to do. She thought about Madge and Lizzie, and their children. And then Ada. Lizzie had told Beatrice about Ada's four babies who were lying in the churchyard.

'Tiny things they were,' said Lizzie. 'All girls, and all not much bigger than your hand.'

* * *

The rain was hypnotic. It hadn't stopped for days. Wrapped in one of Jonathan's weekend jackets, she sat at the window with her nose in the collar wondering how she'd keep going in this place of soil and water. The reservoir was like an icy sheet of metal. In the summer (and it seemed so long ago), there'd been rowing boats, and all-day picnics. If you chose the right spot, underneath the hanging trees, it was almost like being at the seaside, and so private that she and Jonathan had stopped just short of making love on a scratchy tartan blanket.

America, she supposed, was where she'd left it, that jagged grey curve on the horizon, though she'd no real proof, and the postman usually disappointed her, with his lack of real letters. She hadn't heard from Nancy again, and the few letters he did bring were usually bills, or reminders, or statements from the bank account.

'One letter. Just one real letter,' she would mumble, pacing up and down. 'Half a letter. Three words on a postcard. Shucks. What am I saying? *Any word.*'

* * *

'Have you seen how the labels have changed?' said Ada. 'Same food inside of course, or so they're telling us, but instead of the usual, we now have Jack Tar salmon, Patriotic pear halves in syrup, and Victory jellied pork tongue.'

'Who are they trying to fool?' said Madge.

'I like the new tins,' said Lizzie. 'I feel like I'm doing my bit.'

'What? Buying pork tongue with a soldier on the label?'

'Talking of doing your bit,' said Beatrice, 'I was wondering if any of you had thought about taking some employment. For the war effort,' she added.

They looked at her. 'I've got a job,' said Ada.

Lizzie chewed her lip. 'What do you mean? What kind of employment?'

'I don't know. A nurse? Or there might be things that need doing on the farm,' said Beatrice. 'The cows must need milking.'

'They've only three cows left, and Ginny does all that,' said Ada. 'She's been milking cows for years.'

'I have the little ones to think about,' said Madge. 'And my mother. They rely on me.'

'Well, sure they do,' said Beatrice. 'I should have thought about that. So, it's just me then. You think I should do something?'

'Oh, yes, you should,' said Lizzie smiling. 'You'd look lovely in a uniform.'

* * *

She stopped the two o'clock bus and went into town. Women in dull-coloured clothes stared at their murky reflections, or glared at the pale-faced man at the back, clutching at a library book, looking at his knees.

'Asthmatic,' he said to no one in particular, when the bus stopped. 'I'm exempt.'

Beatrice walked behind girls wheeling ash carts. They were whistling. Others shouldered creamy joints of beef, their new-found tender muscles pushing hard through their sleeves.

At the market the fish were sparse, lying between cans of sardines and lobster packed in Newfoundland. They looked nothing like the fish that had sat in chipped ice behind the counter at Franny's.

'Brought in this morning at Fleetwood,' said the man with a wink. 'Fresh as a daisy. Honest. How about a nice piece of cod for your supper? Your husband over there? The fish will cheer you up. You have to keep yourself going, or he'll have nothing to come home to.'

Across the road, the pharmacy sat glittering between V. Edgar Jones Tobacconist and an empty-looking bakery. She stood at the window, with its mirrors and jars. A sign said, *Buy British Goods*. There was an advertisement for indigestion pills, and she wondered if Jeffrey might have painted the kind-looking nurse, holding out a perfect pink hand containing a box of the pills, To

Keep You All In Comfort.

The air was sharp, the sky a wash of blue, and soldiers on leave stood in clumps, cheeks pink, their uniforms slowing girls down like soft khaki magnets. Prickling with cold, she bought *Cinema Chat* from the news-stand, and then, feeling somewhat frivolous, she bought a couple of gramophone records and a tin of new needles. The girl behind the counter looked at her as if she was wasting her money.

'This is an old one,' she said. '"Everybody's Doing It"? Well, they're not any more,' she sniggered.

*   *   *

A cold wind howled that night, banging at the windows where the curtains moved with the draught, nudging at the ornaments. Beatrice was dancing. She was drinking last year's elderberry wine and dancing around the furniture, her eyes flashing, her hair floating loose, flying up from her head, like cotton.

When the record had finished, she slumped into a chair, looking at the ripples in her wine glass. She wrote letters in her head. *Are you in France yet? Or Belgium? Did they send you off to Belgium after all? Have you heard them talking in French? And Nancy, where are you? Did the man who tapped nails into his hands come back to the boardwalk, or did they hide him in a booth, away from all the ladies and the children? He was a strange one all right. Is Ray's lemonade still sour? Did they shoot any elephants? What's the weather like? And what about Franny? Is she still sweet on Mickey Toomer? Did he buy her that fine silk dress that she'd been swooning over? Are the mussels still cheap? Is France how you thought it would be? Were the guidebooks right? Do they eat frogs' legs? Are you scared?*

She fell asleep in the chair, with the glass in her hand. She woke just after two, shivering; the fire was out and the room was so dark that she thought for a moment she was somewhere underground.

*   *   *

Wrapped in a blanket, Beatrice watched the postman moving slowly up the lane. He kept scratching the side of his face. When he reached her door, she could hear him clearing his throat, and the letters sliding onto the tiles with an icy rush of air.

She had to look at them in order. That was her rule. She had to open them in turn without cheating. The first was a bill from the coalman; his smudged black fingerprints were all over the tatty-looking invoice. There was an advertisement for a second-hand furniture sale. A bookseller was getting rid of stock. And then there it was. The familiar slanted handwriting. Her cheeks flushed. It was almost like she could hear him.

30 March 1915

Dearest Beatrice,

Just a few lines to let you know that I am still very much alive and in the pink. The weather has been cruel to us; we've had snow, sleet and frost. When the snow falls, it falls thick and fast. Of course it does make things difficult at times, but it'll soon be the spring and I knew that it wouldn't be easy.

Well, Bea, you'll be pleased to hear I've been promoted. They were right. It didn't take long. I don't know what the lads think. Best not to boast about it. I was supposed to go back to Sandhurst for training, but they needed me here, and so I've had to learn the hard way, on the job.

How are you keeping? Fine and well, I hope. I got your parcel. Everything in one piece, and we all enjoyed the toffee. The little things make a big difference over here.

I have to end this now.

My love to you.

Keep well, keep going.

From Jonathan xxx

She wiped her hand across the page. It was strange to think that he'd touched this paper, and that her parcel had reached him, all that way; it had found him, over the Channel, in a hidden part of France. Her husband was fine, and alive, and he was talking to her. Throwing down the blanket, she pulled on her coat and her grey wool gloves. She was smiling.

* * *

The farmer was sitting on the doorstep, blowing into his tea.

'There won't be any money,' he said. 'Though we can feed you. We need help all right. Jack's in France. Paul and the rest are God knows where, being trained for God knows what. There's just me and Ginny, and Jed. My wife isn't well. She'd help me out if she could.'

'OK, so what would you like me to do?'

'Are you strong?'

'Strong enough.'

'You'll have to see to the pigs, and those pigs can be brutes. We've no horses left, but they let us keep some of the cows and the pigs and the handful of chickens. And then there's all the carrots. They'll want washing and sorting and bagging. The hotels are still fussy. And the hospital. They like their carrots clean because it saves them time and money.'

'I can do that.'

'Come back on Monday. Ginny will find you some overalls. You're not one of those women averse to wearing trousers?'

'I'll wear anything,' said Beatrice, 'if it's right for the job.'

* * *

On Sunday Beatrice sat in her usual pew, watching the women as they arrived, their best shoes tapping, their hands fluttering over their musty prayer books. Soldiers in uniform sat at the back, their smiles fixed, their eyes like a flat stretch of water, while their women held tightly onto their sleeves.

'Beatrice?'

'Ada?'

'Have you heard from Jonathan?'

'Yes.'

'Jim says he's been promoted. What is he now, a sergeant?'

'Beats me, he didn't say.'
'Why didn't he say?'
'He didn't have the time.'
'He has stripes?'
'Maybe.'
'A medal?'
'There was no mention of a medal.'
'So what did he do for his stripes?'
'Ada, I'm sorry, I really don't know.'
'It's probably the way he talks,' said Ada, moving away. 'That's what it'll be. He'll have done nothing more than talk nice. Those bigwigs in the army must think he's one of them.'

The Reverend Peter McNally looked his sombre, war-weary self. He'd been praying extra hard, visiting war widows at all hours of the day and night, and dreaming about Iris, who never went to church and was a sinner. He looked at the congregation with heavy bloodshot eyes. The whisky was medicinal—Dr Burke had told him there was nothing better for insomnia—and so he'd hidden a peppermint inside his cheek as he talked about peace and bravery, and John the Baptist walking through the wilderness. He read a few psalms. Someone yawned. Heads turned. Then the choir stood up, the boy on the end pulling at his surplice, his stomach rumbling for the mutton stew his mother had waiting on the stove, as the reverend read out the names of the valiant missing, presumed dead, while the choir sang 'Abide With Me', and all the handkerchiefs came out.

Outside, the soldiers were shown off, and then quickly pulled away. Beatrice shook the reverend's limp hand, saying nothing. Lizzie was smiling because Tom had written.

'And he drew a funny little picture for Martha. It's her birthday tomorrow. We're having a tea party, nothing fancy of course, we couldn't be doing that, not now, but you will come, won't you?'

'I'd love to come,' Beatrice smiled.

At the bent lilac bush, snowdrops were tucked around the headstone. *Thomas Crane. Four Months. In God's Great Hands. Elizabeth Ann Crane. Twenty-Eight Years. Martin Francis Crane. Sixty Years. Reunited.* The grass was thinning. There was a mossy-looking urn and a few cracked pebbles.

Beatrice walked home slowly. A rabbit ran out in front of her, stopping to wipe its thin grey face, before diving into the hedge. She remembered the rabbit's foot she kept inside her handbag. Her toes were rubbing inside her boots. She thought about the emerald on her finger, bought for a Mrs Crane before her. She looked at the sky. The sun was a flat brittle coin. The breeze like ice. Had the snow started melting in the trenches?

* * *

'You'll have to show them who's the boss,' said Ginny, handing Beatrice a bucket of slops. 'They'll trample all over you, if you let them.'

The pigs were huge, pushing against her legs, knocking her hard into the wall.

'I'll get used to it,' she said, catching her breath and rubbing the back of her head.

'Best time to clean them out is whilst they're eating,' said Ginny, handing her a shovel. 'They don't notice anything when they've got their snouts stuck into their grub.'

The smell turned her stomach, until she really didn't smell it any more. After the pigs, she went into the carrot shed. There were hundreds of them.

'Hose them down,' said Ginny. 'There's a pile of sacks in the corner. They all want filling up.'

By lunchtime she was almost in tears. Her hands were numb. It was like the muddy carrots were laughing at her. She'd spent an hour and a half washing and bagging them up, and the mound didn't look any smaller.

'It's your first day,' said Ginny, handing her a plate of buttered toast. 'I've been doing this all my life. It takes some getting used to.'

'I'll never eat another carrot.'

'You will.'

'Do I stink?' said Beatrice.

'Probably,' shrugged Ginny, 'but what would I know?'

* * *

A framed studio photograph of Tom in uniform stood on the mantelpiece next to Martha's cards, and the pencil drawing he'd sent, a fluffy-looking dog, saying, *A Very Yappy Birthday!*

'I wish my mam was here,' Lizzie sighed to herself, wiping down the table. 'She could have easily caught the bus from town, but no, she couldn't spare the fare. Today of all days.'

The room was crushed with children, and most of them were behaving, trying to keep their best clothes nice, though Bert's shirt was covered in drips of raspberry cordial.

'It's blood,' whispered Billy. 'Let's pretend you've just been shot.' And so they ran outside, where Bert held his heart, staggering, before collapsing onto the ground.

'Well, there's another killed in action,' said Billy. 'Now get up quick, it's my turn.'

Inside, a broken-looking tail was being pinned onto a donkey. A girl called Dot won and Martha started crying. Lizzie looked exhausted.

'Why don't you all share this bag of barley sugar and play a nice game of happy families?' she said.

'If I win again,' said Dot, 'will I get a proper prize?'

The children tired quickly of playing cards and took their games into the lane. Billy and the bloodstained Captain Bert commandeered their army, and soon had everyone marching up and down. A boy called Sam was sick behind a laurel bush. Harry had scraped his leg, and was exaggerating a limp. Martha said that she wanted to be a spy, and as it was her birthday, they'd better let her be one. She set out with a stick.

'I'll report back,' she called over her shoulder. 'Remember, lads, we have to stamp out the Kaiser!'

She walked to the top of the lane, dragging her stick through the newly dried mud. Her eyes settled on windows. Spies could be anywhere. They could be crouching behind sofas and pot plants, or whispering in German just behind the coal shed.

By now, the others were playing something else, but she was a spy, and she wasn't going to stop, because England needed spies. She wished she'd been better equipped. She should have brought a notepad and a pencil, and the binoculars that were hanging in the cellar. But spies had to look ordinary. She whistled. Whistling made you look ordinary. She sniffed. Germans smelled of greasy sausage, or like bacon gone bad. Bert once told her that the Germans melted down corpses to make more ammunition, but she didn't believe him because they wouldn't have the time. She bent to pick some bluebells, her eyes looking right and left. A bird rustled. Then she heard footsteps and froze. Boots. Thick heavy boots. The Kaiser wore boots. She quickly looked behind her. The boots suddenly stopped.

Throwing down the flowers, Martha ran all the way home without stopping, until she stood inside the kitchen, her hands on her hips, panting hard.

'Mrs Crane,' she breathed. 'Mrs Crane's on her way, and you'll never believe me, but she's all dressed up like a German.'

* * *

Beatrice and Ginny sat at the side of Mary's bed. They'd washed and changed their clothes, but the sweet manure smell that was clinging to their skin had refused to give in to the block of yellow carbolic.

'They told me you were working on the farm,' Mary said. 'I tried to imagine you with the pigs, but it was hard.'

'She's doing all right,' said Ginny. 'She's been a real help to Dad.'

'And what does Jonathan think?' Mary pulled the eiderdown a little closer to her chin. 'Him with his stripes and medals, and you up to your knees in the filth?'

'He doesn't know. And I've heard nothing about any stripes or medals, by the way.'

'Ada says he's already a sergeant?'

'Who knows?' said Beatrice. 'He might be.'

'Don't sergeants get stripes anyway?' said Ginny. 'They put them on their sleeves.'

'Al Riley was killed,' said Mary. 'First day he was out there. A bullet, straight through his heart. His mother got a letter from his sergeant. Said he was brave, and that he felt nothing.'

'That's terrible. I'm sorry.'

'You didn't know him,' said Mary. 'He was a private, a nobody, but a lovely bright lad all the same. He used to lodge with Lionel now and then. He was always running away from home, for no real reason at all, like boys always seem to do for the fun of it.'

'He used to scrump our apples,' said Ginny.

'He was nineteen,' said Mary. 'He'd just had his birthday.'

'I was sweet on him once,' said Ginny. 'He had lovely green eyes.'

Beatrice sat looking at her dry, calloused hands. She could hear Ginny sniffing.

'Let's change the subject,' said Mary.

'You know, I've often wondered what Jonathan's father was like,' said Beatrice. 'I never got to meet him. I'd love to know something about his family.'

'We didn't see much of him,' Mary said. 'He was a gentleman. Kind-looking, I suppose. Very slim. He worked in insurance, but I suppose you know that?'

'He was always coughing,' said Ginny. 'Cough, cough, cough, like his wife before him. Or that's what I heard.'

'I was told that his wife died young, and he never remarried,' said Mary with a shrug. 'I don't remember her. She was supposed to have been a beauty, but they always say that when someone's dead.'

'Didn't she like opera?' said Ginny. 'My mother's always saying that she sang like a linnet bird, and that Italian was like a second language to her.'

'It was?' said Beatrice. 'Jonathan never talks about his mother.'

Mary yawned loudly. 'More dead people,' she shuddered. 'Don't you know any funny stories?'

'Not really,' said Beatrice.

'I've heard some funny stories,' said Ginny, 'but I can never tell them right.'

* * *

A week later, Frank came home on leave.

Beatrice was in the shop with Lizzie and Ada was bristling with some important news.

'I have a message for you all,' she said, straightening her apron. 'You've not to go and bother them. Madge has given strict orders. Frank's home because he's hurt.'

'He's been injured?' said Beatrice. She'd seen him arriving in the trap, and her heart had jumped when she'd seen the khaki.

'That's right.'

'Is it bad?'

'Bad enough,' said Ada.

'I'm sorry he's hurt,' said Lizzie, 'but it's good that he's back home.'

'Give them my regards,' said Beatrice.

'Mine too,' said Lizzie. 'Don't forget.'

'I won't. That's if I see them,' said Ada. 'I've had orders too.'

*　　*　　*

She'd been thinking about Jonathan's parents, how they'd lived in this house. Had they left any clues about their lives? Were there sheets of opera music yellowing at the bottom of a drawer? Books written in Italian? Hair combs? Clips? Mr Crane had only died a couple of years ago. There must be something left of him.

She started at the top of the house, a house she'd grown to love, even in Jonathan's absence. She liked the feel of the carved marble fireplaces with their threads of grey and blue, the curling brass door handles, and the worn green cushions on the chairs. Sometimes, she'd stand and look at the stained-glass flowers that were set around the door. If the light was right, they would be pressed onto the walls in shimmering pinks and blues.

In the box room there was a chest carved with grapes and figs and vine leaves, but as far as she could see it was full of cedar blocks and bedding. Another chest had drawers lined with newspaper, but these drawers were empty, apart from a couple of cherubic-looking ornaments wrapped in thick paper.

For years, Jonathan's father had slept in the room at the back of the house. The clumpy double bed with its polished brass frame was stripped, the wardrobe bare, its mothballs hanging from the dusty shoulder rail in sachets. Curled in the corner, like a snake, was a grey silk tie which she unravelled, smoothing it out, reading the stitching on the label that said the tie was a good one and made by Perks of Manchester. How many times had he tied it around his neck? Had he done it the same as Jonathan, chin in the air, not looking?

There were no photographs or daguerreotypes. She had no idea what these people, her new family, had looked like. Nobody had told her. She'd asked Jonathan, 'Do you remember your mother?' and he'd replied, 'Sometimes.'

Recurling the tie, she put it into her own drawer, with her soap-smelling camisoles and underwear. She felt disappointed. The biggest clues had been in the bathroom cabinet, and she'd thrown them out months ago. Camphor rub, bottles of liquorice syrup that had left faint sticky circles on the shelf, a strong menthol liniment, and tucked behind a rolled yellow bandage there had been a cracked invalid's cup.

It seemed that his mother, like her own, had vanished altogether.

* * *

Beatrice felt empty. Lying in bed listening to the creaks and moans of the house, she wished that Jonathan was home, that they were listening to the music she'd bought, or talking, just sitting in the same house. A small injury, that's all he would need, a broken arm, a sprained ankle, perhaps a little deafness in one ear, and it would heal, slowly. They would have time together, and the war would end without him. They could hide.

That night she dreamed about the Island. Nancy was a soldier. She was standing on a soda crate signing up new recruits. Marnie was in a uniform, her black hair cut and oiled like a man's. The sunshine had vanished. It was snowing, but the air felt warm and thick. It was only when Beatrice looked up, that she saw that the snow wasn't snow after all. The sky was dropping feathers.

CAPTURING THE NIGHTJAR

In 1905, it was said that a large flock of nightjars, usually found in Mexico and Guadeloupe, had strayed into the state of Illinois. On Friday 12 May, the *Chronicle* reported that a Professor Henry Ratchett of Pontiac had used his young son's butterfly net to capture one of these strange nocturnal creatures. The bird (a male) was now confined to a large brass cage in his study, from where Professor Ratchett was able to observe this off-course nightjar at close quarters. He was intending to write a major paper on his findings.

In Normal, Illinois, the Lyles' kitchen table was covered in nightjar material. Sketches of nightjars and nighthawks were weighted down with boxes. Books were open at relevant pages, and *full color plates*. Mr Lyle looked more agitated than ever. He didn't wash, rarely ate, and had very little sleep. He had a constant headache, from staring at the thin pale wash of a sky, waiting for night to fall, when these night-flying aerial insectivores would be hunting for their prey.

'Are these birds rare?' asked Beatrice. The birds

in the hand-tinted pictures looked plain and insignificant.

Her father glanced at her, shrugged his aching shoulders and twitched. His throat felt dry. He took a slug of dusty water from a tumbler on the table.

'We certainly have common or garden nightjars in Illinois,' he said impatiently, 'but these have strayed off-course. They should be in Mexico by now.'

'And that makes them rare?'

'In Illinois they are rare,' he said. 'I thought that much would be obvious.'

Beatrice sat watching her father with his stacks of papers, rubbing his hands through his matted greying hair, picking at some aspirin. Every few minutes he'd scribble something into a jotter. At dinner time she tentatively pushed a plate of bread and cheese across his bird-filled horizon. He grunted.

Elijah was lucky, Beatrice thought. Nightjars had probably never even crossed his mind. He was spending a month in Jacksonville with the Church. The common nighthawk spent winters in Argentina.

'Are you going to put one in a cage?' she asked. They weren't at all pretty, like finches or canaries, and she couldn't imagine having a living breathing bird inside the house, singing on its perch, in its own kind of mortuary.

'I just want one,' he snapped, clicking his heels together. 'If this Ratchett found one in Pontiac, then Normal's just an evening's flight away, and they could be sleeping in the garden right now, only they weren't there last night, or the night before.'

'It says here that they prefer wooded areas,' said Beatrice, pointing to *Nocturnal Birds of America*, by J. Pfeiffer Scott (second edition). 'They might be sleeping in Hackett's Wood?'

'Ratchett's bird wasn't in any wood. His was sitting in his garden like a stone, waiting to be picked.'

By nightfall, her father was pacing slowly around all the rooms. He perched on windowsills. He hummed. The stuffed and mounted birds seemed to be watching him. Every so often, he would pause to look up at the sky. The moon, when it eventually appeared, lit up the blue-edged clouds like a lantern.

'The perfect backdrop,' he mumbled.

Beatrice had a stomach ache. Why couldn't her father stay inside the outhouse with his pelts and solutions? His agitation had gripped her. Suddenly, he turned.

'What do you know about the nightjar?' he asked.

'Ratchett's nightjar, or the usual one?'

'Ratchett's nightjar? What do you mean, Ratchett's nightjar? It isn't called Ratchett's nightjar, and it never will be. He hasn't named the species,' he growled. 'It's the buff-collared nightjar, plain and simple. This damn Ratchett isn't an explorer or a naturalist. The man's discovered nothing. Well?'

Beatrice licked her pale lips. She'd been reading about these birds all day. Her head was full of them. 'They do like wooded areas,' she stuttered. 'And they're often called goatsuckers, because they suck the milk from goats.'

'Nonsense, that's nothing more than an ignorant myth. They eat moths and other flying insects.'

'They forage close to the ground?'

'Yes, yes?'

'Their brown mottled feathers make for an excellent camouflage?'

'That's right. Now go upstairs and put on something white.'

'White?'

'White makes a nocturnal bird very curious,' he said, rubbing his hands together. 'We're going to walk to Hackett's Wood and get ourselves a nightjar.'

It was past ten o'clock when Beatrice and her father left the house. Beatrice was wearing a white blouse and a shawl. Her father had tied a bed sheet around his shoulders. Between them, they carried fishing nets, a large basket and a smaller basket containing the five live moths they'd managed to catch from the back of the closet, where they'd been feasting on her father's old collars and neckties. They also had a small jotter pad and pencil, and four ginger cookies to sustain them through the night (Beatrice's idea).

The walk took them past the church, and Bethan Carter's house, where the windows were in darkness, and where the swing, now even more dilapidated, was creaking on its tilted broken chains. Beatrice shivered, tugging at her shawl. Her father kept his eyes on the sky, which he had to admit, was nicely illuminated. Between their hollow footsteps, he listened for the *cuk-cuk-cuk-cuk-cuk-cuk-cukachea* cry of the buff-collared nightjar, who might be above their heads right now, looking for beetles, flying insects and Mexico.

Hackett's Wood skirted the edge of downtown, past Beaufort Street and the Orphan's Home that looked so sinister with all its tall windows flashing in the moonlight. Beatrice kept her eyes on her feet.

The wood was sparse with small dense patches. Most of it had been cut down to make way for the cannery. Beatrice squeezed her net tight as her father walked on ahead, their feet crunching on leaves and snapping deadwood branches. She could smell something sour. Stumps were covered in fungi the size and shape of dinner plates. Her heart was pounding. Her father's sheet billowed in a sudden gust of wind. She couldn't see his bent head, just the sheet hanging ghostlike, until he paused at a large shingle oak, and crouched down beside it.

'Over here,' he whispered. 'This is as good a place as any.'

She crouched down beside him, suddenly feeling the cold, her back resting against the thick bony trunk. Then the sounds came. The crunching, rustling, snapping, crying. The wood was coming to life. It was hiding things.

By now, her father was lying flat out on the ground, the basket sitting ready in the leaves. Beatrice pulled in her knees. What if they weren't the only people in Hackett's Wood that night? Elijah had told her that men lived deep inside the wood, building small shacks out of branches, foraging for berries and wild mushrooms, whispering tales to each other, of how they'd lost their families, or their fortune, their once expensive clothes hanging threadbare from their shoulders.

'Can you hear the cry?' her father whispered. 'Listen carefully. Concentrate.'

She tried. Her teeth were chattering and she could feel things in her hair. She could hear birds all right, but how was she to know if they were nightjars?

'It has to be them,' said her father, slowly edging his way into the clearing with his elbows.

They sat looking at the sky through the knotted branches. The birds were in silhouette, crying and slapping their wings.

'Now keep very still,' said her father. 'They might want to take a closer look at us.'

Beatrice didn't move. Her legs were frozen. She was thinking about the men in their shacks, the moths in the basket and the birds that were moving like puppets in the sky. A couple of minutes later, her father unhooked the lid of the smaller basket, and the moths fluttered out, hovering, dazed in the thin pool of light, before disappearing into the darkness.

'Damn.'

They kept their eyes peeled to the ground, where the birds were supposed to be resting. By now, she could see quite well in the moonlight, and between the mounds of soil and dead leaves, rocks that looked like eggs began to move.

'Oh, Lord,' breathed her father. 'This is it.'

The birds were brown and purring; her father moved closer, the net poised in the air, his arm shaking with the effort of it. She was sure she could hear his thin heart pounding through the sheet. The tension made her ache. She closed her eyes tight. There was a fluttering, and a shrill kind of screaming, as her father dragged the thrashing net towards the basket.

'As easy as that,' he whispered. 'Ratchett and his butterfly net. Some professor. What does he know about birds?'

Feeling euphoric, they made their way home, their white clothes glowing, the basket gently bouncing at her father's side, while Beatrice ate the sweet ginger cookies to stave off the cold. She felt light-headed. She'd braved the night-time wood. Captured a Mexican nightjar. Would Elijah ever believe her?

Down Beaufort Street they walked, their tired feet stumbling over paving blocks, her father's white sheet dragging in the dust. A boy looking down from his shady bedroom window rubbed his tired eyes and thought he must be dreaming.

The house was in darkness, the lamp they'd left shining in the kitchen had died. Exhausted, Beatrice sank into a chair at the table. Her father was still restless. He gathered up some papers and the small twitching basket, disappearing into the night. Beatrice fell asleep with her head resting on *North American Birds.* She didn't dream. She didn't feel anything.

* * *

It was not a good week. The bird they had captured had not lost its way. On closer inspection, the bird in the basket was a whippoorwill, common to Illinois. Her father banged his fist through the porch screen, wailing and cursing Professor Ratchett. He refused to buy the *Chronicle.*

Most of the nightjar books and papers had been thrown to the back of a cupboard. Spines had broken. A couple of them had torn. Beatrice was sure she could smell liquor on her father's sour breath, though she supposed it could possibly be one of the solutions that had soaked into his shirt, something that he'd ordered from a catalogue. These parcels came at least once a month. Beaks and eyes from Jefferson. Chemicals from Duluth. Bags of natural plumage from an office in downtown Monroe.

'Is the bird still alive?' she asked.

'Who do you think I am?' her father said. 'Professor Henry Ratchett?'

'So it's dead?'

'Of course the bird is dead. I specialise in the art of taxidermy. I have no intention of writing any fancy unreadable papers.' And with that, he stood away from the table and swayed. 'I'm feeling rather faint,' he said. 'The floor is starting to dip a little. Perhaps you would do me the great honour of bringing me over a bite to eat? Something plain. I'll be in the outhouse, working.'

'I'll leave it on the step.'

'No,' he told her, 'you'll bring it right inside.'

Beatrice paled. She hadn't been in the outhouse for years. She'd crept around it. She'd peered into the small side window. It was always dirty. The glass was splashed with something that looked like goose fat.

She took her time arranging crackers on a plate, a slice of trimmed ham, a somewhat soft tomato. She poured a glass of fresh water. The jaybird on the counter glared at her.

It was cold outside. There was a sharp snap of wind. She could hear Mr Rickman next door talking about his dog. 'She's getting on, and the poor girl's as blind as a bat, but the wife wouldn't part with her, not for all the world.'

Balancing the glass on the plate, she knocked on the door. As soon as her father opened it, the smell knocked her sideways. The air was clogged with glue, old blood and chemicals. It made her feel dizzy. No wonder her father was swaying.

'Put the plate on the back bench,' he told her, wiping his hands on a torn piece of rag. 'There'll be a space for it somewhere.'

The bench ran along the back wall. It was full of pails, boxes and deep metal trays. She tried not to gag.

'Now, come over to me,' he said. 'This is where it happens. This is where the light is.'

Standing beside him, she tucked her thumbs into her fists. The basket was there, with its lid wide open. The bird they had captured had been pinned onto a board.

'The smell,' she said, looking away. 'Can't we open a window?'

'Are you out of your mind? A small gust of wind could spoil everything. You'll soon get used to it.'

She put her hand on her face. Her eyes were stinging. Her father, with his tools on the table and his torn white overall, looked like a down-at-heel surgeon at the Cook County Hospital.

'I'll talk you through it,' he said. 'See, look closely now, you lay the specimen on its back and part the feathers along the bare area of the breastbone. The opening incision is made from a point at the forward tip of the breastbone, to the vent.'

Beatrice held tight to the table as he picked up his scalpel.

‘It has to be sharp,’ he said, holding it into the light, like an actor. ‘You have to avoid cutting into the abdominal wall, or blood and body juices will run out and damage the feathers. See, this is perfect. Now, pass me the borax, it’ll soak up all the mess and help preserve the skin.’

She pushed the box towards him. She didn’t want to look. Standing with the bird spread open, surrounded by the skulls from other creatures that had been boiled and scraped in the pot, she tried to think of other things. The blue hyacinths in her bedroom. Rose water. The beads her aunt Jess had sent her, small and creamy white, but then they reminded her of the whippoorwill’s tiny eyeballs that were sitting dead and glazed on a plate. She was sure the bird was twitching as she stepped away from the bench.

‘Girls have no stomach,’ said her father to the bird.

Beatrice moved around blindly. Broken skulls in various shades of white sat across a narrow shelf, proud souvenirs, bowls held teeth and bones, and a ferret, mounted on a piece of polished bark, had pins in its eyes and sticks where its toes should have been.

‘It’s drying,’ said her father. ‘Do you think it looks fierce? I’m practising the fierce look for when I get something bigger.’

‘Like what?’

‘A wolf,’ he told her with a smile. ‘Now that would be a challenge.’

He scratched his ear. Beatrice could see a globule of dark stringy blood hanging from his lobe. His fingernails were black with it. Retching into her hand, she grabbed at the door, running through the garden and into the house, gulping all the way to her bedroom, where she plunged her hands and face into the bowl of cold water on the washstand. She stripped off her clothes. They were full of death and chemicals. She kicked them into a corner. They made her feel dirty.

A branch pressed against the window as she pulled on yesterday's dress. There was a coffee stain on the sleeve, but now it felt like something clean, and it smelled as good as the French perfume they sold in Davenport & Lamb, where the salesmen wore oil in their hair and ruby-coloured cufflinks.

She slumped against the window. The outhouse was dirty against the fresh trees and sky. She could see Mr Rickman with the dog they called Bess. What did he think happened in the outhouse? Did he picture trays of seedlings? Soil-stained rakes? A crate of yellow apples?

She stayed in her room for the rest of the day, sitting on her bed, reading Elijah's *Good for the Soul* storybooks. She couldn't face the birds. It was only when she saw her father weaving over the lawn, his hair springing back in the wind, losing feathers, that she braved the wild turkey on the landing.

* * *

Six weeks later, the whippoorwill was fully complete. A ball of brown and cream in a brown-leaf setting. Elijah, back from Jacksonville, admired it.

'You have to look twice to see the bird,' he said. 'The camouflage is excellent.'

Beatrice stood back. She thought the bird looked frightened, and perhaps a little lonely.

'Naturalistic,' her father said, rubbing his hands together. 'One of my very best attempts, don't you think?'

He was more than pleased with himself. He'd heard on the grapevine that Professor Ratchett's specimen had barely lasted a fortnight.

'That would make for a very short paper, and a waste of a good brass cage,' he said. 'And you know something else? If that so-called professor offered me that half-witted buff-collared nightjar, who didn't know the difference between Pontiac and El Paso, I'd be telling him, in no uncertain terms, that I just wasn't interested.'

FRAGILE

Beatrice thought she heard a scratching at the door, then the scratching turned into knocking. It was Madge.

'It's Frank,' she said, looking quickly over her shoulder. 'He asked me to come. He said to give you this.' She held out a piece of crumpled paper. It had been folded and refolded. 'I've read it. I don't know what it means.'

'Come on in, come and sit by the fire,' said Beatrice. 'There's fresh tea in the pot. How's Frank?'

'He's recuperating, slowly.' Madge hesitated before following her inside. 'He has good days and bad.'

Beatrice stood by the window unfolding the

paper. In dark, thick pencil it said: *Did you ever have a twin? Were there more of you? I have seen. I believe. I have missed them.* She could hear Madge rubbing her hands as she read it through twice.

'Did Frank write this?' said Beatrice finally.

'It's his handwriting.'

'I don't have a twin. I've never had a twin.'

'Of course you don't,' said Madge, quickly taking the paper from her and pushing it into her pocket, 'it's just some stuff and nonsense. He's been having lots of peculiar dreams, and the medicine, it's very strong, it makes him ramble on, and then he gets all agitated. I've had to send the boys off to their aunt's.'

'Is he getting any better?' Beatrice asked, sitting at the table and pouring cups of pale-coloured tea. 'What happened to him?'

'He hurt his back,' said Madge. 'He really can't remember how he did it.'

'Was he in hospital?'

'A field hospital. They did what they could.'

'Did he bring back any news?'

'About Jonathan you mean?'

Beatrice looked down, taking a sip of her tea; it tasted of the fields, of the wet world outside. 'Jonathan and the others. Are they still together?'

'I don't know. I wish I could tell you. He's home, but he doesn't want to talk about it.'

'And I've wished for that every hour—Jonathan, back where I can see him. Where was Frank fighting?'

'France.'

'Whereabouts?'

'I don't know. I'm sorry.'

Beatrice looked disappointed. 'I just wanted

some news.'

'I wish I could help you,' said Madge, pushing her cup away. 'I'd better get back.'

'Don't forget to tell him,' said Beatrice, managing a smile.

'Tell him what?'

'No twins, just me.'

Suddenly Madge stopped. Her face was burning. 'Thing is,' she said, 'I was going to ask . . .'

'Go on.'

'There's this word, he keeps on saying this word.'

'What is it?'

'I don't know. It's foreign. French. It sounds a bit like bully bass.'

'Bouillabaisse?' said Beatrice.

Madge looked relieved. 'Yes, that's it, that's the word exactly.' She paused. 'So what is it?'

'It's like a broth,' said Beatrice. 'It's made with shellfish, and fish, it's really very pungent.'

'Are you sure?'

'I'm positive.'

'Fish broth,' she said, shaking her hand and smiling. 'Really? Is that all it is now? A broth?'

* * *

'Beatrice!'

Beatrice turned. Lizzie was leaning over the farm wall, waving at her. Beatrice put down the slop bucket, patted Bertha on the head, and went to see what the matter was.

'It's nothing really,' said Lizzie. 'It's just that Al Riley's mother has organised a spiritualist evening. She's desperate to hear from Al. Her husband doesn't approve, so I said she could have it at my house tonight. We're all going to be there. The medium's quite well known. She's supposed to be very good.'

'Most of them are charlatans,' said Beatrice.

'This one isn't. Ada once saw her at the Varieties. A woman in her row heard from her husband. She knew all sorts of things about him. Even the name of his dog.'

'All right,' she smiled. 'It'll get me out of the house.'

'And you never know who you might hear from,' Lizzie smiled, waving over her shoulder.

Beatrice had met a spiritualist in New York. A Hungarian woman who, for the price of a meal, would hold your hand, roll in her seat and give you messages from beyond in a strange crackling voice. Beatrice had seen women clutching handkerchiefs and swaying in the doorway of the East Side Cafeteria, the medium's favourite place for Polish sausage and borscht. Sceptical men would be found wiping tears from their eyes when she moaned their mother's name, and they would hand her extra money for another glass of wine. Nancy had visited her, hoping to hear from a boy called Eugene Parker, her first love, who'd drowned in a pond, just after his sixteenth birthday. Nancy had bought the woman a two-course lunch, and they'd sat in her favourite curtained booth, holding hands. Nancy was certain that she'd felt strange vibrations, moving up her arms. But she had been disappointed. The woman described a boy, but the boy wasn't Eugene. 'She said he was tall, and thin, like a long piece of string,' said Nancy. 'But Eugene was as stocky as they come.'

* * *

'Are you a believer, Mrs Crane?' said Lionel. He'd been one of the first to arrive at Lizzie's. He'd brought pamphlets about the spiritualist movement, endorsed by his friend Conan Doyle.

'I haven't yet made up my mind,' she told him, which she supposed was the safest thing to say.

Lizzie appeared with a tray of rattling cups and saucers. 'I'm nervous. Just look at my hands. The children are sound asleep upstairs, thank goodness; I don't want to be giving them nightmares. And I've been thinking about ectoplasm,' she said, putting down the tray. 'Does it leave a mess?'

'Is she here yet?' said Ada, pulling off her coat.

'No.'

'Well, let's have a cup of tea anyway, I'm cold to the bone, and some of these mediums don't like to eat or drink before they start performing.'

Lionel cocked his head. 'Performing?' he said. 'These people are special. They are gifted, and they are generous enough to use that gift with others. They're certainly not theatricals.'

Ada held her hands over the small licking fire. 'It's all the rocking and groaning that gets me. Why do they have to do that? When I saw her at the Varieties, she was good, but she was acting like something from *King Lear*. He was on the week previous, shouting and beating his chest in the wind. It fair wore me out.'

'They have to attune themselves,' said Lionel. 'Their body is the vessel for the departed person to use. It's an extremely sensitive instrument.'

'I suppose so,' said Ada. 'Where's Madge?'

'She's going to be here at the last minute,' said Lizzie. 'She doesn't like leaving Frank for too long.'

Mrs Riley appeared, bringing a sudden gust of air. 'The medium's on her way,' she said, unwinding the scarf from around her neck. 'She's at the top of the lane. We should go and knock for Madge.'

'I'll go,' said Lizzie. 'I said I'd tap lightly on the window, in case Frank's asleep.'

'Is his back any better?'

'Madge said he can hardly move an inch,' said Lizzie. 'Funny thing is, I saw them dancing the other night, though I didn't like to mention it.'

* * *

They sat in a circle around the table in the parlour. Lizzie had used her good lisle cloth and her best brass candlesticks. The medium was wearing black. A large cameo brooch was pinned at her throat. She had a long sombre face and tightly scraped-back hair.

'I am a spiritualist,' she told them. 'I am not a Madame Zaza, or a gypsy from the fairground. I'm Dora Barnes. Mrs Dora Barnes, plain and simple. I come with no airs or graces. Now, let us all join hands. We need to make a circuit.'

Lionel nodded sagely, as if he did this all the time. Beatrice remembered Morecambe and wondered if Dora Barnes talked in riddles like the palmist. Suddenly, Mrs Barnes closed her eyes, and let her head flop down, like her neck had just snapped. The women looked around. Lionel had his eyes closed, as if he might be praying. Perhaps they should do the same? With his pamphlets and his nodding, he seemed quite the expert. Mrs Riley was biting her lip. She had a photograph of Al in her pocket. It was her favourite. He was laughing by the boating lake at Barrow Bridge. It had been a good day. Perhaps he'd look down from wherever he was, and remember it?

In the small light from the candles, Mrs Barnes began humming and circling her waist. Her shoulders twitched, then her face, and in a low trance-like voice she started speaking.

'I am here. I am free and ready to hear you. Come. Come to me. Come to me now!'

'Is that her, or the ghost?' whispered Madge.

Mrs Barnes stopped. She opened her eyes, and shook out her hands. 'The connection has been broken. Whilst I am in transit it is most unwise to chatter. Complete silence and concentration is required by all. If you cannot do this, then please leave the circle.'

'Sorry,' muttered Madge.

'Can I ask you a question?' said Mrs Riley.

'You may,' sighed Mrs Barnes, pressing at her forehead.

'Well . . . if we're hoping to hear from someone in particular, should we be thinking about him? Asking him to leave a message?'

'It can certainly do no harm, though I should warn you all, the spirits talk through me. I am not a personal telegraph service. If they want to talk, they'll talk. Many of them prefer to be left alone, and are silent.'

Mrs Riley, looking disappointed, rubbed the sepia-coloured face in her pocket.

'Now, let us reconnect.'

They held hands, looking somewhat chastised, Madge glancing quickly at the clock on the mantelpiece. How long would this take? Mrs Barnes had started swaying again, her face creased and tight with concentration, her breathing becoming louder, and faster, as she called out to the spirits.

'I am with a man,' she said, in a voice that was her own, only deeper. 'He has been a long way from home.'

Mrs Riley opened her eyes, and then quickly shut them again. Her heart was racing. Belgium was miles away, but was nineteen old enough to be a man? The army said it was, and she was sure her Al would think so.

'He was important in life, but now all that has gone.' Mrs Riley's mouth drooped. Al was never important. Not in that sense. 'Is Alice there?' said Mrs Barnes. 'He would like to speak to Alice.'

The women opened their eyes, shrugging and looking perplexed. Lionel and Mrs Barnes were still concentrating, but as it was her house, Lizzie thought she ought to be the one to put her straight.

'There's no one here called Alice,' she whispered.

'Do we have an Alice connection?' said Mrs Barnes, her voice a little strained.

'It's my mother's name,' said Madge.

'It's where my grandma lives,' said Lizzie. 'Alice Street, in Bolton.'

'It's my sister's middle name,' said Ada. Then suddenly she flushed, almost dropping one of her hands. 'My baby,' she swallowed. 'I called a baby Violet Alice. The middle one.'

'Is she this side of life, or beyond?'

'Beyond.'

'The Alice he wishes to speak to is this side of life.'

'I could take a message to my mother,' said Madge. 'I'm seeing her tomorrow.'

'*Alice, I still love you*,' said Mrs Barnes, in a voice like a growling dog. Madge pulled a face. She could hardly tell her mother that. What on earth would her father say?

'The spirit is fading fast. I have another voice, waiting to connect. Let us concentrate.'

The circle squeezed their hands tighter. Beatrice, who was sitting next to Mrs Riley, was sure her hands would be bruised in the morning.

'The voice is a little unclear,' said Mrs Barnes. 'Perhaps the spirit has just passed over. The voice seems to be somewhat dazed, and slightly confused.'

Mrs Riley swallowed. Al had never been good with words. And he'd only been gone a month.

'Please be patient, whilst the spirit tries to connect.'

Mrs Barnes began to hum. 'The spirit is new to the world on the other side,' she said. 'I have a male. He is telling me that he is whole again, in mind and body. He is telling us to believe.'

'I believe,' said Mrs Riley.

'The spirit is sending me music, a signal to you all that it was something he was fond of. I see the colour green. A muddy kind of green.'

'A soldier?' mouthed Mrs Riley.

'The noise is very loud,' said Mrs Barnes, rolling her head as if she was in great pain. 'Oh, the noise! It could deafen you. Speak up, sir, speak up, I can't hear you! The world is exploding! Speak up! Ahh,' she sighed. 'It has quietened. He tells me he has sons. He has two sons. Sir, can you give me their names?'

Mrs Riley sighed. *Oh Al, where are you?* she thought. *Just one word would make all the difference*.

'This new spirit gives me the letter B. His sons are B. Both of them. And you, sir,' said Mrs Barnes, 'do we have a letter for you?' Mrs Barnes' voice was almost singing the words. A gust of wind started banging at the window. 'F. The man is giving me an F!' She was triumphant. 'The letter F is the initial of his name.'

Madge shot up. 'That's my Frank,' she said. 'The B's are for our Billy and Bert. I only left him half an hour ago.'

'It's all right,' said Lizzie. 'It can't be for you, Frank isn't dead.'

'Well, he could be by now,' said Madge, heading for the door.

The others were shaking their heads. 'No,' said Ada. 'It's only his back. He can't be dead.'

'I'm not sitting here taking any chances.'

'Can we have another go?' said Mrs Riley.

'I'll come with you,' said Beatrice, jumping up. 'I'll see you're all right.'

* * *

The wind was whipping down the lane, whistling through the trees, and pushing at their shoulders.

'I knew I shouldn't have left him,' said Madge, dropping her door key and fumbling on the step.

It was quiet inside the cottage. The parlour was

empty, so they went into the kitchen, where there was a bottle of milk on the table, and an open tin of grate polish.

'Frank?' Madge called. 'Are you in bed? Frank?'

There was no one upstairs. By now, Madge was straining not to cry. 'He must have gone outside. Where can he be? He'll be lost in the dark.'

'We'll find him,' said Beatrice. 'He can't have gone far.'

They were halfway down the stairs when they heard him. Madge paled. 'Oh God,' she said. 'Oh God, he's at it again, and you're here with me, to see it all.'

'What do you mean? What is it?'

'Frank isn't dead,' swallowed Madge. 'He's sitting under the stairs.'

They paused outside the door. Madge opened it. Frank was sitting with the coats and boots, he was wearing Madge's Sunday coat, with the squirrel collar, and he was rocking, his eyes closed, singing a lullaby in French.

'This is what he's like,' said Madge. 'So now you know.'

Madge held out her hand. Frank took it. He looked up at her and smiled.

'Come on out, love. You can't be sitting in there all night, in the dark.'

Frank came out, wincing in the light. He had polish on his face, like streaks of dried mud. He was stroking the fur collar and singing in a light, soft voice, *'C'est la poulette blanche, qui pond dans les branches . . .'* Suddenly he stopped and looked at Beatrice. 'Oh,' he said, clapping his hands, 'you've come back. I knew it. I knew you'd come back and I've been waiting and waiting. Where's the other one? The one that can float right up to the heavens and fly?'

'There's only me,' she said.

'No there isn't. There's another one.'

'I'm sorry,' said Beatrice, opening up her hands. 'I'm really all there is.'

'Just go,' said Madge. 'Go on.'

* * *

Mrs Barnes was sipping a glass of sweet sherry when Beatrice reappeared. The seance was over. The spirits had fled for the night.

'How's Frank?' said Lizzie. 'He wasn't dead, was he?'

'No,' said Beatrice. 'He was fine.'

'Thank goodness for that,' said Ada. 'How's his back?'

'I don't know,' said Beatrice. 'He was sleeping.'

'Sleeping's good for the healing process,' said Lizzie. 'That's what my granny always says.'

Lionel was busy with his leaflets. 'I urge you all to take one, to peruse at your own leisure,' he said. 'Any questions, you know where to find me.'

'Do you do private sittings?' said Mrs Riley.

'I can do,' said Mrs Barnes, draining her sherry glass. 'The cost is a little higher.'

'How much higher?'

'A guinea.'

Mrs Riley looked crestfallen. 'A guinea,' she said. 'I don't think I can manage a guinea.'

'I can take it in instalments,' said Mrs Barnes. 'But there are still no guarantees of my making a connection.'

'You could come to the spiritualist church with

me,' said Lionel. 'All they ask for is a small donation.'

'Whatever would the Reverend McNally say? We had no body to bury, but he did a lovely service for Al.'

'It's cheaper than a private sitting,' he said. 'I always go once a month.'

'And have you ever connected?' said Beatrice.

'No,' he said. 'But there are plenty there that do.'

Mrs Riley looked a little happier. 'Let me know when you're going,' she said. 'But don't tell my Vince, or he'll lock me in the house, he'll be that mad at me.'

'Mum's the word,' said Lionel.

* * *

Beatrice watched the stars blinking over the treetops. She was wearing her thickest nightdress, the one she'd bought from a store near Battery Park, and the familiar plain brushed fabric made her feel comfortable as she thought about Al Riley's mother, making her way home in the dark. And Frank. Whatever had happened to Frank? Perhaps the stars were lost souls, she told herself, because their blinking looked forlorn, their persistent messages lost, unanswered, and the sky was supposed to go on forever, and who knew where it was we came from? She believed in Charles Darwin, but she supposed there must be more to it than that, or else why did she cry when she heard a particular piece of music, or ache when someone went away, or laugh at the comedian juggling eggs on the corner of Surf Avenue, his shoes like soft red boats, flapping on the sidewalk?

So there'd been no real messages from beyond. No words from Al Riley, or from Ada's baby girl. She didn't believe, so why did she feel let down? And who had she wanted to hear from anyway? Her mother? Father? Jonathan's parents? Should those departed souls have found Mrs Barnes, giving their approval through her dry and mumbling lips? 'You are all we could have asked for in a daughter-in-law.' She wouldn't have believed it. Not in a million years.

Poor Frank.

She looked across the bookcases. *Saunterings in Florence. Riviera Walks. Alpine Adventures.* She found Jonathan's guide to northern France, and pulled out the map with its black veins cutting through Calais, then on to Lille and Mons. She read about Arras. The Hôtel de Ville in the Petite Place was built in the sixteenth century by Jacques Caron. The fine museum includes a gallery of paintings and the public are admitted every Sunday, from April to September, and on the first Sunday of the month during the rest of the year when, she supposed, the people could sniff and sigh, pausing to gaze at *Portrait of a Woman*, *Tobias and the Angel*, or *Misery and Despair* by Jules Breton.

The wind was beginning to ease. The whistling and banging had stopped. Shivering, Beatrice closed the curtains, as the light from the moon cracked across the eiderdown in thin silver branches.

*   *   *

A postcard arrived, a painting of a soldier saying farewell to his sweetheart. There was no date or postmark, just a smudged blue stamp from the censor. *I will write again soon. Jx.* She worried about it. Why had he used a pencil? It looked rushed, the letters were wobbly, and Jonathan was usually so careful. Was he ill? Was he just about to charge over the top?

'You're lucky to hear anything at all,' said Madge. 'You're lucky he had a pencil, never mind a postcard.'

Beatrice had put the card on the mantelpiece, next to the photograph of Morecambe, but then she had changed her mind, sliding it into the drawer with his other letter, and his old red scarf that still had something of his scent about it, the lime cologne he'd bought in New York, and was mercilessly teased about by the men at the office, who said that he smelled like a girl.

Madge had appeared that morning. She'd lost weight and her hair could have done with a wash. The thin grey circles that sat around her eyes made her face look dusty.

'It's Frank,' she said. 'They're talking of sending him back. A doctor came, all the way from Scotland. Some kind of head doctor. I didn't like him; the man looked very cold and hard, and I wasn't allowed inside the room while he talked to Frank, but I kept my ear to the door. I couldn't hear everything, but he was asking all these questions.'

'He can't go back,' Beatrice assured her. 'Really. They'll see he isn't well enough.'

'The man seems to think that he is. "Complete rest and relaxation is all this soldier needs." I told him everything. I had to. About the singing in French, and the cupboard, and all sorts of other things that you wouldn't like to know about.'

'Nerves?' said Beatrice.

'He called it battle stress, and he's supposed to be an expert on these matters. He said he has to go back.' Madge blinked back her tears.

'Is there no one else you can talk to about it?'

'The man said his decision was final. He signed some papers. He was very curt.'

'What did Frank say?'

'He said "yes, sir", to everything.'

'I suppose that didn't help.'

'We could always run away,' said Madge, rubbing the back of her neck. 'I have an aunt in Kendal. It's a lovely quiet place. I don't think they'd find us.'

'But then you'd always be running.'

Madge looked defeated. 'Perhaps the doctor's right,' she said, almost brightly. 'He might be better after a few more days' rest. He slept like a baby last night.'

Beatrice gave half a shrug. She was picturing him under the stairs in Madge's fur-collared coat singing in the dark.

'You'll still say nothing?' said Madge. 'To the others, I mean?'

'Of course not, if that's what you want?'

Madge nodded. 'It's my boys I'm thinking of,' she said. 'If this gets out, people can be very cruel.'

'They won't hear anything from me,' Beatrice told her. 'I promise.'

'Then I haven't any choice,' she said, chewing the skin around her fingernails. 'I'll just have to trust you.'

*   *   *

'Are you still working on the farm?' Mary asked.

Beatrice nodded. 'I often glance up at your window when I'm mucking out the pigs and wonder how you're doing.'

'I'm all right.' Mary shrugged into the sheets. There was a small blue bottle on the bedside cabinet. Earlier in the day, Dr Burke had brought more envelopes of powdery-looking tablets and bottles of bitter medicine.

'Why do you come here?' Mary asked, rubbing her grazed knuckles. 'It's not that I don't want you here, it's just that it must be awfully tedious for you. You didn't know me when I was well. Why would you want to sit in this room, drink my mother's awful tea and make conversation?'

'I like you,' said Beatrice. 'I like talking.'

'Joanna Brown and Cormac?' she said. 'Was that true? Did you really live in a house with all those dead birds?'

Beatrice rolled her eyes in mock horror. *'Tell me about it.'*

Mary bit her lip. She looked at her knees, two small bumps, poking through the eiderdown. 'When my father ran off with . . . that girl,' she said. 'I told all sorts of fancy stories. First I had him away on business, though where a factory foreman would actually go on business, I've no idea.'

'Other factories?' said Beatrice.

'I suppose so. And then he was out. Just out. People would say, "Your dad not at home tonight?" and I'd have him in the pub playing cards, or fixing my grandmother's back gate, or he'd have gone into town to get his watch mended, anything but the real reason. I couldn't do it. I couldn't say the words, "he isn't coming back".'

'I understand,' said Beatrice.

'You do?'

Beatrice nodded. 'Yes.'

'My father left almost fourteen years ago. On 6 August 1901. The girl's name was Eloise, a lovely exotic-sounding name, don't you think? My mother said she was a snivelling little tart. She actually said those words. I was nine years old, and I wanted to believe her. I thought she must be right, because the girl worked serving beer and wiping tables at the Black Bull Inn, and what kind of employment was that, for a nice sort of a girl? But then I saw her. The day my father came back to say goodbye to me, and to give me those bright coloured stamps with their pictures of fruit and birds, she was standing outside, trying to keep hidden. When I ran upstairs, throwing the stamps behind me, I caught sight of her and she was beautiful, she looked kind, and for a second, I really didn't blame him. My mother has always been difficult. I knew that even then. He painted the door. It was the wrong shade of black. The wrong shade of black! The scent he'd saved up for and bought for her birthday gave her headaches. Small things. They all add up.'

'Is your mother still difficult?' Beatrice whispered, looking towards the door as Mary grimaced and the floorboards began to creak across the landing.

She shook her head, quickly changing the tone of her voice. 'Have you heard from Jonathan?' she asked. 'Perhaps you should start reading proper books now that you're alone? You can escape inside a good thick book. You can forget the real world and its horrors for a while.'

Beatrice nodded. 'Good idea. What would you recommend?'

'*Pride and Prejudice*. You can't go wrong with that. You can borrow my copy, you'll find it on the landing. First shelf down, a red paper cover. It's all alphabetical.'

'What?'

'A,' she said. 'For Austen.'

* * *

From the window at the top of the stairs, if she stretched her neck a little, Beatrice could just about see the front of Madge's cottage door. Dr Burke was still inside. He'd been in there for almost an hour with his black Gladstone bag, and small gold-rimmed glasses that sat on the end of his long Roman nose like a fussy kind of ornament. As soon as he'd gone, his overcoat flapping, Beatrice pulled on her own coat, washed her hands again (the pigs were sticking), and headed over there, making sure that no one had seen her. Madge eventually opened the door, running a tea towel through her fingers, still in her best Sunday clothes, the only clothes she'd let a doctor see her in.

'My last hope,' she said, her shoulders bent, defeated.

'What did he say?' Beatrice asked.

'Physically fit.'

'But what about the other thing?'

'Frank was more or less himself,' she said. 'He

was trembling a bit. He kept saying, "Is it time?" over and over again, but it was as if the doctor couldn't hear him.'

'So he has to go back?'

Madge nodded. 'And what chance has he?' she said. 'Of taking good care of himself, never mind fighting a war?'

'The others will see he's all right.'

'The others will have their own selves to think about.'

'I'll make some tea,' said Beatrice. 'That's what we'll do; we'll all have a nice cup of tea.'

They sat at the table looking out of the kitchen window. Frank couldn't keep his eyes off Beatrice. He looked happy.

'Is it time yet?' he asked.

Outside, a couple of blue tits were swooping around in circles. 'I never would have thought it,' said Madge, almost managing a smile. 'You, the foreign American, making us all a nice pot of tea.'

'I can't get hold of decent coffee anywhere,' shrugged Beatrice. 'Everything tastes like chicory.'

'But there's nothing like tea,' said Frank suddenly, and they looked up at him and laughed.

* * *

Beatrice started running. He was on her doorstep. It had to be him. Out of breath, she slowed at the path, the disappointment taking over as quickly as the excitement had a moment ago. It was Jeffrey. Beatrice glared at him.

'Three days' leave,' he said. He waved a box at her. 'I've brought foreign cigarettes.'

She led him inside, but as the day was clear, and

the sun was out at last, they sat in the garden on the two faded deckchairs she'd found folded in the potting shed.

'So, what news?' asked Beatrice. Now that her disappointment that he wasn't Jonathan had passed, she felt happy to see a friendly face, someone who'd been over there.

Jeffrey shrugged. 'We're desperate for men,' he told her. 'We're losing so many every day.'

'And of course,' said Beatrice, taking a drag of her cigarette, 'that's just the kind of news I need to help me get to sleep at night.'

'Oh, he'll be all right,' said Jeffrey dismissively.

'Is it awful?'

'Hell. Don't ask.'

'Will it soon be over?'

Jeffrey opened out his hands and gave a mournful shrug as they sat in their little blue smoke clouds.

'I read the *Daily Mail*,' said Beatrice. 'They always sound so hopeful.'

'Of course we're hopeful,' said Jeffrey. 'We're always hopeful. Sometimes, that's all we can be, though I'm working with men who surprise me every day, men who make me feel hopeful, and humble, shaming and spurring me on into some kind of bravery. Whatever that is.'

'Let's not talk about it,' she shuddered. 'Tell yourself you're on vacation from all that. You'll be back there soon enough.'

'True. Anyone else home?'

Beatrice looked towards the lawn that needed cutting, then at the trees, their branches like fine bony hands gnawing at the sky. 'Frank,' she said. 'He hurt his back.'

'I'll go and see him.'
'No visitors allowed,' said Beatrice. 'We've all had very strict orders.'
'Best not to incur the wrath of Madge Temple,' he said. 'I'll obey orders, like I usually do these days.'
Later, when the sun had vanished, they took themselves inside.
'It's strange doing nothing,' said Jeffrey, tapping his fingernails on his chair arm. 'It's almost unnerving, not to be looking at the time, or over my shoulder, or sitting in the mud.'
'It goes very slowly here.'
'I can hear every tick,' he said, nodding at her clock. 'Time passing.'
'Take me out,' she said suddenly. 'Take me out to a public house for a glass of gin or something. I'm sure Jonathan wouldn't mind. We shouldn't be sitting here, looking at the clock. What an awful waste.'
'All right, farm girl,' he grinned. 'You're on.'

* * *

Madge watched them go. She was standing in her bedroom window. Beatrice had changed into a blue dress. She was clapping her hands, like a small excited child.
'Sir!' Frank shouted from the bed she'd tucked him into. 'Is it time?'
Madge turned towards him and tried her best to smile.
'Not yet, love,' she said. 'You've days and days ahead of you. You've plenty of time. We all have.'

*   *   *

The pub was busy, but they found a small round table close to the fireplace, Beatrice giving a mock grimace towards the case of stuffed pike and the dusty fox head with its lolling pink tongue and missing glass eye.

'I can't get away from it,' she said, taking a sip from her small glass of ale, which Jeffrey assured her was the only thing in the place worth drinking.

There were other women, glued to men in uniform, laughing, and nuzzling the blue and khaki shoulders, sipping beer of their own with glazed-looking eyes.

'I expect people will think we're a couple,' said Beatrice.

'I expect they will,' said Jeffrey with a shrug.

'I wish you were with him, over there. I'd feel so much better.'

'You would?'

'Definitely. Just look at you,' she said, smiling at his face. 'You are reassuringly unchanged.'

'Thinner surely?'

'Maybe.'

'The food is measly,' he told her. 'By the time the rations reach my station, they've either been dropped into the mud, or half have gone missing. Wet and starving, that's what I am.'

'You're all dry now,' she said, looking into the fire, the thin logs and branches rough at the edges and fraying bright orange, like the filaments in a light bulb. 'And full?'

'Fullish. I don't think I'll ever be really full again.'

'Look, soldier, they have pork pies just sitting on

the bar,' she said, 'and the pastry is thicker than my arm.'

'Sold,' he said. 'I'll take two of them.'

She rolled her eyes at him. The beer was making her cheeks tingle. On another table a soldier had a broken arm and a web of black lines scratched across his cheeks and he looked at Beatrice with hard hollow eyes, before turning back to his beer and a fresh game of cards.

'The world will never be the same again,' she said. 'That's what the papers say.'

'And you know the *Daily Mail* is always right,' said Jeffrey.

'Really?'

He smiled. 'It will be better, yes, it will be so much better.'

'Good, but let's talk about the past for a minute.'

He put down his glass, and wiped his foamy lips with his fingertips. 'What past? Yours? Mine?'

'Jonathan's.'

'Oh? You want to know about his deep dark secret past? It was the same as any other young man's, I suppose.'

'I mean his life. I've been trying to find out about his parents. His family. What were they like? Do you remember them?'

'His mother, not at all, though of course I remember his father very well. He was a dapper-looking gentleman, but he was quiet, and something of a loner. He was great friends with Lionel. You should ask him.'

'He never remarried,' said Beatrice. 'He never got over losing his wife?'

Jeffrey looked hard into his nearly empty glass. 'I wouldn't say that,' he said. 'There were rumours of lady friends, but no one ever saw them.'

'Perhaps that's all they were,' said Beatrice. 'Rumours.'

'Twenty years is a long time to be alone,' said Jeffrey.

An old man appeared with a tray around his neck. 'Whelks?' he said. 'Cockles and mussels?'

'I'll have mussels. And you?' said Jeffrey, rummaging in his pocket for some change. 'I can recommend Ed Pearson's seafood; he's been selling it here for years.'

'And never a dull moment,' the man said. 'I have shrimps, if the lady would prefer something a little more refined?'

'Oh, that's OK, I'll take the cockles,' she smiled. 'You see, I'm not at all refined.'

The man chuckled, handing her a carton and a small wooden fork.

'Now,' said Beatrice, pulling her stool a little closer, 'what about my husband? I'm getting curious. Has he got a murky past?'

'Not at all,' said Jeffrey, lighting another cigarette. 'Though of course, they were all in love with him.'

'Who's all?'

'Madge, and Mary, Lizzie and Ada. They worshipped him. From afar,' he added.

'Only from afar?'

'They knew,' he said, taking another swig of beer, 'that he wouldn't be interested in that kind of girl.'

'What kind of girl?'

'You know exactly what kind of girl I mean,' said Jeffrey. 'Do you want me to spell it out? Lower class. Uneducated.'

'Uneducated? Mary's read more books than I'll

ever manage in a lifetime.'

'And you sold picture postcards,' he said. 'Aye, there's the rub, that's what they can't come to terms with. Jonathan went and married a shop girl after all.'

* * *

It was a dry clear night as they picked they way over the cobbles.

'The stars,' said Jeffrey, suddenly stopping, tipping back his head. 'The stars are very comforting in France. Seeing them blinking by the moon, those very same constellations.'

'What's it like? France?'

He said nothing as they began their walk again. Beatrice could taste the sour bitter beer on her breath.

'Like hell,' he said. 'That's all I want to say. Like hell.'

'But the other parts of France,' she said. 'The France that isn't fighting. Away from the battlefields? Is it beautiful?'

'It's all fighting,' he said. 'It's all mud and hell.'

She didn't say anything; she pushed her hands deep inside her pockets, as their boots made a creaking sound.

Then, 'There was a place,' he said quietly. 'A small place. I can't tell you what it was called. We were marching, the sun was shining, and then the snow, it was coming down in curtains. Some of the locals were standing in their doorways, watching these uncouth British soldiers marching through their shattered lives. A few of the old men were spitting, I can tell you that. Apparently, a month earlier one of the girls in the village had been attacked by a Canadian infantryman and we could feel the hate and tension hanging heavy in the air. We felt sad and somewhat guilty. The cottages were crumbling, the farmers' carts were broken, their horses old and lame. Some of the women were crying. It was a desolate place, until suddenly we turned, and we were at the top of a sloping valley, and beyond there were fields and fields, a small grey church, a farmhouse. It was a beautiful sight. Really. I wanted to sit right there and paint it in the snow. That night we slept in a barn. A woman with a thick blue ribbon in her hair brought us steaming bowls of broth and jugs of red wine. It wasn't much, but it felt like the best thing we'd tasted in our lives.'

They stopped outside Fox Cottage, the wisteria hanging ghostlike from the thick sloping walls.

'Come inside,' he said. 'I'm feeling quite morose.'

'It's late.'

'What does time matter?' he shrugged. 'But I'll walk you home if that's what you want?'

She shook her head, and followed him over the step.

The room was wide, the ceiling low, and the thick distempered walls were covered in paintings and prints. Butterflies. Trees. Insects. There were advertisements for ink, beef tea and dentifrice, Orchid Dusting Powder, liver salts and lamp wicks.

'Those pictures might be selling things,' said Jeffrey, leaning on his messy desk underneath the window, 'but I consider them works of art all the same.'

'You're very talented.'

'Thank you.'

She sat on the sofa, with its scattering of worn cushions, the arms stained with ink.

'I kept wondering,' she said, 'if you might be in an office somewhere, or in a studio, designing war posters, you know, "Send Something For Our Troops", "Save Food", that kind of thing?'

He laughed. 'However lily-livered I might look, I'm far too fit and well for that game,' he said. 'Those studios are full of lame artists, or consumptives, coughing into their palettes.'

'I'm sorry.'

'Don't be. You saw what I was like before I left. You had every reason to wonder.'

'I don't know how soldiers cope. You must all get very frightened.' She paused. 'What do you know about this illness they're calling battle stress?' she asked.

'Not a lot,' he said. 'Though most of them are faking it.'

He went to his drinks cabinet and poured them both a glass of cognac from an almost empty, dusty bottle.

'I'm always wondering what Jonathan might be doing. Now for instance.' She looked up at the clock. 'It's eleven o'clock. It's midnight in France.'

'Perhaps he's sleeping? He's a sergeant. He'll be much more comfortable than most.'

'Really?'

'Oh, yes. Our sergeant, a snappy man called Barlow, has an almost complete china tea set on a dented silver tray, he has pictures on the walls—not very good ones, mind you—he always has a bottle of something, and an almost real bed made from beer crates and wadding.'

'That's one thing I haven't imagined,' she said, rubbing her own aching eyes. 'Jonathan simply sleeping.'

'Of course, at first, you wonder how you'll manage it, then by the time it's your turn to rest, you can drop off in seconds, you could sleep standing up like a horse if you had to.'

'I can't imagine it.'

'No. You wouldn't want to.'

But then, looking at the quivering metal hands on the clock, the small sooty fire and Jeffrey's cap with its badge shining on the desk, she could think of nothing else, and she was sure she could hear the shouting and screaming, the gunfire rattling over their small frozen heads in the trenches.

'Let's talk about something else entirely,' she said suddenly. 'Something frivolous.'

'Frivolous is a word I haven't heard in a long time,' said Jeffrey.

'Then frivolous it shall be.'

'Hmm.' He squeezed the last few drops of cognac into their glasses. 'Let me think . . .'

'When were you at your most frivolous?' she asked, smiling.

'When I was a student,' he said. 'We'd sit on the studio roof drinking cheap wine and smoking these stinking Turkish cigarettes that a boy called Julian would filch from God knows where. They were murder on the throat. We'd leave the windows open downstairs and play gramophone records, lie on our backs and talk nonsense all night. Sometimes we'd dance, right there on the rooftop—it was flat, by the way—and we'd babble on about everything, though it would usually wind up with how our fathers despaired of us ever getting real employment. One boy had been completely disinherited because his parents were so ashamed of him. Funny thing is, they'd spent a small fortune on art, they'd hung paintings on their walls, and admired them, visited the Louvre and so on. Where on earth did they think the bloody things came from? Did these paintings just appear?'

She laughed.

'Artists are wonderful creatures and very much admired,' he said. 'As long as they're not in the family.'

'Were there girls in your class?'

'One or two, and they were lovely.'

'Did you fall in love?'

'Every five minutes.'

'Was there anyone—you know, serious?'

He took a sip of his cognac and put the glass by his feet. 'Yes,' he said. 'There's always one that breaks your heart.'

'Tell me?'

'No.'

He took his empty glass to his desk and started moving papers around, sliding them under the giant conch shell he was using as a paperweight. He put some loose charcoal pencils into a pot.

'It's very late,' said Beatrice. 'I should be going.'

'All right.' He turned towards her and shrugged. 'Frivolity,' he said, with something of a smile. 'See where it gets you?'

* * *

After a day bagging carrots and turnips, Beatrice sat with a glass of warm milk reading *Pride and*

Prejudice. Jeffrey had waved good-humouredly while she was shovelling muck in the farmyard, enjoying the sight of her in muddy overalls. He was on his way to see a cousin whose husband had been killed. 'I didn't really know the chap,' he'd told her. 'But sympathy and respect costs very little.'

The milk made her think about Normal. Glasses left souring on the table. Joanna adding a drop of honey when she'd had her hand stitched. She looked at the scar. It was almost invisible now.

The book had a torn paper jacket and yellow-edged pages. The spine was a shade or two lighter, where it had faded in the sun. It smelled musty. After the first thirty pages, her eyes began to ache. The print was too small and she longed for her magazines. The pictures of showgirls, the chat about horoscopes, or the baby-faced actor who'd left his new wife to set up home with an acrobat. So she gave up, putting the book across the cushions as a small piece of sunlight fell across the jacket. Words appeared. Holding it at an angle she tried to make them out. Scrawled dents across the illustration of a girl in a pale Regency dress said, *Please come home it's killing me.*

* * *

'You've been out with Jeffrey Woodhouse,' said Ginny. 'What would Jonathan think?'

'What do you mean?'

'You think he wouldn't mind?'

'Why should he mind?' said Beatrice.

Ginny shrugged. 'I don't know, but it doesn't seem right to me. Is it different in America?' she asked. 'Do married women go out with other men from time to time?'

'I don't understand. We only went out for a drink. Jeffrey and Jonathan are friends. Can't I be friends with Jeffrey? Who says men and women can't be friends?'

'Nature,' said Ginny, as a pig rolled onto its back.

* * *

'I thought I'd come and say goodbye,' said Jeffrey. 'I've had my five days' leave.'

'Goodbye? It must be England's favourite word.'

'Any news from back home?'

'Nothing,' she told him. 'Coney Island? New York? It's just like a dream.'

'That's exactly how I feel about this place when I'm over there. Is it real?'

'Oh, I think so,' she said, leaning against the windowsill, the light pushing through her hair.

'I'll miss you,' said Jeffrey.

'You will?'

'Yes.'

'Then good, I'll miss you too.'

He smiled. 'I'd better go.' He looked at the clock, then at the picture of Morecambe. 'I'll think of that,' he said.

* * *

Two days later, Frank was sitting at the kitchen table in his uniform. He had an hour before the train left.

'What shall I tell the others?' said Madge. 'They'll wonder why he went off without even saying hello, never mind goodbye.'

'You could tell them that he had to go quickly, without warning, that there was some kind of an emergency? They sent him a telegram? Or I could tell them for you?'

Madge said nothing, putting her lips to her teacup.

'Is it time?' said Frank.

'No,' snapped Madge. 'Not yet.'

'I hear you've been eating bouillabaisse,' said Beatrice.

'Stinking bully bass is all they had,' said Frank, resting his chin on his hands. 'Bony fish heads and guts. They were all dirty bastards, but you're lovely you are, you know.'

Beatrice left them. She sat at her window with an American magazine that was so well read the words were starting to vanish. She looked at ads for grape soda, cotton gloves and washing powder. The latest shades of the season were crash, vivid coral and deep cobalt blue. *Miss Susanna Hearn (Delaware) held her eighteenth birthday party at the Astor Hotel.* Outside, a door slammed and Frank started shouting, No! No! No! *The guests were entertained by the James Baxter Orchestra. Champagne was served on the roof terrace. At midnight, Miss Hearn's father presented his daughter with a Model T Ford. She was said to be 'delighted'.*

THE PRESERVATION OF MEAT

Sunday

On a late-April afternoon, Beatrice and Elijah were listening to the transformation of their father from the corner of the landing. They could hear him batting the dust and the creases from his mothballed clothes; the splashing of water, and the snip, snip, snip of the scissors.

'He's cutting his beard,' Elijah whispered.

'I can smell soap,' sniffed Beatrice. 'Can you smell soap?'

'It's the good soap. It's the sandalwood.'

'Oh, this is going to be some fine trip,' their father was saying through the crack in the bedroom door. 'I was going to write to the keeper, but then I changed my mind, no, I'd much rather meet him face to face. Now, Elijah, don't go all pious on me, if I start telling a few half-truths, don't land me in it.'

'You want me to come with you?'

'You're both coming,' he said, stepping out of his room for a moment, his suspenders hanging loose and his hair dripping wet. 'Didn't I tell you? I've got the tickets in my jacket pocket. The train leaves at eight tomorrow morning. We're staying overnight in a small hotel called the Lemon Tree. It's all arranged, and paid for.'

'But—' Elijah slumped hard against the wall, loosening his collar.

'No buts,' their father said, waving his soapy hand. 'Everyone likes a menagerie, Lincoln Park is one of the best in the state, and the *Chronicle* tells me that the sun will be shining, apart from a brief scattering of cloud, later on in the afternoon.'

'Lincoln Park, Chicago?' said Elijah.

'The zoo by the lake. Everyone's talking about it.'

'Everyone who?'

'Bob Rickman. He tells me they have everything, bears, parakeets, monkeys.'

'The next-door neighbour? When did he tell you about Lincoln Park Zoo?'

'When that dozy blind dog of his lost its ball. I found it in a bush. I threw it back over. He started talking, and I couldn't get away.'

Beatrice took a couple of steps forward, passing the wild turkey and something that looked like a dormouse sitting on a twig. 'What exactly are we going to do at Lincoln Park?' she asked.

'The same as everyone else,' her father said. 'We're going to look at all those animals, we'll buy ourselves a souvenir guide, and we'll eat whatever it is they're selling at the kiosks.'

Elijah looked at Beatrice and gave a helpless shrug. 'What was it you were saying?' he asked. 'About writing to the keeper?'

Their father sighed heavily. He was fully dressed again. His skin was shiny pink and scrubbed. 'Don't you listen to anything I say? I told you. I was going to enquire about their disposal system.'

'Their what?'

'When an animal dies, what do they do with it? It would be a shame to let a good animal carcass go to waste, when I have the expertise to transform it into an interesting, educational, almost alive-looking specimen. Now, Elijah, do you have a tub of hair cream I can borrow for tomorrow? My hair is wild and springy, like I've just had a terrible fright, it needs licking down, I need to look respectable, I need to look like I know what it is I'm talking about, which of course I do,' he said. 'Find the hair cream, Elijah. That's right, you heard. Hair cream will make all the difference.'

Monday

At ten to eight they were on the eastbound platform, waiting for the next Chicago train. Beatrice and Elijah were standing a little way back from their father who was leaning against a lamp post, his hair slick with cream, poring over yet another catalogue that the mail boy had handed him that morning. He was talking to himself and screwing up his face. 'Wire frames,' he was saying. 'Plaster bones? Why plaster? Why not the real thing? It's an animal we're recreating, not a child's stuffed toy.'

They sat in the dining car. The other tables were crowded. Families in their best spring clothes sat quietly, looking through the velvet-curtained windows, the world a steamy blur. Girls in fresh lace collars toyed with their hair, reading the breakfast menu, or their new city guides to Chicago. Beatrice looked at her brother. Elijah was nineteen years old, but he was like a small fresh-faced boy, complete with freckles, reading his book of sermons, smiling and nodding at the pages as if those words could see all those rapt encouraging signs he was giving them. He'd been working with the local minister, who had great hopes for him as a lay preacher. 'You go out into the world and you tell those folks what this is all about,' he'd said, banging his Bible. 'Doesn't matter who they are, where they are, or what it is they're doing. They could be picking cotton, or washing down their automobiles. You reach out and you grab them. You get them to listen, to ponder a while, and to pray.'

Washed and brushed and spruced, her father, she supposed, looked like any other father in the car.

'Ham and eggs,' he was saying, licking his lips. 'You can't go wrong with ham and eggs, even on a train.'

She looked at her reflection in the glass. She was just seventeen, yet she felt tired and worn; her dress had looked fine at home, but now she could see that it was old and faded, and she couldn't help but compare herself to the girls on the opposite table, sisters with hair as light as her own, with pearls in their ears and good-looking clothes. Their mother, a plump woman with a small turned-up nose, kept tapping the table saying, 'Amy, look at that building.' 'Lucille, did we pack our new spring bonnets?' 'Larry, the hotel is in a good district, isn't it? I wouldn't like a repeat of Wilmington, not when the girls are with us, Lord, I simply wouldn't get to sleep at night.'

Beatrice read the menu again. She tucked in the frayed edges of her cuffs, yet she supposed they were lucky. Families all over America were living in poverty. Elijah had told her all about it. How he'd met families who were starving, who were dressed in rags, with nothing on their feet.

'I told them that God would provide.'

'Really?' said Beatrice. 'And they didn't want to shoot you?'

The train rattled on. The waiter brought them coffee, ham and eggs, baskets of bread, curls of yellow butter and preserves. Elijah prayed, while the sisters on the opposite table giggled into their hands. Beatrice turned her face towards the window, losing herself in the fields, houses and the glass that flashed back in the sunlight.

Their father slept for most of the journey. Elijah kept sharpening a pencil, annotating the sermons. Beatrice listened to the other travelling families. 'I've never liked Uncle Claude. Why? Because he spits tobacco juice onto the rugs, isn't that reason enough?' 'Father was in Chicago after the fire, he said he could still feel the heat through his boots.' 'I have a headache, Mama. Mama, I said I have a headache.'

The sun was still shining when they reached Chicago. They rode the crowded 'L' to Harlech Street, where the Lemon Tree Hotel was squeezed between an employment agency and John T. Hooper Optometrist. It was a small, shabby hotel, with a cramped green lobby. The man behind the desk was reading a sports paper, and he handed them their keys with hardly a glance up from the page.

'Second floor,' he grunted. 'Top of the stairs, take a left.'

Beatrice wasn't disappointed with her room. She'd had little expectations. The narrow bed was hard and the window looked out onto a yard full of boxes, but there were no stuffed birds or animals. She found a bent hatpin in one of the drawers and the visiting hours of the Chicago Hospital for Women and Children had been taped across the bureau. Someone had circled the wards for infectious diseases.

'Let's get out of here,' her father said. 'Why waste time cramped up in our pens, when we could be observing wild animals at close quarters?'

* * *

Her father was trembling as he paid the entrance fee. The air was already full of animals, the scent and the sound of them mingling with fried apple doughnuts and a small wind band.

'This,' Elijah whispered, 'could be a very bad day.'

Beatrice felt a little sick. She'd rarely seen so many people. Squeezed into the elevated train, her face almost pressed into someone else's sweaty collar, she'd felt like she was suffocating. Here, children raced around with balloons and wooden tigers. The small lake shimmered like a moving plate of silver as her father strode purposefully towards the large mammal house, the map of the zoo flapping in his hand.

'First stop,' he said, 'the lions. Margo and Mitchell, bought last year from Barnum and Bailey's circus.'

People were already pressed against the bars of the cage, watching Margo and Mitchell sleeping in the sawdust.

'Keep a step back,' a woman was saying to her children, 'they might be hungry; they could soon have both your arms off.' The children squealed, running around in circles.

'They're nothing but a bag of old bones,' a man said. 'Let's go and find something with a little more life left in it.'

Beatrice and Elijah duly looked into the cage, where the lions slept, oblivious to the faces, and to the flies that had settled on their scabby-looking tails. Their father became very still. He was carefully observing the heavy bone structure, the position of the ears, the fine brown lines of their whiskers. He wrote something in the guidebook with a small silver pencil.

'How old would you say they were?' he asked.

Beatrice shrugged.

'They look pretty old to me,' said Elijah. 'I'd say they were ancient.'

'Exactly, and if they came from the circus, then they must be into their retirement years. A lion,' sniffed their father, 'is a distinct possibility.'

Beatrice didn't know whether to laugh or feel alarmed. 'A lion?' she said. 'How on earth would you get a dead lion all the way over to Normal?'

Her father turned on his heels. 'Have you never heard of a crate?' he said. 'The railroads carry hundreds every day.'

'But, well,' she hesitated, 'wouldn't the lion . . . go off?'

'A little preservation is all that's required. Think of meat,' he said. 'Think of all those Virginia hams that go winging their way around the country at Thanksgiving.'

Elijah chewed his fingers.

'What's the matter with you?' his father asked.

'Nothing,' he sniggered. 'I was thinking of Daniel. "Satan as a roaring lion walketh about seeking whom he may devour." '

'My lion will be finished with walking. My lion will be required to do an awful lot of standing. Though,' he pondered, 'lying down might be easier.'

In the next cage a camel stood chewing a wad of hay, its pale pink lips flopping over its teeth, of which it had thirty-four, according to the information sign, and most of them looked broken. The camel (a dromedary) was called Millicent.

'I'm not interested in the camel,' he said. 'I know my limitations. What with its hump and its spindle-like legs, I don't think I could manage it.'

'Hallelujah,' said Elijah.

'The camel certainly looks relieved,' said Beatrice. 'Did you hear that, Millie? You're saved.'

'Stop behaving like a double act and come and find the wolves,' he said. 'It says here they have a pair of grey wolves, and wolves are what I've come looking for. They're my next big thing.'

The two unnamed wolves were in a large, wide enclosure. Hiding behind the logs, they were not a popular exhibit.

'They look like dogs,' said Elijah, squinting. 'Willie Freeman at church is from Vermont. He says he has dozens of wolves in his backyard. He can hear them crying all night long.'

Beatrice shivered, picturing her father on a wolf hunt, net in hand, the moon hanging in the sky, shrouded in a curtain of fine white mist. Would she have to go with him?

'Here, boy,' said their father, crouching by the rails. 'Here, boy, come on now, let me see how you move.'

One of the wolves hunched its way over to a rock. 'Fascinating,' he breathed. 'Look at its slinking shoulders, the loose fur and skin, and that face, so intent and pointed and serious.'

Elijah yawned. A man dressed in an ape costume was handing out monkey nuts. Pink-cheeked girls linked arms; bored of looking through bars, they were skipping towards the ice-cream barrel.

'It says here that their keeper's name is Jed Adams. Do you think he'll be around?'

'What are you going to ask him?' Beatrice worried. 'Should we leave you for half an hour, so that you can go away and find him?'

'We'll all go together,' he said, brushing down his pants. 'You can back me up.'

'Back you up?' said Elijah. 'Back you up, how?'

'I don't know,' he shrugged. 'Just help me out now and then.'

In the distance, by a cage of green parrots, a man in a tan-coloured jacket was sweeping the walkway.

'You work here?' their father asked.

The man slowly raised himself up, leaned his big red hands on the top of his broom, and smiled. 'Sure looks like it,' he grinned.

'You know a Jed Adams?'

'Who's asking?'

'A Mr Ethan Lyle,' he said. 'That's who's asking.'

Beatrice felt a little cold. She kept her eyes on the boys peering through the parrot cage. Suddenly, the birds dived from their perches, a swoop of squawking jade as the boys started moving away.

'Parrots are for girls,' said one of them.

'Ach, they don't even talk,' said another, picking up a stone.

'Is Jed Adams here?' her father asked.

'Probably.'

'So where might I find him?'

The man took out his watch. 'He'll be in his room around now. That's at the back of the porcupine cage. Do you have an appointment?'

'We'll just take our chances.'

'You folks from Chicago?'

'No, sir. We're from Normal.'

'You are? You came all this way to see Jed Adams and you didn't make an appointment?'

'We came to see the zoo,' he said, turning to look for the porcupine sign. 'That's what we came for.'

The man nodded. 'Yes,' he said, 'a zoo is a marvellous thing.'

They walked towards the porcupines with their long sweeping bristles. A short stony path led to the office where a sign on the door said, *Keeper*.

'Looks like we're here,' said their father, straightening out his shoulders.

Jed Adams opened the door, eating a sandwich. He was tall, around twenty-five, with chestnut-brown hair, and a wide open smile.

'What can I do for you?' he asked. 'Come on in, folks, don't be shy, come and step right on inside.'

Beatrice felt embarrassed, the man was eating, they'd obviously disturbed him, and what would he make of her father, with his strange, macabre ideas?

'Jed Adams.' The man held out his free hand, after wiping off the crumbs.

'Pleased to meet you, Mr Adams. I'm Ethan Lyle, and this here is my son Elijah, and my daughter Beatrice.'

Jed Adams nodded towards them, and blushed. His office was small and messy. There were pictures of bears on the walls. Books on zoology were piled on his desk. The room smelled of coffee, turpentine and animal droppings.

'I'm interested in your wolves,' her father said.

Beatrice, squeezing her fingers tight around her thumbs, tried to disassociate herself entirely from the conversation. She studied the bear pictures. *Brown Bear with Cubs. Polar Bear on Icecap*. Elijah stood looking at his feet.

'The wolves?' said Jed, taking a last bite of his sandwich. 'Grey wolves are interesting creatures, though you sure can't make a pet of them.'

'I should think not.'

'We have an information stand. It's very good. You can purchase pamphlets inside the shop, and all at reasonable prices.'

'It's not that kind of query.'

'No?'

'Might I ask how long you've had them here?'

Jed looked puzzled. 'A year. Fourteen months,' he said. 'They settled in well and they've never been a problem to us. They're often restless, but that's wolves for you; they seem happy enough, both of them.'

'And what is their age?'

'Are you an inspector?' said Jed. 'Is this some kind of test?'

'Not at all. I was simply wondering how long you expect them to live?'

'You don't like zoos?' Jed looked uneasy. 'Are you one of those campaigners?'

'I like zoos very much.'

'You do?'

'Sure I do. Who doesn't?'

'Then the wolves are five and six years old. I'll be honest with you, sir, I'm a bear man, and I'm no real expert on wolves, but I'm expecting them to live another four or five years, something like that.'

'Then what happens?'

'Then we either acquire another pair, or we find something else to fill the cage.'

'I meant—' He coughed. 'What do you do with the remains?'

Jed Adams scratched his head. Beatrice had a crick in her neck. Elijah pretended to be interested in a book called *The World of the Captive Mammal*.

'The remains? We burn all the carcasses, Mr Lyle. Or the veterinarian takes them away.'

'Seems such a waste.'

The man laughed. 'What do you expect us to do with the remains, sir? Give them a full Christian burial?'

'Now there's an idea,' said Elijah.

'No,' said their father, 'not at all. You could give them to me.'

Jed Adams got up from the desk where he was leaning and walked around a little. He brushed against Beatrice, making her turn away from the pictures, her face flushing pink.

'So,' said Jed, addressing Elijah, who was just as flushed as his sister. 'What does a man from—where did you say you were from?'

'I didn't. We're from Normal.'

'That figures. What does a man from way out in Normal want with the carcass of a wolf?'

Beatrice decided that she'd have to say something quickly. What must this man be thinking? She gave him a beautiful smile, blinked her wet blue eyes and stopped him in his tracks.

'Mr Adams, my father is a skilled taxidermist,'

she said. 'It's a growing pastime, and something he is extremely serious about. So far, he has rebuilt birds and small animals. Now he'd like something bigger.'

'Yes,' her father said, nodding vigorously. 'That's it exactly. That's the reason that I'm here.'

'I've never heard of such a thing,' said Jed Adams. 'Rebuilt wolves?'

'You've never seen a stuffed and mounted creature?' her father asked, amazed. 'Some of the bigger museums show collections in their natural history department. I myself have seen beavers, wolverines and turtles.'

Jed chuckled. 'Have you seen the size of those wolves, Mr Lyle?'

'The Museum of Natural History in Manhattan has an Indian elephant standing large as life in the lobby,' he said.

'So, where do you plan to show your specimen? Your porch? Now that would be a real nice welcome for your guests.'

'I plan to donate it.'

'You do?' said Elijah.

'Certainly. I would like to give the good people of Illinois the chance to see my art, and to observe the wild wolf without any fear or danger.'

Jed rubbed his forehead and swallowed. Beatrice and those eyes of hers were making him feel nervous. 'Thing is, sir, I don't know why we're even having this conversation. I can't let you have those wolves dead or alive.'

'You can't?' Beatrice felt a sudden need to stick up for her father, though her voice began to waver a little towards the end. 'Are you not in charge of these animals? Animals that will end up being burned?'

'Miss, we are not allowed to give our creatures away, even when they're completely demised. There'd be a risk of disease. It just isn't healthy.'

'Chicago is full of meat packers,' said her father. 'What's the difference?'

Jed opened the office door. A beam of sunlight fell across his face, making him blink. 'There are laws, Mr Lyle, and in four or five years' time, when those wolves are dead, I doubt they will have changed.'

'I don't believe you. Why, if such a law exists then how do these museums get hold of their exhibits? And what about New York? Those big-shot curators and their taxidermists were allowed a fully grown Indian elephant.'

'Perhaps they were friendly with a big game hunter,' he said, showing them out the door. 'Either that, or a circus.'

Beatrice was glad to be outside again. Above her head a lost red balloon shivered in the sky, then got caught up in some branches. She heard the gibbering of the animals, the high-pitched squealing and a slightly muffled roar.

'Well, Mr Lyle,' said Jed Adams, shoving his hands inside his armpits and bouncing up and down. 'Say, you might have missed out on a wolf, but you've certainly made my day. This will do the rounds of the zoo for weeks.'

'Who runs this place?'

'A Mr Ephraim Colt.'

'Then I will write to him.'

'Oh, please do that. I wouldn't want to stop you. He's a hard-working man, and he'll be awfully glad of some amusement.'

'It will not be an amusing letter.'

'Believe me, sir, it will.'

They were at the end of the path when Beatrice took a quick glance over her shoulder. Jed Adams had a hand in his hair. He was smiling and shaking his head.

'It could have been worse,' Elijah whispered to his sister. 'Much worse.'

'The impudence and the ignorance of the man,' said their father with his teeth clenched. 'He knows nothing.'

'I agree,' said Beatrice, 'because, after all, if taxidermy is displayed in an important New York museum, then it's a very serious business.'

Elijah looked amazed. 'Sister, you're forgetting. It's one thing looking at those animals inside a museum, but we have to live with them, and the outhouse is hardly the right place to take a wolf to pieces.'

'Chicken,' their father said. 'I can smell fried chicken.'

'Are you awfully upset?' she asked.

'Not at all,' he told her. 'These ideas have to be explored. Anyway, Lincoln Park Zoo hasn't heard the last of Ethan Lyle. I can be extremely persistent. Now let's go and buy some chicken, I could do with a bite to eat, and it does smell uncommonly good.'

* * *

They strolled around the zoo for another half an hour, but their hearts weren't in it. Gazing at the monkeys, their father looked sad. They were a nice size. They had a curl in their tails, and small, human-like faces.

'I was reading about a man in Seattle,' he told them. 'He stuffed one of these little marmosets and he gave it to his wife to keep as a companion. Now she dresses it in soldier suits and takes the creature everywhere. When she visits friends and restaurants, she hooks it onto a chair by its tail. She once took it to the theatre. The play was by Mr Bernard Shaw. It was very popular. They made her buy the little stuffed monkey a ticket.'

'Really?'

'Oh, yes,' he said. 'Every word is true.'

*   *   *

Chicago was wonderful, filthy and frightening. The air sloped. The wide crushing streets were full of steam and sweet oil, soapsuds, raw meat and wet metal polish, new money clinked, and girls with scarlet lips sashayed their way between street lamps, barrels and freshly slaughtered cattle. Walking back to Harlech Street, they passed bars with open doors, glimpsing men without jackets drinking straight from the neck of the bottle. Beatrice had never seen such a thing. Normal was dry. Outside a particularly lively establishment called Frankie D's Saloon, Elijah stopped.

'Keep up, keep up,' their father shouted, battered by the crowds.

'Wait!' Elijah stood stock-still. 'I can't pass this by. It's too good an opportunity to miss.'

'What? Drinking liquor? Liquor just addles the brain.'

'No. I'm a preacher, I'm going to be a preacher, and I'm supposed to practise my preaching. If I can save just one of those poor damned men from drowning in their sins, then it will be worth it.'

Beatrice felt faint. 'No,' she said. 'No, leave them alone, I want to go back to my room.'

'I can't walk away,' said Elijah. 'I've been called.'

'We can't stop him,' said their father, shrugging and shaking his head. 'The boy has found God, and who am I to say it's a bad thing? The hotel is just around the block, do you think you can find it?'

Elijah nodded. He was rifling through his pockets for his sermon notes.

'We'll see you back at the Lemon Tree, a saloon is not the kind of place for Beatrice to be visiting, even if she is with Normal's John Wesley.'

'They'll kill him,' Beatrice said, walking on.

'Sure they will, like a lamb to the slaughter, but the boy's got to learn.'

* * *

Beatrice was exhausted. Lying on the bed, staring at the ceiling with its dusty yellow paint, and a crack that looked like a hand, she tried not to think of her brother in Frankie D's Saloon, shouting out his sermon to men with bloodshot eyes.

Her father was napping in his room. She was tired, but she couldn't sleep for five minutes in the Lemon Tree Hotel, where the man at the desk was reading about the Chicago Cubs, shaking his head and sighing at the week's poor results, an old man in a striped collarless shirt was coughing in the backyard, rooting through the boxes, and in another room a baby was crying, and a woman with a creak in her voice was singing a song about her poor departed papa. Was this place ever quiet?

She pulled on her boots, now tight against her ankles; she took the thin silver key and pulled her door shut. Downstairs, the man with the rattling pages was drinking a cup of coffee. She could see the street through the plate glass in the door, its flat brown colours, splashes of crimson and the sunshine hanging like a rinsed-out piece of muslin was something you could slice through.

'Excuse me,' she said to the man behind the counter.

'Hmm?' He didn't look up.

'Could you tell me where the nearest church might be?'

'What?'

'I said . . .' she began, as the man lifted his head at last, biting his lip and then looking somewhere else. 'Do you know where the nearest church is?'

'What kind of church?'

'Any church.'

'Well, miss; I guess what I'm trying to say is, are you a Catholic, or Baptist, or a Jew, or something else entirely?'

'I'm nothing,' she told him. 'I just want some peace and quiet.'

'You're nothing? You don't look like nothing to me. St Pius,' he said. 'Will he do? He's the nearest. Turn right out the door, take the first right and St Pius will be looking at you from his shiny white tower.'

The air pressed against her face while billboards advertising chewing gum flashed between billboards advertising shaving soap. A *Tribune* had been taken by the wind, its old news rising as she looked out for Elijah, her eyes aching. She took a right turn. A marble saint holding out his thin pointed hands balanced on a block of white stone. The bricks looked cool. Plants with yellow leaves were curled around the steps and the door was slightly ajar.

Inside, the silence was sudden and her footsteps were so loud she moved down the aisle on tiptoe. The church was almost empty. A woman in a black coat was kneeling near the front and a man was lighting a candle. Beatrice sat towards the back, closed her eyes and drifted. She pictured Joanna making a pudding, a vase of pink flowers, Cormac Fitzgerald twisting his cap in his hands, a breeze in his flame of red hair. He was laughing. He was always laughing. He had radishes in his pockets and shiny purple beans, like Jack before the beanstalk, and when she opened her eyes she was sure she could see him, standing by the font, his hands in holy water, but after she'd blinked a couple of times, it wasn't Cormac, it was the woman in the long black coat genuflecting at the altar.

She felt better. Back outside, the wind caught in her hair and woke her. Through the forest of faces, she saw a red-and-grey muffler, and then Elijah stumbling with his hands in the air, as if he was calling for help.

'What's the matter?' she breathed. 'What's happened to you?' She looked him up and down, but there were no signs of any obvious bruising, no broken bones or bloodied lips. Elijah was intact, his hair still slick with the cream he now shared with his father.

'I can do it!' he shouted, pushing her towards

Harlech Street. 'I really can do it! The Reverend Malcolm Henderson was right. I can reach out and grab them, and if it wasn't for the liquor they'd be saved.'

Back in the lobby, they sat on a worn overstuffed sofa, the same dirty green as the walls. Elijah was panting. There were vibrations in the air coming from his skin like static electricity.

'They didn't want to brawl?'

'Not at all. Heck, they liked me. You know, I really think they liked me. But boy, it wasn't easy. I had to shout to get their attention. I started telling them about temptation, and how it's a weakness that brings them closer to the Devil, and how it separates their souls from their God, and how they can be saved. They laughed, but then they started slapping me on the back and finding me a stool, and then they started saying, "Hush up, hush up, let the boy say his piece. Can't do any harm if we just sit right here and listen." Of course, there were some who didn't like what they were hearing, but they'd taken so much whiskey, they were swaying around like grass in a breeze, and what did they know anyway?'

'So you saved them?' she asked. 'Your sermon worked?' They were alone. The man behind the counter had vanished. She could smell tobacco smoke coming from the office.

Elijah shrunk a little. 'I don't think "saved" is exactly the word I'd use,' he admitted. 'But I certainly gave them all something to think about. We ended with a prayer.'

'A prayer?' she spluttered. 'You actually got those men to pray?'

'Beatrice,' he said, getting to his feet and pacing

up and down, 'what is a prayer anyway? All right, so they might not have got down on their knees with their hands clasped and their heads bowed, but as I was saying the words, it seemed like they were listening.'

'Well,' she said. 'I suppose it's a start.'

'Yes, it is a start, and it was certainly an unforgettable experience. I'd never been inside a saloon bar before, and it was like another world. There were ladies in there, you know, I could see them in the background. They were wearing frills on their dresses and their shoulders were bare. It was all so very immodest.'

'Really? Perhaps you should go back in there and save them?'

'You know, that's exactly what I was thinking,' he said.

* * *

That evening they ate in the hotel restaurant, a small L-shaped room, without a view of any kind, but their father had said that the meal was included in the price, so why waste another cent and boot leather? Most of the other tables were empty. Their father, it seemed, had lost his new enthusiasm, he'd scrambled back in on himself, and as they went through the meal—the bowl of tomato rice soup, the tough piece of beefsteak, and the soggy apple pie—there were no more stories about monkeys dressed as soldiers, how Jed Adams was an idiot, or how wolves were his next big project. He was quiet, leaning on his elbows, looking down at his plate like the man Beatrice knew from Normal, who hardly left the outhouse.

She tried to bring him back.

'You'll have to write a letter to the zoo,' she told him. 'They need telling, and who's to say that Ephraim Colt doesn't know all about taxidermy, and its benefits?'

He grunted.

'I'm going to write about my preaching in a journal,' said Elijah. 'People like reading about these things. They find the words inspirational.'

'Isn't that a little premature?' said Beatrice.

'It has to be recorded,' he said, picking at the meat that had caught between his teeth. 'Because in ten years' time, when I've had a little more experience and I'm writing a serious book, then I can look back on these humble beginnings and use them as a prologue.'

'Where did it come from?' their father said, suddenly looking up and scratching his hair, which was starting to look a little wild.

'Excuse me?'

'I'm talking about God. How did that happen?'

Beatrice put down her fork. The room was quiet. She was sure the woman on the next table was listening, while sawing at her steak.

Elijah didn't say anything for a minute, his face had reddened, and his eyes were staring at the painting on the wall, an ugly-looking picture of a dog. 'God happened like your taxidermy,' he said at last, throwing down his napkin and pushing back his chair.

'What do you mean?'

'What I mean,' said Elijah, 'is He came to fill in a hole.'

* * *

That night Beatrice slept badly. The room was too hot. Pushing open the window, she watched a handful of stars over the dark city roofs. She breathed in the cool night wind, listening to the traffic, the woman in the room above her head pacing up and down. Someone was laughing. A man shouted, 'I'm on the late shift again! Would you look at this list! It ain't right, I'm telling you. My lady friend will kill me.' Beatrice wrapped her arms around herself. Lying on top of the bed sheets, she watched the curtains flapping back in the breeze like thin white sails.

Tuesday

'It's not as bad as it looks,' Elijah said on the morning train home, his voice muffled by the large stained handkerchief that was used more to hide his face than to comfort it. 'I've had aspirin. I can hardly feel a thing.'

'You look like something raw,' said their father. 'You should have quit whilst you were ahead.'

'He's right,' said Beatrice. 'You were lucky they didn't kill you.'

'I'll heal,' he winced. 'I'll heal.'

'Still, you've learned a good lesson,' said their father, opening up one of his bird catalogues, and then reaching for the coffee. 'Girls who wear feathers and show off their shoulders usually have someone else to look out for them, and they sure aren't asking to be saved.'

* * *

'So that's that,' said Beatrice, throwing her dirty clothes into a sack for Mrs Oh. 'I didn't want to go on that trip, but now I sure don't want to be back.'

Elijah was sitting on the end of her bed. His jaw was black and blue.

'Chicago is full of sinners,' he said carefully. 'I thought Normal was bad, with people drinking behind closed doors, and the post office was broken into last week, and Ronnie Weaver is playing around with Jeannie, the candy-store girl.'

'He is?' said Beatrice. 'How do you know?'

'I buy a lot of candy.'

It was raining. The world outside looked drab. A fly the size of a thumbprint went skating over the glass. Their father had holed himself up in the outhouse. He didn't need the hair cream any more.

'I'm going to Cicero tomorrow,' said Elijah. 'Three weeks in Cicero, and then I'm going to ask for a placement right in the heart of Chicago.'

'Look at you,' she said, handing him a bottle of witch hazel. 'You want to go back there and take your chance with the drunks every night?'

'No one said that preaching was going to be easy.'

'Still, at least you're doing something and going places.' Beatrice slumped. 'I'm going to be stuck here in Normal forever.'

He dabbed his face and winced. 'Ouch. You never know what's around the corner.'

'Yes, I do,' she said. 'More dead birds. Or a wolf.'

Wednesday

Books and pamphlets had appeared around the breakfast plates. They were left on the windowsill and in tall dampening piles by the sink. *The Anatomy of the Mammal.* Dissection. Skinning. Skull Cleaning with the Dermestid Beetle. *The Practise of Salting and Tanning.*

Elijah, before leaving for Cicero, had an idea. 'I don't know why we didn't think of it before,' he'd said. 'Why don't you go and buy an animal from the farmer? Tom Hayes will sell you something, he'll be glad of the money. Surely a small calf would be good enough to practise on? And the slaughterhouse would kill it for a very small charge.'

'A calf? Why would I want to recreate a calf?' their father had said. 'I'm not making leather. The hide is too thin; it would need a lot of tanning. If I wanted to start tanning, I'd go and get myself a deer. At least a deer would be something fine to look at on its mount.'

*　*　*

Beatrice could not get away from it. Standing in the butcher's store, passing the time of day with Johnny Eckel as he sliced through the veal, her eyes were trained on the animals hanging from the ceiling on thick metal hooks. Hollowed pigs. Fatty rumps of cows. Hooves still full of brown farmyard mud.

'That brother of yours away again?' he asked.

'That's right.'

'Where to now?'

'Cicero.'

'You ever get away?'

'Not often,' she told him, putting the soft parcel into her basket. 'Though I just got back from Chicago.'

'Ah, now there's a place,' he beamed. 'A city full of meat.'

She bumped into Bethan Carter, newly engaged to a boy called Victor Bloom. She was smiling, and showing off her ring.

'It was his grandmother's,' she said. 'It's a token. I would have preferred something new, but Victor's awfully sentimental. We're moving out to Cairo as soon as the wedding's over. He has a job on the railroad.'

'Egypt?'

'No, silly, Cairo, Illinois. The railroad's booming and Victor's been promised rooms in a house and a real good chance of promotion. He has a brother. Henry. You must know Henry Bloom?'

She shook her head.

'You ought to meet him,' said Bethan. 'You want to get yourself a beau and settle down. I can't wait to leave home, and my brothers, who still drive me mad to this day. So what do you say?'

'Say to what?'

'Henry, silly. Shall I set something up? You and Henry Bloom? Just think, we could be sisters-in-law!'

Beatrice shook her head. 'I'm too busy,' she said. 'I'm too busy to be looking for a beau.'

Bethan pulled a face. 'Too busy doing what, Beatrice Lyle? Housekeeping for your father?'

'No.' She hesitated. 'Thing is, I'm just not really interested.'

Bethan turned. Her cheeks were bright pink. 'Well,' she huffed, 'it just isn't right. Who do you think you are? Everyone wants to be married.'

When Beatrice was almost home, she saw Bob Rickman, the neighbour.

'You get to that menagerie?' he asked. 'I told your papa all about it. We were there last fall. Myrna wanted to bring a monkey home and keep it as a pet, but I told her, I said, Myrna, don't you think we've got enough with Bess in the twilight of her years?'

'The monkeys were sweet,' said Beatrice.

'Sure,' Bob winked. 'But not half as sweet as you.'

*   *   *

The kitchen looked different. The books and pamphlets had disappeared. The table had been scrubbed, she could smell disinfectant, and propped against the fruit bowl was a worn-looking copy of *Human Anatomy*. Beatrice flicked through the pages, and puzzled. There was a marker in 'The Ribcage'. She thought about it. She felt her own bones, sitting like a basket underneath her dress. Animals had ribcages. They worked the same. Was there any real difference? Humming, she rinsed the piece of veal underneath the faucet. She waved at Bob Rickman, who was walking up and down the line of the fence, whistling.

Thursday

A letter arrived. The envelope was narrow and blue, and the sender address said, *Lincoln Park Zoo, Chicago*. She studied it. She held it up against the light. Then she steamed the envelope open.

Dear Mr Lyle,

The keepers and staff of Lincoln Park Zoo thank you for sharing your interest in taxidermy. Unfortunately, we are unable to provide you with any specimens to practice on. It is stated in our regulations (1896) that we are not allowed to pass on any creature. Please do not send a money bill for any transportation, as none will take place. In answer to your pertinent question, we have no demised large birds, particularly the turkey you saw in our local birdpen. The turkey is not ill, as you suggested. Nor do we have any other 'miscellaneous' creatures.

Thank you once again for taking the time to write to us.

Yours in good faith,
Ephraim Colt,
Governor

When her father had read it, he threw it desolately into the air. He looked tired. There was a thumbprint of blood on his forehead.

'Fools,' he sneered. 'The whole damn lot of them are fools.'

'It's only Thursday,' she said, looking at the ink that was smudged around the stamp. 'When did you write to the zoo?'

'When we were there,' he said. 'I got it hand-delivered.'

'Are you disappointed?' she asked.

'Not at all, there are other ways to get yourself a carcass,' he told her. 'And I can think of plenty.'

'Not hunting?' Bethan Carter's uncle went after the whitetail deer in Pike County. He once hit a fellow hunter by mistake, shooting him in the shoulder. They became firm friends. It was on the front page of the *Chronicle*.

'No, I'm not a natural hunter,' he said sadly, shaking his head, and rubbing his unkempt whiskers. 'Guns unnerve me, and anyway, I don't need a huge magnificent creature to show off to the world.'

'I'm sorry.'

'Don't be. I'm still busy with a tern I found the other day, and only a little mangled, yes; I think a cat must have got it.'

Folding clothes in her room, she thought about Bethan, who would soon be Mrs Bloom. She envied her, but not for Victor, who was a sallow-looking boy, with small dark eyes pushing too close against his nose. No, she envied Bethan Carter simply because her life was moving forward, and she was going places, even if it was only to Cairo, Illinois, where the railroads were booming.

In her linen drawer, she found one of her old empty notebooks. Sitting by the window she wrote in it.

Beatrice Lyle. Aged 17.

Seventeen years in this house has left me full of dust. I am always surrounded by dead things, there are so many of them, and they have been sitting here so long, I just don't see them anymore.

I wonder about ghosts. Especially when the house creaks and the windows start to rattle in the wind. Do birds have ghosts? Do they sail through the house when we're sleeping? The turkey, pecking. The raven. The plover with its stack of empty eggs. Do they all come to life? Does my mother?

I miss my mother. I miss her every day. I never thought it would be possible to miss someone this much. Someone I didn't ever know.

Who could take me away from here, like Bethan and her Bloom? Would I ever dare let someone into this feathery mausoleum?

At lunchtime, her father paced up and down, waiting for his veal to be fried, reading *The Structure of Bones,* turning his hands, and then flicking at the air.

He chewed his food noisily. 'This sure is a good piece of meat,' he told her, jabbing with his fork. 'When did you buy it?'

'Just yesterday.'

'Well, there's nothing like veal. See how pale and drained it is? It's young, you see, a baby, yes it's most delicious and tender.'

*   *   *

Beatrice washed the bathroom floor. She spilled a tub of Epsom salts. She folded all the towels that had dried hard and snappy on the line. Her arms ached, and her forehead.

*   *   *

That afternoon, the anatomy book was turned to page 19, 'The Human Skull'. Her father didn't appear at supper time, when it was reported in the *Chronicle* that an eighteen-month-old boy had gone missing that morning from the centre of Normal. His parents were said to be distraught.

She'd had too much coffee. Her hands were shaking, her mind was blurred and her eyes ached. Hadn't she heard the front gate creak around ten o'clock? There was a bag of fruit candy on the table. No one ate fruit candy. The anatomy book had vanished.

'I've brought you a little bite to eat,' she said, knocking at the outhouse door, with a plate in her hand. It was cold, and she was shivering. The bread and cheese were jumping.

'What?'

'I said I've brought you something to eat.' She could hear him chopping and cursing to himself.

She knocked again, and he answered, keeping the door closed tightly behind him.

'This,' she said, holding out the plate, 'see, I've brought you this, a little bite to eat.'

'Did I ask for food? Take it back, I'm not at all hungry.'

'You're still working on that tern?'

'Tern? What tern? Oh, that,' he said, looking

over Beatrice's shoulder. 'Yes, I'm still working on that tern.'

'Would you like a glass of water?'

'No, I would not. I'm busy. Awfully busy and I'm not to be disturbed. Not by you or anyone.'

'All right.' She turned.

'Beatrice, has anyone been to the house?'

'No.'

'Then good. And if someone does come knocking . . .'

'What?'

'Just don't let them in; that's most important. I haven't any time for people just now. And neither have you,' he said.

* * *

She paced up and down, barefoot in her nightdress. She wrapped one of Elijah's old sweaters around her shoulders, looking out of his bedroom window with its good view of the road. Squares of light hung in the air. The hazy yellow windows of the houses down the street. Old Mrs Blaze. Pat and Dolly Fisher. Had they read the *Chronicle*? Had they tutted over their fried-chicken suppers about that poor missing child?

She pressed her head to the glass and waited. What had her father been doing? The shadows were like long arms stretching and pulling her in. There would be strings of people. Swaying lanterns. They'd soon kick that door down. One, two, three. There'd be no real point in hiding from them. The house was small enough. The outhouse was frail. They'd find him. They'd find everything.

Friday

She stayed in bed all day, annoyed by the light that came filtering through the curtains. She could hear Bob Rickman in his garden. She slept. She dreamed about saloon bars in Cicero. Polar bears on ice caps. Wolves. The sky was full of birds, and they were shouting.

Saturday

Her father was still in the outhouse, and although she was sure she could hear him crying, Beatrice felt better. The early-edition *Chronicle* was happy to announce that the missing boy, Nathaniel Scott (18 months, Normal, Ill.), had been found. Oliver Marshall, a retard from Bloomington, was being questioned and detained. Late in the afternoon, it rained. Myrna, the woman from next door, appeared, looking dishevelled.

'Have you heard anything?' she asked. 'Can I come in?'

Beatrice hesitated (she was thinking about her father). 'Of course,' she said eventually, 'sure, of course you can, come in.'

'I'm simply going out of my mind,' said Myrna. 'We both are.'

'What do you mean?'

'Didn't your father tell you? We told him to tell everyone. Bess has gone missing. She's been missing now for days.'

Beatrice sat down, feeling cold. From the kitchen window she could see the outhouse and the plume of grey smoke from its chimney, flattened in the rain.

'Has she wandered off?' she managed.

'Never has done before, and the poor girl's blind and lame, and needs all our care and attention, has done for years. We really don't know how it could have happened. We let her out for ten minutes. The gate was locked, and the garden's so secure.'

'Perhaps she was stolen?'

'Who'd want to steal an old Labrador?' she said. 'Unless it was some kind of awful prank?'

'People are cruel.'

'We've made notices. We're keeping all our fingers crossed and hoping for the best.'

* * *

Beatrice sat in Elijah's bedroom. She looked at the pictures of Christ that her brother now kept hidden in a toffee tin. He was holding out his bloody hands. His hair was golden. Sometimes brown. He looked forgiving. In the light from the rain, he looked sinister. Beatrice closed the lid. He was nothing more than a picture.

By seven o'clock it was getting dark. Beatrice was reading a women's magazine. The words about fabrics and smoked-chicken salad, made her feel better. She read an article called 'Resourceful Women' and a short romantic story called 'Gina Westcott Dares'. Towards the end of the last paragraph, when the heroine goes riding through her thwarted love's garden party on a sleek black gelding, Bob Rickman came leaping over the fence. He was banging on the outhouse door. He had Bess's red collar in his hand.

'Open up, Lyle!' he was shouting. 'I know you know something!'

Beatrice knew the end was coming. Pulling on her blue felt beret, tucking her hair behind her ears, she felt unnaturally calm. The rain was soft. The garden was shining with it.

'What is it?' she asked, running outside. 'Whatever is the matter?'

Bob held the collar in the air. 'This,' he said, triumphantly. 'What was it doing in the trough next to the outhouse? And why won't he answer the door?'

'He's busy,' she said. 'He's working on a tern.'

'A tern? What in hell do you mean by he's working on a tern?'

'It's a bird,' she told him. 'He's making it into a model.'

'Open up, Lyle!' he shouted, rattling the door. 'Bess! Are you in there? Bess!'

Beatrice was getting soaked. She could feel the rain dripping down her face; it clung to her neck, falling into her collar.

'What in God's name is he doing?' said Bob.

'Working. He doesn't like being disturbed.'

'I'll give him disturbed.'

Bob Rickman forced the door, with one sharp kick of his boot. He stood in the gap not moving. The air was full of smoke. Beatrice gave a sudden gulping cry.

'*Jesus Christ*,' said Bob, falling to his knees. '*Oh my God, oh my good God . . .*'

Ethan Lyle was standing in a pool of dark blood. His arms were dripping with it. On his messy workbench, Bess's head was sitting on a fixed metal pole. The golden bloody skin was hanging on the back of a chair. In the shadows, the rest of the dog was boiling in a pot.

When he could move again, Bob Rickman lunged at the dumbstruck Ethan Lyle, who went flying towards the back of the room, where Bess's ribcage and hind legs were bubbling.

'You bastard!' Bob yelled. 'You crazy murdering bastard!'

Ethan Lyle was not a big man, he soon crumpled and slipped, gripped around the shoulders by Bob's wide and shuddering hands. When he eventually found his voice Ethan said, 'There's so much to it, I never realised, I never realised, there was so much to it.'

'Why?' Bob cried. 'Why?'

He couldn't answer. Bob's hands had moved up towards his neck and were holding him tight, so tight that Ethan, struggling to hang onto his life, managed to lose him for a second, before tumbling into the shelf stacked with chemicals. Boxes fell. Bottles smashed. Liquids hissed towards the brazier where they were caught up in the sparks. Ethan slipped. Something tore in his ankle.

'*Oh Bess, oh my God.*' Bob moved backwards in a daze, stumbling out of the outhouse and towards the edge of the lawn; leaning against the picket fence, he had his face in his bloodstained hands, retching.

Beatrice stepped carefully through the door and reached out to her moaning father, who was still on his hands and knees.

'Let me help you. Let me pull you out.'

'Get away!' her father shouted as the sparks suddenly turned into a roaring line of flames.

'Move back!'

'Just get out! *Father, please!*'

Beatrice ran to safety as a barrel exploded, then another, and the outhouse was quickly consumed, the bird skulls on the shelf, the bones in the pot, the dog guts, the head on the pole, and Ethan.

'Almighty God!' Bob shouted. 'No!'

Beatrice ran in a blind panic towards the street. 'Help!' she cried, her voice sounding choked. 'Help! Help! Please! Help!'

It was not a busy street. It was getting past supper time and people were indoors. She ran towards the nearest house, her heart pounding, she drummed her fists against the door, she began to kick at it, but still no one came.

'Anyone? *Please?*' she yelled, pulling off her beret. She turned, then a man appeared, he was running towards her, his shirt tails flapping.

'I could see it from my window,' he said. 'My son's gone to the fire depot. Come on, come on, let's go get some water on it, quick!'

She ran with him, back to the garden, where Bob and Myrna were already trying to throw pails of water over the blaze, but they couldn't get close enough, it was too hot and too late; everything had gone.

'I can't believe this, I just can't,' Bob was saying. 'I didn't want him to . . . I didn't want this, I should have . . . surely he could have . . .'

Beatrice was frozen. 'Yes,' she was saying, over and over, as the outhouse burned, and the fine misty rain turned black. 'He could have.'

LEAVE

140a Oceanic Avenue
Coney Island
Brooklyn
New York

April 30, 1916

Dearest Beatrice,

I kept meaning to write, I always started, sometimes finished, but never quite got around to sending it off. Chances are this might not even reach England.

Ever since the war started, I've been thinking about you, and praying you're both safe. Everything here is strained, it's like people are trying too hard, if you know what I mean. I can only imagine what it must be like in England. I don't know. It's like the world's closing down.

I promised myself that this would be a good letter, a letter to make you smile, but what can I say that will make it any better? Franny has her shutters down and her place is up for rent. She lost both her brothers last year in some filthy Belgium wasteland, and she wants to go back to Dublin to be with her mother, who is crippled with her sadness and has locked herself into the house. So, no more oysters, or bowls of mussels with a jug of cold beer, sitting outside, watching the light on the ocean, and you swimming like a mad thing, and your hair dripping wet. How you didn't get pneumonia is beyond me.

I was still at Cooper's until last fall, but I couldn't face it anymore, though heaven knows those boys need entertaining. Now I'm waiting tables at an eatery called The Tide. It's a new place, and the food stinks, but the owners are good people and it almost keeps me sane.

Other news. Marnie has a baby boy called Jack. Looks just like his father, who's still around, and seems to be treating her like the Queen of Coney Island, now she's given him an heir. (He has four daughters with his other wives.) I had something of a dalliance with a boy from Long Island, but he was only here for a couple of months, and then of course he didn't write, though he promised me a thousand times, and so it meant nothing, and I am still on my own, and in no mood for romancing. Look at where it gets you. Celina has moved into the centre of Brooklyn with a girlfriend and they're the happiest, craziest couple you could meet. The girl's name is Marina and Celina's always joking about where she's going to park her yacht. Marina's very pretty with dark gypsy looks, but has a boyish way about her. She writes poems and stories and some of them have been published in *McCall's*.

We all miss you. On the rare times we're together, we talk about you. It's Beatrice this, and that, and remember the time we . . . well, you know how it goes.

I hope this letter reaches you. It isn't much, but it's something to tell you that you're still in my heart, always have been, and maybe when this whole awful thing is over, we can meet up again, linking arms, and laughing, or just sitting around being quiet. Whatever you want to do. Wherever.

All my love and prayers to you.

From Nancy

She found herself quietly sobbing. It had all happened at once—Jonathan had arrived home yesterday, then the letter. It was early June, and the sunshine had appeared, the rain had dried, and she was sitting in the garden with the warmth on her face, Jonathan pouring drinks, and now Nancy.

'What's the matter, my darling? What's happened?' Jonathan pushed his chair a little closer. He had his sleeves rolled up. He'd just been mowing the lawn.

'Nothing,' she told him. 'It's just a voice from back home, and you're here with me, full of grass stains, and looking so whole and so ordinary. It's wonderful.'

'I don't like ordinary,' he smiled. 'Ordinary stinks.'

'Now you're sounding like an American,' she said. 'I like you being English.'

'Yes, ma'am,' he saluted. 'I'll talk just like the King.'

'I've never heard the King,' said Beatrice. 'But he has a kind enough face, and I'm sure he has the voice to go with it.'

They sat side by side in their deckchairs, Beatrice in her coat, Jonathan in his shirtsleeves—it seemed he didn't feel the chill—and they held hands, smoking cigarettes, watching the early butterflies looping and hovering over the small yellow roses.

'Does it feel strange to be back?' she asked.

'It feels stranger knowing I have to return to the front in less than a week. I feel guilty for leaving them, for being able to sit like this, at home with you, and all the comforts.'

'You deserve a break.'

'It's all part of the game,' he said, flicking ash into the breeze. 'After a big campaign we recuperate, then we come back with vigour, and we need all that vigour in the trenches.'

'Jeffrey wouldn't talk about it. He said it was hell.'

'Did he? I hear he's up for promotion. Hell's been good to him. It's given him stripes and a bed in a chateau, which is where they're apparently sleeping in that neck of the woods.'

'And Frank?'

'What about him?'

'They sent him back. Why? He wasn't fit. He looked terrible.'

Jonathan stood up; folding his arms he walked to the edge of the lawn. He prodded a dandelion with the muddy tip of his boot.

'I saw Frank only last week. He was laughing and joking, you know how he is. Someone had found him a bicycle. He was looking forward to cycling up to the village for supplies. He was glad to be back in the thick of it with his comrades.'

'You'll tell all this to Madge?'

'I don't fancy going out,' he shrugged. 'You tell her.'

* * *

Madge was on her way to the shop. She was slightly stooped with a scarf around her neck. She looked older.

'Jonathan says Frank's all right,' Beatrice said, running over. 'He has a bicycle.'

'A bicycle? What kind of a war is it, when a soldier needs a bicycle?'

'They use them to get supplies,' Beatrice told her. 'They ride up to the village and back.'

'You know more about my husband than I do.'

'Not really. Jonathan won't talk about it, but he wanted me to tell you that Frank is doing fine, he's all in one piece, and he's happy.'

'Happy?' Madge smiled uncertainly. 'Really?'

'That's what he told me, and I know he wouldn't lie,' she said.

* * *

Jonathan was quiet. He kept pressing at his eyes, and pacing round the room.

'What's the matter?' said Beatrice.

'Nothing. It's still in my head.'

She took his hand. 'Let's go and lie down,' she said.

She undressed him. He looked thinner, she could see the shape of his ribs, and his shoulder blades had sharpened.

'I wasn't going to come back,' he said. 'Most of the men were refused leave. One of them, a young lad from Brecon, wanted leave to see his baby, because the little girl has whooping cough. They went and turned down his request.'

'Don't think about that.'

He shrugged her off a little. 'I have to; I have to

keep thinking, because they're my men.'

'You're here now, and you'll be all the better for it.'

He sunk his head into her neck. She smelled clean. He'd missed that wet-soap smell, and although he'd dabbed a little of her scent onto his handkerchief it had hardly lasted the outward journey. She brought his hand up to her breast.

'Lie down,' she said, pulling off her clothes. He did as he was told, but he seemed more intent on the window than on his naked wife, whom he'd been dreaming about constantly since he'd been at the front. In his dreams she was lying beside him. She was an acrobat flying in the circus. She was on a ship, a pale grey smudge on the horizon. She was leaving him.

'I can't,' he said. 'I look at you, and I want you, but nothing happens.'

She tucked herself into him. She touched him, like she used to, but his penis remained soft.

'No hope of a leave baby,' he said, with a grim laugh.

'We don't need a baby,' she said. 'I'm happy simply lying here with you. It's what I've been thinking of for months.'

'I'm tired,' he said with his eyes closed. 'That's what it is, I'm tired.'

Beatrice let him sleep. She poured herself a glass of water, then went back to see him, simply lying there. He was there, but he wasn't; he looked like a shadow, and although she knew she shouldn't, she couldn't help feeling disappointed. 'I'm selfish,' she told herself. 'I wanted all of him, like it used to be.' She sat beside the bed, then moved, because it felt like she was visiting someone sick.

She thought of Frank. 'No, he's not like Frank. He's nothing like that. He's all fine and well. He's just tired.'

* * *

'He looks like a ghost,' said Lizzie.

'What do you mean, a ghost? Ghost, nothing. He looks just like he always did,' said Ada. 'Fit and healthy and strong. Why should he have all the leave? I've hardly heard from my Jim. And he says nothing in his letters.'

'Tom hasn't written in ages,' said Lizzie. 'I hope he's all right.'

'He's too busy doing all the dirty work for Sergeant Crane,' said Ada. 'Sergeants and captains and colonels and the like don't do any fighting. They just sit at their desks and write out all the orders.'

'Is that true?' asked Madge.

'Of course it's true,' said Ada. 'Why do you think your Frank came home with his back all twisted, and Jonathan's walking about like he's been away for a few months on business?'

'Someone did once tell me that the sergeants are nowhere near the front,' said Madge. 'That they're sitting it out in comfort, and they're miles away from the action.'

'True. And they still have all the luxuries,' said Ada. 'Brandy, fancy French wine and roast dinners.'

'And hot baths,' said Madge. 'What my Frank wouldn't have given for a hot mustard bath. A bath would have done his back the world of good.'

'They hardly know there's a war going on at all,'

said Ada. 'Yet they get all the glory. They get all the fancy medals, and the visits from the King.'

'The King?' said Lizzie, her cheeks turning pink. 'I wonder if my Tom has seen His Majesty the King?'

'Oh, he only bothers with the sergeants,' said Ada, bristling.

'But the men who are fighting fair and square, he has nothing to do with at all,' said Madge, joining in, remembering a conversation she'd had with a woman in town. 'He looks at them like they're nothing but a piece of muck on his shiny royal boot. And he won't shake their hands in case he catches something.'

'The King?'

'Yes, the King.'

'But that's awful,' said Lizzie, thinking of the cup with his face on it, sitting on her mantelpiece.

'That's the truth,' said Madge. 'That's the whole sorry truth of this war.'

* * *

He liked seeing her in her overalls, working on the farm. He was proud of his American, doing her bit for England. Ginny came over to him, blushing. She tried to straighten out her frizzy red hair. She quickly spat on her handkerchief, wiping the small muddy freckles from the bridge of her nose.

'Dad says he doesn't know what he'd have done without her,' she said, facing him over the wall. 'She's been a real help. A godsend.'

'Good.'

'She's busy in the shed, but you're welcome to come in for some tea.'

'Thanks,' he said, opening the gate. 'I'd like that.'

They sat by the range. A tabby cat came over and curled itself into a ball by his feet. There was the smell of baking bread; it made him feel hungry.

'How very strange to be sitting here, and my wife out there working hard, it doesn't seem right at all.'

'You've worked hard enough,' said Ginny. 'I'm sure.'

'Well . . .' He shrugged. 'It's all a team effort. It has to be.'

The heat was making him sleepy and the glow from the range blurred his eyes. He lit a cigarette, and offered it to Ginny.

'Thanks. Your wife certainly has some tales to tell.'

'She has?'

'Oh, yes. Her life in America. She keeps us all entertained.'

He could feel his face twitching. 'She does?'

'Of course, we hardly know what to believe half the time. It seems so far-fetched to those of us who've never left Lancashire, never mind England.'

'Yes,' he said quietly, pulling a loose strand of tobacco from his lips, 'America really is something else.'

'Oh, it sounds very free and easy,' she went on, shaking her head, looking at the fat glowing tip of her cigarette. 'And men walking out with women, even if they're married. Apparently, it doesn't matter over there, though I had to keep reminding her that it's different here in England.'

'Pardon me?'

'Over here. It doesn't look right, I told her,

though of course, it's not her fault she's a foreigner and doesn't know our ways yet.'

'What on earth are you talking about?'

'Beatrice and Jeffrey Woodhouse. They spent all his leave together. She said you wouldn't mind, and I'm sure that you don't, but I didn't think it looked right.'

'No, of course not,' he said, looking at the brasses hooked around the range, the toasting forks and irons. 'Thank you, thank you for putting her right.'

'Least I could do,' she smiled.

* * *

'Of course I smell of pigs for most of the time,' she said, her hair wet from the bath.

'Jeffrey didn't mind?'

'What?'

'Ginny tells me that you spent all his leave together.'

'We went out for a drink.'

'Ah,' he said. 'I see.'

She rubbed her hair with the towel. 'So, now they think I'm a harlot?'

'Something like that.'

'And you? What do you think?'

'I know Jeffrey,' he grinned. 'He wouldn't take advantage.'

'And me? Would I take advantage of Jeffrey?'

'No,' he said. 'I trust you.'

'So you damn well should,' she said, but she was smiling and flicking her towel at him.

He watched her combing out her hair. It looked dark when it was wet, and from the back she looked like someone else.

'These tales you've been telling,' he said. 'Do they know about the wings?'

She stopped. 'Of course they don't, I'd never tell them that. I've told them nothing but a few light-hearted stories to keep them entertained.'

'Are you sure?'

'I'm positive.'

'Because Ginny had me worried.'

'I would never tell. It's our secret.'

'It's more than that,' he said.

*   *   *

They sat listening to her new gramophone records. Jonathan could feel the tension slowly leaving his body, though he doubted his ability to make love to her.

'I wish it was over,' she said. 'I wish I knew what it was like. Imagination is often worse than reality, don't you think?'

'It can be.'

'You won't tell me?'

He sighed, taking hold of her hand, marvelling at its smallness, the way his palm could swallow it.

'I won't tell you,' he said. 'Perhaps the very reason we're fighting is so that you'll never really know.'

'Tell me one thing.'

'No.'

'One thing.'

He smiled. 'You won't wear me down.'

'Tell me one thing,' she said, looking up into his face. 'Give me one small thing, and let me have it as a gift.'

He poured himself a brandy. The record had stopped and the room was full of the clock, ticking on the mantelpiece.

'All right. One thing, and don't ask me any more.'

'I'll never ask, I promise.'

He closed his eyes, sitting back against the cushions looking thoughtful. 'I'll talk about Jim and his good friend Solange Devaux,' he said, slowly. 'That will be my gift to you. But you must never repeat this story. Ever. You must never tell Ada, or any of the others. That has to be part of the deal.'

She nodded.

'I mean it.'

'Sure you do, and yes, I promise.'

'Solemnly?'

She smiled, but then her voice dropped. 'On your life.'

In the lamplight, she could see new fine lines running away from his eyes, like the veins on the back of a leaf. He looked into his glass; he took a long sip, and swallowed.

'We'd been shelled, and the place was torn to blazes. Jim and his partner, a man called Potts, had been digging to get the guns into better positions. They're gigantic monsters, these guns, and they were digging for hours, ten feet deep, forty-foot-long ditches. They were good pals. Then Potts got it. Jim was right next to him, and he'd felt the full blast, felt the whole impact of Potts going up in smithereens, the whole sordid mess of it—is this too much for you?'

'No.'

'Jim wasn't the same after that. He could barely keep it together. I thought we were going to lose him; he was like something hollow, and no use to anyone. That night I walked with some of the men up to the village, a tiny place three or four miles away. Jim came with us. It was a bright clear night, the sky full of stars, and a sharp slice of moon. We felt very small. Jim was silent the whole way, though the others were laughing and joking, relieved to be out of the front line for a couple of hours. Jim kept his head down.

'The village was no more than a couple of tumbledown houses and a barn. One of these houses was a café of sorts. Of course, they hadn't much food but it was the wine the boys were really interested in. It was rough, but it could take you out of yourself for a while, and the boys would sit around playing cards, and it helped. There were girls,' he went on. 'A few of the men would take these girls upstairs, and come back down with a swagger. They were not the prettiest, or the youngest-looking girls, but when the men were up there, the girls could be their sweethearts. Needless to say, I was never interested.'

'Of course you weren't.'

'The place was run by a woman called Solange. She was about seventy; at least she looked about seventy, and she was a kind old soul, with not a bad word to say about anyone, including the Germans. "Those boys on the other side are the same as you are; they have mothers and wives and loved ones. They're being told what to do, and you should never take it personally, they're just boys after all, like you." Whatever we really thought, we agreed with her out loud. She could speak very good English. Said her father had taught it to her when she was a child and that he was half-English, and her grandmother had come to France from Norfolk. We had many long chats about this and that, our families, pals, anything but the war, which we could often hear in the distance, depending on which way the wind was blowing.

'She saw Jim. She saw at once how bad he looked, and without a moment's hesitation, she slid her chair over to him, and she began to talk. I watched from the corner of the room, and I could see how he'd closed inwards at first, turning away, and how she'd coaxed him, and then the tears came, and then more talk, until after an hour or so, he was smiling, and laughing quietly, and it looked like he was back again.

'We were there for over a month. He visited Solange whenever he could. They became very close; she was like a mother to him, and he would help her around the place, he would cut meat, he'd chop wood and make himself useful, and he felt better for it. I often found things for him to do up there, getting supplies, and finding petrol for the motorbikes, and so on. Solange Devaux was his saviour. I don't know what they talked about, and I never asked, but I do know that she probably saved his life.

'When we moved up the line, I wondered what he'd be like without her. How would he manage? He had a letter she'd written, and her address. He often looked at it, and I'm pleased to say that nothing changed. He didn't turn inwards. It was as if she'd left something of herself with him. And now he's doing well, he's one of the best men I've got, and he's a credit to himself and the rest of the company.' He stopped. 'Now that's enough, I think, and you won't ask again, because you promised.'

The silence hung between them. Beatrice squeezed his hand to show him that she was glad of the gift, and that she would keep her promise. She thought about Jim, saw him sharpening his butcher's knife, hooking up the rabbits he'd snared, 'because I'm not a real butcher,' he'd say with a wink, and they all knew what he meant. She pictured Solange. She had her grey hair in a chignon. Her hair was always well done, it was something she hadn't let go, as she ladled out bowls of mutton stew, pulled up a chair, and listened.

Jonathan went to put on another record, and then he stopped.

'There's something I haven't told you,' he said. 'Solange Devaux is dead. The village was flattened, a few days after we left. Everything went. According to the corporal, even the biggest trees were lifted.'

'Does Jim know?'

Jonathan shook his head. 'Will Caruso do?' he said.

* * *

'Is my Tom all right?' asked Lizzie.

'Private Blackstock was perfectly fit when I left,' said Jonathan.

'Are you his boss?' asked Lizzie's daughter Martha, who was standing with her arms folded, watching the other soldiers on leave, filing from the church.

Jonathan smiled. 'I suppose so, but not really,' he told her, 'not in the larger scheme of things.'

'What does that mean?'

'He means he's only a sergeant,' said her brother Harry. 'And sergeants aren't the boss.'

'I meant,' smiled Jonathan, 'that your father's boss is probably the King. Or God,' he added quickly.

'Oh, we don't like him any more,' said Martha. 'We've gone right off the King.'

'Martha . . .' Lizzie warned.

'Well, he doesn't like us,' she said, stamping her foot for emphasis and bringing it down a little too sharply, so that a pain jolted through her leg.

'Of course he does. Why wouldn't he? For King and country,' said Jonathan, 'that's what we're fighting for.'

'I thought we were fighting to kill all the Germans,' said Harry. 'Bang, bang, bang, goes the Boche.'

'That too,' Jonathan admitted quietly, as the Reverend Peter McNally cast an eye in their direction.

'Has my dad killed any stinking Germans?' asked Harry.

Lizzie looked away, though she had a hundred questions of her own tucked inside her head.

'Oh, he's killed plenty,' said Jonathan, knowing it was the right thing to say, though Tom Blackstock had been working in communications, in charge of the wire, and rarely got the chance to aim and fire. 'He's a very brave man.'

'Will he get a medal?'

'One of these days he might, who knows?'

'Mr Crane,' said Lizzie inching forwards. 'Sergeant. I mean, Jonathan. How long are you back for?'

'Four days.'

'Why couldn't my Tom come with you?'

'It wasn't his turn, I'm afraid, Lizzie,' he said, biting the inside of his cheek and looking quickly away.

*　　*　　*

'How can she look like that when she spends all week with the pigs?' said Madge, looking at her own dry hands, and then patting down her hair. 'She looks like an illustration. I don't know how she does it.'

'A cheap illustration,' said Ada. 'She's a picture from the comics, parading her husband around, like he's some big prize she's just this minute won, and for nothing in particular.'

'Oh, do you really think so?' puzzled Madge. 'I think she looks lovely. She always looks lovely.'

'Can't you see it?' said Ada.

'See what?'

'She's as hard as nails, that one.'

They stood in a patch of pale sunlight, baulking at the soldiers on leave walking home with their wives and with their proud-looking children swinging on their arms. The reverend, standing by a gravestone, leaning on it now and then, looked ill. Madge had noticed how his hands were shaking as he read out the sermon. His face was the colour of chalk, but there was a dark red flare sitting over his cheekbones.

'I wanted to ask him things,' said Lizzie, who'd left Harry and Martha playing soldiers in the lane. 'Jonathan must know how they're doing, but he just won't say.'

‘I’d rather not know,’ Madge lied. ‘Beatrice said he’s fit and well, and that’s enough for me.’

‘But why should Jonathan Crane know things about our husbands we don’t?’ said Ada.

‘I think we should go over there and ask him,’ said Madge.

‘No,’ said Ada, her large green eyes narrowed into slits.

‘No? What do you mean, no?’

‘What I mean,’ said Ada slowly, ‘is that we’ll go and see him later.’

* * *

It could have been easy to forget the gruelling world of France, sitting dry in the warmth, with a plate of chicken and vegetables, a glass of his father’s forgotten burgundy, and the only smells in the air, of the cooking, the beeswax, the new coal in the fire. Wasn’t this what had kept him going all that time, remembering the small things, dry socks, a plate of clean soup, a mattress? But now he was here the battlefield seemed closer and he could see it, smell it, hear it. He almost gagged over his chicken leg, picturing the bodies resurfacing with each new explosion.

‘Are you all right?’ Beatrice asked.

‘I’m fine,’ he said. ‘Really I am. This is lovely.’

‘So now I’m something of a cook?’

‘A cook,’ he smiled, ‘yes, and quite a farmer too.’

‘I just wanted to do something. Does that sound awfully righteous? I could have gone to the munitions factory, but the farm seemed so immediate, and I knew they needed help.’

‘I couldn’t be prouder,’ he said, raising his glass.

He was suddenly feeling tearful; he was finding it hard to swallow. 'But I don't know what I'm doing here.'

'Recuperating at home.'

'I'm not ill. Look at me—I'm not even tired any more.'

Beatrice wanted to say, you look tired, you look exhausted, but she didn't. She wanted to feed him up, to watch his cheeks fill out.

'Have some more potatoes,' she said. 'Go on, they'll do you good.'

When he reached for the bowl she felt pleased, as if he was a child, not very fond of his vegetables.

The doorbell rang, sounding sharp. Jonathan jumped and rubbed his eyes.

'Should I leave it?' she asked.

'No,' he said. 'You must go and see who it is.'

She felt overwhelmed, as Ada, Madge and Lizzie crowded onto the steps. Ada was smiling, but her eyes were saying something else.

'Is Sergeant Crane available?' asked Ada, in a voice that didn't sound like her own.

'He's eating,' said Beatrice.

'We can wait.'

She let them inside. Jonathan was already standing by his chair, straightening out his jacket.

'We're sorry to interrupt your meal,' said Madge. 'Please don't stop on account of us. We have plenty of time, we can wait in the parlour.'

'It's finished,' said Jonathan, with a strained sort of smile. 'Really, ladies, do sit down. Can I get you a drink?'

They looked at each other. They hadn't banked on hospitality.

'A sherry would be nice,' said Ada. 'Yes, I

wouldn't say no to a sherry.'

'I'll have the same,' said Madge. They looked at Lizzie.

'And so will I,' she said.

'Beatrice?' said Jonathan.

She carefully poured what was left of the sherry into five small glasses.

'And how can I help you ladies?' he asked.

'We want news,' said Ada, a little too forcefully. 'What I mean is, we'd like to know what's going on.'

'We're at war,' said Jonathan. He wondered what these women wanted from him.

'We haven't been hibernating these past few years,' said Madge, her hand tightening so hard around the glass she thought she might have cracked it. 'We do know about the war.'

'Of course you do. What I meant to say is, that we are all under strict instructions not to divulge any information.' He looked at Beatrice. 'Not even to our nearest and dearest,' he said.

'But can't you tell us how they are?' said Lizzie. 'That's all we want to know. Are they still alive?'

Jonathan sighed. 'If you haven't received a telegram, then we have to assume they're still with us.'

'Imogen Parker's husband had been dead for six months before she got her telegram,' said Ada.

'I know nothing about that,' said Jonathan, opening up his hands.

'But you live with them,' said Madge. 'You all signed up together. What were they like when you saw them last?'

'Fit and well,' he said, lighting a cigarette.

'Fit and well means nothing,' said Ada. 'I want to

know about my Jim. What he gets up to. What he's doing. How he's living.'

'What I want to know,' said Madge, 'is how are they coping?'

'As well as can be expected,' said Jonathan.

'And what's that supposed to mean?' Ada was eyeing the leftovers on the table, the fancy gold-edged china and the expensive bottle of wine with its foreign-looking label.

'It means, they're in a battlefield and life is very hard and no one finds it easy, but they're good men, and they're coping. They're a credit to the battalion, and the last time I saw them, they were all fit and well.'

'Like you,' said Ada. 'You look fit and well.'

'Thank you.'

'It wasn't meant as a compliment,' she said. 'If you're so fit and well, what are you doing here?'

'He's on leave,' said Beatrice.

'Why?' said Madge.

'My commanding officer sent me home,' said Jonathan. 'A small break.'

'Oh, a small break?' said Ada. 'We used to have one of those at Easter. We'd go and see my brother Vernon in Chester.'

He closed his eyes. 'I've been working on a very difficult campaign,' he said quietly. 'I worked hard. They sent me home. I'll be working twice as hard when I get back to the front.'

'And my Tom won't?' said Lizzie as her chin began to quiver. 'Doesn't he work hard enough?'

'Of course he does.'

'I just want to see him. Our children are missing their dad. When will it be Tom's turn?'

'That I can't say,' said Jonathan.

'But what would you do?' said Beatrice suddenly finding her voice. 'What would you do if you were out on the battlefield and you were going to be sent home for a while? Would you say, hey, no thanks, I'd rather stay here than go back to my loved ones?'

'Beatrice . . .'

'Of course we wouldn't, but we just want to know when we'll see them again,' said Lizzie. 'Is that so much to ask? Don't they get a turn?'

'Honest answer? Not always. They've had breaks of course. They've spent days away from the battlefield and they've been given time to rest and recuperate.'

'They have?' said Lizzie.

'Of course. We don't expect a man to carry on non-stop without a respite.'

'What do they do on these breaks?' asked Madge.

'Chat, play cards, rest up.'

'My Tom never said anything about that,' said Lizzie, picturing him in his shirtsleeves, a handkerchief on his head, sprawled out on a beach, like Morecambe, only warmer. 'You mean they get a little holiday?'

'I suppose you could put it like that.'

'Some holiday,' said Ada. 'I bet they'd rather come home.'

'Yes,' he said. 'Of course. I'm sure that they would.'

'Like you,' said Madge.

'But he's different,' said Ada. 'He's a sergeant. He isn't a nothing, like our men.'

'Your men aren't nothing,' he paled. 'Your men are everything.'

‘So why are they treated like muck?’

Jonathan sat down. His head was swimming. He could see Tom scrambling underneath the wire, Jim with a spade, digging graves in the mud, Frank, wandering, smiling, singing nonsense French and being overly brave because he just didn’t care any more, because perhaps all the world was dying?

‘Your husbands are treated well, and they are all well respected,’ he said, draining his sherry. ‘I admire them.’

‘I admire your motor car,’ said Ada. ‘But your motor car is a thing. It isn’t a human being, and the way you talk about Jim and the rest of them, it’s like they’re objects, and they’re there to be used like the rounds of ammunition in your guns.’

‘You’re talking like you don’t even know them,’ said Madge. ‘I thought they were your friends. Your old pals. Isn’t that what you called them once upon a time? Not good friends perhaps, but friends all the same. Didn’t you invite them here now and then? Didn’t you all get tipsy, laughing and joking and smoking fine cigars? Or were you doing your duty?’

‘Of course not, and I’m sorry if I’ve offended you,’ he said, rubbing his forehead. ‘I’m extremely tired just now.’

‘Then isn’t it lucky you have a nice warm fire, a bed upstairs, and a wife to go in it?’ said Ada. ‘Sweet dreams, Sergeant Crane. Come on,’ she said to the others. ‘We’ll be going. We’ll let Sergeant Crane get his beauty sleep.’

As the door closed he threw his sherry glass against the wall. The splinters looked like ice shivering on the sideboard.

‘I’ll be leaving in the morning. It isn’t right. It never felt right.’

‘I know.’ She closed her eyes.

He sat down, hunching up his shoulders tight. ‘You don’t know. How could you? No one knows anything,’ he said. ‘No one knows anything about the bloody awful mess we’re in.’

‘You could tell me?’

‘I can’t,’ he said, with his head down. ‘I just don’t know the words to describe it.’

Ten minutes later he was smiling again. He’d washed his face and he’d given himself a good talking-to in the small bathroom mirror.

‘Play some more of your music, darling,’ he said, opening another bottle of wine. ‘Go on. I don’t know what got into me. And what about dessert? We didn’t even start our dessert. What is it?’

‘Canned peaches,’ she said, sliding the record from its thick cardboard sleeve.

‘Good,’ he said. ‘I’ve been dreaming of peaches for days.’

* * *

The women huddled together. They were looking back at the light shining in the Cranes’ bedroom window, Ada remembering how she’d once climbed onto Jonathan’s shoulders, and how she’d felt tall and full of the sky, and they were joined up like a giant, until he was laughing so much that his knees gave way, and as soon as she’d slipped to the ground he’d gone running back to wherever he’d been before, brushing down his shoulders, and Ada already forgotten.

‘It’s only just getting dark,’ said Madge, looking

up at the sky. 'But you can see the moon and stars already.'

'It's getting dark all right,' said Ada, 'but I don't mind walking in the dark.'

They wanted to stay outside, to look at the water, and the deepening indigo sky. Why go back now when Lizzie's mother had the children? At home their small summer fires would be dying, their rooms empty, and their single supper plates were already washed and stacked beside the sink.

'It might be over by next week,' said Lizzie. They were sitting on the wall, linking arms. 'Next week we might be celebrating.'

'You'll give yourself an ulcer if you keep on thinking like that,' said Madge, absent-mindedly rubbing her stomach. 'All that hoping for nothing.'

'But it has to end sooner or later,' said Lizzie. 'Doesn't it?'

Ada took a long look over her shoulder. 'Some people don't even know that it's started.'

'I think you're wrong about Sergeant Crane,' said Lizzie.

'No I'm not,' she said.

A breeze began to whip across the water, making thin grey waves. An owl swooped from the trees. Silent. White. Then suddenly the moon disappeared as they pulled their elbows closer, pressing themselves together, until it felt like they were breaking.

BE GOOD OR BEGONE

Brooklyn, New York
16 July 1911

The Brooklyn air was thick and heavy, and she felt all the weight of it as she pushed her way towards Renton Street, the address on a piece of paper screwed up tight in the warm sweaty crush of her hand; she'd already asked twice for directions, but the first time the man spoke no English, and the other, a woman fanning her face with a chop suey house menu, shrugged her shoulders and shuffled into a tiny piece of shade.

She walked a little further. Her small heavy case was biting into her palm, and her feet were cramped and pinched inside her boots.

'Excuse me,' she said to a man washing down a window. 'I wonder if you could help me? I'm looking for Renton Street.'

He turned round and wiped his forehead with the window rag. 'It's full of grime but it's cool,' he explained, 'and I'd rather be filthy and cool than dying of the heat. You looking for Renton Street you say?'

'That's right.'

'What do you want over there?'

'A hotel,' she said. 'The Galilee Hotel. Do you know it?'

'I don't know no hotel, but I do know Renton Street,' he told her, wringing out the rag and dipping it into the pail of murky water by his feet. 'This place is full of pickpockets, so keep your eyes open and all your wits about you. Next block up, take a right.'

'Thanks.'

'It's the Russians,' he said, turning back towards the window, 'the Russian gypsies are full of tricks, and they can con you, and you think you're being entertained whilst they're emptying out your pockets. You've got to admire them,' he grinned. 'Those gypsies are dripping in style.'

She shifted a little. There was nothing in her pockets to pick, apart from a torn white handkerchief that was none too clean, and a gum wrapper.

'You watch how you go now.'

She walked a little further past a row of brownstones and a man sleeping rough on a pallet. The back of her neck prickled with the heat, the sky pressed down, and all she could think of was an icy glass of water and a bed.

Renton Street looked empty. The houses on either side were thin and shambolic. A shop selling sliced Italian sausage had thick iron bars on the door.

The Galilee Hotel was at the end of the block. It was a tall narrow building, the fancy masonry, the flowers and diamonds were broken at the edges, and the paint was cracked and blistering on the sills. A sign in the window (cardboard, handwritten) said, *Be Good or Begone*. Beatrice tried to smooth out the creases that had been sitting in her clothes since yesterday and nervously pulled on the bell.

A woman appeared, and in the haze, and with the pale blue wash of her dress, she might have been floating over the doormat.

'I'm Beatrice Lyle, from Illinois. My brother arranged everything. Elijah Lyle. Did you get my letter?'

'Yes,' the woman said, opening the door a little wider. 'You're the preacher's sister, I have been expecting you all day. I made a simple light lunch, just in case you should appear on time, but as you didn't, the lunch will now be supper.'

'I'm sorry.'

'Don't be,' she said, ushering her inside. 'The good Lord provides and nothing goes to waste.'

She led Beatrice into what appeared to be the parlour. It was a plain room, with four hard-backed chairs and a table. A bunch of white flowers (unidentifiable) were wilting in a pickle jar.

'Questions first,' the woman said, producing a notepad from her pocket. 'Glass of water later.'

Beatrice nodded, and unstuck her lips.

'My name is Miss Flood, I am the proprietress, I am not the owner. The Galilee Hotel is owned by the Methodist Mission of America. You are still a Methodist, I take it, as stated in your letter?'

'Yes, ma'am.'

'Then you'll understand and believe in our rules, as well as abide by them?'

'Yes.'

Miss Flood laughed a little. 'You don't know what these rules are,' she said, covering her mouth with her fingers. 'I'd hold my tongue and look at them before agreeing to anything, if I were you.'

She handed Beatrice a slip of paper. The rules went over the page. Beatrice read the first three, No Alcohol. No Tobacco Products. No Callers. The rest of the rules appeared in a blur, as her eyes skimmed over the words, Noise and No, No,

No.

'You agree to all these rules?' she asked. 'You believe in them?'

'Yes.'

'Then sign your full name here. Your room is on the third floor. You'll find a jug of water to refresh you, though I doubt that it's still cold. You are lucky,' she went on. 'You were supposed to be sharing with a Miss Brownlow, but Miss Brownlow has now left us.'

'She has?'

'Yes. She is now somewhere in Sheepshead Bay, doing nothing at all that is good for her.'

On the way to her room Beatrice passed dusty hollow squares where pictures had once hung, candlesticks surrounded by mounds of tallow drippings, and a large oilcloth banner that proclaimed, *Put Down That Glass & Go*.

'Here we are,' said Miss Flood. 'Room 9.'

The room was larger than Beatrice had been expecting. There were two iron beds—one stripped—a chair and a plain set of drawers. The window looked onto the street, and the buildings opposite, with all their shutters and pulled down blinds, seemed to have little life inside them.

'Mealtimes are printed on your guest sheet,' she said, pointing to a large piece of paper sitting on the lopsided bureau. 'Everything else is explained. If you require me in between times, my room is Room 1. Please knock.'

'Thank you.'

'Thank the Lord,' she said, without the slightest hint of irony.

Beatrice collapsed onto the bed. Every bone and muscle ached. She untied her boots. The water in the jug was warm and tasted dusty, but it ran down her throat and uncaked her tongue. She closed her eyes and tried to fall asleep, because surely she was ready for it?

Her eyelids were heavy, but her head was too busy. She was in New York. The place people wrote about in those monthly magazines, where buildings sat tall, side by side, shining in the light like arms full of jewellery. Where were those buildings? The houses on Renton Street, Brooklyn, were taller than most of the houses in Normal, but they were dull-faced and crumbling, and as for the windows, many of them were cracked and broken, patched up with brown paper card, and all of them scorched with the dust. She yawned. Perhaps those other, shiny buildings were just around the corner. When she felt rested, she would go out and she would look for them.

* * *

She woke to the sound of someone hammering on her door. She had a crick in her neck and her arm felt numb from where she'd been sleeping on it. For a few seconds she was in her room in Normal, with the birds just outside, peeping around her door with the eyes that saw nothing.

The hammering again. Rubbing the back of her neck, she went to see who it was. An oldish-looking man with flat grey hair and a threadbare suit shifted from foot to foot. His shoes were the smartest thing about him. They were all buffed up and shiny, and she couldn't take her eyes off them, until she remembered that she hadn't even washed her face or changed out of her clothes, and she must look such a mess.

'I've been sent to get you,' he said.

She looked up from his feet, surprised. 'You have?'

'It's time for dinner,' he told her. 'Six thirty p.m. sharp.'

'It's that late?'

'It is.' He held out his hand. 'Elliot Price.' He bowed from the waist. 'The redeemed Elliot Price.'

She tried to do something with her hair. She could feel it slipping over her forehead and falling over her collar. 'The redeemed?' she smiled, adjusting her hair clips and following him out onto the landing.

'That's right. I was an actor on the vaudeville circuit, serious roles you understand; I was never much of a hoofer, even in my early days, though goodness knows, I tried. I played all the heavy dramatic scenes, they were my specialty, and I made something of a name for myself. Do you ever go to vaudeville?'

'No,' she said, shaking her head.

'Never mind, you're missing nothing, and neither am I. It's where I fell from grace. Those bleary-eyed characters got to me, and they wouldn't let me go. Men who'd lost their sons. Kings who were losing their lands. I played Hamlet for three whole seasons, and I'm sorry to have to tell you that I brought him home with me. Night after night, I was melancholy, and I was always asking myself questions that could never be answered. When it all became too much, I sought solace,' he told her, pausing for a second by the large oilcloth banner. 'And I'm sorry to say I found it in the wrong place.

I hit the bottle. I was sozzled from morning till night. I began to slur my words. Those lovely long vowel sounds I'd become so famous for were sliding all over the place, and there was not a thing I could do to stop them.'

'I'm sorry.'

'Never mind sorry,' he said, opening the door to the dining room, where it appeared the rest of the hotel sat waiting for her, 'I was saved by the Lord. By the Methodist Mission of America, who told me to put down my bottle and start looking at the Word. Not the word of Mr Shakespeare, or those other great dramatists, whose characters I was slowly but surely murdering, but the word of the Bible, the only true piece of literature that's been printed and bound in a book.'

'Amen,' said a woman on the nearest table. She was sitting straight-backed, and staring at her shiny empty plate.

'Mrs Mitchell,' said Elliot. 'Mrs Mitchell is another permanent guest. Mrs Mitchell, let me introduce Miss Beatrice Lyle. You are a Miss?' he added. 'You don't look like you're married, and I see you aren't wearing a ring that means you are promised?'

'No,' said Beatrice shyly, 'I'm not married.'

'I was never a drinker,' said Mrs Mitchell. 'I'm here because I was married to one, and under the influence of it he took everything, including my three sons, who followed their father like sheep, and went to live with him in some dreadful flimsy shack of a house on Hawaii.'

'Hawaii?' said Beatrice. 'My goodness.'

'He read a book about the Sandwich Islands,' she said, opening out her napkin. 'Said he liked the look of the palm trees, but I know for a fact he had no real interest in those trees whatsoever.'

'No?'

'No. Palm trees, nothing. It was the nearly naked natives circling their hips in those little grass skirts with those fancy scented flowers tucked behind their ears he was thinking of.'

Beatrice shook her head. The other guests were politely looking away. Elliot guided her towards an empty table.

'You can sit here with me,' he said. 'This table has a good view of the street, and though it might not be Broadway, or west of Chatham Square, it still has its God-given qualities. Like that tree,' he nodded. 'And that hazy strip of sky.'

The sky was certainly hazy, and even at this hour the heat still poured through the glass, turning the small pat of butter into a rancid yellow pool.

'In my actor days, I used to eat out all the time,' he said. 'A three-course meal at midnight was nothing out of the ordinary, though it played havoc with my digestive system, and I was nursing an ulcer for years. Actors work very strange hours, they move from place to place, and they like to be sociable. Sociable didn't suit me in the end. Sociable wore me down. I never knew when to say no. Of course,' he added, 'not all actors are demons. I knew some lovely actors who preferred a cup of tea and an early night, but I have to say, they were very few and far between.'

'It sounds exciting, the world of the theatre.'

He frowned. 'But my dear girl, have you not been listening? The theatre was my downfall. It very nearly killed me.'

'I didn't mean—'

'For what we are about to receive,' began a voice on another table, which started a wobbly chorus, 'may the Lord make us truly thankful. Amen.'

'Fish,' said Miss Flood, hovering with a tray. 'Fish, boiled potatoes and cabbage.'

'Most nutritious,' said Elliot, rubbing his hands together. 'What kind of fish is this?'

'I don't know,' said Miss Flood, 'but it's white.'

Elliot Price looked satisfied as he carefully sprinkled a little salt onto his three bruised potatoes.

'Miss Lyle,' said Miss Flood with a smile, 'I managed to rescue your lunch.'

Her lunch had been two cheese sandwiches. The bread was hard and curled, but Beatrice thought they looked better than the fish, which appeared to be little more than a steaming pile of bones.

'So what brings you to this place?' Elliot asked. 'We all have a story to tell. Apart from Mr Brewster,' he nodded towards a man in the corner, 'who refuses to divulge any more than his surname, and who's to say it's his real one?'

'It isn't much of a story. My brother is a preacher. My father died in tragic circumstances, and I was left alone.'

'Really?' he said, widening his eyes. '*How tragic*.'

'There was a fire,' she told him, picking at the bread. 'I have no other family, at least none that I could really turn to. Afterward, I tried keeping house for a while, but it was difficult, and lonely. I closed up most of the rooms. An elderly neighbour employed me, and I ran errands and kept her company, but then she died. My brother went to Chicago, where he's preaching and working with the Church. I wanted to get away from Illinois altogether.'

'And you chose Brooklyn?' he said.

'I wanted to come to New York,' she explained. 'My brother arranged all the details. It was either this, or Hoboken.'

'Hoboken,' said Elliot, using the handle of his knife to scratch behind his ear. 'I know that place. You made the right decision.'

'I don't know. Have I? It doesn't look like the New York I was expecting.' She glanced outside the window, where a woman in a dirty grey dress was dragging her children in a line; she had five, and at least two of them were crying.

'But this is Brooklyn,' he told her. 'This is the real thing. It's New York without all the hard glamour and the falseness. Was that what you were after? The glamour that is Broadway, Manhattan? Times Square?'

'I don't know.'

'Brooklyn's a good place to start again,' he told her. 'Almost everyone in Brooklyn has come from someplace else.'

'I was born here,' snapped a voice from behind them. 'I was born around the block, and my father too.'

'Miss Stanley was born here,' said Elliot. 'A true Brooklynite. Let us not forget.'

'Though my mother came from Poland,' she said with a shrug. 'Warsaw. But she soon lost her accent, and she always made sure that she looked like an American.'

'Bravo,' said Elliot, scooping up some cabbage. 'There's nothing better looking than an American.'

* * *

It was quiet in her room. She could hear nothing behind the walls, or above her, not a footstep, a cough, or a rattling. What did the others do after supper? Did they stay in their rooms? Sit chatting in the parlour? Did some of them have jobs? And what on earth did they all do for money?

Beatrice sat on her bed. The pillow was hard. *Property of the Galilee Hotel* was stitched into the corner. In her case there was a notebook full of plans, but they didn't seem to belong to the New York she'd just landed in. The plans in her notebook involved Tiffany & Co., where she would work selling diamonds. She'd studied Elijah's book of rocks and minerals. For the past three years she'd stared hard into the window of the jewellers in Normal, where Mr Boris Kosch displayed his rings on velvet cushions, gold chains hanging from little metal trees, and his wife would serve tea (Russian-style) if you were making a purchase and taking your time about it. 'It's all part of the service,' she'd smile, as girls stood hunched over cases, blushing and biting their nails, their fresh-faced boys behind them worrying about the cost, because was a ring really needed after all?

But Tiffany & Co., advertised in her magazines, was the most spectacular store. They sold jewels to rich New Yorkers. Maharajas. The British aristocracy. Pencil-line drawings showed women with furs around their necks, pouting their heart-shaped lips, their hands full of bracelets, *'Oh, I'll take the lot!'* she says, one foot on the running board of her automobile. *'It's hard to choose at Tiffany's!'*

Beatrice had seen herself holding out those trays

of diamond rings. She knew about carat and the different shades of rubies. She'd used cold cream on her hands, and manicured her nails, because she knew appearance was important, it was the little things that made all the difference.

She went outside. The air was cooler now. She could see Elliot Price talking to Miss Flood in the dining room, using his hands, like they were spelling out the words. Miss Stanley was sewing in the parlour, her mouth full of pins, her forehead wrinkled; pulling out the needle like it pained her.

From the top of the step she could see all the way down Renton Street. The air sat on the rooftops and shimmered. A group of boys were kicking a flat-looking ball and men strolled by in summer straw hats with fancy walking canes. It seemed the street was coming to life. She could hear trombones and the sound of the seagulls as they drifted into shore.

'The meals stink,' said a voice behind her. 'Me? I go to the Jewish bakery whenever I can. At least those bagels taste of something.'

Beatrice turned. A girl around her age was standing with her arms folded. She had dark curly hair and a round plump face.

'I'm Lydia. I'm only here until the day after tomorrow, that's when my dear, dear papa will be coming to pick me up, and take me home to Kirksville, Missouri, where I shall certainly die from boredom within the first three weeks. Missouri stinks,' she said. 'All of it.'

'What are you doing in Brooklyn?' asked Beatrice.

'Me? I'm on a little vacation.'

'Really?'

'No. Real reason? My mother ran off with a travelling salesman. Fell madly in love with a man selling buttons. Can you imagine? My father was so ashamed he almost shot himself. But he didn't,' she added, rolling her eyes as if he should have done it. 'Now my mother is travelling all over America with a trunk full of buttons and bows and her eyes full of love hearts. My father said he needed time to adjust to this new situation, so he sent me away to an aunt, who wasn't even home when I got there. She has this big fancy house near Central Park, but there was no one inside it, not even a girl washing dishes or polishing the floor. And that's how I ended up here, and it's a dump, if you don't mind my saying so. Are you a Methodist?'

'I suppose so. Are you?'

'You have to be to get into this place. So, yes, I suppose that I must be.'

They sat by the door, Beatrice tracing her finger in the dust. 'It isn't at all like I thought it would be,' she said. 'Brooklyn, New York.'

'You ever been to Manhattan?'

'No.'

'That's where it's all supposed to be happening, but the people over there, they've got bigger problems than me. They're all too busy trying to make themselves a quick buck, or showing off their fancy clothes or admiring their reflections to look at you twice. I spent a night in Manhattan, all by myself, because I figured if my aunt ain't home yet, then come night-time, she might be, and so I walked around a while, took in the sights, and then went back to Central Park, and there was still no answer. The windows, and believe me there were plenty of them, were black. A woman appeared from next door with a wheezy Pomeranian bitch under her arm, who looked at me like I was nothing, and couldn't believe it was my relative she'd been living next door to all these years. Anyway, it turns out that my aunt is in the Hamptons for the summer, wherever that might be.'

'Did the woman help you out?'

'You've got to be kidding. The woman threatened to report me for loitering if I was still there when she got back. Her dog started snarling, and let me tell you, that fluffy little dog had teeth that looked like razors. I didn't hang around.'

'What did you do?'

Lydia sighed as she leaned back on her hands and looked up at the sky. 'I walked around Manhattan for a while. I got a cup of coffee. I didn't have the money for a room, but I'd heard that New York stays open, so I figured I'd just walk around, buy a sweet roll and a couple of coffees, and wait until morning.'

'What happened?'

'You want to take a walk?' she said. 'I talk too much. I know I talk too much and then people make their opinions, and I'm usually the bad mouthy one they try and avoid at mealtimes. Take your friend Mr Price, for example.'

'He's hardly my friend.'

'Whatever. That man turns his nose up whenever he sees me, like I smell worse than a dog's behind, just because I don't read Shakespeare, or whoever it is he's talking about. He thinks he's English. Have you noticed that yet? Anyway, I know things about Mr Price he wouldn't want nobody else to know about.'

'Like what?'

'Like, I'm talking too much already. What about you? I'm bad at asking questions, I'm so terrible, really I am; don't take it personal, I usually forget.'

'I'm all right.'

'Is that all you can manage, "all right"? You're creating quite a stir, you know. I saw them all looking, even Mr Brewster had a funny little twitch at the side of his mouth, and usually that man is like a stone, so you made an impression in there, believe me.'

'I look a mess,' Beatrice said. 'I've been in these clothes since the day before yesterday.'

'Who was looking at the clothes?'

They walked towards Prospect Park. The streets were full of people. Men sat on upturned crates playing pinochle and poker and girls jumped in and out of skipping ropes singing songs in other languages, their plaits bobbing high in the air like question marks. People shouted from window to window. 'You know what the time is?' 'Henry Schwimmer, he don't know nothing!' 'She always plays the innocent, have you seen the look on her face when she comes tiptoeing home in the dark?'

Beatrice felt dirty. A man was having his hair cut, right there in the street. Her head felt itchy, it really needed washing. Lydia looked so clean; she could almost hear her squeaking.

'We'll sit in the park if you like. Brooklyn's emerald. That's what Miss Flood calls it.'

'I'd like to work with jewellery,' said Beatrice as they reached Prospect Park where the grass looked nothing like an emerald. It was dry, and yellow and brown.

'Who wouldn't?'

'No, really. I'd like to work in a jeweller's store.'

'You want to get yourself over to the diamond district. Mind you, they usually employ their own, so I wouldn't be getting your hopes up.'

'I want to work at Tiffany & Co.,' said Beatrice, looking at her fingernails which were already in need of some repair.

'Oh, I've heard of that place right enough,' said Lydia, waving to a woman selling pancakes. 'I've heard they won't let you in through the door unless you've got at least a thousand dollars in your purse.'

'Really?' said Beatrice. 'How do they know?'

'Oh,' she said, with a shrug, 'they can tell just by looking at you.'

They sat with the grass prickling under their hands.

'It's been a long few days,' said Beatrice.

'What are you going to do?'

'Look for a job. I'll have to.'

'I'll come with you,' said Lydia. 'I like jewellery stores. Not that I've ever put a foot inside one.'

'Did you see Tiffany & Co. when you were in Manhattan? They have a new store at Fifth Avenue and 37th Street.'

'No. Jewels weren't exactly on my mind. I did see Macy's,' she said. 'Now that store really is something else. It sells everything under the sun.'

Beatrice fell back onto her arms, until she was lying down. The park was busy. She could feel a rumbling, the stamping of children's boots begging for taffy and ice cream, the wheels of the perambulators as drowsy-eyed babies sucked in the air. She was so tired now, she was drifting and the ground was opening up, taking her in and wrapping her, while the sky above her head sat on her face like cotton.

* * *

'You look like something glowing,' said Elliot Price.

The next morning, Beatrice was wearing her smartest and cleanest summer dress. She'd washed her hair in the basin. Her skin smelled of cheap lemon soap.

'I'm looking for employment,' she told him.

'I know the girl who washes dishes at Carson's. They might need more help. I could always ask.'

Beatrice shook her head. 'I'd like to work in a jewellery store,' she said, looking at her hands.

Miss Stanley appeared. 'Jewels? Jewels are expensive and frivolous; the world does not need jewels.'

'The world does not need a lot of things,' said Elliot, 'but having them helps us through the day.'

'Like alcohol.'

'No,' he told her, 'like books, paintings, and sticks of cotton candy.'

'Useless things,' she said, turning and walking away. 'And the only books I own are religious or instructional.'

'I need a job,' said Beatrice. 'I'll try the jewellery stores first, because I've kind of set my heart on it, but if nothing happens then I'll have to look elsewhere.'

'Good idea. I'm sure the only thing that will stop

you getting work in a jeweller's is that you'll shine brighter than the jewels they have on offer, and you are not for sale.'

Lydia put her head around the door. 'Ready?'

'Are you looking for a job as well?' asked Elliot.

'No chance. Pops will be here tomorrow, and I'll be heading back to Missouri where I can sleep all day and dream of my Prince Charming.' She winked at him. 'But you'll know all about that,' she said.

'What on earth are you talking about? The girl talks in riddles.'

She took Beatrice's arm. 'Come on, kid, those diamonds won't sell themselves. You could have sold at least a dozen rings by now.'

'I'm nervous.'

'Nervous? What for? It's only a jeweller's,' said Lydia. 'It isn't life or death, it's just a store.'

* * *

Tiffany & Co. was sitting in the place where the buildings shone, though the sidewalks were jammed with so many people and it was hard to breathe in the heat, let alone stop and look up at the shine.

'This city must have more glass than any other city in the world.'

'We're here,' said Beatrice, her throat a little tight. 'We're at Tiffany's.'

'That's what it says on the sign.' They stood gazing into its wide bow-shaped windows. Lydia whistled softly. 'They just don't look real,' she said. 'See those diamonds? They look like clumps of glass.'

Beatrice could feel her hands sweating. She'd reshaped her nails with an emery board. Hands were important in the jewellery business. Even if you were selling a necklace, it was the hands that clicked the clasp into place.

'Are you going in?' asked Lydia. There were men on the door with stiff waxed moustaches and braid around their collars.

'Do I look like I have a thousand dollars?'

'I'd believe you.'

Lydia stepped back. She said she'd wait for her in a nearby coffee house. 'It doesn't look like my kind of place after all,' she shrugged. 'It looks more like a museum than a place that's selling things.'

Beatrice took a deep breath. Why should she be nervous? She could always say she was browsing, looking at the jewels, which were there to be looked at under their glass domes and cages, because if you didn't look, then how could you buy?

The men on the door nodded her inside.

I've made it, she thought. *I look a thousand dollars*.

The room was wide, it smelled of limes and the fans above her head droned, she could feel her hair moving; the glass glittered, and under the glass, diamonds had been set into gold and shaped into flowers, birds, faces. Octagonal boxes were inlaid with ivory and pearls the size of pigeon eggs sat with icy strips of sapphires.

'Can I be of any assistance?' A man with yellow-coloured eyes appeared. He was the smartest-looking salesman that she had ever seen. 'Would miss like to see something special?'

'No thank you,' she told him. He nodded and

turned on his smooth-sounding heels. A clock shaped like an owl began to chime in the corner. She was sure its head was moving.

* * *

'What do you mean you didn't ask about a job?' said Lydia. 'I can't believe you didn't ask about a job.'

Beatrice looked into her coffee cup. 'Job or no job, I wouldn't be happy there, even with all the jewellery. It felt cold,' she said. 'Cold enough to snap you.'

'So what are you going to do now? Try another store?'

She shrugged. 'I'm rethinking the jewellery business altogether,' she said. 'It wasn't how I thought it would be.'

'It was only one store. One big store. Don't give up. There are plenty of other places selling diamonds.'

She shrugged. She'd lost all of her enthusiasm. The man with the yellow eyes had said everything here is hollow.

'Don't look so worried,' said Lydia, licking her finger and dipping it into the sugar bowl. 'New York is full of employment. Granted, it's also full of people looking for it, but half of them can't speak English yet, and the rest aren't as pretty as you.'

'You don't have to be pretty to get yourself employed.'

'You're new to this,' said Lydia. 'You'll learn.'

This was the New York that she'd imagined, but it wasn't as clean as the place in her magazines, where the air was full of window shine, scent of Araby and the occasional glimpse of an Astor. A man stood in a doorway with a toothpick and a board saying BUY UNION CIGARS. People rubbed against each other. Lips sparkled. Plumes of steam spouted from the underworld. The stores sold everything. Antiques. Devilled crabs. Fading yellow roses.

'I know,' said Lydia. 'Let's go where the air is fresh. I was there on Saturday. You don't need any money, once you get to it, the whole place is one big sideshow and you can see it all for nothing.'

'You can?'

'It's called Coney Island,' she said. 'You ever heard of Coney Island? It's back over Brooklyn way, so we won't be late for dinner, and Miss Flood won't lock us out.'

'She locks you out?'

'Only happened once,' said Lydia. 'And it wasn't my fault I was late, I got lost, I'm new to New York, so what does she expect?'

'You seem to know your way around.'

'What else have I got to do all day? It's best to get away from the others and their banners,' she said. 'I really can't face walking up and down with "Prepare to Meet Thy God" above my head.'

* * *

The air was sharper at Coney. It was like another country as they stood looking at the water, where the ferry boats were sounding their whistles and the tramp steamers moved through the haze.

'Come on,' said Lydia, pulling on her arm. 'Come and be amazed.'

The boardwalk was busy. Children screamed, men tipped their hats and Beatrice felt her face burning. Girls in stockings and ballet shoes wore fancy white collars, crisp as pastry frills, and a man beside them shouted, 'Come and join us for the five o'clock show! These girls can dance! They can sing! They can perform acrobatic miracles for you to swoon and sway over!' Painted boards advertised Mermaids, Elephant Boys, Corn on the Cob. A tattooist from Scotland was hitching up his round pot belly and smoking a cigar. His assistant had his shirt wide open to show the strings of bluebirds that flew around his neck. He had anchors and small dripping hearts stabbed with jewelled daggers. A blue-grey galleon had pride of place on his flat solar plexus.

'Oh my,' giggled Lydia. 'Just look at him will you, he's a living piece of chintz.'

Beatrice felt dizzy. She could taste the salt water on her lips. Stinging. The chattering voices, the long high-pitched screams droned, and in the distance the booths and curving roller coasters were hanging in the sky; a warm tickly feeling crept across her stomach.

'Where does this place end?' She squinted. She could see a woman with gemstones dotted in her hair, her blue cape waving, and her feet invisible as she danced along the boardwalk.

'End? It doesn't end,' said Lydia. 'It stretches. Look over there. Over there you have your Dreamland. You have your Luna Park. This place goes on and on.'

They stopped for a cheap lemonade. The long polished counter was like a busy road, with its sliding cups and tall glasses, bowls of saltines, coleslaw and spicy fried chicken.

'If only the smell would fill you up,' said Lydia.

'Are we really in Brooklyn?'

Lydia smiled. 'It's not exactly Renton Street,' she said, 'but it says Brooklyn on the map.'

'Will you miss it?' Beatrice asked. 'What are you going to do with yourself in Kirksville, Missouri?'

'Stagnate. Unless of course we have to move because of our very shameful circumstances. I can't get a job, that's for sure,' she said, pulling a chunk of ice from her glass and sucking on it. 'Genteel ladies don't work. Genteel ladies stay home and embroider things and play the pianoforte and so on.'

'I can't imagine you doing all that.'

'Look, I might not seem all that genteel to you, but believe me, in Kirksville, Missouri, I'm more than highly refined.'

Beatrice smiled. 'I wish you weren't leaving.'

'Me too, but all good things have to come to an end. *Farewell, Miss Flood and the Hotel Galilee! Farewell, Mr Price!*' She said it in the style of a tragedian, the back of her hand pressed against her forehead. 'Come on, it's getting late, we'll miss tonight's delicacy if we're not careful, and we'll go to bed rumbling.'

'Can't we stay a little longer? I have some money; we could go and see the mermaid.'

'All right,' she shrugged, 'who in their right mind would say no to meeting a mermaid?'

* * *

There was a small queue outside the booth where the large painted board showed a mermaid combing her long yellow hair, sitting on a rock. Dripping gold letters proclaimed she was *The Siren of the Sea! Stolen for Your Viewing Pleasure by the Sailors Who Fell Under Her Spell . . .*

'Only two at a time,' the man was saying as they shuffled down the line. 'Three if you're very, very quiet. The mermaid's awfully sensitive, you know; she's not used to being on dry land.'

'What's her name?' asked a boy.

The man hesitated. 'Well, we don't rightly know,' he said, scratching his chin. 'Problem is, she don't speak no American, she only speaks mermaid.'

The boy looked impressed.

'Do you think she's for real?' Beatrice asked.

'I don't know, but this place is chock-full of mystery. When I was here last week I saw two women stuck together from the hip, they were laughing like they hadn't a care in the world, one of them was eating a corn dog. It was a very peculiar sight.'

They held hands and squeezed them as they entered the booth, where a tight narrow space led to a room of blue light.

'It smells like the bottom of the sea,' whispered Lydia. Her skin was now turquoise. Beatrice held out her fingers and watched the light ripple. It felt eerie. From the corner of the room they could hear a splashing sound. They squeezed their hands tighter.

The Siren of the Sea was sitting in a tank, on a stool that had rocks piled around it and at least ten inches of Hudson River water. She was small and hunched, wearing a wig that covered her chest and fell down to her waist. Her face was old and drooping, and when she smiled, her teeth were like tiny yellow pearls sitting in her gums. She wore a short flouncy skirt, its fraying hem embroidered with exotic-looking seashells. Her small bony legs were joined from her sore-looking knees. There were no shiny emerald scales or a pretty flapping tail. Her feet came apart at the ankles, sticking out at right angles. Most of her toes were fused. The mermaid coughed, and her leg shot up in a spasm. Beatrice and Lydia ran.

'She must have thought we were frightened of her,' Beatrice said, her hands on her knees, her heart pounding.

'But I was,' said Lydia, catching her breath. 'Weren't you? That woman is a freak.'

*   *   *

Elliot Price was sitting on a chair by the door, reading *Let the True Light In*. There was a gravy stain on his jacket and a small shiny hole had wormed its way into his right knee. His shoes, a bright deep chestnut, were perfectly clean and glowing on his narrow crossed feet. He looked up and slipped his thumb inside the pages of his book.

'How's the jewellery business?' he asked.

'I didn't like it,' she told him, shading her eyes. 'Truth is, I didn't even ask.'

'Never mind, never mind, something will turn up; meanwhile, there's always the Galilee.'

Lydia smirked. 'I'll be out of here by ten o'clock tomorrow morning, if not before.'

'I'll miss you,' said Elliot.

'I don't believe you.'

'Of course I will. I mention you every single night in my prayers.'

‘Why?’ she said, stepping over him. ‘Are you praying I won’t blab?’

‘I don’t know what it is you’re talking about,’ he said. ‘I pray for all the lost souls inside this hotel, always have done, always will.’

‘Do I look lost to you?’ she said, heading for the stairs. ‘I’m here; I know exactly where I am and exactly where I’m going. I’ve never been lost in my life.’

‘Oh, she’s a live one all right,’ said Elliot, unhooking his thumb from the book and opening out the pages. ‘Don’t let her lead you astray.’

‘Talking of being led astray, what happened to Miss Brownlow?’ asked Beatrice.

‘Oh Miss Brownlow,’ he said, dropping his head. ‘Miss Brownlow disgraced herself.’

‘How?’

‘Oh, the usual things; liquor, a good-looking boy, and the rest, as they say, is history.’

* * *

She stretched out on top of her bed. It was late and the walls were patched with shadows. She could hear a man shouting in Yiddish in the street, it sounded fast and furious and the words more interesting than English, the way they worked around his tongue like he could taste them. A door slammed. Then silence.

Lydia had been quiet all evening. She’d worked through her meal (corned beef, potatoes and carrots) without relish, but left nothing behind, not one speck of beef, not a single dot of carrot. She’d sulked with her arms folded when Miss Stanley had said that the place simply wouldn’t be the same without her, and she'd gone to bed early, leaving her bag in the hall, a dusty-looking carpet bag with a mended leather handle.

Beatrice had walked around the block, watching the sky change from blue to orange to something that looked like a bruise. She'd seen Miss Flood and the others marching down the street with their banners, dodging dried beans and insults. A man had been sitting on the pavement eating a bowl of spaghetti. He had his shirtsleeves rolled up. His arms were the colour of caramel. He'd looked up from his bowl and nodded. *'Questo un la sera bella.'* And she'd nodded back, because whatever it was he was saying, he sounded as if he were right.

The hotel was quiet. A dog was barking somewhere around the back. She closed her eyes. 'This is my home, this is where I live, this is my home, *this really is my home.*' The words were a mantra she didn't quite believe, and she felt panicked when she remembered that everything in Normal had gone. The furniture auctioned, the house—eventually sold to a family called Robinson, who had come from Carbondale and didn't know the details, and didn't seem to mind the charred square of garden, and the rumours. Her aunt in Springfield had sent a note of condolence, and said she understood that after three long years it was only right that Beatrice should move on. *I don't know how you lived in that place for so long*, she wrote, *you are right to want to leave it*. But she offered no kind of help or accommodation. Her brother had fled to the Church, and to the Reverend Malcolm Henderson who had prayed with him, talking of salvation, finding Elijah a place in Chicago where crime and insobriety were rife, where they needed the enthusiasm and the energy of the youngest, fittest preachers to set the godless onto the path of true light.

Eventually, she fell asleep. She dreamed fitfully. She was eating spaghetti, wearing silk ballet slippers and standing on a horse. The tattooed man appeared. He unbuttoned his shirt. He smiled at her. Then, shaking out his collar, he started setting free the birds.

* * *

Lydia had gone before breakfast. After the prayer and the plate of toast and shrivelled eggs, Miss Flood announced that Miss Lydia Shields from Missouri was no longer a guest at the Galilee, and that she should not be allowed inside the premises if she reappeared. 'Under any circumstances.' Beatrice suddenly felt sick.

'Why?' she asked. 'What has she done?'

Miss Flood cleared her throat a little. 'In a word,' she said, 'absconded.'

A large black fly was dancing on the tablecloth, which Miss Flood eyed suspiciously before banging down her fist.

'I don't know what you mean,' shrugged Beatrice, 'wasn't she supposed to be leaving this morning anyway?'

'She was supposed to be leaving at 10 a.m.,' said Miss Flood. 'She was supposed to have been collected by her father, a Mr Henry Shields. She was not supposed to be leaving at 1 a.m., collected by some unknown shadow loitering about in the yard.'

Elliot Price pushed his plate to one side. 'Well, there we have it,' he said, producing a crumpled handkerchief from his pants pocket, and dramatically blowing his nose. 'Another one bites the dust.'

'But what will her father think?' said Beatrice. 'He'll be devastated.'

'Miss Lyle,' said Miss Flood, slowly shaking her head, 'don't you see?'

'See what?'

'There is no such person as Henry Shields from Missouri. Never has been. Who knows who Miss Shields really is, where she comes from, or what she might be called. Thanks to the protection of the good Lord Himself, we were not robbed, or murdered in our beds, though I must urge you all to check through your belongings, and report what is missing.'

'Lydia wasn't a thief,' said Beatrice. 'I'm sure she wasn't a thief.'

'Who knows who or what she is?' said Miss Stanley, with her arms folded. 'I agree with Miss Flood. That girl could be anything.'

'Of course, the Galilee Hotel is not a prison,' Miss Flood added quickly. 'We took her in. We took nothing. The least she owes us is her honesty.'

'But are you sure her father won't be coming here to get her?'

Miss Flood rubbed and twisted her hands, like she was washing something out. 'I am positive,' she said. 'Henry Shields is a fictional character.'

Beatrice went outside, breathing hard in the freedom, the large expanse of blue and white sky.

No one else had appeared the slightest bit concerned for Lydia's safety. They'd tutted, shaking their heads with a knowing smile here and there, as if they'd expected something like this was going to happen all along, and that the alias Lydia Shields was now somewhere being sinful.

'I've heard about girls like Lydia Shields,' Miss Flood had said. 'The things they get up to are enough to send them dancing all the way down to the Devil.'

'It's Miss Brownlow all over again,' said Miss Stanley, and there had been something of a smile sitting in the corners of her narrow colourless lips.

Beatrice walked without knowing where she was going. Every so often she thought she might have seen Lydia, laughing on the corner, pushing back her curls.

She took the ferry to Coney Island, because it was the only place she could think of, and one of the few places she knew how to get to. The ferry was already crowded. Children danced on the spot, squashed between bodies in their best Coney clothes. There was no sign of Lydia, but she might be there already, eating fried chicken, or queuing for the elephant boy.

Her head was full of colour. Crowds pushed together speaking in languages that Beatrice didn't recognise. The scent of horses mingled with salt, the perspiration, the coils of smoke winding in the air, snake-like and smelling of charred beef and spices. Beatrice, pummelled by elbows and shoulders, passed plaster minarets, bands with dancing monkeys, a woman playing a polished gold harp, the Pavilion of Fun, bronze-lipped fish, tail-to-tail elephants, the Ferris wheel, and people, old and young, rich and poor, sniffing the air, eyes wide, lips trembling, because what they'd heard was true, this place really was heaven on earth, the sun was shining, and they were strolling in it.

Her eyes ached with looking for Lydia and she could feel the sweat sticking underneath her arms. So many girls had round smiling faces, dark curls and green summer dresses. A stall selling cheap souvenirs said *Help Wanted*. She hesitated. She watched the girl behind the counter in a pink-and-white striped apron selling kaleidoscopes. A boy kicked his mother's shin. *I want one of those. I want one, I want to get one now!* She walked away. She could always walk back.

By the time she'd reached the heart of the park, cricking her neck at the revolving airship tower, she'd been sung to by a man from Bombay (he was also carrying a snake), shouted at by a woman selling paper concertinas, whistled at by a group of boys, followed by a man with a glass of Turkish coffee, and squashed against a child with a pink marshmallow cupcake. She couldn't stand a moment longer. Her feet were throbbing. She found a quiet dark corner in the Memsahib Tea Parlor. Here the air rustled. She ordered iced tea, pressing her hands against the cool wooden table, pressing them back to her forehead, transferring the change in temperature. An English accent said, 'Like the old days, only cleaner.' A waitress moaned, 'Juss leave me alone, willya? I've got no change, I've got no change, I'm tellingya.'

The frozen tea brought a sharp pain to her forehead. Sitting behind her eyelids were points of reddish light and she rubbed them into blurs.

'Are you waiting for someone?' said a voice.

Beatrice looked up, shaking her head. It was a woman. 'Mind if I join you? I'm looking for the darkest corner, and you're in it. I shouldn't be here, I should be standing in my booth, but I haven't felt right all morning, and now I'm starting to swoon.'

The woman sat down. She was a little older than Beatrice. She was wearing a blouse that had *Nancy* embroidered on the collar.

'I'm baking,' she said, stirring the fat slice of lemon that was sitting in her soda. 'Truly. This heat is killing me off.'

'Do you work here?' asked Beatrice. 'Here at Coney?'

'For my sins.'

Beatrice looked into her tea. She took a sip. The woman smiled.

'Are you here like the rest of them, for pleasure?'

'I don't know.'

'Funny answer.'

'I sort of came looking for somebody.'

'Find him?'

'It was a girl. We were staying in the same hotel, then she disappeared.'

'This place, it sucks you up,' the woman said. 'Some people come here for an hour, and they're never seen again. I'm Nancy, by the way. Nancy Karlinsky.'

'Beatrice.'

'You look the smart type,' said Nancy. 'You work in Manhattan?'

'No,' Beatrice told her. 'I only just got here. I'm looking for a job.'

'Are you fussy?'

'Depends.'

'How would you like a job selling postcards? My boss will have to see you first, he'll have to give you the once-over, but he's been moaning about wanting someone else since the start of the season. How about it?'

'Postcards?'

'Views of Coney. Luna Park by night. People like postcards.'

Beatrice didn't hesitate. 'Yes,' she said. 'Selling postcards. I could do that.'

BRINGING BACK THE PAST

'Mary's asking for you,' said Lizzie. She was covering her head with her coat, sheltering from the rain. 'I've just been there. Have you heard? She's on death's door. I know she's been there a few times before, but this time she's almost inside it.'

'She's asking for me?' Beatrice had been cleaning all day. Her apron was grey; her hands were sore and her nails were full of silver polish. 'Do you think I should go?'

'Yes.'

She pulled off her apron. 'Should I change?'

Lizzie shook her head.

'Then I'll just wash my hands and brush my hair a little.'

'I don't think there's time,' she said. 'Come on.'

They ran through the warm, fine rain. In the parlour, the doctor was sitting with his coat off, his waistcoat unbuttoned, sipping a large glass of port. 'Just to keep out the weather,' he explained, nodding at the window. 'This summer rain's worse. It's the change, you see; it gets into the bones.'

Mary's mother offered Lizzie a chair. 'Oh no,' the doctor waved. 'Elizabeth can sit here with me. How are those two little rascals of yours? Harry and George?'

'Harry and Martha,' said Lizzie, shyly perching down on the sofa with a cushion in between them. 'I have a girl and a boy.'

'Ah yes,' the doctor twitched, pushing his glasses further up his nose with his finger. 'One of each, how thrilling.'

'And Mary?' asked Beatrice.

Her mother looked down at Beatrice's boots, and then slowly raised her red eyes. 'She's waiting for you,' she said, rummaging up her sleeve for a handkerchief. 'Can't speak of anything else.'

'Might I go up?'

The doctor cleared his throat. 'I must warn you,' he said, taking a slurp from his glass, 'she has little time left with us.'

'I'm sorry.'

'I never thought it would come to this,' said her mother. 'Don't upset her. Be careful what you say, and if she starts rambling . . .'

'It's the morphine,' said the doctor. 'That's all it is, the morphine.'

Beatrice felt more than a little nervous walking up the stairs. The cottage felt different, the small deep-set windows looked smaller and there was a creaking as she knocked at Mary's door and walked straight in.

Mary was almost invisible. It seemed like her

eyes had slipped to the back of her head. Her hair had been wrapped in a thin muslin towel.

'I'm here,' said Beatrice.

'I wanted you to come,' said Mary. 'I've been asking all day. Is the door properly closed?'

Beatrice looked behind her. It was slightly ajar. She closed it.

'Two things,' said Mary. 'I want you to tell me another story. I want to be able to think about something other than this world when I'm slipping away. And I want you to find my father. It's important to me,' she said. 'I want to know he'll be there at my funeral. I know where he lives, I've always known. I have his address. Here.' She took a slip of paper from underneath the blanket. 'Will you promise?'

'I'll do the best I can.'

'I couldn't ask the others, they know Mother, but I know I can trust you. Tell me you'll do it.'

'I'll do it.'

'I believe you.'

Beatrice sat on the chair by the bed.

'I'm not in any pain,' said Mary, 'but I can feel myself slipping, and it isn't wholly unpleasant, so don't think that I'm lying here in torment, because I'm not.'

Beatrice nodded. Her mouth felt dry. 'So, you want me to tell you a story?' she said, wondering how she would manage it.

'Would you? It doesn't have to be a happy story, the sort that will make me smile, and feel better. I want it to be a long story, one that will stay with me, a story I can think about, and go over all the little details when I'm lying in the dark.'

'If that's what you want, then I'll tell you the

story of Marta and Magda, the Hungarian Siamese twins who fell in love with the same man.'

'Yes, tell me that story, but don't tell me if it's true, or if you are making it up. I want to believe in it.'

'Oh, but you can, because Marta and Magda are real, and they're still living on Coney Island, New York, working on the hoopla stall.'

'Really?'

'For sure,' said Beatrice. 'Even as I speak, Marta will be collecting up the hoops whilst her sister holds a box out for the dimes.'

*   *   *

Two days later, Mary's bed was stripped, and the house looked empty from the outside. Beatrice took out the folded piece of paper. The address was a street in the centre of town, a crooked row of terraces with roofs the colour of ox blood.

'Mr Fell?' Beatrice asked.

'That's me,' he said. He was fastening his collar. 'I'm not in the mood for a talk about God. Or are you selling something?'

'No. It's about your daughter, Mary.'

The man stopped what he was doing. He looked frozen. 'She's dead, isn't she?'

Beatrice nodded. He leaned against the peeling door frame, looking somewhere over her head. 'Who are you anyway?' he asked.

'I was Mary's friend. I'm sorry, I didn't come here to shock you. I thought you might have heard already.'

'From her mother, you mean? There was never any chance of that.'

‘Can I come in? I won’t stay long; it’s just that I promised Mary that I’d speak to you.’

She followed him inside. The room was small and sooty. Toys were strewn across a large horsehair sofa and the grate was full of ashes.

‘My wife’s out with the little one,’ he said. ‘I’m on my way to work; I’m a porter, at the town hall, I’m on the afternoon shift. Can I get you a cup of tea? I’ve time for a cup of tea.’

‘I’ll make it,’ said Beatrice.

‘No, you won’t,’ he said. ‘The kitchen’s like a pigsty.’

She heard him running water and pulling out the crockery. When he came back with two small cups, she could see he’d been crying.

‘I wanted to see her,’ he said, rubbing his eyes with his knuckles. ‘I know I did wrong, but it had nothing to do with Mary. I missed her so much I ended up in the hospital. Ulcers,’ he said. ‘I was all twisted up inside.’

‘She talked about you. She said she didn’t blame you, and that she would have done the same.’

‘And now she’s gone for good,’ he said, ‘and there’s not a damn thing I can do to make it up to her.’

‘There is one thing. She wants you at her funeral, and I made a solemn promise that I would get you there.’

He pulled in his lips and looked into his teacup. ‘She wouldn’t let me. She’d put her foot down. Cause trouble.’

‘Your wife?’

‘No,’ he said. ‘The other one.’

‘Not at the funeral. She’s your daughter too.’

‘When is it?’

'Thursday. I hope you don't mind, I've written down the details.'

'You were her friend, you say? Are you a foreigner?'

'American.'

'Still, I'm glad she had friends. It must have been a lonely life, cooped up in that bed. Sometimes, I'd go and stand across the lane, and look up at the window. Watch the lamp going on and off. I saw her once. At least, I think it was her. She was brushing her hair. She had lovely brown hair.'

Beatrice didn't say anything. He looked at the clock.

'I have to be going,' he said.

'Are you sure you're all right?'

'It's better than sitting here, thinking things that shouldn't be thought.'

'You will be there on Thursday?'

'I'll be there. I'm her dad. It's the least I can do.'

* * *

The sun was shining on Thursday as they followed the hearse, through the village, around the scented lanes, and into Heapy where they stepped aside, and the pallbearers (three elderly men from the funeral home, and Lionel) took the small, light coffin onto their shoulders, walking behind the Reverend McNally who read the twenty-third psalm so fast, the words meant nothing. Beatrice kept her head down. Through the little crowd of black, she'd seen Mr Fell, skirting around the edges.

They gathered at the front of the church, where Mary's mother was being supported by the doctor.

The coffin, with its small sprays of flowers, was the size of a malnourished child. The Reverend McNally looked down at his notes, belching quietly into his hand.

'Let us remember our dear departed loved one and friend, Mary Ann Fell, who lived in Anglezarke village all of her life, and was loved and cared for by many.' He looked up at the congregation, his eyelids drooping; it was like he had run out of steam. 'We brought nothing into this world, and it is certain we can carry nothing out. The Lord gave, and the Lord hath taken away; blessed be the name of the Lord.' He paused. 'Let us now sing hymn number 329.'

It was a quivering congregation who sang 'Abide With Me'. They had no help from the choir, who were on a charity picnic, in aid of the widows and war orphans. The organist stuttered over the keys and the timing was out.

* * *

Mr Fell was noticed at the graveside. After Mary's mother had thrown in her handful of earth, she looked across the faces to where her former husband stood with his hands cupped and his eyes lowered. She looked liked she'd been stung.

Afterwards, when the reverend had disappeared into the vestry, where he could loosen his robes and sip a little drop from his flask, and the mourners had nodded their silent prayers into the deep rectangular hole that was slowly being filled by the gravediggers, Mary's mother lunged at him, before he could quietly slip away.

'Who told you?' she hissed. 'Who said you could

come?'

He shook his head, and shrugged his heavy shoulders, because words were no use; he was here and there was nothing more to be said.

'You've sullied it. My own daughter's funeral and you've made it something filthy.'

'How?' he asked, wiping his sweaty forehead with a handkerchief. 'I've kept my distance. I wanted to be here. She wanted it.'

'What do you mean, "she wanted it"? Since when have you bothered with what we ever wanted? How do you think I feel? Look at them all, staring at me and remembering my shame. Making me out as the fool you left behind.'

'Mary wanted it. She wanted me to come, more than anything.'

'How did you know that she wanted it?' she asked. 'How?'

He didn't say anything, but he looked towards Beatrice. Mary's mother swung round. 'So that's what you were plotting,' she hissed. 'Who are you anyway? Who are you to decide things about my life, when we don't even know who you are?'

Shaking her head, her eyes stinging, Beatrice began to walk through the graveyard and out into the lane. Mr Fell followed her.

'I'm sorry,' he called.

'Don't be,' she told him, pulling off her hat. 'Really. You mustn't be sorry. You did the right thing, and whatever anyone says, I only kept my promise.'

* * *

From the back-bedroom window she watched the

linked throng of black filing into Mary's cottage, where they would sip what little sherry could be found and nibble on whatever could be made with the rations. Ada had donated a tin of corned beef, a jar of raspberry jam and a box of sweet wafers.

Beatrice walked from room to room, peeling off her gloves, listening to the birds, feeling the streams and squares of sunshine melt across her face. She lay across the bed, and catching sight of her reflection in the mirror, she was startled by how black she was, like a long narrow crow.

And later, she could hear them in the distance, the cottage door banging, the shuffles on the gravel that paused outside her gate, before crunching off again. The mutterings, the talk fuelled by drinking sherry in the daytime, the bitter aftertaste from the poor bereaved mother.

Then from the kitchen table, where she was half-heartedly chopping a salad, she could hear something clicking in the hallway, and lying on the doormat was a piece of torn yellow paper telling her in no uncertain terms that she was *Nothing But A Traytor.*

LETTERS TO ELIJAH

Galilee Hotel
Renton Street
Brooklyn
New York

July 25, 1911

Dear Elijah,

I have news from New York! Not only did I arrive here safely, thanks to all your arrangements, but I have managed to find myself employment, and although it isn't in the jewelry store that I had once imagined, it's a respectable business, and from Monday of next week, I shall be selling postcards to the tourists who flock to Coney Island.

Miss Flood, here at the Galilee, went more than a little pale when I told her. She said that Coney was a place full of heathens and wickedness, but I assured her that it is really not the case. The resort is full of families, who are looking for a break from their regular routines, and are here simply to have fun, and who says that good healthy fun is a sin?

Talking of sin, how are the not so good people of Chicago? I hope they are listening to you, and not throwing things at you, as I have heard of some preachers being hit upon by missiles, and one young Wesleyan who ventured into the Bronx was killed when he was pushed into a butcher's store window. Best not to think on that.

The people here at the Galilee have all been very kind, though in due course when I have earned enough, I hope to move out and into accommodation of my own. It is only right, that once you are earning, your place should be taken by someone less fortunate, though having said that, the other bed in my room has always been empty.

I often think of you in Chicago. Have you ever been back to the zoo? Or passed the Lemon Tree Hotel on your travels?

New York is all that I hoped it would be. It is not just a tall place made of metal and glass, but it is also a place of small things. Streets are like villages, where people speak in several languages, and the stores sell the kinds of foods the immigrants are familiar with, and the New Yorkers are getting to like. Brooklyn is a sprawling, dusty place, but there are trees, some that look like umbrellas, and there are green places, and people lolling around in their doorways, hoping to pass the time of day.

I must go now. I promised Miss Flood I would set out the tables for lunch.

Thank you for all that you've done for me, in finding my escape.

Love and plenty good wishes,

Beatrice

July 30, 1911

Dear Elijah,

I do hope you received my last letter. Mr Price who is also a guest at the Galilee tells me that new preachers are often so busy they can only pick through their mail every other week. Well, if that's so, you'll have an awful lot of reading to do.

Mr Price, a retired vaudevillian, seems highly knowledgable about all things. He says that actors have to be like a sponge. He has given up the world of the theater, but he has kept a scrapbook full of cuttings from 'my past life', as he puts it. The pictures show him dressed in baggy suits and bowler hats ('apprentice') and Elizabethan costumes, with frills around his neck and black lines beneath his eyes ('master'). He looks at these pictures fondly, but says the way of life very nearly killed him, and led him into all sorts of temptation and paths full of evil that he does not wish to revisit.

As I wrote in my last letter, I am now a salesgirl. I started the job Monday. It is harder work than I imagined. People like flicking through the boxes and the stands, their fingertips full of frankfurter grease, and we sometimes have to be firm, because who wants to send dog-eared pictures of the beach to the folks back home? At certain times of the day the customers have to wait in line. The girls I work with are the pleasantest, friendliest girls you could wish for, and my boss, Mr Cooper, is a gentleman, though we see him very rarely as he has another booth on Surf Avenue that requires his special attention. The first card I ever sold was a picture of the Chute Tower and Lake Dreamland by Night. The lady said they were from Philadelphia, and they come to Coney every year, though they suffer with the heat something terrible. I think you would like it here, perhaps when you have finished your training, and are looking for a break away from Chicago, you could come and see it all?

Well, Elijah, take good care of yourself,

Much love to you,

Beatrice

August 6, 1911

Dear Elijah,

I must write and tell you about what happened here last night. I was walking home from my shift, and I have to say, after being on my feet for so many hours I was feeling somewhat exhausted, so it took me a while to figure it all out. Just as I was approaching the hotel, I could hear something of a commotion. Not a fight exactly, it was more like moans and pleading. I stopped. At the side of the hotel is a small narrow alleyway, and in this alley a young man was calling up to a window. I must say, I was feeling somewhat giddy at the prospect of listening to this Romeo calling to his Juliet. (Please don't judge me on this, Elijah! It appeared to be a bit of harmless fun . . .) Anyway, I stopped in the shadows to hear a little better what this young man was saying. I can't remember his exact words, but they went along the lines of 'but you promised', 'you mean the world to me', 'I've been waiting, and hoping', and so on. But the most thrilling thing of all was wondering who this young man's 'amour' might be. There were several possibilities. There was Miss Flood herself of course, but I assumed at once that this was highly unlikely, and although everyone deserves love and romance in their lives, I couldn't picture her entertaining this (remarkably handsome, from what I could see) young man for more than two minutes. Miss Flood is a paragon of virtue—if a little abrasive. This left Mrs Mitchell, who is still reeling since her husband left her for the beauty of the islands of Hawaii, taking their children with him, or Miss Stanley. Now, Miss Stanley is around forty years old, and I have heard that some women of this age prefer younger men . . . am I gossiping too much for your liking? If so, then screw the letter up right now, put it into the trash, and forgive me. You're still with me? Then I'll continue . . . Miss Stanley is tall and slim, with hair the color of chocolate, and although her teeth are somewhat crooked, she is not unattractive. The young man, with his hat in his hands swaying from one foot to the other with his head tilted toward a window on the second floor, seemed in pain with all this pleading, words of wishful thinking, and cries of broken promises. I tried to listen to the voice that was telling him in no uncertain terms to 'get lost', but I couldn't quite make it out. There was a low kind of mumbling, a voice I didn't recognize at all, but I presume it was because his ‘Juliet’ was trying her best to be discreet, and worrying about the other guests, who were probably attempting to sleep, or reading, or some such. When I saw the young man had lost all hope of a meeting, I hurried off.

This morning when I sat with Mr Price having breakfast, I looked around the room, to see if I could perhaps detect some lovelorn expression, or exasperation on the face of Miss Flood, Mrs Mitchell, or Miss Stanley, but they appeared to be munching stealthily through their toast and sipping at their juice in just the usual manner. Mr Price kept yawning. I asked him if he’d been kept awake last night, and he seemed to redden a little, and so I asked him if he knew if any of the other guests had a beau. I made it sound like a very innocent question, and one that I wouldn’t be at all shocked or disgusted to hear if it were true, because I know that even the strictest of Methodists are allowed to have beaus, because it is only human nature after all. He seemed to choke a little. ‘Oh, I very much doubt it,’ he said, looking over his shoulder. ‘Whatever makes you think that?’ And so I told him about the very handsome young man, who’d been calling up to a window last night. ‘He looked very handsome you say?’ he asked, with a little shake of his head. ‘Oh yes,’ I told him. ‘I only saw him in the shadows, but he had the profile of a real Prince Charming, make no mistake.’ Mr Price licked his lips, smiled, and quickly drained his glass of orange juice. ‘Perhaps this young man was swooning around the wrong hotel?’ he shrugged. ‘Perhaps the object of his affection was really residing in the Somersby Hotel? It's a very similar building and only the next block down, and in the half-light, and in such a heightened state of emotion, things can become somewhat blurred and confusing.' And I must admit, when I looked around the room again—Miss Flood wiping down the tables with a dishcloth drenched in disinfectant, Mrs Mitchell scratching her neck, and Miss Stanley picking out the crumbs from her rather crooked teeth, I had to admit that Mr Price was probably right, which somehow seemed a shame, and I went upstairs, feeling strangely disappointed.

On my way to work, I thought about Normal, and it felt more than a million miles away, and that has to be good thing, hasn't it? Do you miss it? I must admit that I sometimes wake up in the heat, listening to the traffic, to the people shouting in the street, and I think, 'I'm tired and I want to go home,' but then it passes, and I enjoy this new place all over again. The sights and the sounds. Really, Elijah, you wouldn't believe the things I see on my way to the booth. Today, for example, I passed a magician picking cards from people's ears, a camel, an opera singer in a big black cape, a man swallowing swords, and a young girl dressed as a tree, complete with initials carved into the bark, and a bird's nest! It really is a fascinating place to work, and it beats the little streets in Normal hands down.

Take good care of yourself, Elijah, and keep yourself safe.

All my love, Beatrice

August 11, 1911

Dear Elijah,

Last night I went out dancing for the first time in my life! My head is still spinning with it all, and you mustn't think that I was unchaperoned because I was with half a dozen girls and even Mr Cooper came for the first half an hour. I was dressed very modestly, and did not act in any way improper. Don't I sound pompous? Why I feel the need to assure you, I don't know. What I do know is that I sometimes feel my minister brother sitting in judgment on my shoulder, and as I've no one else to look out for me, I really should be grateful, yet it can also be unnerving—do you know what I mean? Or am I babbling again?

The dance was held at a place called the Bavarian Palace. And inside and out, it really does look like the kind of palace you might see illustrating traditional fairy tales and the like. It has cloud-topped turrets, and the walls are painted with alpine scenes that look so real you can sometimes feel quite chilly, which, let me assure you, in those crowds and at this time of year is a blessing.

I was asked to dance at least a dozen times, and I accepted most, encouraged by my friends. The young men, all of whom were extremely well behaved and proper, came from different walks of life. I can't remember them all (see how popular your sister was!) but there was definitely a student from Princeton, a strapping blond baseball player, an encyclopedia salesman from New Jersey, and an Italian waiter, who works in his father's spaghetti house. It was very noisy, with the band and the crowd, but I think his name was Luigi, and he congratulated me on my neat and dainty way of dancing, though I am sure he was being polite, because the only other time I've danced was way back in Normal with Bethan Carter, waltzing up and down in her yard.

I stayed late, drinking fruit juice and punch. We ate fried chicken and noodles and we girls laughed and talked about all kinds of nonsense.

This morning I woke with a headache, but it was the kind of headache that makes you smile, because you remember why you have it, and somehow it was worth it, and though I know you think that punch is a sin, it was really quite delicious, and refreshing, and it has not made me hanker after anymore, or stronger, liquor. (Please don't worry. I know all the pitfalls, and I will be very careful.)

I was in another world at breakfast. Couldn't stop yawning. I am sure the others must have noticed. Mr Price did not appear. When I asked Miss Flood where he was, she said she had really no idea, but that he was probably 'lying in' and he would have to go hungry.

I must get myself off to work.

Please don't worry or despair, I am still the same old (young) sister you saw off on the train.

Let me know how you are, when you can.

Love and best wishes,

Beatrice

August 15, 1911

Dear Elijah,

I hope you are not working too hard. I would love you to pick up your little pile of mail and write and let me know how you are doing. I picture you all the time, stopping crowds, talking with all your heart exposed about the word of God, what it means to you, and what it means to many. I just wish I had your conviction. I sometimes feel that I have let you down, and I hope you don't think too badly of me, or spend too long praying for my soul, because I'm sure my soul is still pretty healthy, considering.

News here from the Galilee. Mr Price has left in mysterious circumstances, and I must admit, I am more than a little worried about him, because it seems so out of character. When he didn't appear at breakfast, four or five days ago now, nor at lunchtime, or for dinner, Miss Flood went from agitation to anger (lamb chops don't fry themselves!). Eventually, after much knocking and calling, she took the skeleton key and let herself into Mr Price's room. We found her later on, white-faced and shaking in the parlor, where Miss Stanley had to fetch a glass of iced tea and a water biscuit.

Apparently, the room had been stripped and all his things had gone. There wasn't a note, but the window was open, and she assumes that he shinned down the drainpipe in the dead of night, though Miss Stanley and myself don't believe it. Mr Price is sixty-three years old. How would he get down the drainpipe, along with his clothes, his extensive collection of toiletries and his very thick scrapbooks? Anyway, why did he have to leave like that without saying goodbye? Miss Flood assures us that he didn't owe any money. He didn't need to escape when there's a perfectly good front door. It is all very puzzling.

I liked Mr Price. He seemed so easy to confide in, and he was full of stories about his past tempestuous life, and how he found salvation when he was in his darkest hour. So I wonder what has happened. I wish I knew where he was. I hate to think of him sunk once again and alone. He's the second person to have disappeared since I got here. (By the way, all that we have left of Mr Price is a large tin of shoeshine he'd left at the bottom of the wardrobe, and half of that had gone.)

Mr Brewster left. Have I said that already? He went to stay with his brother who owns a carpentry shop. We do have a new guest. A Miss Holland, who used to be the nanny in charge of four small girls, but ran away when the father of these girls started harassing her in a most indecent manner. Why are people always running away? Thank goodness for the refuge of the Galilee. Miss Holland, after her ordeal, is still a bag of nerves. She started crying over her plate of bean stew yesterday, and I tried to make light of the situation by assuring her that the food wasn't always quite as bad as this, and that I knew a good little store that sold the most delicious cream-cheese rolls, and I would treat her to one. Much to my chagrin, she bawled even louder, and I got a ticking-off from Miss Flood who quickly came to Miss Holland's aid with a newly ironed handkerchief and a murky glass of water.

How is Chicago? Am I talking to myself? Is it warm? Hot? Indifferent? It is so warm here that I often feel like I'm melting. The air sits so tight it's like walking through sheets drying on the line. Writing that made me suddenly think of Joanna. I can see her now, her arms plunged in a tubful of soapsuds, and beating out the rugs hanging on the line. I wonder how she is?

And you. How are you?

Please, please, write when you can, even if it's to tell me you are too busy to write, and to stop asking you so many stupid questions! I just want to hear.

I miss you. I miss Papa.

Love, Beatrice

August 30, 1911

Dear Elijah,

I didn't write for a couple of weeks, because I thought, if I don't write to him, perhaps I'll hear something back. But still no word.

We had the most tremendous electric thunderstorm here yesterday. It was like the sky was crashing down, and we all had to rush around trying to save the cards from melting into nothing, and we ended up huddled under the canvas awnings watching the strips of jagged light over the ocean, and when the rain came, it was so thick and straight it sounded like the boardwalk was being hit by balls of glass.

It must rain in Chicago. Tell me about it.

Your loving sister,

Beatrice

September 8, 1911

Dear Elijah,

It has been a strange, cold day. It is half past ten in the evening, and I am writing this facing the window of my room, with the drapes open, and the world below me still moving about as if it were late afternoon.

At eight o'clock this morning, a policeman appeared, with his cap under his arm, which Miss Flood took straight away to mean he was the bearer of bad news. And he was. He was here to inform us that Mr Price had been found dead under an 'L' pillar. He'd been badly beaten about the face. We all felt very shaken and had to sit down, even Miss Holland who had never met Mr Price went as white as a sheet and was trembling. The policeman could offer no real details of the assault. There were no witnesses. All he knew was that Mr Price had been found at four o'clock this morning by a man on his way to his shift at the fish market. Then the policeman coughed, and the noise made us jump in our seats. 'Why do you think Mr Price was wearing female cosmetics?' he asked. We were silent for a moment, and then Miss Flood sat a little higher in her chair. 'Mr Price was an actor,' she informed him, with a certain sense of dignity. 'I believe it is customary for actors to apply a little greasepaint?' The policeman nodded, made a note of it, but he didn't look entirely convinced. When he had gone, we all went to our rooms. I cried for Mr Price. But I also cried for Papa, and then for myself. I just couldn't help it.

Where are you, Elijah?

Write to me.

All my love,

Beatrice

September 12, 1911

Dear Elijah,

I have not given up on you, so please don't think I'm going to stop all these letters, because I'm not. Who else really knows me in this world?

The weather (why do people always talk about the weather in their correspondence?) is cooler, and much more refreshing, and the sky is no longer shrouded in a hazy kind of blanket. After work, or in between shifts, I often sit with the girls (their names are Nancy, Marnie, and Celina), and we pass the time of day, watching the crowds go by with their sunburned cheeks and hopeful expressions. I also like to walk along the beach, especially when the people have all but disappeared. It's a good place to think, with the ocean often pressing at your boots, and the curve of the horizon reminding you how great the world is.

The hotel is a somber place to live right now. We were informed that Mr Price's body had been released for interment, but that no one had come to collect it. Miss Flood offered to contact an undertaker herself, because she couldn't bear the thought of a committed Methodist and friend being treated as a pauper. When she arrived at the mortuary, she was informed that the deceased had finally been taken away by his younger brother. Miss Flood was unhappy, and said she felt strange and perturbed because Mr Price had always told her that he was an only child. 'He said that being an only child was what led him into the world of the theater,' she told us. 'That because he had no playmate, he had to read and use his imagination a little more than was good for him.' Miss Holland talked about body snatchers, which only made things worse. The mood at supper time was black.

I had been thinking about leaving the hotel and perhaps finding a room in a (respectable) boarding house, but at the moment I think that Miss Flood and the others need all my support. My room here is light and airy, and I like looking down at the street where I can watch the people come and go. As I am writing this, a group of women are standing on the corner, looking dangerous, smoking cigarettes, holding them high, and laughing through the fine gray plumes like conspirators. I wonder what they are saying? One of them, a plump redhead, is holding her stomach as if she might break

herself in half with all the carrying on.
Well, Elijah, need I say it again?
Write to me soon.
I miss you,
Love Beatrice

September 17, 1911

Dear Elijah,
Wishing you a very Happy Birthday. Please find enclosed a picture postcard of the Dreamland Dock. It is one of our most popular cards.
Love and best wishes,
Beatrice

September 25, 1911

Dear Elijah,
I met a Wesleyan preacher today. He was visiting cousins who have a balloon and trinket stall on the park. He has worked in many cities and has written books about his travels, one in particular, *People Preaching*, is apparently very well known. Do you know it? I asked him if he had ever visited Chicago, and he said, ‘Once or twice.’ Of course, I asked him if he’d met you, and he told me that he’d met hundreds of people, and couldn’t recall them all. Perhaps you remember him? His name is Todd Grammar, a tall man with a long pointed face and thinning brown hair. He is about fifty years old. He has a wife called Olive. It would be nice

(and comforting) for me to have the connection.

Love, Beatrice

October 10, 1911

Dear Elijah,

Papa's birthday. Did you remember it? I tried to go about the day as usual. Work, then I swam for a while at the Lido. Did I ever tell you that I'm now a strapping swimmer, attempting all sorts of hair-raising dives and twists under the water? It didn't work. I sold postcards and thought about the birds. The gulls were crying hard, and that didn't help. In the water, the spray from my arms became the dust in the air from the bonfire. All these strange reminders. Now I intend to go straight to bed. I will not dream. I will think about jewels sitting in velvet-lined boxes. Colored polish on fingernails. Roast-beef hash. The sweet Italian children playing hopscotch on Mulberry Street. Acrobatic dancers. But best of all, and hardest of all, I will do my best to think of nothing.

Your loving sister,
Beatrice

October 20, 1911

Dear Elijah,

I had my photograph taken today with a sweet little monkey called Pom. He was wearing a red suit, like a bellboy, and reminded me of a story

Papa once told us. His fingers gripped tight around my neck, and his breath smelled of garlic and bananas.

Later on this afternoon I am going with my friend Nancy to look at a room near Ocean Avenue. It is reasonably priced, close to work, and I will still be able to visit the folks at the Galilee Hotel.

I will send you my new address, if I decide to take it. Nancy has seen it, and she says it is clean and the furniture looks almost like new.

Best wishes,
From Beatrice

Room 18
Talbot House
Western Drive
Brooklyn
New York

October 30, 1911

Dear Elijah,

Please find enclosed my new address. I left the Galilee a couple of days ago. Miss Flood was very sweet and made a plate of vanilla muffins, and then there was lots of embracing and a few blurry tears from Mrs Mitchell, who said she felt like she was losing one of her children, all over again. (Something of an exaggeration, as I hardly spent any time with her, but I went along with it, dabbed her teary eyes, and promised her I'd return very soon for a visit.)

My room is lovely, and all my own, paid for by my wages from the booth. Now that the season here has all but ended, Mr Cooper transfers his stock to his other booth, and we sell birthday and anniversary cards, correspondence paper, books and stationary, and so on.

I hope this letter finds you well. I have something of a head cold, but I have been sipping lemon, honey, and warm water, recommended to me by the lady who lives next door, who says it is probably the change in my location, and the sudden drop in temperature.

Best wishes,

Beatrice

November 4, 1911

Dear Elijah,

Gray skies and rain. I visited the Galilee this morning. There were three new people, so it all felt very different. Miss Flood was busy making a banner, emblazoned with the words *God Is Good For You!* They all seemed pleased to see me, though Mrs Mitchell shook my hand as if I were a stranger.

I like watching the rain. From my window, I can see other windows, and people passing between them. There is a big bay horse in the yard, wearing a black coat, and stamping at the growing pools of water.

Do you have a window?

All my good wishes to you, Elijah,

From Beatrice

John Wesley House
Pickford Square East
Chicago
Illinois

December 1, 1911

Dear Miss Lyle,

I regret to inform you that I must return all correspondence sent to Mr Elijah Lyle. Mr Lyle arrived at John Wesley House on July 20. The next evening he went out with a Mr Frank Hooper. They were last seen at the Horseshoe Tavern, behaving in a very unchristian-like manner.

We have done all we can to try and locate your brother, and to assure his safety, but we have not been able to do so.

God be with you.

Yours faithfully,
(Rev.) Bernard J. Scott Esq.

BUTTERFLY

'The thing is, we don't need you at the farm any more,' said Ginny, awkwardly. 'You see, we've agreed to take on some injured men who aren't fit to go back to the quarry, but they can see to the pigs, muck out the stables and do all the rest of it.'

Beatrice nodded. She'd seen the men hanging around the gate. They'd looked wizened and older than their years. One of them had jaundice and a cough that rattled so hard in his chest it was like he was spitting out the bullets that hadn't quite killed him off yet.

'They need employment,' said Beatrice. 'I understand.'

'We haven't the money to pay you. I'm sorry. We haven't the money to pay the men either. We're giving them free bed and board, that's all.'

'I didn't expect money,' Beatrice told her. 'Don't worry about that.'

'Who said I was worrying?'

Since Mary's funeral, Beatrice had been walking on eggshells. She would give Ada her shopping list and while Ada collected the tins and bottles in grim silence, Beatrice would say such inane things as 'Isn't this sunshine lovely?' or 'You're looking very well today.' But there would be no replies to any of these, as Ada would bang down the box of soap powder, almost smashing a bottle of vinegar, and a jar of pink salmon paste. In church she would say good morning to all the ladies, and though they'd say 'good morning' back, they'd look distracted, like something was playing on their minds. At the end of the service, the Reverend Peter McNally would be gazing over her shoulder as she asked him how he was, and he would tell her he was well, all the while looking at Iris engrossed in a bag of something sticky, licking the tips of her fingers and giving him a look that was bordering on the lascivious. Iris had recently let the vicar do something that he'd only ever dreamed about. 'It's this war,' she'd said, hooking up her corset. 'It makes you look for comfort, and bugger all the consequences.'

Now it seemed that Beatrice's longest

conversations were with strangers. The lady selling cotton reels on the market, who'd talked for a good twenty minutes about her baby grandson who had yet to meet his father. 'He's the spitting image of my son-in-law,' she'd said. 'It's a shame really, because he's nothing much to look at.' Then there was the man who'd sold her his last copy of *Woman's Own,* who'd said his son was in hospital with a shoulder wound, and he'd never thought he'd be so grateful for a shoulder wound, but the hospital was miles away and how were they supposed to get to the other side of Manchester to take him a bag of grapes and something for his pipe now and then? On the bus home, the woman sitting next to her was crying. Beatrice offered her a handkerchief. 'Oh, I'm not sad,' the woman said. 'I've just heard from my son for the first time in months. A tatty little postcard it was, but it was his handwriting all over the back of it, so it proves he's still alive, and there's me thinking that he couldn't be.'

At home she either talked to herself or wrote letters. She wrote to Nancy, telling her about Mary. She wrote to Jonathan sounding bright and breezy, with news about the fruit she'd managed to grow in the sunny corner of the garden. 'Small pots of very tiny strawberries, raspberries winding around precarious-looking canes, and blackcurrants—though most of those are rotten.' For the first time in years, she wrote to her aunt in Springfield, Illinois. She told her about Jonathan, how he was fighting, how she was now living in England, and hoped her aunt and her friend Alicia Wellaby were in the best of health. The letter ran to seven pages. It didn't fit inside the envelope, and she worried about postage. In the end, she didn't send it; instead she used the back of the pages for shopping lists, sums and reminders.

The gramophone stayed silent, the records stacked and occasionally dusted, especially now the sunlight showed up all the dirt. She didn't play the records because they reminded her that music should be shared, at a concert, a dance, or with the intuitive tapping of fingers on the four chair arms. But then she caught herself, one long light evening, walking about the rooms, wringing her hands, and the words 'bad acting' came to mind, so without a second thought, she lowered the needle and the air was full of a shrill-sounding woman singing 'Alexander's Ragtime Band'.

She began exploring the surrounding countryside, and though it occasionally felt hostile with its brambles and stings, she refused to take it personally. In the bright summer light, the waves appeared blue, matching the sky in their sharp choppy brilliance. Birds chattered in the trees, invisible in the froth of jumping leaves, filling Beatrice's head not with the macabre images from her past, but with a host of chattering women, cheerfully telling each other about a dress they'd just made, or how well their sons were doing, or how their husbands didn't know the half of what they did around the house, and as soon as they came back through the door, they were messing it all up again.

Beatrice found herself a wide smooth stone, and went there every day, with a blanket and a piece of bread and cheese. She liked the way the trees closed in around her, and then the water opened up, and the sky dipped down to meet it. The trees and the hills on the other side made her think of dabs of paint. Sometimes, she'd look at the water and forget about the war, then it would come back to her with a jolt, and she'd try to remember what life had been like, without the constant worry of death and destruction. It must have been wonderful, she thought. It must have been so easy, to get up in the morning, knowing that everyone around you would be safe, and all you had to do was bake bread, say, polish the brasses, or heat water to scrub the tide of grey sitting around your husband's dirty collar. Who cleaned his collars in the army? Did they worry about washing in France? Did they have a bar of soap? She threw a couple of stones into the water. If they do have soap, she thought, you can bet it won't be Woodbury's, 'For the Skin You Love to Touch'.

Sometimes, she fell asleep by the side of her rock, holding onto its smoothness as if it was a pillow, and waking with an ache in her neck and her hair caught up with twigs. It was Martha who found her.

'Are you dead?'

Beatrice opened her eyes. 'I don't think so,' she said.

'I thought you must be,' said Martha. 'Because I've been watching you for a really long time and a butterfly was sitting on your skirt, a big blue butterfly, the size of my hand, and you didn't move at all.'

'I was fast asleep,' said Beatrice, sitting up and rubbing the back of her neck. 'I always fall asleep just here.'

'It's the fresh air that does it. That's what my mam says.'

'And your mam is right.'

Martha shrugged and walked to where the water was licking at the stones. 'You don't really believe that,' she said. 'You don't even like my mam.'

'Of course I like Lizzie. She's lovely.'

'You don't like anybody. That's what Auntie Ada says. You think you're better than everyone else. Mind you . . .'

'What?'

'You do look like a princess.'

Beatrice laughed. 'Thank you,' she said. 'I'll take that as a compliment.'

'So you're not a princess?'

She shook her head. 'No, I'm just an American, a long way from home.'

'But this is your home, isn't it?'

'I suppose it is,' she said, picking leaves from her skirt. 'Trouble is, I keep forgetting.'

'That's my trouble too,' said Martha turning round. 'I keep forgetting what my dad sounds like. I can remember his boots, his big clomping boots, but I can't remember his voice.'

'He'll come back to you.'

'He might,' she said. 'If the Germans don't get him.'

They stood side by side watching the water for a while, the dragonflies, the splashing on the stones, the way the waves seemed to change colour, from brown to green, to a sludgy kind of grey.

'Do you know any Germans?' Martha asked.

'No,' said Beatrice, shaking her head. 'Not one.'

'What do you think they look like?'

'Like we do.'

'Do they want to kill us? Would they like us all to die? Not just the soldiers?'

Beatrice put her arm around the girl's small shoulders. 'I'm sure they wouldn't want us all to die,' she said. 'And I'm sure the British soldiers don't want all the German people to die either. I know I don't.'

'Just the bad ones,' said Martha.

'Just the bad ones,' said Beatrice.

They walked around the edge of the reservoir, the ferns dipping their fronds into the water, the birds still chattering about the price of meat, and the merits of National War Bonds.

'Do you know something?' said Beatrice. 'When I come here, I like to forget all about the war. I pretend it isn't happening.'

'Can you do that?' said Martha.

'Sometimes. If I try hard enough.'

'I'd like to do that,' she said, picking the head off a daisy and tearing the petals apart. 'It gives me nightmares,' she admitted. 'And it makes Mam cry.'

'Then let's talk about something else,' said Beatrice.

'Like what?'

'How about . . . Professor Hubert, and his world-famous flea circus?'

'Will it make me itch?'

'Oh no,' she said, sitting down on the bank. 'Because all of his fleas are very well behaved, and they all work under glass. Apart from the main attractions,' she added. 'They work on a special baize carpet, and they're the most talented, and the most disciplined, and they would never jump onto your arm or make you itch, because they're extremely dignified fleas.'

'Have you ever met them?'

‘Many, many times,’ said Beatrice, ‘though I’m particularly well acquainted with Captain Thunder who shoots out of a cannon and lands on a flying trapeze.’

‘You know Captain Thunder?’ Martha sighed, leaning backwards. ‘You know all the best people. None of the fleas that I’ve ever met can swing on a flying trapeze.’

*   *   *

The next day must have been the hottest day of the summer. The sky shimmered, clearing into a blue satin sheet, the sun flat and brittle, waking the village early with its sharp metallic rays.

Beatrice sat in the garden, watching the bees chasing pollen, the scent of the magnolia so strong it changed the taste of her tea. She picked a couple of raspberries. She walked around the edge of the lawn, popping them into her mouth.

Inside the house she shivered in the gloom and waited for the postman, who eventually appeared up the lane, red-faced and sweating, with nothing more than a pause at her gate to wipe his face with an already sodden handkerchief.

At ten o’clock she rolled up her blanket, packed her bread and cheese and a flask of lemonade. She passed the men on the farm moving slowly in the heat. She often missed the pigs, and the jobs that took your mind off everything, but the men needed work and she didn’t begrudge them it. She climbed over the hawthorn-trimmed stile and through the swollen trees towards her stone. In front of her, the water hardly moved at all, but the heat prickled as she sat and opened out her collar;

pulling off her boots and unrolling her stockings she felt the warm mess of stones creeping in between her toes. Then, as she tilted her face, she did her usual thing of thinking about the war for at least ten minutes, so that later, she could push it all aside and remember things from way back, or look at things now, or even dare to think about the future. Sitting back on her hands she thought about Jonathan, fighting in the sunshine, because surely the sun was shining like this in France too, drying out the mud and staining his skin a sweet olive brown? Was it worse in the sunshine? Did the heat make them faint inside the thick woollen cloth of their uniform? Did they have their summer kit yet? She thought about the girls in the munitions factory. She'd heard that the chemist's daughter had been killed in an explosion, 'Another casualty of war,' she'd said to the assistant, with his tremor and his tiny wire-framed glasses, but 'Oh no,' he'd said, 'she's a casualty of Mr Horace Blenkinsopp, who had been most remiss in acquainting her with all the safety rules, and in my opinion is now nothing more than a murderer.'

Closing her eyes she wondered if she ought to volunteer at the hospital, where the wounded were often miles away from home, and needed help with the little things, like the reading and writing of letters, or a chat to make the day go by. But she knew she was romancing, with her visions of a neat blue dress and the red cross on her apron, floating down the ward like a lovely apparition, when the real truth was gruesome, and nothing more than mopping up, and laying out, or running after doctors and changing mouldy dressings and although she hated herself for it, she knew that she would never be able to stand up to the job, and therefore would be useless as a nurse.

She lowered her flask of lemonade into the water, grinding it into the stones. Flattening out the blanket, she sat against the bark of a tree watching the birds bobbing gently on what little waves there were. It seemed almost impossible that there was a war going on. Perhaps it had ended and she didn't even know about it. She hadn't read a paper in two days.

A heron appeared, and she saw her father with his scraggy unkempt hair chasing after the bird with a net that was too small and flimsy, and she smiled, but then she quickly closed her eyes, where she could picture him doing ordinary things, like eating a meal, lacing his boots, or blowing into his coffee.

'You're here again. I didn't think you would be, but you are.'

Beatrice opened her eyes and smiled. Martha was holding out a fat bunch of buttercups.

'Why wouldn't I be here?' she said, taking the flowers and putting them under her nose. They smelled of warm fields and dust.

'Grown-ups say one thing, and then they do something else.'

'Sometimes we have to. Thanks for the flowers. They're very yellow. I like yellow.'

Martha sat on the stone with her chin in her hands. 'I've escaped,' she said. 'Harry's at war with Billy and Bert, and I'm supposed to be the prisoner.'

'Won't your mother wonder where you are?'

'No.' She shook her head. 'She's washing all the

windows and I'm just playing out.'

'Any more news from your dad?'

'We had a letter last week. We sent him some Oxo.'

'He'll like that.'

'Will he know what to do with it? He can't even make himself a sandwich.'

Martha picked at the stones, stringing them out into lines. The sun was hot even in the shade, the birds had dry throats, and the insects hummed like fans.

'What are you thinking about?' asked Martha.

'That I shouldn't be here, doing nothing at all, that I'm lazy and I really ought to be working.'

'Doing what?'

'I don't know.' Beatrice hitched up her skirt. Her legs were the colour of milk. 'Rolling bandages. Packing equipment. Anything.'

'Ginny let those men have your job,' said Martha. 'I don't like them. The one with the yellow skin told Harry to bugger off, and those aren't my words, I'm only repeating what he said.'

'Sure you are. I know that.'

Martha looked at Beatrice with her bare legs, her stockings stuffed into her boots, and she began unlacing her own.

'Hadn't you better tell your mother where you are?'

'Is it dinner time?'

'Not yet.'

'Then I'm playing out,' she said. 'That's all I'm doing. I'm just playing out.'

The heat became painful. Beatrice thought she could feel the ground moving, it was like she was sitting on a soft wide hammock. She rubbed her eyes, hard.

'Don't you wish we had ice cream?' she said. 'I do.'

'I don't have it much. Sometimes Mam will get a brick and we have to eat it quickly, and I always get a headache.'

'What's your favourite flavour?' Beatrice asked.

'Flavour? It's just white.'

'Vanilla.'

'Is it?'

'Probably. What other flavours do you like?'

'I don't know any other flavours. Do you?'

Beatrice nodded. She saw the board in the window of Manfredi's, the painted bowls and fruit. 'I know hundreds. Let's see now, there's raspberry,' she said, counting off on her fingers, 'pistachio, chocolate, mocha, hazelnut, coconut, strawberry, lemon, banana, apricot, cinnamon, blueberry, toffee, cherry, apple cake—'

'Apple cake? Really?'

'Yes.'

'I wish I lived in America.'

'It's only ice cream.'

Martha walked to the edge of the water and dipped her feet in it. 'Ouch,' she said, 'it's freezing.'

'I used to swim all the time in New York,' Beatrice told her. 'Almost every day.'

'I can't swim very well,' admitted Martha. 'I don't like the water on my face. Are you coming in?'

Beatrice hesitated, but the heat was too much. The water was humming cold, and without hesitation she sat right down in it, and then floated on her back as her light summer skirt began billowing around her. Martha laughed. 'I never thought you'd do that,' she said. 'I thought you'd be tippy-toeing around the edges, just like my mam always does.'

Beatrice dipped her head inside the gentle ripples, bringing it out, gasping, unpinning her hair, flipping back her neck and letting the water spray in a fine shimmering arc. The weight of her fingertips pressed down into the cold, and she laughed.

'My teeth are chattering,' said Martha. 'I have pins and needles.'

'Yes,' agreed Beatrice, 'but it was worth it.'

Shivering, they lay side by side on the blanket. 'We're like a couple of seals,' said Beatrice.

'You are,' said Martha. 'I'm only wet up to my knees.'

'Ah, well,' said Beatrice, twisting and squeezing out her hair, 'we'll dry.'

As the drops of icy water evaporated from her legs, Martha looked across Anglezarke, throwing up her arm in a dreamy kind of gesture.

'My dad once swam all the way across there,' she said. 'Granny was stamping her boots, screaming and shouting, but my dad was just a dot bobbing up and down. He couldn't hear a thing. He was ten and he was in trouble for something. I think he'd dropped his dinner plate, and his mam went mad, and they started arguing and he just ran out of the door, and down to the water where he jumped in and started swimming until he reached the other side. Everyone came to watch, and when he got out, dripping and panting, and rolling onto the stones because he was that exhausted, they all began to cheer, which made Granny even madder, and she gave him a good clip around the ear before she let him have a towel.'

'That's a wonderful story,' said Beatrice. 'Is your granny still alive?'

'No, she died last year. Kidney trouble, whatever that means.'

'I'm sorry.'

'She was old. She always smelled like the back of a cupboard.'

Beatrice pulled up her sodden sleeves and squeezed the water from her hem. 'Both of my grandmothers died when I was three,' she said. 'I don't remember them at all, though I'm told they looked after us for a while, when my mother died. They died the same year. One collapsed at her front door. One collapsed in her garden, when she was picking out some roses. They were still in her arms when they found her, or so my papa said.'

'Your mother died?' said Martha, struggling with the words. It was the worst thing she could think of, her mother lying stock-still in a coffin. 'When?'

'The minute I was born,' said Beatrice. 'My fault.'

'But you were just a tiny baby.'

Shrugging, Beatrice pursed her lips into something of a smile, all the time thinking that babies were dangerous things. By now, the sun was making the world a blurred-edged kind of place. Her legs felt weak. The reservoir was dissolving into pools of coloured flakes.

'I didn't tell,' said Martha, looking at her hands, 'about yesterday. I didn't tell anyone that I'd seen you, though I was dying to tell Harry about Captain Thunder. I nearly did, I had to keep biting my lip.'

'It's nice to have something for yourself, but perhaps you ought to tell your mother, because she might not really approve.'

Beatrice, her shoulders steaming, retrieved the bottle of lemonade, and they drank it, three gulps each, laughing at nothing at all, so it looked like they were drunk on it. In the distance, behind the clumps of trees, the church bells were ringing.

'Dinner time.'

'I don't want to go.'

'You don't,' said Beatrice, 'but you have to.'

Martha pulled a face. 'Oh I'm going, I'm going,' she muttered. 'I know you want your peace and quiet, and all of them sandwiches for yourself.' Suddenly, she stopped. 'You're lovely, you are,' she said, before running through the trees towards the track where Harry had last been seen parading with his rifle.

Beatrice stretched. Her clothes were drying fast against her skin as she ate her bread and cheese. The sky was taut. The bees were sticking to the lavender. A butterfly appeared; it was wide-winged and blue, like the one that Martha had described the day before, and it hovered over the water before landing on a stone, its wings like a cut of good cloth, with a thin line of violet and a dusty turquoise haze. Butterflies were finer than birds. People collected them. They had them pinned and pressed behind glass. *Delicate.* They made pictures. Brooches. They decorated their hats with them. When Beatrice had asked her father why he had none in his collection, he'd puffed and grunted saying, 'Not enough meat.'

There was a gust of warm wind and the wings rippled, like water on stone, as the butterfly quivered, then flew towards the trees in lazy zigzag lines.

Yawning, and with her head in what little shade she could find, her legs and arms covered in her flat dampish clothes, Beatrice dozed. Her broken dreams seemed long and full of detail. Tom was there. Young and freckle-faced. He was swimming away from the war, shouts in German behind him, and then cries from his angry battalion, and then his mother, slapping her hand against a rolling pin, but Lizzie was urging him on. 'Go on,' she screamed. 'Go on! Go on! Or they'll be catching up with you!'

And then of course there was Coney, ubiquitous, shimmering, larger than life, if that were ever possible, with the man from Donegal shelling peanuts, whistling a tune that all the men were whistling that August, a watered-down tune from the Follies. And behind him, a man she'd danced with (Arnold? Archie?) holding out a picture, saying, 'It's the best one of the set,' and she could see it, she was there, and Arnold/Archie was wafting the photograph gently in the air, and she was flying from the paper, her wings rustling like a breeze in the trees, her hair flying backwards, a battered stream of gold.

She woke up panting, and for a few long seconds she was looking at another stretch of water, and the birds in the trees were twittering about *Florida oranges, sticky hands, would you like to try your luck, sir?, this is the park that was burned, have you seen this place in the night-time, you really oughta, there are so many bulbs it's like walking under sunshine.* She looked at the sky. There was still nothing in it. Her clothes were dry and creaking and her skirt felt like paper.

Brushing herself down, she rubbed all the contours of her face, feeling slightly sick. The air was fat with flies, and they settled on her arms before scattering like dust. She should go back now. Change her clothes. She'd wash her hair in cold water with the last amber squeeze of orange-oil shampoo. Then she would write a letter to Jonathan and reread the ones he'd sent to her. She shook out the blanket and rolled it. She bent to get the wilting buttercups. It was only then that she saw the small pair of boots and the stockings. *Martha.* She must have come back when Beatrice was sleeping. Shielding her eyes she walked to the edge of the trees calling, 'Martha! Hello, Martha! Are you there? I'm leaving now.' There was the rustling of the branches, the cool brown stripes, and the birds shaking themselves out, calling through the bars of shade, but not a sound or a glimpse of the girl, so she walked to the edge of the water where the shore curved, but all she could see were the bare stony banks, the pale burnt grass and the trees.

She would not panic. Why on earth should she? Martha was probably up on the lane by now, running away from her brother. Leaving the boots and stockings, Beatrice made her way up the bank, climbing over the stile to where the lane was empty. She could hear one of the men on the farm shouting. 'Ted, is this pig supposed to be panting like this? It sounds like an engine. Ted? Are you listening? It doesn't seem right to me.' She turned back. Martha wouldn't have gone this far without her boots. The lane was full of stones.

She called her name again, squinting through the

bushes, the thin mossy shadows that were spreading out in fingers. A breeze had come from nowhere; the water was rippling, the abandoned stockings quivering like little black mice.

'Martha?' she bellowed, feeling the thumping of her heart in every part of her body. 'Where are you?'

She walked into the water. The breeze was whipping her hair into her eyes. 'Martha!'

And then she saw the flash of white. It looked like a bird. A swan. Beatrice stopped still, straining her eyes. A swan, or Martha's white arm? It was moving with the current. Taking one last look behind her she pulled off her boots, wading out past her knees before dropping forwards, gasping with the cold, and with every icy stroke she thought *Martha,* whose swimming wasn't strong, she was small, she didn't like to feel the water on her face. The birds scattered, squawking. Treading water she tried to see where the white arm had gone to. It seemed to be floating away.

The drowning white arm turned out to be a seagull. As soon as the bird heard the beat of her hands it flew up from the water. Beatrice was startled. She looked around but there was nothing, only the reservoir and the horizon with its thick clumps of trees and the dusty-looking shoreline. Exhausted, she turned onto her back. There were clouds in the sky now, ragged-edged, the breeze pushing them out as if they might have been sails.

She crawled out of the water, groaning, rolling onto the stones, heavy with water and coughing with exhaustion, her clothes wrapped around her like rope. Eventually she managed to sit up. Without the sound of the water, the world felt empty. Time hadn't moved. The boots and stockings were still side by side and her clothes were covered in mud.

'Look,' said Martha, 'I found him for you.'

Beatrice turned. Martha was standing behind her on the bank, grinning, her hands cupped in front of her. 'Have you been swimming again?' she said. 'You look terrible.' She crouched down on her knees. 'I went all through the woods, but it was difficult, I didn't have a net, but I wanted you to see it, are you ready?'

Beatrice nodded. She was shivering. Slowly, Martha opened up her hands, and there was the butterfly, sitting still across them, the blue wings stretching, a lake between her fingers, until it gave a sudden jerk, flying towards Beatrice, landing on her breast for a couple of seconds before taking off again.

'Wasn't he beautiful?' said Martha.

'Yes,' said Beatrice. 'Like a torn-off piece of sky.'

'You've ruined your skirt,' said Martha, rolling a stocking over her hand. 'You're like a scarecrow. You know something?'

'What?'

'If I looked like you, my mam would probably kill me.'

ILLUMINATION NIGHT

Brooklyn, New York
Spring, 1912

Mr Jesmond Duncan Cooper had been married, but his wife had recently left him for a surgeon.

'That's right,' he said, 'a legitimate surgeon, and a man like me can't hope to compete with a book-reading lifesaver, and if she wants to spend her evenings washing the blood from his jacket and talking appendectomies, then that's entirely up to her.'

'Do you miss her?' asked Nancy.

'As much as any man would miss the girl he'd chased and loved and married. I miss her presence. The way she quietly filled up a room. She had a lovely singing voice,' he said. 'And very small ears.'

Outside the window of the Cowrie Shell Café, couples stopped to stare at the man swallowing swords, and every so often a ripple of applause would patter through the high window, and the man would take a bow, showing them where his hat was, before starting all over again.

'He sure would put me off my beefsteak,' said Mr Cooper, watching the show. 'Luckily I know all his tricks. Those gleaming swords are fakes. Every single one of them. The blade simply rides into the handle. I know the man who makes them. He has all kinds of neat contraptions sitting in his workshop. He makes those cabinets where it looks like people have been broken into three.'

'How do they do that?' asked Beatrice.

'Mirrors mostly,' he said, cutting through his steak. 'Thing is, people want to believe, and on the whole, they don't start looking for the answers.'

'And if they do?' said Nancy.

'The mirrors are good enough to fool them; heck, people get fooled by their own damned mirrors every day.'

'And what does your mirror say?' asked Beatrice.

Mr Cooper looked up from his plate. He rubbed his chin carefully. 'The mirror on my wall,' he said, 'laughs at me from time to time, but on the whole it tells me that I could do better.'

They finished off their supper. Mr Cooper, it seemed, was in a more than generous mood, closing the booth early, ordering a bottle of wine and paying for their meal.

'I'm not good at being alone,' he said, tapping a new cigarette onto the back of his hand. 'Oh, I'm all right for a little while, I'll sit and eat, have a drink, and read the paper and so on, and then,' he said, striking up a match, 'I'm afraid I start to rattle.'

Marnie appeared. She sat down next to Mr Cooper who immediately poured her a glass of wine.

'I've just finished,' she said.

'How did we do?' he asked, narrowing his eyes through a puff of grey smoke.

'I sold over fifty. Celina's still over there. She signed a few. They liked the old ones better.'

'How many did she sign?'

'Twenty?'

'You didn't leave her on her own?'

'Billy was with her. She says she'll be over in twenty minutes and can she have the chicken platter?'

Sighing, Mr Cooper looked out of the window. The man with the swords was taking a break. He was drinking a soda and rubbing at his throat, as if those shiny false blades had made it something raw.

'Fifty is not a lot of pictures,' he chewed. 'Last month, we sold well over two hundred, in one day.'

'It's been quiet,' said Marnie, sipping her wine, 'that's all and it's still so early in the season; it happens.'

'Was it quiet yesterday?'

'A little.'

'And the day before?'

'It isn't our fault,' she said, pushing her glass around. 'We do the same as always.'

'I never said it was your fault, I'm not blaming you, honey, really I'm not, it's just business, and it's getting me into thinking that we need a different tack.'

'I don't do no moving around,' she said, finishing off her wine in one fast gulp. 'And neither does Celina. We both agreed. Moving isn't right.'

'I wouldn't move for anyone,' said Nancy. 'Not an inch.'

'I'm not talking moving, or anything else that goes down the road of the downright indecent. We're artists. What am I always telling you? We're not selling filth. I don't know,' he sighed. 'Order the chicken platter and get one for yourself. We'll have another bottle of wine, and then maybe my brain will start ticking, and I can think up a way to earn us more money.'

'Didn't the booth close at eight?' Beatrice had been listening for the last couple of minutes, but was struggling to piece together what she'd heard.

They looked at her. Mr Cooper shrugged, taking a long hard drag of his cigarette. 'I have another interest,' he said, pulling loose tobacco from his tongue. 'The girls work for me, only business isn't strictly booming at the moment.'

'More postcards?'

'Postcards and pictures,' he said, looking at Nancy who raised her eyebrows, giving him a helpless kind of shrug. 'Why don't you take her on a stroll over there, if you think she'll be all right?'

'At last. Sure she'll be all right. Beatrice Lyle might look like an angel, but she has something of a wicked streak.'

'I do?'

'Of course you do, and you know it.'

They walked arm in arm. The fairground was quiet. The Scottish tattooist waved with his painted right arm.

'I think I know what you do,' said Beatrice, stopping suddenly. 'I think I've always known.'

'You have? Well, gee, Beatrice, you coulda said something. I wanted to tell you months ago, because I hate keeping secrets, and I'm sorry.'

Beatrice narrowed her eyes. She felt slightly sick. 'I don't want to go there and I certainly don't want to do it.'

'Of course you don't, but just wait and see.' Nancy squeezed her arm. 'Come on, we're almost at the booth.'

It looked like all the other postcard booths. Cooper's Holiday Cards was tucked between a shellfish bar (closed due to illness) and a vendor selling flags.

'Hey, Nancy,' he said, 'how are things?'

'Business isn't great,' she told him. 'How's the flag game?'

He waved one half-heartedly, a limp Stars and Stripes. 'People like waving them,' he said. 'Goodness knows why, but I'm glad.'

They went through the small tight entrance. A girl Beatrice hadn't seen before was sitting at a counter, a stand of postcards in front of her, the same picture postcards that Beatrice had been trying to sell all day.

'You just missed Billy,' said the girl. 'He went to meet his son. Celina's still here. She's getting herself fixed up, and then we're closing.'

'Sold any more?'

'Five,' she said. 'But three were double-size.'

Celina appeared through a drape at the back of the room. She was straightening her hair.

'Oh.' She stopped. 'Beatrice?'

'I've finally come to show her what it's all about,' said Nancy, parting the drapes behind her.

'I can't wait around, I'm starving,' said Celina, packing up her little mirror and fishing for the earrings she'd left inside her pocket. 'I'm going straight to the Cowrie.'

'Your chicken platter's waiting,' said Nancy. 'And so is Cooper, who is racking his brains trying to think up new ideas.'

'New ideas?' she yawned, pushing in her earrings. 'Oh, I'm way too tired for that.'

At the back of the drapes there appeared to be a small waiting room and another draped entrance. Across the wall there was a line of chairs, and a table with a jug of water and some tall glass beakers.

'Sit down,' said Nancy. 'Go on. I won't be a

minute.'

Beatrice felt cold. The floor was full of cigar butts. When Nancy reappeared, she was holding a black leather box.

'Don't look so worried,' she said, taking the chair next to her. 'You look like you're waiting to have a tooth pulled.' She took off the lid. 'These are the pictures,' she said, handing her the first one. 'Me.'

Beatrice looked down. It was Nancy. She was standing in the nude, her long hair loose; she was draped in a piece of white gauze. She stared. She couldn't say anything.

'You're shocked,' said Nancy. 'I should have known you'd be shocked and I'm sorry.'

'No,' said Beatrice. 'No, I'm not shocked, I like the picture, I don't know why, but I do, you look lovely.'

'Lovely? You think so? Really?'

'Absolutely.'

'Sure, I've seen worse,' said Nancy. 'I've seen the nasty types of pictures that get handed round the park, but that's not us at all. Mind you, we're not exactly illustrating the New Testament.'

'But I've seen more flesh on a painting,' said Beatrice. 'This looks kind of classical, and I guess someone has to pose.'

'True. And I don't look at all bad, though Marnie looks great, you should see Marnie.'

Marnie was wearing a veil, as well as her draped piece of gauze. She was standing against an Arabian background, a pale-looking desert and a painted group of palm trees.

'Inspired by the Orientalists,' said Nancy. 'Those fancy-looking paintings are full of girls in harems.'

Beatrice looked up. 'So, what's behind the

curtain?' she asked. 'Is that the photographer's studio?'

'Not exactly. A man called Maurice Beckmann takes the pictures. He has a set-up in the Bowery. Maurice is a real good sort, and he makes you feel at ease with his jokes and his singing. He has an old piano in the studio. It doesn't feel seedy. He sees it as something artistic.'

'So what is behind the curtain?'

'It's where we pose,' she said. 'Some gentlemen just buy the pictures, some get them signed, and some pay extra to see the model live. We stand on a podium,' she said. 'They're not allowed to touch.'

Beatrice took a few moments to take this in. 'But aren't you scared?'

'I was the first few times, for sure, but Billy's always there, in case someone's had one too many drinks and they start misbehaving. I don't really think about it any more,' she said. 'Sometimes, I'm up there in my little bit of gauze and I'm thinking about my shopping list, what I'm going to buy for my supper.'

'Do these men ever say anything?' she asked. 'Make comments?'

'They're not supposed to speak, and most are good and don't, but a few do try to make me blush, but then Billy tells them to shut right up or to leave.'

'Who is this Billy?'

'He used to be a boxer. He's a grandpapa now, but still as strong as an ox. He's very respectful; he even keeps his eyes on the ground, though he really doesn't need to, as he's seen it all before, at least a hundred times.'

'But how do they know?' she asked. 'How do

they know where to come?'

'We have cards printed, and they're given out across the park, mostly by the tattooists, or the barbers, or the men running the taverns. They're very discreet. Cooper pays them a small amount. It isn't just us,' Nancy said, 'they're handing out dozens of cards all day, for all kinds of different services.'

'Why didn't you tell me? You could have told me. You're all in on it, and now I feel such a fool.'

Nancy shook her head and took hold of Beatrice's hand. 'No, you're not a fool. We wanted to tell you, all of us, but Cooper made us promise. You must believe me, Bea, there were times when I nearly told you everything, and I don't know why Cooper was protecting you, but all I can say is, I'm sorry. We're still friends, right?'

Beatrice looked up at her and smiled. 'Of course we're still friends. We'll always be friends. What do you take me for?'

* * *

The sky was fading and a ghostly moon sat like a thin piece of bone between the clouds. They sat outside Franny's Oyster Bar, wrapped in their coats, with a bottle of cheap red wine. When the lights came on, there was a roar from the crowd and thunderous applause.

'Illumination night,' said Nancy.

Beatrice picked at some peanuts, licking the coarse salt from her fingers; she put a pile onto the table, making the shape of a small crooked heart.

'I couldn't do it,' she said.

'It didn't cross my mind for a second that you

would. You really don't have to. Mr Cooper employed you to work in his everyday booth, and you're good at your job, and he's happy.'

A group of men passed, tipping their new spring boaters. One of them, tall, with an elaborately waxed moustache, gave a little bow before catching up with the others.

'Do you ever get recognised?' asked Beatrice.

'I have done, once or twice. It's a peculiar feeling. One day I was buying apricots and a man came in with his wife, they were buying a bag of cherries, and she was chiding him for choosing the ones that weren't ripe, and I caught his eye, and he smiled and I knew that I'd seen him before.'

'You didn't mind?'

'How could I? And to tell you the truth, I kinda liked it!'

* * *

Midnight in her room, and she undressed slowly, draping a sheet across her shoulder, then she stood on the soda crate she'd been using as a table, wishing she had a larger mirror. There was a small light from her oil lamp. The shutters were closed and she could hear the woman next door talking to her cat. She smiled, licked her lips and pouted a little, but it didn't feel right. She shook out the sheet until it covered most of her front, imagining a man sitting before her, his hat on his lap, his warm perspiring forehead, the tremble in his hands, and she suddenly felt powerful, her body tingling as she stepped down from the crate and went to find her crumpled nightdress. Lying on her bed she began to feel aroused, picturing the men staring at Nancy, Marnie and Celina, and she could see herself stepping up onto the podium, her clothes hanging behind the screen, every last stitch, the gauze barely scraping at her breast. She pressed herself into her pillow.

* * *

Mr Cooper had arranged to meet them at Franny's. He arrived fifteen minutes late, pushing and panting, elbowing the waiting customers and the waitresses with their precarious-looking trays.

'I'm sorry, I'm sorry,' he said, fanning his face with his hat. 'I got talking, and one thing led to another, and I've arranged for Maurice to do a couple more pictures based on a different theme.'

'What theme?' Nancy looked sceptical. She was sitting with Beatrice. Celina and Marnie were still at the booth, selling panoramas and the usual pictures of Coney.

'I need a lemonade,' he said. 'Spring weather? It's like walking through hell out there. Get me a lemonade, Franny, a tall lemonade with a straw and plenty of ice.'

When he'd got his breath back, he wiped his face with a paper napkin and smiled at them. 'Japan,' he beamed. 'Japan is all the rage. Fans. Cherry blossom. Those white-faced little geisha girls.'

Nancy swished a chunk of smashed ice around her glass. 'I don't look Japanese,' she said. 'Look at me, Jesmond. I come from Milwaukee.'

Beatrice took a sidelong glance at her and smiled.

'Don't matter one jot,' said Cooper. 'Maurice has a trunk full of jet-black wigs and those kimono things they wear. Straight from a production of *Madam Butterfly*. Real authentic stuff. Production had to close early, due to technical difficulties.'

'And the twist is?'

'Twist? What twist?'

'Oh, come now, we always have a twist. Will the kimono be undone, sheer gauze, or will I be carrying it over my arm and protecting what's left of my modesty with a large paper fan?'

Cooper took a long sip from his drink. 'I leave all those details up to Maurice,' he said. 'He's the one with all the artistic know-how, and the eye for detail. I'm just a postcard seller.'

Nancy laughed. 'And I'm the Queen of Sheba.'

'Now there's an idea,' said Cooper. 'Royalty.'

*   *   *

Maurice Beckmann's studio was a large open room at the top of a dusty warehouse. Below him, Abel Singer had his clothing business, his machines running twenty-four hours, and you could hear them day and night, humming like wasps through the loose knotty floorboards.

'He won't mind my being here?' said Beatrice.

'Of course not, why on earth should he?'

Nancy pushed at the door with her shoulder. The room was light and long. It smelled of wood and face powder. Scenery was propped against a wall, painted backdrops, plaster columns, drapes of plum-coloured velvet.

Maurice appeared; he was twirling a paper umbrella and walking towards them with tiny mincing steps. 'Welcome to Tokyo,' he bowed.

'Sayonara,' said Nancy. 'This is Beatrice, by the

way; she's come to watch me being debauched.'

'Come, come,' he said, 'it's all completely civilised. We drink tea. I play a little piano—'

'And then I take off all my clothes.'

'So ends a perfect day.'

The tea was already in the pot. Maurice went to find another cup as Beatrice walked around. Across screens there were hundreds of pictures of girls, dimple-cheeked, holding ostrich feathers, open newspapers, naked, dressed in men's suits, holding fat fluffy cats, bamboo canes, lollipops, puppy dogs, bottles of champagne, a pair of white doves.

'Are you in the postcard-selling business?' asked Maurice.

'Oh, she's strictly legit,' said Nancy, taking a sugar cube and pushing it through her lips.

'That's right,' Beatrice told him. 'I sell the sorts of cards you can send back home to Mother.'

'How very nice for Mother.'

The sun came through the high windows in straight blocks of light. She could see the specks of dust; a small brown spider hanging from a thread.

'And where does Mother live?' he asked.

'She doesn't,' said Beatrice. 'But I come from Illinois.'

'You have a wonderful face.'

'Leave her alone,' said Nancy. 'Just pour the girl some tea.'

Beatrice knew he was looking at her. She could feel it when she was staring through the window at the crumbling brick wall, into her flowery china teacup, or at the scenery, with the corner of the desert showing, a blue sky, sand, the sharp green leaf of a palm tree.

'Do you think it'll work?' asked Nancy. ' "The Pleasures of the East"?'

'Japan's everywhere,' he said. 'I'm thinking of getting some bits of bamboo furniture, what do you think?'

'For the picture?'

'For my rooms.'

'Bamboo?' said Nancy. 'I wouldn't like to sit on it.'

'There's a wonderful shop in town, it sells the lot, lotus-patterned wallpaper, teapots and bowls, tatami mats, hand-painted shoji screens. Everything is beautiful.'

'Sounds expensive.'

'Yes,' said Maurice, 'but it's travelled.'

'So have I,' said Nancy. 'Didn't you know? I came all the way from Milwaukee.'

'And then you landed in paradise.'

Maurice pulled out the folded kimonos. They had labels saying *Authentically Made in Kyoto*. 'Kyoto, New Jersey,' he said. But they were beautiful, pale and embroidered with cranes, blossoms, tiny foam-capped waves.

'I thought tastefully suggestive,' said Maurice. 'What do you think? It seems to be your forte.'

'All right, all right, I'll see what I can do.'

Nancy sat in a dressing gown, painting her face with the sticks of ivory greasepaint; Beatrice sat at the window while Maurice found a gramophone record, Enrico Caruso singing 'Mi par d'udir ancora' from *The Pearl Fishers*.

'I would love to take your photograph,' he said. Nancy looked up from her piece of mirror, but she didn't say anything.

Beatrice folded her arms. 'I'm neither brave nor

bold,' she told him.

'Your face, that's all I need, your face. What do you say now? Can I?'

He pushed his camera towards her. He walked around with his arms folded, while she played with her lips, looking at the ceiling.

'Relax,' he said. 'You don't even have to smile.'

She tried not to think that she was going to be a picture as the flash lit up the room, the thin sulphur smell wafting over her face.

'See,' he said. 'All done. That didn't hurt now, did it?'

Nancy's face was a white oval mask. Her lips shaped into a small scarlet heart. She had a wig in her hands. 'This hair weighs a ton. Feel it. It's full of clips and slides.'

'That's why they're all small in the East,' Maurice told her. 'The decorations weigh them down.'

He dressed a set with a plain sky backdrop. 'Forget Mount Fuji, we'll let the costume do the work,' he said. 'A sky is a sky is a sky.'

With the wig and the kimono, Nancy was transformed. She held a paper fan. Maurice pushed the kimono down over her shoulders; you could see her creamy skin, the curve of her breasts, her leg pushing out through the sea-patterned silk.

'You'll sell out in a week,' said Maurice. 'The real Madam Butterfly. The one that sailor saw when he got her home at night.'

'This kimono,' she grimaced, 'it smells of Doctor Porter's Liniment.'

'All the more reason to get out of it.'

*   *   *

From the booth Beatrice could see the railings where people leaned, pushing their heads together, an arm loosely curled around a waist. Here, children rattled the metal with sticks and spades while their fathers looked for the ferry, and their mothers worried about change, or the streaks of sweet ice cream that sat around their lips—but by now the children were wise to the great white handkerchief that came out of the mouth of the bag, damp on the end and smelling of powder and peppermint.

Standing against the counter with the cards in her hand, she pictured herself on another kind of postcard, hand-tinted gentlemen's relish, her face being thumbed, pored over by men in sweaty jackets, magnifying monocles, slavering, inside pockets, the card eventually hidden in a desk drawer, a diary, a shooting magazine, or added to a collection, brought out with the cigars, heads in a circle; that one last glass of brandy.

'He only took your face.' Nancy was behind her. She was putting cards of painted kittens on a small revolving stand. 'Anyway, he's supposedly an artist,' she said. 'He's had his pictures used as illustrations in all sorts of fancy magazines. He's acquainted with the English aristocracy; they're very open-minded over there.'

'You mean they're all filthy devils?'

'I don't care. I hope they are. Happen I quite like the idea of some lord or other getting hot under the collar over one of my pictures.'

'Perhaps the King keeps you tucked inside his wallet?'

'Now wouldn't that be grand?'

Cooper appeared at closing time. He was in what

passed as his Sunday best with a wilting white gardenia in his buttonhole.

'Who's the lucky lady?' asked Nancy.

'You are,' he said. 'You and Miss Lyle.'

'What are you talking about? I thought you had your eye on Violet Murphy? She was at Mitzy's last night, and she was asking after you.'

'She was?' He touched the gardenia. His ears were turning pink.

'Sure. It was Jesmond this, and Jesmond that. I really think you should ask the poor demented woman out to supper.'

'That I might,' he said. 'But tonight, it's your turn.'

'Why us?' asked Beatrice, locking the door. 'Did you hear about the man from Boston who bought forty-five pictures of Brighton Beach and twenty-one pictures of Dreamland?'

'He did?'

'Yes, apparently, he cuts them up and makes them into art.'

'Now I've heard everything.'

They each took an arm and strolled past the booths and rides, the Ferris wheel with the gold-coloured lanterns, and boys loosening their collars outside the Hall of Many Dreams where girls with lace-edged dresses danced barefoot, swooping over the stage in cartwheels, hollering and winking their large lazy eyes at the audience.

'I'm taking you to Falco's,' he said. 'You can have anything you like off the menu—the world, as they say, is your oyster.'

'Have you been drinking?' said Nancy.

'I hear there's an opium den at the back of Steeplechase Park,' said Beatrice.

'Well, if there is,' said Cooper, 'I haven't found it.'

Falco, in his expensive-looking suit and swinging gold fob watch, greeted Mr Cooper like an old, long-lost friend, showing them to a table near the window with a view of the ocean.

'Two very beautiful ladies,' he said, offering them a menu. 'What a lucky man you are.'

'I like to think so,' said Cooper, wondering if it was the kind of restaurant where you could take off your jacket without it looking impolite. How did the other men who were dining, and all in their jackets and waistcoats, manage to look so comfortable in this heat?

'So what goes?' asked Nancy. She'd already made up her mind to have the lobster à la crème. 'You can't fool us. You want something.' Then her face fell. 'Are we losing our jobs? Is this your polite and very generous way of saying, get lost?'

He coughed, knocking over the salt cellar, immediately taking a pinch of the salt and throwing it over his shoulder. 'Of course not,' he said, wiping his fingers on his pants. 'I just need a little time to talk, to mull over some things that have been sitting in my mind.' He smiled expansively at Beatrice. 'I have seen your photograph,' he said. 'Maurice couldn't wait.'

Beatrice blushed, still looking at the words printed on the menu. She wasn't used to seeing pictures of herself. In Illinois the couple of photographs that had stood in dust-caked silver frames had shown her as a wide-eyed child with ringlets and nervous-looking hands. In her room, tacked above the fireplace, there was the picture of her with the monkey, but she was laughing, her face was somewhat blurred, and the monkey was all you really looked at.

'You have?'

'Oh, don't sound so worried, I bet you look like a doll,' said Nancy.

'Wine? Food?' Falco beamed. 'My chef recommends the paprika pork. I myself like the salmon.'

They ordered. Mr Cooper looked nervous. As soon as he'd seen one of the other men in the room pulling off his jacket, he did the same, then immediately regretted it, picturing the pools of sweat that must be spreading from his armpits. He poured wine. The bottle was beaded with cold. He felt better straight away.

'Do I look all right?' Beatrice asked. 'On the picture?'

'Stunning.'

'What did I tell you?' said Nancy.

'Maurice is an artist,' said Cooper slowly.

'So I've heard,' said Nancy. 'But if he really is an artist, why does he have to keep reminding us all the time?'

'I don't know,' said Cooper, rubbing the back of his neck. 'But you must have heard? He has a friend in Manhattan, a successful publisher of books. He's a very rich man, and his books are sent all over America, from east to west, and north to south.'

'So?' said Nancy, who didn't like books, they made her feel uncomfortable, and they were always so weighty, sitting in your hands like dry musty stones.

'So, Maurice tells me that we could be part of them.'

'We?'

'Certainly.'

'I don't write,' said Nancy. 'I mean, I can write, only I'm not much of an author is what I'm trying to say.'

'Me neither,' said Beatrice. 'Just think of all those words . . .'

'Girls,' said Mr Cooper, who was suddenly feeling hotter. 'I am not talking about the words. I am talking about the pictures.'

'Ah,' said Nancy. 'Now I don't feel so guilty for ordering the most expensive thing on the menu. You want to use us. You want to put us into his book.'

Cooper looked more than a little embarrassed. He drained his glass of wine and poured himself another one. Above him, a small wooden fan started twitching.

'Your kimono pictures are selling like hot cakes,' he said. 'Even Marnie and her snake in a basket can't outdo Japan, but it's Beatrice the man wants, only Beatrice.'

'Beatrice doesn't do pictures,' said Nancy, feeling like she ought to speak up for her friend. 'You know she doesn't. You can't make her and you can't buy her off with a plate of fancy fish and salad.'

'I have no intention of doing so,' he said, as their meals appeared from over their shoulders, the waiter setting down the plates in silence, his hair so damp and shining it looked like it had been painted onto his head. Beatrice was disappointed. Why had she ordered the salmon? It was sure to be full of those fine hairy bones that you were supposed to crunch your way through, only she never could. She suddenly lost her appetite.

'What kind of pictures?' she managed.

'Don't even think about it,' said Nancy, tucking into her lobster. 'I don't know what you've been plotting, Jesmond,' she said, 'but it has to be a no.'

'Your name is Beatrice Lyle?' Cooper asked Nancy.

'I feel responsible,' she said. 'I found her. You employed her to sell your holiday cards, nothing else. I don't want Beatrice thinking that she'll lose one job if she doesn't take up the other.'

'What kind of pictures?' Beatrice repeated. Was no one listening to her?

'Well . . .' Cooper said, finding the whole thing very difficult. Why did Beatrice make him feel nervous? 'Maurice showed your picture to his Manhattan friend, who got terribly excited. He has an idea.'

'Oh, I'll bet he has,' said Nancy.

'It has something to do with wings.'

'Wings?'

Beatrice turned her head towards the ocean where the gulls were circling; tonight the waves looked brittle, like they could snap right off and cut you.

'Angel wings,' he said, cutting into his steak, which he saw was a little too rare for his liking. 'The kind that sweep down to the floor.'

'And that's all I'd be wearing?'

'Need you ask?' said Nancy.

'Of course,' Cooper went on, 'it will be extremely artistic and tasteful. The wings would be made by a top theatrical costumier. There will be no . . . how can I put this?' He coughed into the wide chubby cuff of his hand. 'There will be no explicit, suggestive or, dare I say, vulgar positioning. Nothing sleazy,' he whispered, turning beetroot, wishing he'd ordered a jug of iced water.

'She'll look angelic?' Nancy smiled. 'Only she won't be wearing any clothes?'

'Yes, yes,' he said.

'So, if she were to say yes, which she won't, what's in it for you?'

Cooper's smiled wobbled. His steak was hard to swallow. 'The pictures will be made into postcards. And if she were willing, then she would be my main attraction.'

'If *she* were willing?' said Beatrice. Why were they talking about her as if she wasn't even there?

'He means the podium,' said Nancy. 'The swish of the velvet curtain. He wants you in the flesh. He wants to put you onto the stand.'

'Anyway,' said Cooper, 'let's enjoy our food for now, my steak is magnificent, the chef is from Rome, did I tell you that? Apparently he's won prizes for his pasta; the wall is full of medals.'

Beatrice pushed her fish around. She could feel her heart beating hard against her ribcage. She hadn't taken her clothes off for anyone. Not since she was a child and Joanna had rubbed her shoulders with the block of carbolic, telling her stories about girls who didn't wash behind their ears and the trouble they got into with the things that started growing there.

'Of course,' said Cooper, 'I'll happily show you one of his books. I have a copy at home. A very handsome collector's edition.'

Beatrice nodded. She'd been right, the fish was full of bones.

'What's the point?' said Nancy. 'You'll only make her feel worse. She's young. Younger than I was when you first asked me to pose, and anyway, I was a bad sort, and Beatrice is almost an innocent.'

'I am?' she said. Of course she knew what Nancy meant, and she was right, but it didn't make her feel any better, hearing them talk as if she wasn't in the room. And what did 'almost' mean?

'You aren't?' grinned Nancy.

'It doesn't matter what I am,' she said, rolling a bone between her fingers. 'I want to make my own mind up, and I'm more than capable of saying a polite yes or no.'

'Of course you are,' said Cooper with something of a smile. 'Now, shall we look at the desserts?'

*   *   *

Mr Cooper lived above a large flower store. The doorway was strewn with flattened petals. A sign said: *Fresh Bouquets* and *Tributes.*

'I try to keep the place as homely as I can,' he said. 'When Mrs Cooper left me for that book-reading, butcherous quack, I must admit, my world went a little downhill for a while, but then I pulled myself together, and now I employ a woman called Hanna to sweep the place out once in a while.'

Beatrice followed him upstairs. Nancy had gone over to Mitzi's where she had a date with a boy from Cypress Hills.

'You'll be safe with Cooper,' she'd said, fussing with her hair before she left. 'He's nothing but a lamb.'

The landing smelled of rotting flowers. Petals stuck to the dark cracked tiles like giant white thumbprints, the wallpaper was a trail of greying violets, and outside number 6 there was a large domed cage full of small green finches.

'The birds belong to the Carlottis,' he told her, opening his door. 'They own the flower store and they've always been generous. When I was at my lowest ebb they brought me plates of lasagne and iced coffee cake. They give me buttonholes and leftover stems, and they're always so cheerful, I think it's working with the flowers that does it, they always have a smile, or they're whistling.' He was talking too much, and he knew it.

'Yes,' she said. 'Flowers can have that effect.'

It was not a bachelor's room. Mrs Cooper, it seemed, had left something of herself behind, her small china ornaments (cats mostly), the pictures that hung across the walls with thick velvet ribbons, a plump shepherdess looking for her flock.

'Do sit down,' he said, indicating a sofa pushed against the wall and plumped with so many cushions it looked like it was bursting. 'Would you like something to drink? Can I get you any coffee?'

She shook her head.

'Then I'll bring the book right over,' he said, scraping his hands together, and then tugging on his cufflinks. 'That's what I'll do then, yes.'

She watched him on his knees, fumbling with a small gold key, unlocking a bureau cupboard. It seemed that the book was somewhere at the back.

'Of course, I've only borrowed it, it has to go back to the publisher, I promised I'd take good care of it, apparently it's awfully expensive.'

'Really?' She could see his hands were trembling as he began fumbling and slowly unfolding the paper it was wrapped in.

'It's like nothing else you've seen,' he breathed. 'It's beautiful.'

He sat it on his knee. It was an inch thick, bound in soft red leather and embossed with gold. It was simply called *Filles*. Mr Cooper wiped his fingers on a handkerchief before turning the first page.

'Best to be careful,' he said. 'Grease is a terrible thing.'

She was surprised, because at first glance it looked like one of the books that had lined the pale oak shelves in the front room in Normal, the room that was home to the prettiest birds in the house, canaries and small parakeets bought from the store on White Sail Avenue and then gassed in the outhouse. These books were never read; they consisted of volumes of poetry (Sappho, Baudelaire, Shakespeare) and classical mythology, and they had nothing to do with taxidermy, bird structure, or any biblical works. The only one Beatrice had ever seen her father glance at was that containing the story of Icarus. 'How that damned fellow ever thought he could fly is beyond me,' her father had said, slamming the book shut and sending a shower of dust motes towards the cock-headed parakeet in the corner. 'Wax and goose feathers will get a man nowhere. Did the man have hollow bones? *Tsk.* If he'd bothered dissecting a bird, then he would have known he'd end up on the floor, sun or no burning sun,' he'd said as a long ray of light came flashing through the window.

Mr Cooper turned a thick vellum page. *For Your Entertainment.* There were at least a dozen girls looking like black-and-white paintings, their names appearing at their feet in fine gold-printed calligraphy. *Aurora. Leilani. Delfina.*

'Nom de plumes,' he said. 'It's de rigueur. They all have them.'

Aurora was standing against a large paper sun. She was beautiful in a haughty kind of way, and with her frizzed light hair falling to her feet, she stood with her arms outstretched, one finger beckoning, her lips a little open, as if she was just about to say something, a name perhaps, or 'I want you'.

'What do you think of Miss Aurora? Isn't she simply magnificent?'

Beatrice nodded; she was looking closely at her nakedness, wondering if her own body matched hers in any way, comparing the size of her breasts, hips, the way her pubic hair was shaped into a sharp black triangle, because imagine removing your clothes and revealing something that was not quite right, then the flinch of the photographer, the putting away of the camera, the opening of the door, and *You are not quite up to scratch.*

'She looks like a queen.'

'Yes? You like her? You have to admit, it's all very well done, in a most artistic professional manner.'

She nodded. Mr Cooper turned the page. There were words now. Beatrice read the first few lines. '*Come with me, to my room at the top of the tower, where I will undrape myself for your private pleasure. Here in my boudoir I will dance. I will show you all my naughty secrets. And then I'll become your plaything . . .*' Beatrice paled. Aurora now had her back to the camera. She was looking over her milky shoulder, her loose hair trailing over her large dimpled buttocks.

Mr Cooper looked a little warm as he wiped his hand across a cushion before turning another page.

'Very tasteful,' he said, as Aurora draped herself over a couch, her finger on her nipple. 'Like something from a gallery.'

Beatrice said nothing as he went from page to page, constantly wiping his fingers, his face becoming pinker as Leilani appeared, a riding whip in her hand, her pale plump legs astride a pommel horse.

'Magnificent,' he whispered. 'What else can I say?'

'Can I look on my own?' said Beatrice.

'Of course, of course, what was I thinking? Read it alone by all means, I will pour myself a nip of brandy; it helps me sleep at night.'

She wiped her hands. The book was heavy, and it left the smell of leather on her fingers. It felt rich and expensive. These girls were full of money. Delfina had dripping wet hair and a towel over her shoulder; a hairbrush sitting like a paddle in her hand. Then there was Clio, Stella, Allegra and Ianthe. Smiling Ianthe was lying in a field with the glimpse of a river behind her. A girl called Persia was standing with her hands inside a large fur muffler. She had no body hair at all. Allegra had ringlets. She reminded Beatrice of a girl she'd been at school with. A fussy little girl called Betsy. Clio was the coy one, looking caught out, and trying to hide her ample breasts with her wide stretched hands.

'I've finished,' she said, closing the book at last. 'Thank you.'

Mr Cooper came back, his breath full of brandy as he started folding the paper around the book like a blanket.

'I have to be most careful with my loan,' he said. 'Yes indeed. These books sell for over a hundred dollars a time. That's right. Over one hundred dollars. You see, they're all limited editions of the highest quality and only the very rich can afford to look at these tempting beauties.'

'And us,' said Beatrice.

'Indeed, and in that we are nothing but privileged.'

When the book was safely locked away, Mr Cooper put his hands behind his back and gave her a serious look.

'What do you think?' he asked. 'Would you like to be published? There's money in it.'

'I don't know,' she told him, feeling a little panicked. 'I really don't. I need more time to think. It isn't something I ever imagined myself doing, or even looking at for that matter.'

'Quite. I understand. Please take as long as you like.'

'I might say no.'

'Of course you might, and if no is your answer, then no it will have to be.'

'And I can still work in the booth?'

'Absolutely. You're my best postcard seller.' He smiled, wishing he had a cigar. 'Just don't tell the others that I said that.'

* * *

He walked her home. The moon was cut in half. A couple were walking their dog, humming their way through the shadows.

'Can I ask you something?' said Beatrice.

'Of course, fire away.'

'What did Mrs Cooper think about your business with the girls? Was that why she left you?'

He stopped for a moment. The couple with the dog were laughing in the distance. He could see the feather bobbing on the woman's little hat.

'Mrs Cooper left because she fell in love with someone else and there was not a damned thing I could do about it,' he said. 'My wife admired the postcards. She saw the art in them, and she got on well with the girls, sticking them all into a cuttings book, which she appears to have taken with her, and which I am sure that filthy surgeon is enjoying as we speak.'

'She didn't mind?'

'Not a bit.'

'She was a respectable woman?'

'Miss Lyle,' said Mr Cooper, 'my wife said prayers before every meal we ate, including milk and cookies. She had me kneel down at the bedside. She was a warden at the children's home.'

'She was?' said Beatrice. 'Then I'm sorry that I asked.'

'Don't be. It's true that my wife was a Christian woman, but what kind of a wife leaves a note for her husband propped against a jar of strawberry and apple jelly saying, I've taken everything I want. I'm in love. I'll post the key through the letter box. Sincerely, Charlotte Cooper? And you know something? It's the sincerely that gets me every time.'

Mr Cooper left her at the door. The cat was washing its small pointed face on the mat.

Upstairs, she didn't light the lamp; she poured a glass of water, undid her collar, and slept in her clothes, in the moonlight.

ALL THOSE THINGS THAT YOU MISS WHEN THEY'VE GONE

1. The Chance to Use Your Voice

They'd had so little time, and in the long quiet evenings Beatrice often felt cheated as she looked back on their old conversations.

'Rome looks interesting,' Jonathan had said, studying his travel guide. 'What do you think?'

'Rome?' she had said, with a frown. 'Rome is full of broken buildings and men who wear cologne but who think that they're gladiators.'

Jonathan had given her a look. She could picture it. Raised eyebrows and a kind of sideways glance. They had teased each other and laughed. Now, the room was quiet, because the walls didn't roll their eyes, and the furniture was only required to stand where it was put, unable to chat about Mr Jackson's lack of insurance, the ridiculous price of petrol, or how lovely Beatrice looked with her hair down. These days, if she wanted to hear voices after supper, she'd have to talk to herself.

2. A Husband's Paraphernalia

Open jars of hair wax.

Coins thrown across the top of the tallboy, windowsill, bureau, kitchen table; any flat surface that was within close reach of his hand.

Suspenders.

Gold Flake cigarettes.

Oil-stained rags.

Automobile parts.

Empty whisky/wine bottles lined outside the garden shed and catching rain (because they might come in useful, but he didn't have the shed key to hand).

Cufflinks, collar studs, collars.

The small gold ring on his right little finger.

Spent matches thrown across the top of the tallboy, windowsill, bureau, kitchen table; any flat surface that was within close reach of his hand.

Tobacco tins.

Chewed toothpicks.

Safety razors.

Boot black.

Whiskers clinging like dust to the bowl.

Black socks and long johns.

Hands, fingers.

His tongue.

A hundred other things.

His penis.

3. Sharing a Meal

It seemed like the neighbours were talking to her again, or at least they'd forgotten that they weren't.

'Of course I have Billy and Bert to feed,' said Madge, leaning against the counter, fanning her face with her hand and wondering if the potatoes in the sack were really as green as they looked. 'But it isn't the same. I miss that time just before five o'clock, when everything would be done and I could set the table, pour Frank a glass of beer, and have myself a sit-down for five minutes before serving up. He likes a good meat pie,' she said. 'Cow heel, tripe, kidney, all the usual things. And when it gets to summer, on a day like today, he likes nothing better than a slab of pork pie with a piece of cheese and pickle. Though he can't abide salad, says it's all water, and there's no taste in it.'

'Now with my Jim,' said Ada, 'everything has to be hot. He says it's not a real meal unless it's been heated right through. I'd be sweltering at the stove slicing spuds and carrots, sweat dripping into the broth. Lord,' she laughed. 'I'm sometimes that sweaty I don't need to add any salt or seasoning at all.'

'I like sitting down to supper and chatting about the day,' said Beatrice. 'I do miss that.'

'Oh, I don't sit down with him.' Ada looked surprised. 'He likes to eat on his own, in peace, with the paper, he likes reading about the crimes of the day and working things out. Says he could have been a detective. He knows all the ins and outs of police work. Though we do sit down at Christmas,' she added. 'If we're not going visiting.'

'I always eat with our Billy and Bert,' said Madge. 'Frank or no Frank. It makes life easier. Either that or standing up in the kitchen.'

'So you always eat together?' Ada asked

Beatrice. 'How on earth do you manage it?'

'Yes,' said Madge. 'Have you nothing better to do?'

'No,' said Beatrice, trying to think. 'Not really.'

* * *

Later, when Beatrice had eaten a piece of broiled chicken and tomato, staring at the empty chair opposite, she remembered planning menus on the ship. In the middle of the night she'd crept from the side of the bed and, with what little light there was, she'd looked again at the *Good Housewife's Manual* with its new-paper smell and printed sample menus. Monday: *Breakfast:* Omelette, beef sausage, toast with preserves. *Dinner:* Roast loin of mutton, mashed potatoes, buttered cabbage. Victoria sponge cake. Cheese. *Supper:* Cold cuts, crackers, beef paste. And she'd tried to picture herself in a kitchen, chopping and boiling and roasting. Back in Normal, she'd only cooked simple meals. A fried piece of meat or a sandwich. Most of the time her father didn't notice what was on his fork. Why make an effort? Then there was Coney, where the food was ready to eat. Nuts were roasted and scooped into bags. Potatoes were fried in the deep oil that Sammy Foyle had bought from the warehouse and heated that morning. She'd admired the noodles hanging behind Mr Song's head as she'd ordered her tub of chow mein.

'What on earth are you doing?' Jonathan had said, rubbing his eyes, his feet stretching into the cold rumpled space in the bed. 'Come back here, I'm missing you.'

She'd closed the book. 'I'm preparing myself. I

need to be able to cook you a proper meal from scratch.'

'Oh, I'll survive,' he'd yawned, pulling back the sheet. 'I managed before I met you, and look, I grew into this big strong man, and I never went hungry, not once.'

She'd smiled, feeling something of a lurch from the ship. 'Well, you know as well as I do, Mr Crane, there's a first time for everything.'

4. Skin

He looked better with his clothes on, or with his clothes coming off; the jacket then the collar, his suspenders hanging down below his waist. It would make her skin prickle and her throat tighten. She would remind herself, sitting on her stone looking at the water, or propped on two pillows with the curtains closed, or sitting in the bath, on a deckchair in the garden, walking down the lane, staring at the sky. She had liked his clothes before she had liked anything else about him. They had looked so immediately English and well made, and with his jacket slung over his shoulder she could see the hand-stitched lining, the hidden pocket, a striped satin blue. His oval-shaped cufflinks had winked at her. He wore new summer brogues that made a shushing sound on the boardwalk. But now his civilian clothes were hanging in the wardrobe. She could touch them. Read the labels. *Bolam & Son. Made in London. Farnam Gentlemen's Outfitters. Oxford.* She could put her nose against the sleeves. She could wear them. And she had.

'All that's missing is the skin,' she told a plain

white collarless shirt. The skin had gone for now, but she had it in her head, like everything else it seemed, there was room for it, the solid curve of the shoulders, the dark hairs sitting at the back of the neck, almost invisible, the moles, freckles, the pale brown lake behind his left knee, the veins on his feet, the small smooth mound of his stomach. She folded the sleeves of the shirt behind its back. She ran her fingers down the spine of cracked buttons, pressed her hand against the front, soft and hard, soft and hard, and still the shirt said nothing.

5. Savings

'Mrs Crane,' said the man from the bank tapping his fat inky fingers, 'you have more than enough funds to lend some to the nation. This war,' he said, with something of a whisper, 'is costing over one million pounds a day.'

'War bonds, war loans, war savings certificates, I've really no idea what my husband would have asked for,' she told him.

'They're all pretty much the same,' he said, 'and a double investment, for your family, and the nation.'

She wanted to ask him, will we get it all back if we lose? Will the Germans take it? Will it matter? And what if we win? Will we get interest? And what if I need all the money after all? Behind the man's head hung a row of framed certificates, an etching of Britannia, and a sheet advertising war savings certificates, a picture of a father with his children. Save for their Education and Give them a Start in Life. The boy looked like Elijah. The girl had a ribbon in her hair.

'We'll take the savings certificates,' she told him.

'Excellent choice,' he said. 'Have you brought your chequebook?'

6. Family

Beatrice had never held a baby. Her family was so small and far apart that babies were something of a rarity. Of course, she'd seen acquaintances pushing their creaking perambulators through the streets of Normal, and she'd stopped and glanced inside, giving appreciative nods and comments to the small pink heads that looked somewhat crunched on top of the pillow. Babies were dolls.

'Three years ago today,' said Ada without looking round. 'My last one, my Rose.' She was on her knees doing something with a trowel. The gravestone looked too bright against the mildewed weather-worn slabs that surrounded it.

'I am so very sorry,' said Beatrice, who had come wandering into the cemetery at the end of her walk. 'I don't know what to say, I know nothing about babies and how it feels to have them, or to lose them, so I can only imagine your sorrow.'

Ada stopped what she was doing and rolled the trowel into a dirty piece of hessian. 'Oh, but you will have them,' she said, 'and yours will grow up into little people like they usually do.'

They sat on a bench looking out across the cemetery. There was the slow steady whirr of a lawnmower in the distance.

'It's peaceful,' said Beatrice, sitting on her hands.

'But I hate this place,' said Ada. 'Sometimes I think I'll never come back, because what's the point of fussing over babies that don't even know you're their mother?'

They sat in silence. The sun was burning their faces. They could see Mary's grave in the distance, the grass still broken; a vase of brown stems sitting crooked and missing most of their petals. At the top of the hill there were several new white crosses for the soldiers that had died of their injuries in the local infirmary.

'We've been lucky in this war,' said Ada, standing up.

'Yes, we have been lucky.'

'It won't last. The odds are stacked against us.'

'It might last. It has to.'

'Look,' said Ada, clutching the hessian wrapped trowel to her chest, 'I'm telling you it won't.'

7. Reassurance

'Jim, Frank, Tom and the rest, they'll come back in one piece. Of course they will. We all will. Heavens, they're only part of the battalion. I've lost other men. Plenty of other men. Their luck will last. And mine. We'll come marching home one day, arm in arm, and you'll see us for yourself.'

He would say that. She could hear the confidence in his voice and a touch of anger at her lack of faith. His fist would be drumming into the chair arm. 'You must listen and believe,' he would say, 'because there is no doubt about it, what I'm telling you is true.'

8. Exterminator

He would stamp on all the cockroaches. (These her very worst enemy, she would rather have a thick-tailed rat than a cockroach.) Set traps for the mice that ran into the house from the fields. Scoop spiders the size of his hand from the bathtub. Remove flypapers. Collect earwigs. Powder bluebottles. Wasps. Beetles. Woodlice. Etc.

9. Inspiration

After studying the weather reports and looking long and hard at the sky, he would then remind her of the last picnic they'd had. The poached trout. Sweet apples. That bottle of gooseberry wine. The blanket that was folded in the box was snagged with dried grass and thistles and he would shake it out, whistling. Eggs would be boiled. Sandwiches cut. The basket, smelling of other picnics, and with specks of stale crumbs in the latticework, would be packed. *It's too heavy,* he would grimace. *How much do you think the two of us can eat? Honestly.* He would walk with a tilt for the first couple of minutes, then he'd forget, and looking at the sky they'd head towards the stile, to the part of the reservoir they felt was their own, and perhaps it really was possible that no one else had discovered it. The way the trees spread across the shore like curtains. Shiny brown stones, smooth as a carpet. In the distance, a single rowing boat, the arms and the oars clipping the water, like they were dredging up silver.

10. Protection

She saw the telegram boy, how he'd sacrificed what was left of his cigarette, throwing it into the lane before scratching under his cap and knocking at the door. Ada had taken her time. Didn't people know that she was busy in the shop? All right, so there weren't any customers, but things needed doing, the shelves needed cleaning, those tins gathered dust, a bottle of gravy browning had been leaking over the tiles. Floors didn't wash themselves.

Her head had appeared. The boy had his arm out, he was looking down at his boots, he'd been doing this for three months, and he never knew what to say. He looked up slowly, listening to the birds. There was a rustling from the breeze that caught the back of his neck. Eventually a hand grabbed at the envelope and the door slammed shut in his face. Still, it could have been worse. A week or so ago, he'd been spat on.

Beatrice couldn't move. 'Is he going to turn around? Will he come here? Will he? Will he?' Then the relief as the boy retrieved his cigarette and walked back towards his bicycle. Her nails were pressed hard into her hands. She should go and fetch Madge.

Madge said nothing, but swept past her, running towards the shop, her own front door still open. Beatrice sat on the step. She could hear Billy and Bert squabbling over something around the back. A catapult. A peashooter. Something. When Madge reappeared half an hour later, her face was grim and she was tutting at the world that still appeared to be turning, the bees around the lupins, the white birds in the sky.

'How is she?' Beatrice asked.

Madge looked her in the eye as her voice began to tremble. 'Jim's dead. Perhaps they all are.'

'No, don't say that.' Beatrice wrapped her arms around herself; she started nervously stamping her feet.

'They might be. How should we know? Ada's beside herself. Trouble is, she's still got hope where there isn't any. "Missing Presumed Dead." What kind of wording is that to put on a telegram? You should hear her. "Perhaps he's just lost?" she keeps saying. "They're only presuming that he's dead. He always was a one for getting lost. Remember that time in Morecambe on his way back from the amusement arcade? We were waiting for an hour. Remember that? You see, that's the thing with my Jim, he doesn't know his left from his right." '

'I'm sorry. Poor, poor, Ada.'

'Poor all of us,' said Madge.

PHOTOGRAPHS

Brooklyn, New York
May, 1912

The night before the photographs, she had taken off her clothes in front of Nancy.

'I need to prepare myself,' she'd said. 'Tell me if I look right.'

Nancy had walked around and nodded, and then

she'd gone and spent her wages on two bottles of good French wine, and tried to dissuade Beatrice from doing any pictures.

'It's my fault,' said Nancy, struggling with the cork. 'You're a good Methodist girl and I've ruined you.'

'I don't feel ruined. Is this what ruined feels like?'

'Yes.'

'Then I'm very disappointed.'

'I should know, I was ruined long ago.'

'But you liked it.'

'Sure I did.'

'Then why can't I?'

'Because you're a good girl, and that's why they want you. You look like an angel, even without those blessed wings, and men with dirty minds get a kick out of that.'

'I just want to give it a try.'

'Why? Do you need the extra money?'

'Not exactly.'

'Then stick to selling pictures of the funfair.'

'It's too late. Those wings were made to measure.'

'It's never too late,' said Nancy. 'You didn't sign anything?'

She shook her head.

'Then you shouldn't feel obliged.'

'I don't, I really want to do it.'

'Look, Bea, I'm telling you, it won't just stop at the pictures. There's the podium after that. Think how you'll feel standing in the full heat of the summer, or freezing in the fall wearing nothing but those goddamn heavy wings whilst men look you up and down, slavering into their filthy bulging laps.'

'I can take it if you can.'

'But I'm as hard as nails,' said Nancy. 'Look at me.'

Beatrice sighed. Her room looked smaller tonight. The window with its view of the dusty yard, like an eye that needed washing. The wine had left a dull metallic taste in her mouth.

'So, where has it come from?' asked Nancy. 'You wanted to work in a jewellery store. You told me. I could ask Abe Templeman. He owes me a favour. He has an uncle in the gold trade.'

'I changed my mind.'

'Your brother is a priest.'

'Preacher. Well, he was.'

'Same thing. Are you doing this to punish him?'

'I've thought long and hard,' she said, 'and believe me, it has nothing to do with either you or my brother.'

It had been a month since she'd sat with Mr Cooper looking down at Aurora with her pale translucent skin and thick wavy hair. She had bought herself a notebook and a hard leaded pencil that sometimes tore the paper. She'd scribbled things down. There was the life she could have led. She pictured Bethan Carter, that old ring on her finger, and a house beside a railroad track. She thought about her family. What would they think? When she looked at herself in the small cracked mirror in the bathroom down the hall, she didn't see any of them, but was she really so different?

She dreamed about her father who would be sitting at the table, his sleeves rolled up to the elbow, opening a parcel, spilling its contents, a hundred glass eyes, bouncing like hail and blinking over the floor tiles. Walking to work, she would watch all the birds that had perched across the railings, and as they cocked their heads at her, she would picture them on stands, immobile, unblinking, feet wired and glued, their feathers tinged with borax, their beaks from a place in Duluth. And then there was Elijah. He was being pummelled by a crowd. He was uncurling his shoulders until his back was ramrod straight. He was standing on a bar stool singing, 'And Can It Be?'

'You know something,' she told Nancy, who by now had wine-stained lips and heavy-looking eyes. 'The only thing that's bothering me are those wings. They reek too much of home. Will I look like a fool?' she asked. 'Tell me.'

Nancy shook her head and yawned. 'A fool? You won't look like a fool. You'll look like something that has just dropped down from the heavens.'

* * *

The room was full of people. Mr Cooper was pacing up and down, chewing an unlit cigar. Maurice Beckmann was setting up his camera in front of a blue-and-cloud cloth. Girls in snowy-white aprons sat on stools next to dressing tables that were covered with unopened sticks of greasepaint, skin creams and bowls of fine powder. There were screens. Trunks (*of what?* she had puzzled). A table stacked with combs, brushes and hair oils had been pushed against a wall. The goose-feather wings, made by Eton & Foster, Fifth Avenue, New York, were hung on a tall wooden stand, like Gabriel himself had just gone to take a shower bath. They reached past her ankles and weighed twenty pounds.

The philanthropist from the heart of Manhattan reached for her hand, and dropped his head into a bow. 'Miss Lyle, we are more than thrilled to have your company,' the man said. His name was Laurence Hoff. He spoke with something of an accent—*German? Hungarian? Swiss?*—and with his sweep of yellow hair and fading blue eyes, he looked like an older, fainter version of the man advertising spearmint gum on the billboard at the Dreamland entrance to Coney.

'There are so many people, I just didn't realise . . .'

'Miss Lyle,' he said, taking her by the elbow and leading her to a plump velvet chair in the corner, 'take a seat whilst I explain how things are done.'

She did as she was told. Her mouth was dry and she had to stick her tongue between her teeth to stop them from chattering.

'As a boy I worked at the opera,' he told her, pulling up a stool. 'Of course, I was merely a lackey, sweeping, cleaning, moving things around. I would take flowers into dressing rooms. Deliver telegrams. I'd make sure the leading man had his tin of favourite lozenges. It is not a myth. Oh no. Actors can be demons. Let me tell you, backstage in a theatre there is nothing but madness and chaos. It's a noisy pandemonium full of heavy machinery, crashing scenery, the colourful shouts from the stagehands. Of course, sitting in the stalls with your box of violet creams, you would never, ever know it. At the front of the stage there is peace. The scenes drop from the fly tower with little more than a swish, the orchestra hums, and the stage has been transformed into a magical place, a box where the story can be told, and the audience are lost in it. And that's what we have here.'

'We do?'

Beatrice looked around. A man in a pair of grey overalls was pushing some screens that had something to do with the light. The floor was being painted. A girl was saying, 'Did you get the magenta? I meant stick number five. *Five.* The real magenta, not the one that looks like an orange.'

'When we have prepared the way, then we will all depart, leaving you in the capable hands of Mr Beckmann and perhaps another female, to help you with your things. After all this crazy chaos, you will have peace, calm, tranquillity. You will feel relaxed. Only then will you change into "Angel".'

Beatrice walked over to Nancy, who was sitting on the window ledge with a glass of iced tea, looking sceptical.

'Didn't have none of this when I was turning into a geisha,' Nancy said. 'It was just you, Maurice and that cranky-sounding phonograph.'

'It's scary.'

'You want to scoot?' said Nancy.

Beatrice shook her head. 'It's just stage fright,' she said. 'It'll pass.'

Maurice had done some sketches, showing Mr Hoff what he hoped the pictures would look like.

'I've kept it very simple,' said Maurice. 'See? That face and those wings will say everything.'

'And the rest,' said Hoff.

She changed into a blue-and-green kimono and as a girl with cold hands sculpted her hair, she and

Nancy talked as if they were sitting in the beauty parlour, and sure enough, another girl appeared to do her nails.

'Can't you do me as well?' asked Nancy, spreading her fingers like starfish. 'My nails are crying out for some attention. Look at them.'

'They look better than mine,' said the girl.

Beatrice's head ached. It had been pulled and scraped until her eyes watered. Her scalp had been rubbed. Stray hairs plucked. Something smelled of fish oil.

'Do I still look like me?'

Nancy shrugged. 'Like you,' she said, 'with a gloss on.'

She could hear Cooper laughing with Mr Hoff, a kind of hollow guffaw that said he was nervous. Had he handed back the book? Did he still have nightmares about grease on the pages? 'The slightest blemish and I'll have to pay the full amount,' he'd said, 'and it's an amount that will have me penniless and living back with my folks in their dreary deadbeat stretch of Idaho which would not look well on a postcard.'

'Would you like something to eat before I do your face?' a girl asked. 'We have a cold plate, noodles, chicken, fruit. If there's something else that you'd like, I can always send out for it.'

She managed to nibble at some warm black grapes, though she thought the skins might choke her.

'You all right?' asked Maurice. 'Look, honey, when all these people have gone it will be like playing dressing up, hell, I'll even take my clothes off with you if you like.'

'Oh, Lord,' said Nancy rolling her eyes. 'Please

tell him, no.'

'I'm fine,' said Beatrice. 'Really I am.'

With the girls fussing around her, pulling at her, telling her what to do—*look up, down, bring your lips together, can you let your head drop forwards?*—she felt calmer, because they were moving her along, they had taken complete control.

'Time for us to go,' said Mr Hoff, clapping his hands. 'Come on, folks, let's get out of here, and give the girl some privacy. You have your friend and Dulcie. Dulcie has worked with us on our last three books. She'll put you at your ease and have you looking beautiful. More beautiful,' he added, tapping the side of his nose. 'That's what I meant to say.'

Her heart began to beat inside her ears when the doors were closed for the last time and a thick black curtain was pulled tight across them. She took a few deep breaths. She could feel her knees shaking.

'When you're ready I'll help you with the wings,' said Dulcie, 'though we might need Maurice, those things are awful heavy.'

Maurice was winding up the gramophone. 'We have all the time in the world,' he said, folding his arms and studying the backcloth.

'I'm fine, let's do it,' said Beatrice. 'Let's just get it all done.'

Stepping behind the screens she took off the kimono and Dulcie dabbed her with powder. 'The hair will be painted over on the plates,' she said, nodding at the space between her legs. 'If Mr Hoff decides to sell your pictures to Europe then they'll paint it back on.'

The room was warm and Beatrice began to feel

strangely relaxed as Dulcie helped her on with the wings. Nancy was chewing gum and reading *Love Story* magazine, doing her best to look nonchalant. Maurice was fiddling with the camera.

'And here we have you,' he said, as she stood on the painted marker cross. 'The angel, Beatrice Lyle.' The music swelled, reminding her of the thick rolling waves on Brighton Beach, the white marble clouds hunched shoulder to shoulder, and as the camera flashed she opened out her hands, she held a scented arum lily, she moved her arms wide, like they were another set of wings.

'You've done this before,' he said.

She felt different. Not an angel. Nothing like an angel. She could look straight into the lens, opening her mouth a little, because now she was being someone else, someone who could stand naked in front of strangers without so much as a blush (she'd imagined herself shaking and sweating and pink). She'd seen those girls hanging around the back of the theatre, shivering, adjusting their flimsy-looking costumes, chatting, yawning, lighting each other's cigarettes, they had looked so different in the daylight, that spark wasn't sitting in their eyes. And then the curtain rose.

When Maurice, Nancy and Dulcie started clapping, she was startled, suddenly feeling the weight of the wings on her shoulders, the heat of the lights pressing onto her face.

'All done,' said Maurice. 'Congratulations. You were nothing but magical.'

'We're done already?'

'You've been standing there for over an hour,' said Nancy, stretching. 'Don't you think an hour's long enough?'

Behind the screen, pulling on her clothes she felt deflated and exhausted. Fastening the buttons, tying her boots, she was Beatrice again, the girl from Normal, Illinois, missing her father, her brother, who had no real family, who sold pictures of the funfair, and who lived in a room decorated with small pink shells she'd picked up from the beach.

'Mr Hoff wants the pictures as soon as possible,' said Maurice. 'I'll let you know when they're ready.'

She walked through the whispering lobby with people clapping her on the back and saying her name over and over in all kinds of accents, *Bay-ha-treece, Bay-ha-treece, Bay-ha-treece!*

Mr Cooper was sitting outside with his hat on his knees playing pinochle with two strangers he'd just met on the street. He looked crumpled.

'Can I walk you somewhere?' he asked, standing up and brushing down his pants.

'Champagne?' said Mr Hoff through the cranked-down window of his automobile; he'd been waiting in there, drinking Florida orange juice, reading, *You Are Your Own Success.* 'I know a wonderful little French place, looks like nothing from the outside, but it's just like stepping into Paris.'

'No,' said Beatrice. 'I'm going to go for a walk. But thank you all the same.'

Mr Hoff waved his hand, said something to his driver, and the car moved away.

* * *

'You said no to champagne and Paris?' said Nancy.

'Are you nuts?'

They walked towards the coast, past doorways smelling of cabbage. A man with a little silver box and red beefy ears was talking to a ghost, and marching down the road there was a small church parade with songs that she recognised.

'Regretting it already?' said Nancy.

'Not at all.'

'You look deadbeat.'

'I have a headache.'

'You want to go home?'

'No,' she said. 'I want to go look at the ocean.'

The beach was quiet. Nancy began to fidget, plucking at her sleeves. 'I promised someone,' she said. 'I hope you don't mind? You should have gone out for champagne with your Mr Hoff; I can't believe you turned him down.'

'It doesn't matter,' she said. 'Go ahead and keep your word.'

'You don't mind?'

'Of course I don't mind. I'm happy.'

The ocean trembled as a woman with a dachshund under each arm picked her way over the sand and a lonely-looking boy sat untying his boots, peeling off his socks like they were another piece of skin. Rolling his trousers to the knee, carefully, painstakingly, he walked into the flat lick of waves, lifting his feet and shaking them out. The water looked icy.

The boy made her think about Elijah. What would he make of her now? Would he quickly disown her? Pray for her soul? Would he slap her? Would he even care, cavorting in a saloon bar in an unchristian-like manner? She had to smile at that.

The sun was fading as she walked towards the

trolley. A family was sitting outside a restaurant eating fried oysters and chicken, and she watched them for a while behind a menu screen, the woman with her wide speckled arms, clucking over a bone, the husband with a handkerchief tucked into the front of his shirt, his lips shining, picking something from his teeth, his sons with burnt necks, like stalks, asking for more lemonade.

*   *   *

She found herself in a familiar part of Brooklyn where the sky was still full of heat and unspent rain. Here, the shoeshine man had given up for the day, already tasting his supper, imagining his new wife happy just because he was home and how wonderful was that? Beatrice sat in a coffee shop and ordered a piece of cherry pie and ice cream, but when it came it turned her stomach, and she sipped her scalding coffee watching boys racing in a splintered orange box cart, and a woman washing her doorstep, occasionally rubbing at her shoulders and looking to the heavens. *Just burst,* she was thinking. *Just burst.*

Walking through the neighbourhood, she could feel her skin moving beneath her clothes, wondering if people could see through her, and would they know what she'd been doing, and could they smell the hidden shame in it?

The Galilee Hotel had lost yet more of its shine, and those windows that every so often had glinted and gleamed from pails of soap and water and the elbow grease lent from a hymn-singing Elliot Price, were so full of dust you could write your name on them, weeds were pushing through the cracks like yellow withered hands and there was broken glass strewn by the door.

She rang the bell before fishing for the handkerchief in her pocket, carefully collecting the broken shards, though one had pierced through the cotton and cut her finger, and without another handkerchief to bind it, it was dripping into the dust.

'Yes?' A woman appeared. 'Can I help you?'

Beatrice took a small step back. She'd been expecting one of the old crowd.

'I used to live here,' she said, instinctively putting her finger into her mouth, and sucking on it. 'Is Miss Flood around?'

'She might be,' said the woman, tightening her lips. 'Shall I go fetch her?'

'Might I come in?'

'No,' she said. 'I'm not allowed to invite strangers through the door. Not any more. You see, people take advantage,' she said. 'They say they're selling hymn sheets, but they've never seen a hymn sheet in their lives.'

'I'm sorry. Do you have a sticking plaster?'

'I suppose I could ask.'

'Miss Lyle,' said Miss Flood, when she eventually appeared. 'It is you. I thought it might be. Come in. How is that . . . place?'

'Coney Island? I suppose it's still dazzling.'

'You don't say? I thought it might still be blinding the innocent; now let me get you that sticking plaster.'

'There was broken glass beside the door,' she explained, holding out the handkerchief. 'Best to wrap this in newspaper or something.'

'Newspaper? We don't have newspaper. Those

things are full of filth and sensation. Though there might be one or two pages that the meat came in.'

Beatrice felt strange. The hotel was the same, but different. The wallpaper was so familiar, that tear in the corner, the small piece of damp that looked like a face, it made her heart jolt. Then they went into the dining room, and her eyes fixed onto the table she'd shared with Mr Price.

'Have a seat,' said Miss Flood, taking the glass-filled handkerchief and returning with a sticking plaster and a jug of water. 'You must let me know how you're getting on, over there.'

'Over there' was said with such a shudder that Beatrice suddenly thought, What if she knows everything? And she pictured herself an hour or so ago, standing in the nude, brazen and ungodly, and she could feel her face burning. The other woman was hovering in the doorway, pretending to read a sheet of notices.

'I'm doing OK,' she said quickly. 'Yes, I'm still selling picture postcards. Just views of the beach and the fair and the ocean. You know, Miss Flood, some people have never seen the ocean, and they're very popular cards.'

'I expect they are, for those people who can read and write.'

Beatrice wrapped the plaster tight around her finger. She hesitated. 'I was wondering,' she said. 'Have I got any mail?'

'Nothing,' said Miss Flood. 'Are you expecting something?'

'I was hoping to hear from my brother. I sent him my new address, but—'

'Preachers have their minds on higher things,' said Miss Flood. 'They've no time for letter writing.'

'So he hasn't been here?'

Miss Flood shook her head. 'No,' she said. 'We haven't had a preacher here in months.'

FALLING

Letter to Ada Richards

FRANCE
4 August 1916

Dear Mrs Richards,

It is with real sorrow that I write this letter, for it brings you I am afraid very bad news about your husband Private James Richards.

He played a very gallant part in the attack which we made against the German position last Monday. He was with a number of men who marched up the line and I am afraid he did not return and had to be reported as Missing Presumed Dead. I am deeply grieved to tell you that this is indeed the case as his body was recovered a couple of days ago.

I cannot tell you how sorry I am, in fact I can assure you that there is not one amongst us who doesn't feel his death as a personal blow. Everyone thought so much of him, and admired his fine sturdy character, and his resilience and ever-unfailing cheerfulness. He was a brave soldier and a fine example to all.

I wish I could help to soften the hardness of your sorrow. There is one comfort at least in knowing that he gave his life in a sacred cause fighting for Right and Justice. It is the greatest sacrifice a man can make.

All those who have fallen on the field of honour in this world war, though perhaps they know it not, are following the path of self-sacrifice and of duty which Our Lord Himself once trod, they are following in his Footsteps and are helping Him to pay the price of the world's salvation.

Let pride then be mingled with your tears. Your husband was laid to rest in a little military cemetery at Bertrancourt by the side of several of his comrades who have died so that England might live, and a cross now marks his grave. His soul we commended to the loving care of Our Heavenly Father, who will keep him until that day when you will find him again never more to be parted.

May God comfort and protect you in your sorrow is the prayer of all who knew your husband, and especially of you, in truest sympathy,

S. T. F. Wilson
Chaplain, C of E
2nd Battalion, Lancashire Fusiliers

Letter to Ada Richards

FRANCE
5 August 1916

Dear Ada,

It is with a heavy heart that I write to inform

you of the death of your loving husband Jim. I cannot begin to tell you how much he will be missed by us all, and there is not a day goes by when we do not talk about him. All our prayers and thoughts are with you.

Jim was a first-class soldier, he was brave, a good companion, and he fought with pride and honour. Let me assure you that he did not suffer; his death was quick and clean. The chaplain was near him, gave him comfort and prayed for his soul.

As you know, Jim and I were good friends and we would often reminisce, and he would sing and keep our spirits up. The trench is a quieter place as the lads do not feel like singing without him. It goes without saying that Frank and Tom, and the other men from the village and nearby, are devastated.

I won't talk about God, because it is not my place to do so, but I hope that you manage to find some comfort in your sorrow.

Yours, in all sincerity,

Jonathan Crane

Parcel of Personal Items Belonging to Private James Richards (deceased)

Photograph of a woman, inscribed, *Love Ada.*

Photograph of a woman, inscribed, *Best wishes, Mam.*

Tobacco tin.

Wallet, containing a letter and several sheets of notepaper.

Small leather purse.

Letter to Beatrice Crane

FRANCE
10 August 1916

Dearest Beatrice,

I will be sending this letter with a man called Bosley who lives on the outskirts of Bolton and is being sent home due to the death of his wife (measles). What I am going to write will not compromise the country, the war, or the army in any way, but I hope to dodge the censor. If I don't, then so be it and I do hope the letter will still make sense to you with all the black ink and spaces. I will not name specific places, because they do not matter. I want to write about Jim.

By now Ada will have received the telegram, and perhaps the letter I sent as the man's captain (more promotion, simply due to lack of men), and the letter that was penned by the chaplain. Jim's personal items have also been sent home, and though I know nothing of that, I do know that on the Monday he left the trench, he put all his personal effects into a tin biscuit box he'd found and left it with another private, which was unusual, though no one seemed to remark upon it. The writing of letters to widows, mothers and sisters is something I have had to do more frequently in the last few months. Usually, a few compassionate lines will suffice, but when it is regarding one of your own, the words seem either meaningless, or like weapons waiting to ignite. That sounds trite. I knew him well. I could have called myself a friend.

As you know, I am not a religious man, though I do attend church because I think it is the right thing to do, showing a sense of community spirit, yet here I have looked for faith and I have spent many hours talking with the chaplain. In letters home, and in dealing with the dead and injured (some worse than dead), it is hard to speak the truth. We write about bravery, 'giving their lives', honouring their country, and of course, this is usually right and true, yet what about the rest of it? This is what plays on my mind day and night. This war is necessary. I know that. But what about the pain, the waste and the tragedy? Will no one away from the battlefield ever know the truth? I have now seen so much of hell that I am numbed by it. I think of little else. This place is my life.

But Jim. I remember Jim from childhood. He was, what? Five years older than me, and as a child, five years turns you into an adult. When I was still at school ('you middle-class over-educated lot!'—I can still hear his voice), Jim was a working man, had been for years, and I would see him walking home, covered in quarry dust. When he was eighteen his father died and left him the shop. I would watch him from Dad's window, or from that corner of the garden with the view down the slope. He seemed so grown up and worldly-wise with a swagger in his walk, a sack of rabbits over his shoulder, or one or two pheasants that the farmer let him bag. And then, of course, he had

Ada.

Ada is the same age as me. We often played together as children, I can't remember our games precisely, but she was not a sissy, and so they were the usual rough-and-tumble affairs, chasing and tag and so on. I must admit to you now that I was a little jealous when they started walking out together, not because I was in love with her, or had any feelings for the girl, but because I wanted to be man enough to have a girl myself, someone to walk arm in arm with under the moonlight—I'd read fanciful stories and saw myself as quite the catch, but that's youth for you. And then they married, and of course I wished them well.

By this time I was working at the office with my father and I was away a lot, travelling back and forth to London. I did have girls, and I've told you all that. London was my Coney Island.

When Dad got ill, I stayed at the house, as you know, and reacquainted myself with the village. I was told (by all and sundry) that it would never work, and that 'a man like me' could not go back to the playmates of his childhood, because what would we have in common, there would be resentments, and so on. I took no notice. I would happily sit in the Coach and Horses with Jim and Tom and Frank, and they would ask after Dad's ill health, and sympathise, and tell tales of losing their own fathers (Tom and Jim), or they would joke and play cards and take my mind off it. Whether they saw me as something of an oddity I really don't know. What I do know is that they were kind, and showed me nothing but the hand of friendship. I'm sure you will have seen this for yourself.

And then how many times had I met Jim in the Coach and Horses to wet a baby's head? Four? The first was all laughing and hearty slaps on the back, and almost drowning Jim in beer, and then he'd start singing, his hair often dripping with ale, and that voice could set a man dead in his tracks, because it was so rich and unexpected. The next time a baby was born, our celebrations were quieter, more humble affairs. And then there'd be the wake.

Jim sang here. Sad songs, which could have the men weeping for all they'd left at home. And what is it we miss? Loved ones of course. And simple things. The smell of the world from the open back door. Freedom of movement. A bed. A plate of clean bread and cheese. Then there were the happy songs, to keep our spirits going. Then later, he talked a lot about the babies he had lost. He said he could remember each face perfectly. The chaplain prayed with him. And so did I.

Jim was a good man. On Wednesday 26 July, he was sent along the line. It had been silent for some time, an eerie kind of silence that meant there was trouble brewing. From our positions we could hear it all going off, and then we were shelled.

A few hours later, several men returned with the stretcher-bearers. 'We're not all here,' they were saying. 'Most of us have gone.' Then all hell broke loose, and the shells were coming over in no uncertain fashion. There was little I could do. The other line had collapsed. There was no sight of Jim, though a man called Dorgan swore he had seen him alive.

Almost a week later, and with no real hope, we were able to dig our way over, and his body was eventually recovered. How I felt when I saw what was left of him under that scrappy piece of tarpaulin I can't tell you. His face was only just recognisable. His limbs gone. His torso like a battered piece of meat. I wanted to scream and shout, to cry and beat my chest, but I did little more than retch and carry on with my duties. This is what it means to be a soldier in this army and part of me was shamed.

For Ada's sake I ask you not to speak of this. Save her from the truth, because what good would that do her now? She that has been left with nothing, not even a child to comfort her in this her darkest hour. And please never speak of the other things I told you. The Frenchwoman. Keep your word to me, as I had promised Jim faithfully, and so let them both rest in peace.

I am well enough, I have a tiny shrapnel injury which isn't worth writing home about, a scratch on my back that was dressed. My spirits have been low for some time, but I constantly think of home, that great sheet of water, and you.

I must end now. Bosley is here, and I must hand this over. I don't know why I want to escape the eyes of the censor. For once, I want to keep my thoughts private, and between us.

And they, my thoughts, are with you,

I love you.

Your own,

Jonathan Crane

THE ANGEL OF BROOKLYN

Brooklyn, New York
Summer Season, 1912

The book was heavy and it was bound in soft kid leather, like the one that Mr Cooper had shown her, but the title wasn't *Filles,* like the books that had gone before it, it was simply *Angel*, because all it contained was Beatrice Lyle, standing in her wings, her eyes the colour of cornflowers, her hair tipped in gold.

She'd turned the pages slowly. She'd looked at the angel with her lily, her outstretched hands; the glance over the shoulder that was supposed to be coy, but actually looked mysterious, as if she was looking at someone else. The girl standing in the picture appeared pure and blessed, and perfect, there was not a mark on her skin, not a mole, a vein, or any of those tiny heart-shaped freckles that sat across her hips. When it came to the podium, wouldn't those men be disappointed? Would they ask Mr Cooper for their money back?

She had stared at *Angel* for hours. She liked the feel of the book. It was heavy and it looked real, legitimate, a book that could be flanked by the classics, pressed tight between Scott, Defoe and Thackeray. Why would it have to be hidden? It didn't seem right. Weren't there nudes all over New York? They were hanging in the county hall, town hall, in libraries, in dimly lit galleries where scholars went with tablets, scratching things in pencil and poring over their notebooks.

*   *   *

Beatrice was about to brave the podium wearing a set of wings based on the original model, but lighter.

'And a pair I can afford,' Cooper told her. 'The price those other wings cost, they might as well have been made out of gold.'

She had vomited. Pacing around in a dressing gown she had her hands pressed together, as if she might be praying.

'What are you doing?' said Nancy. 'Just sit down for five minutes. The first won't be in for at least twenty minutes. Have a glass of water.'

'I have to keep moving,' she'd said. 'If I stop, I only feel worse.'

'You still want to do it?'

'Yes.'

'Honest?'

'Yes. What did I say? It's just stage fright. That's all it is now, it's stage fright.'

'The first on the list is a man called Mr Lambton,' said Nancy. 'You're lucky. He's extremely courteous and he's never been any trouble. He's been coming since we opened.'

'I won't look at him,' said Beatrice.

'No. There's a black spot on the wall the size of a nickel, I usually look at that.'

'What if I start shaking?'

'Then you move a little.'

'I thought you didn't move?'

'When I say move, I mean you turn your head or

your shoulders, or you take a small step to the side. You don't have to do a dance.'

'How will I know when his time's up?'

'Marnie will ring the little bell.'

'What if he's seen all the postcards? He'll know I'm not that perfect.'

'Who is? It's the real you he wants to see, and you'll be flooded in blue light, and that always helps.'

'Blue light? Won't that make me look cold? Or dead?'

'Will you just stop and listen to yourself?' Marnie appeared with a small glass of hock. 'Drink this and shut up. Jeez. You're worse than all the divas at the Met.'

'I am?'

'Of course not,' said Nancy. 'She's joking.'

* * *

The angel was in position before the door opened. Billy nodded, turned round and stood facing the curtained-off door. She felt safe with Billy. In front of him she didn't feel naked, he looked so solid and trustworthy and ready to do battle for her honour. Nancy came and spruced up her wings.

'Ready?'

'I'm ready.'

When Mr Lambton appeared through the drapes she couldn't help looking at him. What sort of man would pay to look at naked girls? In one swift glance she had taken him in. He looked prim, a bookish kind of man with buff brown hair and a jewelled tiepin. Married, certainly. Mistresses, probably. He was well dressed and wore an expensive-looking fob watch. He folded his hands on his knees like he was sitting in church waiting for the priest to begin his morning sermon. She stood looking at the nickel after that. What did she think about? The way the man's boots creaked. The words of 'O for a Thousand Tongues to Sing'. Then she counted her heartbeats until the bell rang on number 64, and the man rose from his seat, bowing towards her and Billy before disappearing silently through the curtain.

'I'm going for a quick cigarette,' said Billy. 'The next isn't due for another five minutes.'

Beatrice sat on the edge of the podium with a wrap across her front. Five minutes. It wasn't worth unhooking herself from the wings. Nancy appeared.

'He was more than happy. He bought the full set of cards. How was it?'

'It wasn't at all bad, he looked nice, a gentleman.'

'You weren't supposed to be looking.'

'Oh, like you never do. What about the dish from Montreal?'

Nancy blushed. 'He took me out once or twice last season—just don't tell Cooper, he's bound to bite my head off. He was sweet all right. I took him over to Franny's, we ate crab salad and played gin rummy all night, and he didn't beat me once.'

'And that's all?'

'He was an honourable gentleman,' said Nancy. 'Though heaven knows I tried to change his mind, he wouldn't hear of any shenanigans, which I suppose is just as well, though it didn't stop me being heartbroken when he went and caught the train.'

'I'm going to keep my eye on the wall from now

on,' said Beatrice.

'Good idea, but you won't.'

That first night was the quietest she'd ever know; a blushing boy, still in his pale summer cap, hardly looking at her at all, biting his lip and peering over his shoulder as if someone might catch him; a grey-haired stick of a man, wiping his face with a handkerchief; she went through the lyrics of two Wesley hymns and Joanna's recipe for butter cake and thirteen beats of her heart before the bell rang for that one. There was a man who looked like a teacher. A man too fat for the chair, he tried to squeeze himself into the seat, but thought better of it and spent his four minutes holding onto its back, tapping his fingers which Beatrice noticed were like uncooked sausages. The last man of the night kept sighing. It made Beatrice want to giggle, but she kept her face straight. He smelled of the tobacconist's on Main Street in Normal, and she remembered the jars of twists, the rows of new pipes, and the man behind the counter, his moustache stained yellow, his eyes with milky lenses.

'Congratulations,' said Cooper. 'They all bought something to take home with them—even the little runt managed to cough up for "The Lily".'

'At least they didn't laugh.'

'I've had one laugh at me,' said Marnie.

'Nerves,' said Nancy.

'Either that, or I looked like an ape.'

They drank wine that night, all of them crowding onto one of Franny's boardwalk tables, pouring red wine until the sky felt sharp and the moon started tilting. There were bowls of clams and oysters. Celina's pretty girlfriend fell asleep on her shoulder. Even Lottie, the girl with the stiff upper lip who was in charge of the season's appointments, drank so much wine and water she had to spend the night above the oyster house dreaming she'd been thrown into the hold of a liner. Three days later, Beatrice Lyle was famous.

*　　　*　　　*

Word spread quickly. Those nights when she was behind the scenes, changing Nancy into a geisha, or Marnie into something that might just resemble a lady from the Orient, the men looked so disappointed, sitting chewing their fingernails, flicking over the cards of Japan and the desert, trembling over the ones slotted into the back of the box, still sharp-edged and ink-smelling. Those cards would have to do for now, but where was the angel in real life? Where did she live? Was she here? Was she sitting behind the curtain? They'd heard so much about her. There'd been whisperings in clubs, saloons and barbershops. The tattooist had etched more angels in the past week than he'd done for six months; all of them blonde and blue-eyed, they were flying over shoulders, kneeling on forearms and praying on bulging chests.

The disappointed asked to see Cooper, who would offer them double appointments, and some would try to pay for triple, though Cooper would have to decline. 'I'm sorry,' he'd say, 'I can't expect my angel to stand still for twelve minutes. It's inhumane.'

'She could sit down? Lie down?'

'She could float?'

'Hover?'

'Dance?'

'She could kneel at my feet, or wherever she feels most comfortable.'

'Eight minutes is enough,' said Cooper.

'What if I came in first and last?'

'Then I could come second and next to the last?'

Mr Cooper rubbed his chin and thought about it. 'Don't see why not,' he said. 'It seems like a fair enough solution all round.'

* * *

'What do you mean, envious? I'm not envious of Beatrice,' said Marnie. 'Why should I be envious? I don't want to be famous. I don't even want to be looked at any more come to that, though I can't say I haven't enjoyed it. No. All I want is a man who'll look after me a damn sight better than my da ever looked after my mam. He doesn't even have to be handsome, though I wouldn't like a baldy. Don't laugh. I have a thing about eggheads, probably because my da was one, and he was a real bag of shite.'

'She's my friend, my pal,' said Nancy. 'She hasn't changed, not one bit, of course, she's too nice to be in this business, but aren't we all? I'm not a bad person. I have morals, and if I lie down with a man, then I do it out of love. We all need some loving in our lives.'

'True,' said Celina. 'But I've never liked men in that way, they're so flat. Their faces hurt. They smell of oil or liquor, or they stink of chewed cigars. I like curves, real curves, breasts, soft skin and shampoo. I couldn't be jealous of Beatrice, because if the truth be known then I'm more than a little in love with her, and that girl could pierce any heart, man, woman, cat, dog . . .'

'I just don't want you feeling put out,' said Cooper, not daring to admit that perhaps he was a little in love with Miss Lyle himself, though surely she was young enough to be his daughter, and wasn't he almost stepping out with Violet Murphy? He'd taken her dancing. He'd bought her a box of fancy crystallised fruits and he'd even made friends with her mother.

'I'm not put out,' said Marnie. 'I'm beat.'

'True,' Nancy yawned. 'I've never sold so many postcards in my life.'

'And that's why,' said Cooper suddenly, 'I'm giving you all a raise.' He hadn't planned to, but the words had tumbled out.

'You mean all of us?' said Celina.

'Why not?' said Cooper. 'The money is pouring in like sunshine.'

'But isn't it all for Beatrice?'

'Beatrice might be on the pictures, she might be standing in her wings, but it's a team effort,' he told them, patting his top pocket, looking for a cigar. 'Someone has to distribute advertising material, and that entails a lot of walking and some persuading, someone else has to take bookings, let the gentlemen inside, as well as selling the everyday items—I see the little girl with the sand pail is selling awfully well at the moment. Billy has to keep extra guard. And then there's the pouring of the wine, and the entertaining that needs to be done whilst the angel signs her pictures. Yes,' he said. 'You all deserve a raise, and I want to say thank you for everything you've done.'

'Can we go now?' said Celina. 'I'm supposed to be meeting a girlfriend.'

'Of course you can go,' said Cooper, trying his best not to look too shocked. Celina with a pretty girlfriend would take some getting used to. 'But if you'd like to stay, then supper is on me.'

'It is?' said Celina. 'Well . . . I might as well eat first, the girl can wait, she's let me down a couple of times and I really fancy a ribeye.'

'You don't have to keep buying us food,' said Nancy.

'I know, but I don't like eating alone.'

'We can pay for our own,' she told him.

'I could run to a small hamburger,' said Celina. 'All right, all right, I can pay for a steak.'

'Next time,' said Cooper. 'Next time.'

*   *   *

So now Beatrice worked most evenings, and the other girls were eventually phased out, though they didn't seem to mind, they were being paid much the same, and in between fluffing feathers, making appointments and emptying out ashtrays, they could sneak off for ten minutes here and there, they could make their own appointments, eat a bowl of chow mein, put their heads around a dancing show, or say a quick hello to Franny who'd be waiting later on with a tray of chinking glasses and stories about men who after one beer too many were convinced those wings were real.

Of course, not all of her visitors were gentlemen. Surely that went without saying? She'd had men rubbing at their crotches, she'd had them whispering, 'open your legs for me', 'bend over', 'kiss me'. She'd had men crying into their handkerchiefs, or their outspread hands, blubbing at their guilt, because it was the first time they'd seen a woman naked, because even their wives of twenty years kept some part of themselves covered, and the lamps would be extinguished, or because she looked so good and wholesome and clean, not like the woman he'd had standing up for half a dollar, swaying and tasting of gin underneath the boardwalk that time when he was desperate. Oh, she'd had a lot of men crying over her.

*   *   *

'You've taken to this, like a duck takes to water,' said Cooper. 'I'll say it once, and I'll say it again, when it comes to the mystery of allure, you're a natural.'

And so it seemed. When the last man of the night had vanished, slotting his precious cards into his wallet, she would lift off her wings, sign more pictures, then, feeling light-headed, she'd walk over to Franny's. And with her hair pinned up, her dress down to her ankles, she would look like anyone else, though she'd seen men blush and turn their heads away, or nudge the other fellow at their side, or stand open-mouthed, or start smiling like a loon, but none of them had bothered her, they'd merely let her pass.

She liked to go dancing. At the side of the hall, she would sip her glass of wine, letting the music flood through her. The dancers on the floor had a kind of giddiness that was infectious, and she would be grabbed up by the hands, or by a stuttering young man, or a friend, and she'd either shake her head or be swept along with them. She never looked at the time. She slept for most of the day.

*   *   *

'You must come and listen to this,' said Nancy one night through the music. 'Come outside, come quickly, come on, all of you.'

And so they were led away from the dance hall to the other side of the boardwalk where an accordionist stood on his silver-painted box, his boy selling sheet music, collecting up the change.

'What are we here for?'

'Just listen,' said Nancy. 'Just listen.'

The man pushing and pulling his accordion was looking at the rooftops, tapping his left foot, singing.

'There was an angel down Brooklyn way,
She ruffled her feathers and bade you to stay,
But when you looked up she had floated away,
And all that was left was her halo . . .'

The others were laughing, and clapping, and although Beatrice stood listening with a small frozen smile on her face, she was white-faced and shivering, like the sea behind him, the birds following the fishing boats, the faint hollow moans of the dance hall they'd just left.

'You're more than famous,' said Nancy, putting an arm around her.

'Is it any wonder?' said Celina with a sigh.

'I wish they were singing about me,' said Marnie. 'What I wouldn't give to be in a song.'

When Nancy had walked her home later that night, Beatrice watched her shadow turn around the corner and then she grabbed her coat and walked towards the ocean. It was almost morning and the world felt at peace. The dairyman, still smelling of the fields, rolled his sloshing churns across the grey cobbled yard of the coffee house. A boy wiping sleep from his eyes had a sack full of newspapers, and he walked bent like an old man, straightening as his load lightened, reading new headlines in between deliveries. WOMAN DROWNS AT GREAT NECK. BOOKSTORE BURNS. LITTLE BOO WINS TALENT SHOW. A dog trotted towards the railings, pushing its face between the bars, staring at the water breaking gently over the stones.

Sitting on the steps leading down to the beach she put her chin in her hands and wondered what she was doing with her life, and what it all meant anyway. If she was a bad person now, why did she feel so good about herself, and did that make her into something even worse? She sighed. Even worse than what? She was still a virgin. She hadn't accepted the few furtive offers that had been thrown at her across the curtained room. She'd kissed a couple of boys in the corner of the dance hall, she'd held their hands and wondered if these gestures might lead into romances, but these boys were usually visitors heading home the next day, and it had been their transient state that had given them their boldness in the first place. A boy called Trey had nervously touched her breast, but she was sure that one or two fumbles with a trembling clammy hand wouldn't lead her into damnation, though the wings might do it.

'You're out early,' said a voice behind her. 'Or have you not been home?'

She turned. It was a man she'd seen at the dance hall. He'd been sitting in the corner with his sweetheart on his knee. She'd noticed him because of his laugh and the way that his girlfriend had let down her hair shaking her head like it was full of something rattling.

'I went home for two minutes but I didn't like it,' she told him. 'I came straight out again.'

'May I?' Nodding, she moved to give him space, rubbing her eyes and looking at the thin line of froth on the tide.

'It's hypnotic,' she said.

'My father has a yacht. Every July through August he thinks that he's Columbus.'

'And you?'

'I'm not much of a sailor,' he said.

Beatrice pressed her hand against the weather-beaten step; she could see the neck of a bottle pushing its way through the sand, a candy wrapper, a broken shell that looked like a miniature trumpet.

'So what are you doing out at this hour?' she said. 'Don't you feel like sleeping it off?'

'Sleeping it off? Did I look drunk to you in there? That's terrible.'

'You saw me?'

'Of course I saw you,' he said. 'And I would have been sober if it wasn't for the vast quantities of mediocre champagne that I'd consumed.'

She smiled. 'You left your girlfriend sleeping?'

'Oh, it's all very proper. My girlfriend is sleeping at her parents' summer house. She has to be in bed before midnight or she'll turn into a pumpkin.'

'That was the carriage,' said Beatrice. 'The girl changes back into poor Cinderella.'

'And there's me thinking that she was about to become a vegetable. Would you like to take a walk?'

'Would your girlfriend mind?'

'Probably, but like I said, she's sleeping.'

The sky was washed orange, the sea molten, the sun quivering at the edges as if it was still making up its mind whether or not to appear. Their boots made a soft crunching sound. Beatrice stopped to pick up a seashell.

'I collect them,' she shrugged.

'When I was a boy I wanted to be a collector, though I'd no idea what it was that I wanted to collect. A cousin of mine was very fond of bottle tops. And I was quite keen on stamps until I asked my father about them.'

'What did he say?'

'He told me that the only thing really worth collecting was money.'

Beatrice looked at her seashell. It was white with green edges. 'In some far-flung place this seashell would be currency,' she told him. 'I could use this fragile, beautiful thing to buy me a ticket for the opera.'

'Do you like the opera?'

'Not really.'

'Me neither.'

They could see Ivan opening up his coffee house, lumbering over the sand with the board, the smell of coffee winding like a thin brown toffee-coloured line through the breeze, his white apron flapping.

'Are you the angel?' the man asked, holding out a

chair while Ivan stood wiping his hands behind the steamy counter.

'I'm Beatrice Lyle,' she said. 'And you are?'

'Conrad Hatcher the Third.'

'How very grand.'

'Not really. It's a new family thing. The other two Conrads are still living. Of course, there's my father with the yacht, and then my grandfather with his telescope.'

'So you all share a love of the ocean?'

'My grandfather uses his telescope to spy on all his neighbours, my father uses his yacht to show off to his, and I just like the look of it.'

'Are you on vacation?'

'I'm here for the summer. So, are you?'

'Here for the summer?'

'The angel?'

'Yes.'

'They said that you were.'

'They were right.'

Ivan appeared with the coffee. 'Early birds,' he smiled. 'Have it on the house.'

She put her hands around the cup letting the heat sink into her bones. A man passed with his dog. He was looking over his shoulder.

'I didn't think it would turn out like this,' she said.

'Like what?'

'I didn't think it would get in the way of my life.'

'And how does it do that?'

'Even if people don't know who I am, then I think that they do.'

'Like that man with the dog?'

'Yes.'

'I'll bet he knew,' he said.

Beatrice sighed. 'So, what do people think of me?'

'That you're the most beautiful girl in Brooklyn.'

'No, really.'

'That you're the most beautiful girl in Brooklyn.'

She could feel her mouth twitching. She took a sip of coffee.

'They have the wrong impression,' she told him. 'They must do.'

'They have eyes.'

'Yes, but what do they see?'

He closed his own eyes and smiled at her. He took a lump of sugar from the small glass bowl. 'Ah,' he said, 'you want me to tell you that they all think you're a whore, that they think you're a wanton type of girl to do such an immodest vulgar thing as to take off all your clothes and wear a pair of wings, and then,' he said, 'then you can tell me that I'm wrong.'

'Yes.'

'Well, I won't.'

'Why? Because it's true or because you don't want to hear of my objections?'

'Because I don't really care,' he said. 'You are what you are, that's all.' He yawned. 'Would you like a pastry? I would love something oozing with vanilla. Or chocolate. It's the champagne. Once the headache goes, then the hunger sets in.'

'What were you celebrating?'

'Nothing. I'm from Cos Cob, Connecticut. In Cos Cob, everyone drinks too much champagne. There's a store that's open all through the night just to sell its bottles of seltzer. It's a sickening, decadent place.'

'I'm from Normal, Illinois. No liquor allowed.'

'So you're all clear-headed and wise?'

'Absolutely.'

'Perhaps I should move there?'

'Oh, I think that you should,' she said.

They ordered a pastry, chocolate for him, and almond for her, and they ate self-consciously, pulling the flakes of yellow pastry from their lips, the sky brightening above their heads into a washed-out shade of blue.

'Would you call this breakfast, or supper?' he asked.

'Breakfast,' she said. 'I had my supper hours ago.'

'Are you going to sleep today?'

'Probably.'

'Me too. Though it's hard to sleep in the daylight.'

A trickle of early-morning walkers had appeared, looking for newspapers, flasks of orange juice and breakfast. A red-sailed boat was bobbing on the ocean, a man was raking the sand.

'I really ought to be going,' said Conrad. 'I'm glad I got to meet you, and you're nothing like I thought you'd be.'

'You thought I'd be what? Let me think now . . . Vulgar? Uncouth?'

'Cold as ice,' he smiled. 'Aloof.'

'Oh, I've tried aloof and it's boring.'

'Might I walk you back?'

'Back where?'

'To wherever it is that you're going.'

'I'm going home.'

'So, might I?'

'If you like,' she said.

He took her arm over the sand. They passed a

barefoot man in a dinner suit. A girl in a cheap-looking dress was chewing gum, an empty bottle of vermouth at her side.

'I've been an insomniac all summer,' said Conrad. 'I have a million and one things on my mind. I don't want to go back to Harvard, though I know that I'll have to in the fall. It's a requisite.'

'To what?'

'Everything.'

'I should have known,' she said.

'Known what?'

'You look like a Harvard man.'

'I do? And what does a Harvard man look like?'

'He looks rich and full of the sun,' she told him. 'Sort of glowing from the inside.'

He pulled a face. 'I've never liked Harvard, and I like it less now.'

'So what are all these other things that are playing on your mind?' They'd reached her door. The numbers had sand sitting in their curves. The paint was flaking.

'Too many things to tell you.'

'Really?' She opened the door. 'You want to come up?'

He hesitated. 'All right,' he said. 'I will.'

The room was warm. The open drapes had let in a blanket of sun. She opened a window and they could hear the clopping horse being led away to work.

'I like your room.'

'It's small.'

'It's like you.'

'Coffee?'

'If I have more coffee then I'll never sleep again.'

She looked at him. He was tall and wide-shouldered. His clothes said jaunty American, jaunty rich American. She suddenly felt poor.

'Won't somebody be wondering?' she asked.

'Where I am? No.'

'Your girlfriend?'

'Marianne will still be flat out. She sleeps until noon.'

'So what do you want from me?' It was a line she'd picked from a magazine. It sounded awful. She turned towards him. She could feel a nerve twitching in her neck.

'What do I want from you?' He sounded puzzled. 'Nothing. Anything. I don't know, I mean I like you, but I'm supposed to be in love.'

'I like you too,' she told him. 'I've never been in love.'

'I don't believe you.'

'It's true. I've never even had a beau.'

'Are you kidding me?' He touched her hand.

'Absolutely not.'

He looked her in the eye. 'Is it hard? Taking your clothes off in front of total strangers?'

'I don't take them off in front of them. I would never do that. Removing your clothes is far too personal. It says something.'

He began to unbutton his shirt until she could see a long deep V of honey-coloured skin. 'Like this?'

'Yes. But you're in love.'

'I know I am,' he said.

* * *

It was a long, strange summer, the summer Conrad Hatcher (the Third) broke her heart, though she told herself that he didn't mean anything at all, he was one of those experiences in life that you had to get through. She was now officially bad. She'd slept with him fifteen times. She wasn't married. Conrad had a girlfriend, and though they weren't yet engaged, she still saw herself as an adulterer.

'So, you are in love with him?' said Marnie.

'Not at all. I like him. Liking him is more than enough.'

'So why did you leave the dance hall when you saw him arrive with his party? Why didn't you just go up to him and say a quick hello?'

'He was with his girl.'

'But if you aren't in love with him then what does it matter? Hell, last season I went out with a guy from downtown. He was married. I liked him. He made me laugh and he set my heart racing, but I wasn't in love. And I had no shame. Hell, I'd go out with him and his wife and the rest of their pals, and we'd have a high old time of it.'

'I don't like seeing him with her. I feel guilty.'

'You mean jealous?'

She shrugged.

'He likes you?'

'More than likes.'

'So why doesn't he leave her?'

'It's the money. The life.'

'What do you mean, it's the money? You mean you aren't rich enough?'

Beatrice sighed. 'Oh, it's fine to fall in love with the Angel of Brooklyn; let's face it, he isn't the first and he won't be the last, but he knows it's just a fantasy. I'm not the sort of girl you can slot into your real life. He has a house overlooking Long Island Sound. They have yachts. Maids. What would Papa say?'

'Then he's a beast.'

'He's a nice beast.'

'You're in love with him.'

'I know I am.'

'Then there's only one thing for it. You mustn't see him again.'

'But he goes back in two weeks.'

'Look, honey, two weeks is a whole relationship for some people. Celina swaps her girlfriends every weekend. Say goodbye now. The sooner the heart breaks, the sooner it will heal.'

'Do I have to?'

'It's the only way to do it. Heck, he deserves it, that's what you have to keep telling yourself. You need to toughen up.'

'But I'll miss him.'

'He was never yours to miss.'

* * *

She waited three days. She slept with him again.

'You were talking in your sleep,' he said.

'I was? What did I say?'

'Lots of things. I couldn't make them out. Something about cake. Danish sultana cake and muffins. And then you told me to be careful.'

She let him take her to the Old Russian tea rooms where they danced to the orchestra and she wore a string of pearls that Mr Cooper had lent her. 'Just don't tell Violet Murphy.'

He cried when she eventually told him; blubbing into his hands, he told her that he hated what he was and everything about himself.

'I wish I could leave Marianne and walk out of

my own life,' he told her. 'I love you.'
'No, you don't,' she said.

*   *   *

That night she became more daring in her wings. She felt reckless, and dirty. When a raw-faced youth appeared, shuffling through the curtains, pimpled and unsure of himself, she touched her breast for him. She could see his face redden. She licked her lips. Then she opened her legs a little wider. His jaw dropped. He put his hand to his throat. Then he smiled.

SECRETS

When the Reverend Peter McNally read out Jim's name from the roll of honour, there was a wail from the back of the church. Ada had dyed her best clothes black the day she'd received the official letter and all hope had gone. The dye had stained her hands; it had left inky coins on her elbows and shadows on her yard flags. She was wearing her aunt's jet brooch and she'd lost so much weight it looked like she was drowning in all that dark material. Beatrice didn't turn to look. She kept her head down as she listened to the now depleted choir. Most of the boys' voices had broken, some had been called up, and the rest were at home because they didn't like church any more; it was a cold depressing place even in the sunshine. The reverend often snapped at them. Arriving late, pushing on his dog collar, he'd sometimes have to hold on to the lectern just to keep from slipping down the step. Some said it was because he'd lost his nephew at the Somme, others had seen a depleted bottle of gin in the vestment wardrobe, though they hadn't said anything, imagining what it must be like, sitting with mothers who were crying over sons they'd never see again, children the image of their fathers asking questions about God, because where did He fit into all of this? Hadn't they been in church every week since they could remember? All those prayers and the hours spent in Sunday school crayoning pictures of Moses. Didn't He owe them something?

'I'm so very, very sorry,' said Beatrice on her way out, because what else could she do? The women were standing huddled, arms clasped tightly around Ada, their own clothes while not exactly black were the darkest they could find in their wardrobes, their faces moist with heat. Only the children were running around as usual.

'I told you it wouldn't last,' she said.

'Yes,' said Beatrice, 'and I'm sorry you were right.'

She walked home with Lionel, who'd only come to the church as a mark of respect for Ada, because he now favoured the spiritualists, and spent every Thursday and Sunday evening sitting in their small red-bricked hall waiting for a medium to bring the other world a little closer.

'It's all scientific,' he explained as they made their way down the lane. 'It isn't mumbo-jumbo. The reason why people are so sceptical is because table turning has always been open to such trickery. Magicians can use their skills to make things appear, for things to knock and float, and so on. People like magicians because they like being entertained, knowing nothing's as it seems, so when the trickery is revealed, they lift up their hands and applaud, and then they say, "I told you so."'

'Do you still believe in heaven?' she asked.

'I believe in another world,' he told her. 'Yes, I believe it is easy to get there, it is like walking through a curtain.'

'And God?'

'And God is just there in His glory presiding over it all. With spiritualism, we simply cut out the middleman; we have no need for a priest, because we can hear it for ourselves.'

'But the medium? Surely that's your middleman?'

'The medium is the vessel and what we see or hear is not open to interpretation, it merely is.' Lionel clasped his hands behind his back and looked down at his shoes, the laces in his left boot had frayed and were trailing over the stones. 'Would you like to come in for some tea?'

Lionel's cottage was neat and full of things. While the kettle boiled and Lionel opened the caddy, Beatrice stared at all the books and ornaments, the jug depicting the entrance to the Liverpool and Manchester railway, a tourist map of North-East Yorkshire, coronation buttons, cycle routes, guides to ornithology.

'I am something of a hoarder,' he admitted. 'My father was the same.'

She joined him at the table. There was tea and a plate of cream crackers. The cloth was snow white, and she tried to imagine Lionel on washday with his posser and packets of starch. How did he manage it?

'It's an awful time,' he said. 'It's a time when we often don't know what to say for the best, though of course I gave my condolences to Ada, knowing as I spoke that words mean very little and it's such a terrible thing.'

'Yes, and then I feel guilty for thinking, thank God it wasn't Jonathan.'

He smiled. 'It's human nature. You've nothing to feel guilty about.'

They stirred their tea, the spoons clinking loudly against the pale yellow cups. Lionel looked at her, and then looked away again. He looked older than she remembered as the daylight dug into his tired puckered skin; it made his hair translucent.

'You knew Jonathan's mother and father?' said Beatrice.

'Yes, I knew his father very well.'

'Tell me about him. Please? I've heard he was a gentleman. Jonathan always speaks fondly of him, and I know he must have had a very difficult time, losing his wife so young, and then bringing his son up alone.'

'It certainly wasn't easy,' said Lionel. 'I was his friend, and he could always turn to me, though what did I know about boys? Of course, I remembered my own childhood, my brother, my cousins and our friends, but that was all so far away. He missed Eliza. He felt nothing without her. Hiding his misery from Jonathan he'd throw himself into his work.' Lionel went to the window and looked towards the lacy clouds. The sky was trembling. What did it matter now anyway? 'He met a woman called Margaret Milton,' he began.

'She lived in Manchester. He met her at a supper party the year after Eliza died. They formed a remarkable friendship. He kept a picture of her hidden in his wallet, and from what I could see she was a charming-looking woman and not at all hard-faced, or indeed coquettish.'

'So why didn't he marry her? Widowers remarry all the time. It's perfectly acceptable and I'm sure Jonathan would have been more than glad of a stepmother.'

'Margaret Milton was already married,' he said. 'I suppose you're very shocked?'

She shook her head. 'Not at all. These things happen.'

'Her husband was a brute. He often left her high and dry. She had a big house with extensive grounds, but she had to live off meagre rations, due to lack of funds. In the winter she froze and Martin would find her huddled under rugs wearing her hat and layers of clothes. Her husband was a partner in a pharmaceutical company and he travelled through the Continent with his pamphlets and his potions, picking up things as he went along, including debts and several mistresses. Margaret was miserable, but he wouldn't divorce her. He said he simply didn't believe in it. It's true, she could have dragged him through the courts but she had two small children to think about, a boy and a girl, and her family thought highly of her husband, and she didn't want to shame them. Martin was in turmoil. When Jonathan was in bed we'd sit by the fireside and he'd unburden himself. I believe he was deeply in love with the woman.'

'Did he ever tell Jonathan?'

'No.'

'So what happened? Did they have a lifelong affair?'

Lionel shook his head. 'Martin loved her, but he hated himself for what he saw was his weakness. He felt that it was wrong to have relations with another man's wife, whatever the circumstances. There were lies. Secrets. In the end, he had to give her up, for his own sake, though she begged him not to. There were letters and pleadings. She said that as far as she was concerned she didn't have a husband, but of course she was married, and Mr Milton with his changing morals, his hold on his wife and all those hollow promises was always there, lurking like a sinister shadow in the background, and so Martin had to end it.'

'That's a very sad story,' said Beatrice. 'I'm sorry.'

'Several years later she died of tuberculosis in a clinic in Austria. She was little more than forty, yet it was a comfort to Martin that she was in the right place. It showed that someone had cared for her.'

'I'm glad you told me.'

'He was a good man. You won't say anything? To Jonathan, I mean.'

'No,' she said, 'not a word.'

*　　*　　*

'I keep thinking about Tom,' said Lizzie. 'I was worrying before, but now that Jim's gone, it's a thousand times worse.'

'We need more distractions,' said Beatrice.

'Like what?'

'Picture shows? The varieties? I felt better when I was working with the pigs because it sure is hard to think of anything when you're being butted by a sow.'

Lizzie smiled. They were sitting in her parlour. Harry and Martha were staying with their cousins, and she'd invited Beatrice over.

'At times like this I wish I lived in town,' said Lizzie. 'My mam and dad still live in town and all they have to do is walk out of their front door and they're looking at the picture house.'

'I'd be there every night,' said Beatrice.

'So would I,' said Lizzie. 'If I could afford it.'

There was a knock on the door. Lizzie went to open it.

'Ada?'

'Can I come in?' she asked. She was wearing a washed-out-looking dress and holding a leather wallet, which she slipped inside her pocket.

Lizzie nodded. 'Beatrice is here.'

As soon as Ada walked into the room Beatrice felt uncomfortable. She stood up, sat down, she didn't know what to say. Lizzie poured tea and offered a plate of biscuits.

'How are you feeling?' Lizzie asked Ada.

'Sometimes better, sometimes worse,' she said, taking one of the biscuits and snapping it in two. 'One good thing. At least I know. The wondering and waiting was making me sick. I couldn't get to sleep at night. I'd pace up and down, I'd be wearing out the floorboards. I knew that telegram would come, it was just a matter of when.'

Beatrice knew how she'd felt. She was always at the window, leaving warm greasy marks on the glass. There had been no more letters or postcards. At night she would sit up late reading old magazines, listening to music, tidying the cupboards, anything, because lying in bed was no good, she'd close her eyes, open them, watch the shadows from the moon, listen to the owl, the ticking of the clock, and when eventually she did fall asleep, she would dream, and sometimes Jonathan was at home and there wasn't a war at all. They were travelling in the motor car. She wanted to see Wales. They had children. A girl. A boy who looked like Elijah, and sometimes it was Elijah, saying grace, reading *The Life of John Wesley*, then saying prayers and requiems for all the dead birds, he was digging shallow holes and giving them a funeral.

For something else to look at, they took their chairs into the yard where they sat in squares of pale sunshine with the scent of the dusty lilac bush.

'I don't know what I'm going to do,' said Ada. 'I thought this was it. Me and Jim. The shop. Our trips out to the seaside. We went to Blackpool one year. It's like Morecambe, only faster.'

Lizzie looked pained. 'I've never been to Blackpool,' she said.

'They buried him, you know,' said Ada, not looking at Lizzie or Beatrice, but at a small lick of cloud above their heads. 'They had to, and I'm glad of it, but it doesn't seem right, he's such a long way from here, and how will I ever get to visit him? They're going to send me a picture of the grave. A picture isn't the same. It doesn't seem real. And I would have liked to have seen the coffin going in, though now that I think about it, I don't suppose he had a coffin, did he?'

'They would have given him a coffin,' Beatrice nodded.

'Yes,' said Lizzie, 'I'm sure of it.'

Ada narrowed her eyes and rubbed at her arms.

'Are you getting cold?' asked Lizzie.

'Cold?' said Ada. 'I'm always cold.'

They sat looking at the wall, with the moss, the white lilac and a thorny-looking rose bush. Suddenly, Ada reached into her pocket and brought the wallet out.

'This was Jim's,' she said. 'They sent it back to me. It's a good one. It's from Letterman's in town. It was a Christmas present from his mam.' She opened it out. Beatrice thought she was going to be sick, right there on her boots. Lizzie paled. There were some pieces of paper folded inside it. 'Letters,' Ada said, embarrassed to see her own handwriting. 'And this.' It was a smaller piece of paper. She unravelled it. Beatrice's stomach dipped as soon as she saw it, but she didn't say anything.

' "Solange Devaux, 20.30," ' she read. 'French. I wonder what it means? It sounds like a place. I'll bet that's where they were fighting or where they were going off to. I wish I knew where it was.'

Suddenly Lizzie smiled. 'I know—you could look it up for her,' she said to Beatrice. 'You have all those travel books.'

Beatrice pursed her lips together and gave a little smile. 'Yes,' she said. 'If I have a map of France.'

Ada looked at her. 'Thank you,' she said, with a begrudging kind of smile. 'It would mean a lot to me.'

* * *

It was getting late. Beatrice did a long slow circle of the village, pausing to look at the water with its small inky waves. She passed the cottage where Mary had lived and through the open curtains she could see Mary's mother and the doctor, sitting side by side on the sofa. A ginger cat was stretching on the doorstep, rattling its claws. She didn't know what to think. She looked at the sky; a single star was out.

It was another warm night. Beatrice fell asleep, then woke up with the sheets on the floor. She'd been dreaming about Normal. She was in a dirty room and a man was in the doorway with a bar of buttermilk soap.

She lit her lamp and read her magazine for a while. When she closed her eyes they were full of gold buttons, feathers, a map of northern France, and in between Bracquemont and Reims was a small black dot that turned into the village of Solange Devaux where soldiers passed between stations, where they could fill their canteens, smoke cigarettes, and talk about nothing, everything, or what it really felt like to be walking in the mud, spitting out rainwater, watching death, dodging bullets, terrified, and all of this such a long way from home.

WALKING IN THE DARK

1. Walking in the Dark

It was always light in Coney. Walking home, the sky might be the colour of a telephone, but there'd always be something else to light your way, and not just the moon or the stars; this light was coloured, and at quarter past midnight, when they turned out all the bulbs, it seemed like they'd left the ghosts of themselves behind, that the boardwalk was glowing, that the air was still full of it, like the phosphorescent mist Beatrice had seen all those years ago hanging like a shroud in Hackett's Wood. But she knew better. She knew that the light came from the tucked-away places down the side streets. Shen Yip had a string of red lanterns outside his shaky-looking bar room where you could sit on dragon-patterned cushions smoking opium pipes with thin-faced men who talked about poetry and ghostly apparitions. The tattooist couldn't sleep. He'd leave a blue bulb shining by his doorway. Sailors who'd docked for the night could crawl their way over and by morning they could have sirens on their arms, a rose-entwined anchor, or the name of their sweetheart over the initials of the last one. Abdul the Turk slept through the day. He'd eat his breakfast at supper time, a plate of cheese and grapes, or an apricot pastry, then he'd sit by his door watching the crowds walking back to their rooms. Later, he'd light his lanterns and set the kettle on the stove. He'd make mint tea. He was famous for his tea. If you'd been working late, if you were an insomniac, if you were alone with a problem, or you just needed a little company, you could pull on a pair of slippers and a robe and make your way over to Abdul's. He didn't care about your clothes. He usually wore a djellaba. Sometimes he slept in it. He was often alone, or he would sometimes have company, but he'd always have room for one more. He always had tea.

There were lights everywhere. In hazy late-night

bars. On funny-face torches, the latest craze of the season. On buggies. Automobiles. Ferry boats. In windows where people packed items into stiff cardboard boxes. Where the baker was just starting his shift between the hot black ovens and plates of rising dough. The twenty-four-hour dentist had a blood-red light in his lobby that made the people who were holding their cheeks and moaning with the worst pain they had ever known, even worse than childbirth, turn right around again, looking for the drug store with those little paper packets that might just do the trick.

Beatrice knew all these lights. The gambler's, the whorehouse, the shaky-handed abortionist—who'd once shown Nancy fake certificates, telling her he'd been a bona fide physician when all he'd ever worked on were the horses at the racetrack—the blind woman who used candles to show the world that she was still alive, the coffee drinker, the man who was reading his way through the library and was on his way to C. Beatrice knew all these lights, because she was looking for the darkness. In the darkness she wouldn't be distracted. She'd be alone. She could ask herself questions and think long and hard about the answers.

When the lights went out across the park, fizzing on the wires, she'd put a small fruit knife in her pocket and walked down towards the shoreline. There were shadows. The shush-shushing roll of the sea at her feet. Pinpricks of light in the distance showed fishing boats. The moon was a scratch. There was a twinkling from the pierhead where the rod and line fishermen were sitting with their bait. But it wasn't nearly dark enough. There were the lights shifting from the far reaches of the boardwalk. She could see her hands in front of her face, and when her eyes adjusted, the world was clear as daylight. It made her think about other people. The things she could see. The sign that said *Mabel's Hot Rolls. Buy Our Crab Cakes. Drummond's Wines and Liquors*.

She walked down the darkest-looking side street she could find, her hand on her fruit knife feeling nervous. She could hear something humming, talking behind windows with the shutters pulled down, and then a wailing. She squeezed the fruit knife tighter. There were men on the corner, she could see the jagged outline of their faces, a soft low groaning; these were the drug addicts who came looking for their own kind of darkness, and in the morning the men taking out their trash would find them on the sidewalk, still slumped inside a bruised kind of daze. Beatrice walked quickly with her head down. A single light bulb still quivered on the sign for Frankfurter Heaven. The men ignored her. The hungry ragpickers. The drug addicts. They were floating from the kerb. They didn't need shoes because they were dancing with the girl who sang songs about the boy she'd left in Donegal and they were the boys come to get her.

She went home. The street lights were lit, and they poured through the window as she made herself a blindfold. The blindfold nearly worked. She made herself another one and pulled it very tight. She sat against the wall with her eyes closed. Two blindfolds. Darkness.

In Normal she had wrapped herself in night-time. She'd had long conversations with her mother who'd told her that if she was still alive the first thing she'd do would be to get rid of all the birds.

It wasn't easy in Brooklyn. She had to throw away the pictures seared behind her eyelids. Nancy, hooking up her wings. Conrad with his hair wet. The men on the opposite chair were cracking their knuckles, rubbing their watery eyes, looking at the picture of her that was supposed to be hidden, and taking it away with them for as long as their memories (or their wallets) would let them.

She tried to relax. The room was quiet enough and she wanted to see her father. Not the man in the outhouse with the blood on his apron, the man who forgot to wash from one week to the next, reading manuals in the half-light, but her father at his best. Holding her hand on her first day at school, the only man in a room of clucking mothers. Why had she forgotten that? Then hadn't he dragged her to see Elijah's only attempt at sport, a fielder in a baseball game, sent off with a headache at half-time? She'd stood on the sideline, bored, but her father had cheered his encouragement, whooping like a madman, hitting Elijah on the back as if his small attempt had made all the difference. She folded her arms around herself. Tight. She saw her father laughing; he was slapping his knees and laughing. What had been so funny? She tried to imagine a time before the birds, a time when he'd stood behind his polished desk with a shiny fob watch, and he'd swung it on its chain while the boys were doing a test. In those days he must have woken early, making sure to trim his beard. He was well respected. Genteel ladies would knock at the door and ask him to tutor their sons. He would come home with a toppling mountain of copybooks, sitting up late, reading every word, and being vigilant with his marking. He would grin over supper. So what happened?

In the darkness, Beatrice sees his face. He's young, but already looking worn. And now the neighbours have stopped leaving baskets of food, they've stopped coming over with their offerings of cake, fish wrapped in paper, loaves of bread, or 'Won't you let me clean the kitchen for you?'

Beatrice wipes her fingers across the taut blindfold. She feels small sitting there in the dark. For years she has tried to think up alternative versions of her life. Her father remarrying. Why, there were plenty of eligible young women in Normal. These women went to church, fluttering in their best white clothes, like moths. They taught school. They had hope chests. She might have had a stepmother. Her father would have stayed at the front of the classroom with his fob watch and in place of the birds there would have been dainty ornaments or brightly polished spaces. There would have been other things. Birthday parties. Visits from new relations. Brothers and sisters. Something like a home.

But what is the use of thinking like this? There was only then. There is only now. *And what would you think of me now?*

2. The Joys of Fan Mail

Dear Angel,

You made me happy.

Spike. (I was wearing a red necktie and

suspenders.)

Dear Brooklyn Angel,

I would like to take you home with me. You could lie in bed all day doing nothing. I work in maintenance. I would bring us food from Mr Chow's, he makes the best rice noodles. You wouldn't have to do nothing. I can clean. I have a nice place. If you crane your neck out, you can even see the ocean. I would buy you presents. Anything you want. It wouldn't be such a bad life. What do you say?

Jake Jackson

Dear Blondie,

I wish that fella didn't charge so much. I would see you every day. I dream about you. Oh boy, the things you do in my dreams! I sat with you on Tuesday. I'm the boy with the irons on my legs. I had polio, but things are looking up. I can get about. I can do almost as much as the next man. I can even kick a ball. Well, thanks for making this the best vacation of my life!!!

I won't forget you.

Paul

Dear Angel,

I think you should let me take you out. I could show you a real good time. They don't call me the horse for nothing! I'll be waiting by the Ziz coaster. Shall we say midnight on Saturday? I'll walk right up to you. I know what you look like. Though I might not recognize you with your clothes on!

See you Saturday,

Billy (the horse) xxx

Oh Angel from the highest heavens,

You touched me last night. Not in the physical sense, but right down deep in my heart. I got your message. I know what it means all right, so you needn't worry yourself about that. I counted the blinks, like you wanted me to. I feel the same. What shall we do? Thing is, I've been married fifteen years this next fall and she's not a bad person, but she isn't an angel either. What I'm trying to say is, that's not for you to worry about. We haven't had intercourse in a while. She's like a sister to me. We'll figure something out.

Twenty-nine blinks.

Yr Lionel

Dear Miss,

Divine things must be loved to be known.

J.V.

Angel,

I spent my last cent on you. I think you should do more than just stand there like a statue. I'm telling you this for your own good and if you don't listen then you'll go out of business. I've had girls for less than half the price you charge (some French) who will let me do anything I want to them. Looking at you, it's like sitting in a church. For that price, I would at least like a bit of a feel-up.

Robbie

Miss,

Love's heralds should be thoughts
Which ten times faster glide than
the sun's beams

Driving back shadows over
low'ring hills;
Therefore do nimble-pinion'd
doves draw love;
And therefore hath the wind-swift
Cupid wings.
From an admirer

Dear Angel of Brooklyn,

You are one sweet creature. I would like to have you as my pet. I have a dog. I'd treat you better than my dog. And I love that dog! I'd like to put you on a leash and take you everywhere.

I am touching myself as I write this.

Buggs

Angel,

I am leaving my girlfriend tomorrow. I have all yr pictures. I'd rather have yr pictures than my girlfriend. She's a prude.

I love you,

Eddy

Dear Angel,

I sat there and I wanted to put it in you.

Thought I'd tell you.

You are the best-looking thing in America.

RJ

Dear Angel of Brooklyn,

Will you marry me?

Dr Victor P. Holcombe (New Jersey)

Dear Angel,

Are you the girl who works in Lyle's Cafeteria?

I've bet five dollars that you are.
Jackie

3. The Bone Yard

There really were quiet places at Coney. There were corners where you could just sit and drink a carton of lemon, rub your head and hide yourself from the crowds. Most people who worked on the park knew where they were. The broken bench by the forgotten rock pool. There was an abandoned chalet near the Alpine railway. Once upon a time there had been a disused bandstand, it had been a good place to creep to because there you could stretch out and the rides were nothing but hums, the people all gone, the occasional screech from the coasters, but you could cope with that because you'd be relaxed and lying down, hands underneath your head, looking up inside the roof that had been painted black with silver constellations, and though the paint was flaking and some of the stars were missing, you could still spend your lunch break looking at Venus. Then they pulled it down. So now, her favourite place was what they called the Bone Yard.

Behind the steeplechase and the fence where they'd hung *Keep Out* and *Danger* signs stood the warehouses and mechanics' yards. Here they kept the tools, the grease that slicked down the tracks, the rows of mechanics' uniforms that hung in bottle-green lines; there were oil cans and safety harnesses, rule books and books that told you what to do in an emergency, just in case you'd forgotten all your training, and you couldn't remember the weight-and-pulley system of the cars, or the way to pummel a person's chest if their heart had stopped beating, or *in case of electrocution*.

One of these warehouses was home to the broken-down rides, the rides that had lost their shine, or popularity, or the scenery that needed mending, the metal palm trees that were waiting for a repaint, a mountain in need of more snow, a skeleton with half its bones missing (some pranksters had taken off the skull and were walking around the park with it like Hamlet).

Beatrice liked the quiet of the Bone Yard. The mechanics were rarely in there, preferring to work out of doors, or to take whatever it was they were fixing into one of the smaller warehouses where they could chew the fat, keeping the doors open for a gulp of fresh air and a view of the ladies who sometimes walked past. Beatrice would nod to Blake, sitting bare-armed in the gatehouse, and she'd step inside this hollow-sounding dreamland where her footsteps would rattle. She would walk around, as if she were at some fancy museum, stopping now and then, looking up at the giant flaking lips of the empty-headed clown. She liked the way the sunshine pierced through the holes in the wall, shooting things.

4. Gold Teeth, Bare Feet and Muscles

Behind the double blindfold she could see them all again. Some of them were blurs, sitting there like nothing. Others? Well. She'd had a bad day. It had been one of those days when it had been almost impossible to stare blank-faced at the nickel-shaped spot on the wall. Billy had a headache, and she could see him rubbing the back of his neck every few minutes. Did he have a glass of water? Would he be better off sitting down? Would he be all right if it came down to a fight? Not that there'd ever been any fights. Just a few scuffles from men who'd thought their time wasn't up, or who'd been making crude remarks, or spitting onto the floor. 'We do not stand for spitting,' Billy had said. 'Gimme a break,' said the man. 'I have to do something.'

'Would you like some aspirin?'

'Nah,' said Billy. 'I don't believe in aspirin.'

'Are you going to be all right?'

'I won't let them near you if that's what you're thinking,' he said. 'Anyway, it's my own fault, I deserve all the pain, I stayed up late drinking vodka, playing cards with Marta and Magda, and I swear they can read each other's minds, they had me over a barrel.'

Billy was all right, but Beatrice couldn't keep her eyes from wandering. She began to look at the men instead of over their shoulders. And then, when she went back to her room for a nap, they were there again, sitting in front of her, and they were hardly daring to blink—they didn't want to miss so much as a second of their allotted time—they were licking their lips, opening their mouths, hands on their knees, staring.

The man with the shiny gold teeth opened his mouth and a fat row of metal flashed at her, his tongue rolling over his gums, slowly, then quicker, as her eyes had darted back to the nickel and she'd tried her best to focus on the wall. He looked like a sailor. His skin had been burnt by the sun, and not just for the season, it had a battered look, like leather. Then his fingernails started tapping on the teeth, like he was playing some kind of xylophone, and Billy had started to rub the back of his neck again, and the teeth were nibbling the man's bottom lip in a way that suggested something else, until Beatrice was counting off the minutes. Her favourite girls' names. Her classmates in Normal. Aileen. Annie-Mae. Gemma. Bernadette. Recalling the menu at Franny's, placing an order, French-style mussels, fried potatoes, a small glass of beer, and how much would it come to, and when Billy opened the drape, she'd almost said, that's a dollar fifty to you.

Then, as if that wasn't enough, twenty minutes later came the man with bare feet. A respectable-looking gentleman, if there ever was such a thing inside this booth, sweating in a formal-looking suit, loosening his collar, he could have stepped right out of an office, he could have been a lawyer, a medical man, a dusty-fingered librarian. He had a pleasant kind of face. A neatly combed moustache. And then she had noticed his feet.

They were bare. She quickly looked down at her own bare feet. Then back towards his. They looked strange. Naked. The way they jutted out from his dark formal pants. They were long, and pink, and hairless, and he kept digging his big toes into the floor, twisting, like he was trying to make a couple of holes, then all his toes would ripple, like some underwater creature; she couldn't take her eyes off them. Where on earth were his shoes? How had he walked here? She looked up. He was smiling. Wriggling his toes and smiling. It was a most extraordinary sight. When Billy eventually moved towards the curtain, he consulted his pocket watch and nodded at her courteously before disappearing through the drape.

'Did you see him?' said Beatrice. 'What did you think of that?'

'That his boots might be pinching?'

'It looked obscene,' she said.

Still, the day wasn't over and after two quiet, nondescript men when she'd been able to look at the nickel at last, figuring out where she was going to eat that night (Riccardo's Spaghetti House), the muscleman appeared. He was short and squat. Strutting like a crow. He looked uncomfortable in his clothes, as if his skin was trying to burst out of the tightly stitched seams; he kept adjusting himself in the chair, grunting slightly, looking hot. Billy shuffled. He didn't like men who might be able to take him down—mind you, size wasn't always the issue. The muscleman looked harmless; he was well turned out, and at least he was wearing a clean pair of boots.

After a couple of minutes the man began unbuttoning his jacket, but this didn't disturb her, after all, it was another uncommonly hot day, and who could blame the guy? Then the jacket went over his knee. Then a couple of buttons were popped on his shirt, then a couple more, until before she knew it he was opening up his shirt, pulling out his bulging arms with their shiny sprouting veins and sitting in his vest. What was Billy doing?

The man grinned. He began flexing his arms at her, the way a strongman might impress the crowd. Beatrice closed her eyes. When she opened them again she tried to fix her stare on the nickel. Billy hadn't moved. She couldn't say anything. She'd promised herself at the start that she would never use her voice unless it was absolutely necessary, and she still wasn't sure that it was. The man was in his chair. He hadn't threatened her in any way, he was simply showing off his muscles and stroking them like kittens. He was grinning at her, as if to say, 'So what do you think of them?' She gave him a half-smile. What if he turned nasty?

Just before his time was up he gave them one last long loving stroke, pulling on his shirt, taking his time with the buttons as if it were part of the act; he seemed to be breathing heavily, or was she imagining things? No, he was definitely panting. He removed his jacket from where it was lying on his lap, rubbing the bulge that was now sitting in his pants for all the world to see, shaking out his legs. She looked away. Billy opened the drape and when she looked back he was gone.

'Did you see that? He took off his clothes,' said Beatrice. 'I thought I was going to faint. Why didn't you do something?'

Billy rubbed the back of his neck and swallowed. 'I was all set to dive in, but do you know who that was?' he said. 'I didn't recognise him right away, but that was Beansy Tombs the champion strongman and wrestler. I thought it best to keep my mouth shut. He's a dangerous type. He knows all the famous criminals; plays around with the big boys.' Billy shrugged. 'Look at it this way, let's be grateful he didn't touch you up, he didn't cause any trouble and he left when his time was up. That's all we could have asked for in a punter.'

'Beansy Tombs?'

'For sure. He's always in the papers,' said Billy.

'I'm surprised you didn't recognise him.'

'I'm surprised they let him in.'

'They wouldn't have had any choice,' said Billy. 'And if it was Nancy who took the booking, well, let's just say he has a way with all the ladies.'

'He does?' She shivered, pulling a wrap around her shoulders. 'He sure did nothing for me.'

Later, in Riccardo's Spaghetti House, sitting in the corner booth, she was sure she could see him again, between the pictures of olive trees and a gondola shaped from glass. She was sure she could feel his bulging piggy eyes, looking her up and down, and it made her feel cold. Wasn't that him on the opposite table, laughing with a brittle-faced woman, drumming his big fat hand on the table, making all the waiters jump? She asked Marnie.

'Nah,' she said. 'That's the guy from the circus. The one the clowns jump all over, using him like a springboard. I can't remember his name, it's Tommy, or Timmy, or something.'

'Timmy? He doesn't look like a Timmy,' she said, twisting spaghetti round her fork.

'It's Toby,' she said. 'I remember now.'

'Did you see Beansy Tombs?'

'No.' She rubbed her eyes. 'But I know a girl who went out with him for a while—apparently he's as sweet as anything once you get to know him. He treated her real well, bought her all sorts of fancy things with French words on the boxes, and he asked her to call him baby boy—you know, when they were doing it—and he slept with his thumb in his mouth and she had to tuck him in real tight cooing like his mamma. Mind you, I swore on my life I'd never tell, so you'd better swear back, or I'll be in awful big trouble.'

‘He didn’t look like a mamma’s boy.’

‘Oh, they never do,’ she said, searching for a cigarette.

Beatrice remembered it all, pressing her fingers over the blindfold, feeling the small oval bulges of her shut-down eyes. She liked the ragged edges, the way the knot pushed on the back of her head like a finger, but it didn’t keep the pictures out, however tight she pulled it. Still, it made her feel secure, because although she’d thought about other things, the cops, the fights, the pawing, one thing she hadn’t thought about were those men who could breeze their way past Mr Cooper, and ask the world for anything.

5. The Strange Phantom Weight of her Wings

Some days Beatrice Lyle spent so long standing in her white feathered wings she could feel the pull of them long after Nancy, or Celina, or Marnie had unhooked her. After she had combed up her hair and she was walking fully clothed doing the ordinary things in life, like buying boot polish, or paying her rent, or telling the man selling spearmint on the news-stand that she thought the rain clouds looked ominous, though she’d be glad of a downpour, because the world could do with a wash. Sometimes, she found she was patting herself on the back, just to make sure she hadn’t left the blessed things on, though of course she knew they wouldn’t sit under her dress, and she was only being foolish. But the feeling was so strong. Standing at the pierhead looking out at the slivers of light on the ocean, she thought she could feel the wings twitching, like those gulls cocking their heads, their black beady eyes staring at her, their own white wings folded tightly at their sides.

In her dreams she was flying (of course she was—apart from anything else, her pillow was stuffed with goose down), and it was the easiest thing in the world, and she wasn't the only one. Nancy had wings, and Celina, and Mr Cooper, they were all circling and diving, from one place to the next, and even Beansy Tombs had a pair of wings, though his were like a buzzard's sprouting from his short muscled back looking dirty.

6. Wife

She said, 'I want to see what my husband saw. I want to see what's killing us.'

Billy glanced over his shoulder. Beatrice felt sick as she looked straight ahead at the nickel. She could hear the woman breathing, and sighing now and then. Beatrice took a long glance at her. The woman was red-eyed. She looked hungry, she looked like she hadn't slept for weeks.

Beatrice wanted to say a lot of things. She wanted to say, he doesn't know me and I don't know him. Really. I'm nothing to him, whoever he is, I never have been, and if something is killing you, then how can it be me? I've never touched him, cared for him, showed him any kindness, I haven't been there for him, shared a meal, a walk, anything. He doesn't know my name. Not really. I don't know his. I never will know his. But she couldn't.

7. More

According to Mr Hoff, Mr Cooper and Maurice, *Angel* was so popular—especially in Germany—that extra copies had been printed, and they were clamouring for more. The book had been out for a year. It had sold in gentlemen's clubs, through word of mouth, at society meetings (photographic and otherwise), it was known in gentrified circles, and was the talk of New York, Boston, and those newly developing parts of Los Angeles, where the artistic, theatrical, film set were living. The book had been exported to Europe, and Mr Hoff's Paris office had been inundated with requests. They would like to see their 'Angel' in the flesh. They would like another volume.

'They would like to see more of you,' said Mr Hoff, pacing up and down his office, opening a window, lighting a cigar, abandoning it, pulling down a blind.

'More pictures?' said Beatrice.

'More of you,' said Hoff.

The room was wood-panelled, and everything looked expensive, from the green leather seats, to the gold-framed scenes of huntsmen at chase, and the ivory inlaid humidor that Mr Hoff kept stroking with his fingers.

'What I am trying to say,' he coughed, 'is that some of our European friends think the photographs are a little too chaste.' He rummaged in his desk drawer. 'What they would like is a little more of this.' He slid across an envelope. 'Open it up,' he said. 'Take a look.'

The girls on the pictures and postcards were

naked, but they were also doing other things. The pictures were graphic, they were kissing men, other girls, they had their legs wide open, they were touching themselves, bending over; all in all, they were pornographic. They made her stomach turn.

'I just couldn't,' said Beatrice.

Mr Hoff smiled. 'You have a big following,' he told her. 'Everywhere I go, people are talking about the Angel of Brooklyn. Heck, they're even singing about her, and on the other side of the river, I hear there are cheap imitations.'

'There are other angels now, yes.'

'So . . .' he breathed, turning his back on her for a moment. 'We need to rethink our game. We need to find you another venue. A real venue.' He turned round and grinned. 'I was thinking of the Ritz Hotel.'

'Manhattan?'

'Of course, where else? Think about it. Everything about you says Manhattan Island. And wouldn't you be so much more comfortable in a suite than standing on a box like you're part of a travelling freak show? In a first-rate hotel you would be able to entertain your guests who would be willing to pay much more for the comfort and the privilege.'

'Entertain them, how?'

'Like any hostess,' he said, flicking up his hand. 'You could set them up with drinks, cigars and so on.'

'You mean I'd be a prostitute?'

'I never said that. The term I would use is "exhibitionist". Think about it. Think about the money you would make, why, you'd be able to set yourself up nicely in a very good apartment in the best part of town, and if the book is anything to go by, this time next year you could be riding in an automobile, you'd be dripping in so many jewels you would need an armed escort.'

'What about Mr Cooper?' she asked.

He sighed expansively. 'What about him? Jesmond Cooper is nothing but a small rat on the sidewalk. He owns a little sideshow. Sideshow, nothing. His business was rumbling along before you appeared, and I'm sure it will rumble on again.'

'I like Coney Island.'

'Of course you do, my dear, it's all you've ever known.'

'I feel comfortable there.'

'Standing on your little box?'

'Yes.'

Mr Hoff sighed. 'If only you could see it.'

'See what?'

'You are living and working in the gutter,' he told her. 'You are a lily in the filth of the fairground and the people who come to stand and gawp are the lowlife of this world, with their grubby pockets of change, they are the unwashed and unpleasant of America.'

'I don't have to touch them.'

'You wouldn't want to. Truly. The gentlemen I am talking about are rich, clean and well living. They're from the oldest, finest families, they own land, companies, and what's more, they are all in love with you.'

'In love? No, they are not.'

'All right, all right, so they're in love with an illusion, but think about it, think of your new status in this world, and the power you'd have over some of the greatest men in America. We'll meet again, that's what we'll do. We'll have cocktails. Have you ever tasted a real cocktail? The bar at the Ritz is sublime. I can show you the suite. Have you ever been inside a hotel suite? The Ritz? It's like walking into paradise.'

'I don't think so.' She hesitated, she pictured the rooms, those jewels she'd seen in Tiffany's, the strings of giant pearls.

'You don't think so?'

She shook her head. Why kid herself? She knew she would not be able to do it. Those photographs had shocked her. Some of them were so graphic they looked like illustrations from a doctor's manual.

'Whose paradise is it?' she asked. 'Mine, or yours? My answer is no.'

'Couldn't we reach a compromise? The photographs say? They'd take half a day. You'd outsell the Bible.'

'I don't think so.'

'You've really made up your mind?'

'Yes.'

'Then you're a pretty little fool,' he said, grinding his teeth and showing her to the door. 'That's all there is to it, you're a fool.'

8. The Englishmen

Nancy and Celina were ill—they'd been to a party somewhere along Ocean Avenue, a girl who was moving out to France was celebrating, and they'd eaten some clams that had turned them inside out.

'I know you're our star attraction and all that,' said Mr Cooper, looking at his hands and plucking at his fingernails, 'and you're lovely, but I have no one else to do their afternoon shift. You'd be selling the usual trinkets. Would you? Could you? Please?'

'Hmm,' she said, patting him gently on the shoulder. 'I think I can remember how to do that. I keep my clothes on, don't I?'

He smiled. 'You know, you really are an angel,' he said, grimacing at the cliché.

It was early September, and the crowds were changing into huddles. The sky was still blue, but the air had a fresher feel to it and when the sun went in you could see the beachfront shivering.

'I come here every year,' one of her customers told her. 'I met my husband at Coney. First time I saw him, he was riding on an elephant. He died three years last May. I still come. I rent the same room, I go on the Dragon's Gorge, I take a walk through the Hall of Mirrors, the Cakewalk, all the old favourites. I eat Franny's chowder, and I feel him sitting right there beside me, I have to keep telling myself not to order the chowder for him, though I sometimes feel I'd like to.'

The woman bought a postcard of Lake Dreamland and a cowrie shell necklace. Business was slow. Beatrice tidied the stock drawers. She dusted down the ornaments, the little pot cats that had Coney painted on their backs, the Negro dolls, the smiling elephants that opened out into tiny manicure sets and mirrors. Later, she stood outside the booth with the cards in her hand, walking up and down, talking to the woman selling lucky charms and heather, the man on the frankfurter stall who was waiting to hear who'd won the three o'clock race, and then there was the man playing sad songs on the corner, for no reason in particular, 'only it's a sad song kind of day'. She watched the dancers from the Show Hall, smoking pink cigarettes; a girl called Kathlyn waved at her, she was the girl who wore the birdcage on her head and danced in the peacock ballet. 'You have customers,' she mouthed, pointing back towards the stall. Then she winked.

Beatrice held out the cards as the two men stood looking at the window, with its shelves of bottled sand, Coney Island teaspoons and racks of picture postcards. One of them had his hands in his pockets and she could see the edge of his jacket shivering in the breeze, the well-stitched lining, blue and cream, then he slipped it off, hooking it over his shoulder, and his oval-shaped cufflinks were winking at her.

'Can I help you?' she said.

The other one turned to her and grinned. 'Oh, I hope so,' he said. *English,* she thought, *or a very good New England.* 'We're looking for some cards.'

She moved a little closer. She pulled out the stand and brought the boxes towards them. 'We have hundreds,' she said. 'Help yourself.'

She watched them turning the stand, pulling out cards and whispering. Their clothes looked well made. Rich even. The one with the jacket over his shoulder handed her half a dozen cards and she slipped them into a printed brown bag and helped him with the change.

'Nickels, dimes, cents, dollars,' he shrugged. 'I'm still not used to it. I've been weighed down in change for a week.'

'Then I'll know it's you,' she said. 'If I'm walking down the boardwalk and I hear somebody clanging.'

'Oh he clangs all right,' said his friend. 'By the way, do you know a chap called Butch?'

The clanging man looked embarrassed, and he stepped away, looking through the window again, examining all the small painted bottles and the seashells.

'Butch? Does Butch spend his days cutting hair?'

'So you do know him?' he said. Then his voice turned into a theatrical kind of whisper. 'Thing is, whilst we were getting ourselves shaved yesterday, this chap Butch mentioned another type of postcard.'

'Oh? You want something a little further afield? New Jersey, for example? We do have a couple, though they're never very popular. We have Manhattan too. Let's see, we have the Tribune Building, and Madison Square Garden . . .'

'I like Madison Square Garden,' said the friend at the window.

'These cards don't have buildings on them,' he said, pulling in his eyebrows.

'They don't?' said Beatrice.

'At least, I don't think they do.'

'Ah, you mean the boardwalk? The clear blue ocean? Our world-famous roller coasters?'

'I mean people,' he said, looking more than a little hot under the collar. 'I mean ladies, mostly.'

She smiled gently, because enough, she supposed, was enough. 'Well, sir, if you're thinking of the type of postcard I think you're thinking of, then you'll have to go to our other outlet after seven o'clock. Here's where it is,' she said, handing him a sheet. 'Ask for Mr Cooper.'

'I will,' he swallowed. 'And thank you.'

She watched them walking down the boardwalk, the way the blue-white jacket was swinging, the way their summer brogues went shushing over the dusty wooden planks. The friend looked over his shoulder. She looked away. A new piece of sun was burning into her face. A girl was turning the postcard stand. 'I want five,' she was saying, 'and they have to be the same, or I just won't hear the last of it.'

It was a long afternoon, but somehow she didn't mind the few customers, overdressed now the sun was out again, panting at the counter with tales of lodging houses and the family back home. She bought a lemonade and held the cheap paper cup into the sunlight, wondering what it would have been like, sipping champagne cocktails at the Ritz with Mr Hoff and all his rich New Yorkers. She watched the one-armed bartender laughing with his sweetheart. She waved at the tattooist, shivering at the birds still dancing beak to beak in circles round his neck. 'How ya doin', Bea?' he called. 'Oh, I'm just fine,' she shouted back and he saluted her. It would be nothing like this, she thought, as Marta and Magda called out to her, sharing a bottle of soda, a straw at either side. It would be nothing.

She hadn't told Mr Cooper or the other girls about Hoff's proposition. She'd said no, so why should she mention it? It made her feel uncomfortable and it would make them feel worse.

Nancy appeared, walking slowly. 'Thanks,' she said, limping behind the counter. 'I'll just sit with you for the last half-hour. I needed to get out of my room, it was like the walls were throbbing, I felt terrible just lying there waiting for it all to subside.'

'I won't mention clams,' said Beatrice. 'Or seafood in general.'

Nancy put her head in her hands. 'And they looked so good,' she groaned. 'Mind you, it could have been the wine, we drank an awful lot of wine, and I danced with a boy with hair the colour of carrots, and he reminded me of home.'

'But you hated it at home.'

'The nostalgic, fictional home,' she said. 'The home where Papa's a good man, Mamma makes biscuits, and there's a piece of fancy lace sitting at the window.'

* * *

That night, hooking herself into her wings, she thought about her own lost home. She pictured another family living in the rooms, holding hands, saying grace, eating at the big kitchen table that had been sold with the house, her own and Elijah's initials carved underneath with a whittle knife—had they discovered them yet? She wondered who might be sleeping in her room, with the window looking out onto the scorched piece of garden where the grass had never regrown. What were they dreaming in there? What would they be thinking, looking up at the cracked plaster ceiling? And when the house was quiet, could they hear the gentle fluttering of wings, could they feel a small draught moving over their faces, a twitching whirr of feathers, softer than a bat?

'How are you feeling?' she asked Nancy, who was

helping her with her wings.

'Shaky.'

'Are you seeing the carrot boy again?'

'I don't know,' she said. 'I really can't remember. I'd better ask someone. I'll ask Celina, she's out there looking unacceptably healthy, selling pictures to two Englishmen. We managed to get them in tonight, and by the looks on their faces you would have thought it was just turning Christmas.'

Beatrice blushed. 'I know those men,' she said.

'And they're not half bad-looking,' said Nancy. 'But you know what the English are like.'

'Like what?'

'Cold fish. They're all soft soaking lips and cold sweaty palms and no real substance, so be warned.'

'I'm warned,' said Beatrice. 'Who's first on the list tonight?'

'An old guy,' said Nancy. 'Says his name is Mr Finnegan, but I know better. I remember him from the old days, his name is Mr Ronald Penn and he's a headmaster, a naughty headmaster who was struck off for something seedy and unspoken, so there.'

'Oh, there's no fooling you,' said Beatrice.

She stood looking at the nickel, feeling her ankles tremble; she could hear the headmaster sniffing and licking his lips, then she could hear voices outside the booth, all the chattering and laughter, and she tried to make them out. Who was it talking to Nancy? She wished she was out there, instead of up on her podium, voiceless, like a statue, because tonight, it seemed, she really felt like talking.

'What are they saying?'

‘They’ll be talking about nothing,’ said Billy.

‘But can you hear them?’

‘Sure I can hear them, I hear them every night, they’re standing around just passing the time of day, flirting a little and pouting, keeping the men smiling, reminding them of the no-talking, no-touching rule, which has to be a good thing, and then they sell them all the cards, which is an even better thing. What’s gotten into you tonight?’

‘I don’t know,’ she said. ‘Nothing.’

Towards the end of the night, the first Englishman appeared. It was the one with the straw-coloured hair who’d asked about the pictures.

‘Oh my,’ he’d said, then, ‘Sorry.’

She didn’t look at him. She could feel her heart beating, and she wondered if he could see it, pumping at her breast. When Billy lifted the drape at the end of four long minutes, he said, ‘Thank you. Thank you very much.’

There was a small break. Half a cigarette for Billy and a sip of water for her. Then the other man appeared. She glanced at him. He’d changed into a pale linen suit, the Englishman abroad. He put his fingers to his lips, he looked embarrassed, but then he was smiling, and somehow she couldn’t help but smile with him. He had something over his knees, and when half his time had gone he held it up. She looked. On a crumpled piece of paper he’d written, *Will You Go Out With Me?*

She shrugged.

He turned the paper round. On the other side he’d written, *Please?*

She smiled. Shook her head. Then she nodded.

He blinked his wet eyes.

He was smiling like a cat.
What else could she do?

9. Walking Out

'You're not clanging. I'm very disappointed.'

'I left all my change in a bowl. I don't think clanging's dignified.'

'I suppose not. Unless you're a bell?'

'A good bell has to clang at least every hour, that's true.'

They had arranged to meet the next afternoon. They were strolling along the boardwalk, the sun warm; all the clouds had vanished.

'So where's your friend today? The one who doesn't clang at all.'

'Freddy is out with a girl he met last night. He seems particularly smitten, for Freddy.'

'He's not the impressible type?'

'He's very hard to please. At least he used to be.'

'And you?'

'Oh, I'm easy, always have been, though I do have a penchant for girls who wear wings.'

'Been out with many?'

'Forty-five.'

'Including me?'

'I've known you twenty minutes so that would be presumptuous.'

'You're a gentleman?'

'Of course. Isn't that why you came out with me?'

'No. I particularly liked your handwriting.'

'Most women do.'

'Shall we go and look at the ocean?'

'Why not? Where I'm from the ocean is called

the sea, and it's only ever blue three times a year, usually in August.'

'The New York Atlantic isn't always blue. You might be heading for disappointment. It's more like oil and ink. So, how do you like America?'

'I'm in love with America. Really. I don't want to go home, but I'll have to eventually. Freddy is staying. He's the lucky one. He's going to California to manage an orange farm for his uncle.'

'Oranges? Sweet. Can't you go with him?'

'No. I have to go back to England. I have work. A house. A life that I'm happy with.'

'What's it like?'

'England? It rains a lot. Especially in Lancashire, which is where I'm from, and where I'll stay, though I would like to travel, I'd like to see the world.'

'Me too. I'd like to see China, and India. And England. You see, I'm crazy about the rain. I like walking in it. It makes me feel alive.'

'You'd be full of life in Lancashire, there'd be no stopping you, and look, there's your wonderful ocean, which today is the colour of curaçao, apart from the ferry which has an unhealthy look of the chimney about it.'

'Would you like to get a drink and talk about the ocean?'

'A drink? Yes, I'd like a drink, though the ocean talk I can do without, too many people have tried talking about the ocean and they've all failed miserably, apart from Mr Herman Melville who did a most spectacular job.'

'So what shall we talk about?'

'Oh,' he said, 'I'm sure we'll think of something.'

*   *   *

‘So what did you talk about?’ said Nancy.

‘Everything. I don’t know why, I couldn’t stop. He knows everything already. The birds. Elijah. Everything.’

‘What’s his name?’

‘Jonathan,’ said Beatrice. ‘And doesn’t it sound so . . . well, English?’

‘Sure. So when’s he heading home?’

‘A couple of weeks. He’s supposed to be heading over to Boston, then onto California.’

‘Supposed to be?’

‘He wants to stay here.’

‘Oh my,’ said Nancy. ‘It’s Conrad all over again.’

‘I don’t know. I don’t know what to do.’

‘Tell him to go to California. That way, he can’t blame you when it all goes wrong.’

‘How do you know it’ll all go wrong?’

‘He’s a tourist. He’s English. It has to.’

*   *   *

‘I can do without California,’ he said. ‘What’s it to me? I’ve already had enough of Freddy. He laughs like a crazed hyena. Have you noticed that? And the girls. He seems to have lost all his pious inhibitions somewhere over the Atlantic. The girls are worse than him. I swear the last one he went out with was a donkey in a party frock.’

‘California sounds exciting.’

‘Does it? Sounds like a dreary desert to me.’

‘But you have a ticket?’

‘I can afford to lose a train ticket. I’ll have you

know, Miss Lyle, that I'm a man of independent means.'

'What does that mean?'

'That I'm fairly well off and I don't have to rely on my father, which is a jolly good thing, seeing as he died last January.'

'I'm sorry.'

'Thank you.'

They walked for a while. The breeze was cool. He pulled his scarf around her.

'It's the end of the season here,' she said, 'but it'll still be warm in California, hence all the oranges.'

'I'm not overly fond of citrus fruit. Unless it's in marmalade. I am missing marmalade.'

'What else do you miss?'

'By that look in your eye, Miss Lyle, I take it you mean, *who* do you miss? Well, no one,' he said. 'Two years ago I was in love with a girl called Jean Hebb. I was smitten for a while, but then I called it all off.'

'Why?'

He looked sad for a moment, rubbing his eyes and pulling on his lashes.

'I put up my hands. I let her down badly. I simply wasn't bothered enough any more. And for a lifetime together, you have to be bothered. After all the flirting, she was dull. Her conversation was nothing more than gossip, needlepoint and her brother's cricket scores.'

'Were they good scores?'

He smiled. 'I really can't remember. Other people's cricket makes me yawn. So, you see, it was entirely my fault. I fell for the pretty exterior, the coy flutter of her big brown eyes, but under all that there was nothing.'

'Nothing? Well, I hate to disappoint you, but there's not a lot to me.'

'You've already given me enough to think about to last me half a lifetime.'

'Only half?'

'I need something to look forward to. I'll save half a lifetime for a little more conversation.'

'Mr Crane,' she said, 'you do know that half of Coney Island is in love with the Angel of Brooklyn?'

'Are they really?'

'Why act so surprised?'

'Is this the flirting part of our acquaintance?' he said. 'Shall we have done with it? Shall we just be ourselves?'

'Flirting can be exhausting.'

'So what shall we have for lunch?' he said. 'Take me to Franny's. I've heard so much about it. Let's go and eat, I'm starving.'

* * *

The day that Freddy set out for Boston he left two snivelling girls at the railroad track, both unaware of the other's existence. He'd told one to sit in the waiting room, and one to wait on the platform, and then he kept flitting between them, until the train began to move and they both ran up to the window, beating their chests and wailing. Jonathan and Beatrice stood and watched it all while Freddy waved and gave a helpless kind of shrug, safely in his carriage.

'Look out, California,' said Jonathan. 'Here comes the new Casanova.'

'Was he like this in England?'

'In England he'd never been kissed.'

The girls appeared to be cat-fighting, one of them was spitting.

'Charming,' said Jonathan.

'That's American girls for you,' said Beatrice. 'Haven't you noticed? We're altogether an uncouth bunch when it comes to love and war.'

'Uncouth is better than boring, but only just,' he smirked.

* * *

It was Saturday, and still the busiest night of the week at Coney. Beatrice was working until past ten o'clock.

'I don't feel right,' she told Nancy.

'He doesn't want you to do this any more?'

'He hasn't said that. It's me. I've started feeling like I'm dirty.'

'You don't look dirty,' said Nancy. 'You look cleaner than Ivory soap. Don't let him change you; you've known him how long? Ten minutes. And he'll soon be on that ship crossing the Atlantic. Do you like him better than Conrad?'

'I think so. Yes, I'm sure of it. It feels like the danger has gone. I feel like I've known him for years, and that he's part of me. Now I'm sounding trite.'

'He doesn't have a girl back in England? A wife?'

'He says not.'

'He can say what he likes, he's a long way from home.'

'I believe him.'

'Of course you do,' she said. 'Anyway, tonight we're going to the Alabama Hotel, we're all going, and I know you bought a new dress, so you can't change your mind. It's the biggest night of the season. Bring lover boy along. I'd like to get to know him. I'm a very good barometer when it comes to Englishmen. I've kissed a few, and to tell you the honest truth, I wasn't all that keen.'

The Alabama Hotel was a tall pink building full of shiny glass baubles, an orchestra which had made several phonograph records and bedrooms with balconies overlooking the ocean that could be rented by the hour. The staff were used to guests arriving incognito, and at least once a week they'd see men in false moustaches and women with wide paper fans and fat-brimmed hats called Mrs Betty Jones (Wisconsin). Tonight the guests were wide open and ready to party, invited every year by Rudy Catelli, the owner, who'd been born and bred on Coney and not in Alabama, and he saw it as his way of saying thank you to the people out there who made it what it was.

They arrived late. Nancy, Marnie and Celina were already in a crush of champagne in a room full of washed-off greasepaint, booming voices and pinched feet. The dance floor was tight with couples shuffling around to the music, more talking than dancing, the clowns pressing tight to the Russian trapeze girls, the lion-tamer crying over the one they had to shoot, Marta and Magda in white tulle dresses dancing with Riccardo and Milo, the juggling trampolinists, their small hands crushed against the warm black felt of their jackets.

'It's so chaotic,' said Jonathan, pushing his way through the crowd.

'Yes, isn't it wonderful?' said Beatrice. 'I know

everyone in the room, including the man with the tray of dirty glasses, that's Mauro, he wants to work with racehorses, it's a big dream of his.'

Jonathan looked at her as if she'd gone mad. 'Waiters? Racehorses? How do you know all these people? Have they seen you in your wings?'

'Of course not. Take Mauro over there. I eat in his father's restaurant all the time, and sometimes we stay there for hours, drinking wine and talking.'

'You drink a lot of wine?'

'No more than most,' she said, taking another glass of champagne. 'Thank you, Paul,' she said. 'You should sneak off outside and grab one for yourself.'

'I might do that later on,' said the waiter. 'Look at me, Bea, I'm red hot and parched.'

'You really do know all these people,' said Jonathan.

'I told you that already.'

They made their way over to Nancy. She was eating shrimp rolls and pulling off her shoes.

'They cost a week's wages and they're killing me already.'

'Where's Mr Cooper?'

'Out with his lady friend. They're taking in an opera. Something to do with a ring.'

They danced. They held hands. They picked at the table with its plates of prawn mousse and crackers, spicy bologna, balls of sticky rice.

'I've eaten the strangest things since I got here,' said Jonathan. 'Food from China and India, and some salty Russian things.'

'What do you eat back in England? Hot roast beef?'

'Yes, of course, and steak and kidney pudding,

lamb pie, cow heel, and all made at home in the kitchen. Have you ever rolled a piece of pastry?'

'What? Are you kidding me?' she said.

Their throats were raw from the shouting. In a corner Marta and Magda were sleeping under a coat made of silver-fox fur. It belonged to Rochelle Baker, the girl who sang the songs that broke men's hearts every night at eight at the Gala Show Theatre; she didn't need her coat, she was wrapped in Solomon Rox the ringmaster up in Room 63.

'We're going up top,' shouted Marnie. 'Are you coming?'

Jonathan looked worried.

'She means the roof,' said Beatrice. 'There's a garden up there. It's sure to be quieter than this.'

They followed Nancy up the rickety fire escape, holding bottles of wine under their arms. They passed girls rubbing their eyes and crying into serviettes, couples kissing, a waiter with a plate of lobster tails, and a skinny crying cat. The rooftop was empty and the quiet made their heads ring. They leaned over the balcony and looked down at the boardwalk and the blue-black ocean with its lines of shivering foam.

Marnie pulled out the musty daybeds and set them into a circle. 'We should have come up here hours ago.'

'But then we would have missed Lottie singing and who would have guessed that she couldn't hold a note?'

They lay flat on the beds. There was a faint hum of voices, the hiss of a fountain, and the ghostly rise and fall of a piano. Celina started humming. Then she turned onto her front, propping her small boyish chin in her hands.

'So you're in love with our Beatrice?' she said.

Jonathan was looking at the fountain. 'Is that all right with you?'

'Of course it is,' said Celina. 'Though it's hardly surprising because everyone she meets falls in love with her a little, and one day she's going to be swept right out of here and we'll miss her.'

'Oh, have another drink,' said Beatrice. 'You're starting to sound maudlin.'

'Maudlin always comes after a party,' said Jonathan.

'What are English parties like?' asked Nancy.

Jonathan laughed. 'I can't speak for the nation, but the parties I've attended have been sedate affairs, where the occasional youth will have one too many to drink and he'll throw it back up on the doorstep. Someone will play the piano very stiffly and the men will talk about the girls in their lives who don't exist and never will, and there might be a dance, but nothing too daring.'

'And that's as good as it gets?' yawned Celina. 'I thought the English were decadent?'

'Only in London,' said Jonathan. 'It never quite hit Lancashire.'

'It will,' said Nancy. 'It will.'

'The world is spinning,' said Beatrice. 'Can you feel it?'

Marnie giggled. 'Definitely.'

'We should have more men up here,' said Nancy. 'How come we only have Jonathan?'

'Because you're all unlucky in love,' said Beatrice.

'And you're not?' said Nancy.

'Not any more,' said Jonathan, who gripped tight

onto Beatrice's hand.

'Oh, we'll see how it ends,' said Celina. 'I thought I'd found true happiness with little Martha Frupp, but then she went and got herself engaged to that giant Irish navvy, can you believe that?'

'I've seen him,' said Beatrice. 'He looks like he's made out of steel.'

'And she bangs that piece of metal three times a day.'

The stars above their heads were soft-looking, though it might have been the wine, making the world felt-edged and fuzzy. Marnie was sleeping, or rather she'd passed out, her mouth open a little, as if she was just about to say something.

'Like a baby,' said Nancy.

Below them, the party was winding its way home, with its yawning trails of laughter, jilted shouts and scuffles. An automobile backfired.

'Like a gunshot,' said Celina.

Beatrice looked hard at the great expanse of sky; a cloud appeared, it was shaped like a wishing bone.

'I'm going to find a girl to kiss,' said Celina, touching Beatrice's forehead. 'Any girl, and I'll pretend I'm kissing you.'

Beatrice closed her eyes. She could feel Jonathan moving at her side. The fountain stopped, a door slammed, and through an open window a girl was shouting in Spanish.

10. Letter

November 1, 1913

Dear Elijah,

I don't know why I'm writing to you, but I have decided to send this to your old address in Chicago. Time has passed and they might have heard something. Firstly, I want you to know that whatever you've done and wherever you've been I'm not here to judge you. We're human beings, we make mistakes, we branch out, and we want to feel alive. Believe me when I tell you, I'm none too perfect myself.

I've been working at Coney this past couple of years, where I have the greatest friends, and I'd never been happier until I came home from work last weekend and I wondered how long it was all going to last, what the future held, and what if I was still here when I was thirty, or forty, or worse? What kind of life will I have? I've seen some of the showgirls turn their nose up at marriage. They say they're not ready, but secretly they're thinking, 'You're still a waiter/a baker/a sausage vendor.' You see, they're dreaming of bigger, better things, because they've read stories about Broadway, and closets full of mink, and men with long automobiles, and diamonds in their pockets. I want to shake them; I want to say, 'Since when have those guys ever bought tickets for a half-hour show in Brooklyn?' But I know. They just wouldn't listen. They'd be hurt.

I want to move on, but I'd be letting people

down. Mr Cooper has been good to me. He's given me everything. And the girls. The girls are my sisters. And the people who come to the stall—well, I might as well be honest with you, it's not a stall anymore, it's a sideshow—they'd be disappointed too. I've talked about it with a man who might be my chance to leave it all behind, and he says, 'Would they miss you? Is it really you they're coming to see? Or is it just a girl, standing there. Any girl. Would they even notice that you'd gone? Even those that have been three or four times. Would they really be looking so hard at your face? And the girls. If they are your sisters, wouldn't they want you to be happy, to get ahead, and make something better of your life? You can write to them. Even visit them one day. America is staying where it is. We'll know where to find them.' Oh Elijah, he goes on, and on. He's English. They don't say much. But when they do . . .

I'm going to think about it. Really I am. I lie in bed at night trying to block out the world that I'm living in, and the one I've left behind (only because it hurts), and I think about the future. Sometimes I want it badly. Sometimes I feel I'd be leaving you.

Wherever you are, and whatever you are doing, be it preaching in a small church or chapel, mending boots, or loving lots of girls, dancing girls, or otherwise, I want you to know that I love you. I have never forgotten you. You are part of me. Part of what we lived. I am always here (wherever that might be), and waiting for you, and hoping.

Let me know how it goes.

Your loving sister,
Beatrice x

PS Due to my success at work, I have managed to save a great deal from my wages. I want you to know that I have put it into a bank account, and if I do go to England and you would like to make the trip to see me at some later date, I will be able to buy you a good return ticket. You mustn't protest! Seeing you again is what I want most in the world, so in taking the money, you'd be doing your little sister a favor! I live in hope.

From, Bea x

BROKEN ENGLISH

The women talked. They sat with their hands curled around their teacups, searching Ada's face, because she was a widow now, and presumably bereft. Did she really look any different?

'I want to do something for the war effort,' said Lizzie suddenly. 'Beatrice is right. We need to do our bit, if we're going to win this war.'

Shrugging, they sat in silence for a while. They sat looking through the shop-door window. The weather had turned cold again and Lizzie's heart contracted at the thought of not seeing Tom, and the way another year was passing by without him.

'I can't think of anything,' said Ada. 'What could I do?'

'I know a girl who works on the trams,' Lizzie told them.

'The trams? I'd rather die than be a clippie,' said Madge, then realising what she'd said, she covered her bright pink face with her hand. 'What I meant is—'

'What about collecting for the charities?' Lizzie enthused. 'I've seen girls in town rattling tin cans and selling paper flags.'

'Who'd look after the children?' said Madge.

'We could knit,' said Ada, pleased with her idea. 'We could knit scarves and balaclavas and mufflers. The soldiers would be glad of them.'

'I could send one to Tom,' Lizzie smiled.

'They're for everyone,' said Madge. 'You can't pick and choose.'

'And we wouldn't have far to go, we can sit knitting and chatting, and we'd still be doing something,' said Lizzie. 'Do you think Beatrice can knit? Do they knit in America?'

'I doubt it,' said Madge. 'They buy everything from catalogues over there.'

'How do you know?'

'My mam's next-door neighbour told me. Her brother-in-law's cousin once knew a Canadian.'

'We should ask her. We'll need to collect wool.' Lizzie was looking through the window at the sky. It was full of dark jagged clouds and the wind was starting up. 'We'll need a lot of wool if we're going to save all those soldiers from the cold.'

*   *   *

They made signs and tacked them onto their windows and onto the bulletin board at church. *Wool Wanted. Help Keep Our Soldiers Warm.* The reverend said he thought he might have a jumper that had seen better days. He was looking well, people had noticed how his cheeks had lost their flare, his eyes looked more alive, and when he read the eulogy he didn't slur the words. After losing her brother in Ypres, Iris had decided that she'd been right all along, and that life really was for living. She'd told the reverend (or 'my Pete') that if he was ever going to make an honest woman of her, he'd better start looking after himself, and she would help him do it. The vicarage was now filled with dishes of stew, calf's-foot jelly and flasks of beef tea, brought over on trays in the guise of 'help your neighbour'. Iris would return at nine to collect her plates and whatever else the reverend might like to give her. She'd sometimes run him a bath. Iris and the few inches of warm sudsy water helped him to relax, more than anything that came from the neck of a bottle. Sometimes she'd share it. 'It's all part of the war effort,' she'd giggle. 'Don't look so bashful. We're saving water, aren't we?'

The weather was cold and crisp. The women, wearing their thickest coats and gloves, wondered what it might be like in the trenches. They'd heard about last winter. Of how the soldiers had to break ice to wash their faces. How the frozen ground had cut them.

The cold and black skies made people generous and scared, and Ada would find bags of wool on her doorstep, or odd socks, or jumpers that were almost worn out. Lizzie had donated a few of the children's outgrown woollens. Beatrice had found an old green cardigan, and Ada had pored over the label stitched into the collar saying, *Tobias J. Snowdon, Pure Wool, NY.*

'What did I say?' she'd said. 'Catalogues.'

Sitting in a circle, they unravelled wool until their fingertips were raw.

'It can't last much longer,' said Lizzie.

'They'll be worn out by Christmas,' said Madge.

'They were worn out last Christmas.' Ada reached for another old sweater and began cutting at the sleeve.

'All this fighting,' said Lizzie. 'All these months, years, if only they'd known.'

'They still would have signed up,' said Madge. 'Every single one of them.'

*   *   *

'It's a bit cramped, but we should all fit in somehow.'

It was the first meeting of the knitting circle and they'd arrived at Ada's with their bags of wool and needles.

'It's cosy,' said Beatrice.

They looked at her. Ada pushed a broken chair against the wall. The children were playing in the yard.

'Talk about elbow to elbow,' said Madge.

'I'm doing scarves,' said Lizzie. 'Scarves are good and quick.'

'Don't they have to be khaki?' said Beatrice. 'Don't they have regulations?'

'Well, you should know,' said Ada, unravelling a hairy ball of claret-coloured wool. 'You're married to the boss.'

'A scarf's a scarf,' said Madge. 'They should be grateful for what they get.'

'I wouldn't want my Tom getting into any

trouble,' said Lizzie.

Ada swallowed a laugh. 'Court-martialled for wearing bright blue,' she said. 'He'd never hear the last of it.'

Their needles began clicking. Beatrice knew how to knit, but she couldn't take her eyes from what she was doing, unlike the other women who could have done it blindfold, apart from Lizzie who appeared to be struggling.

'Those three young lads from the quarry are dead,' said Madge. 'It was in the paper last night.'

'They can't have been old enough?' said Lizzie. 'Can they?'

'Well, it's too late now, whatever their age, they won't be getting any older.'

'How's your Frank's back?' said Ada. 'Have you heard?'

Madge grimaced, but then she smiled into her wool pile. 'He knows how to suffer in silence,' she said. 'That's his trouble. He doesn't want to let all the lads down.'

'That's your Frank all right,' said Ada. 'He always was a martyr to the cause.'

Their needles filled the room with their hollow clicking sound. Madge was humming. Lizzie was tapping feet.

'By the way,' said Ada suddenly, 'did you find that place on the map?'

Beatrice looked up. 'No,' she said, 'I couldn't find it anywhere.'

'What place?' said Madge.

'In Jim's wallet there was a scrap of paper with some French words on it. It was where they were fighting. I wanted to see it on a map. I showed it to Beatrice. Are you sure it wasn't there?'

'Positive.'

'Strange,' said Ada.

'I have a map of all the battlefields,' said Madge. 'I got it free with the *Daily Express*.'

'Solange Devaux,' said Ada.

'What about her?' said Madge.

'That's the place.'

'No, it's not.'

'How do you know?'

'It's a name,' she said. 'Solange is a French name. I've seen it before. In a book. Or was it in an operetta? I used to go all the time with our Vi before she moved to Blackburn Road.'

'It's a place name,' said Ada.

'It's a girl's name,' said Madge.

'Since when have you been the expert in French?'

'I'm not.'

'Is that right?' she asked Beatrice. 'Is Solange really a French girl's name?'

'I don't know,' said Beatrice, dropping another stitch. 'I've really no idea.'

'I don't believe you,' said Ada, looking pale. 'You seemed so sure it was a place. You agreed with me.'

'I thought it was a place.'

'Well, it's not,' said Madge. 'I could have told you that, with or without my free map of the battlefields.'

'Why did Jim have the name of a French girl in his wallet?' said Ada, putting down her knitting. 'Why would he?'

The women said nothing, because they didn't know what to say. Their needles were growing hotter in their fingers. The hard wool was scratching their skin.

'It'll be something and nothing,' said Lizzie.

'Of course it will,' said Madge.

But Ada could already smell her cologne, and by the time the women had gone, their fingers aching, their heads ringing with the French name they'd never heard of, she could picture Solange Devaux; she could see her tiny pinched-in waist, her eyes that were deep and blue, and her small oval face that resembled Beatrice Crane's. How could he not fall in love with her?

Ada paced up and down. She held the piece of paper to her nose, to the light, tracing her fingertip over the words as if they might turn into an image, or into a voice that would speak to her in lilting broken English. She looked at herself in the mirror, her enormous eyes, she supposed, took up too much of her long narrow face, and then there were the tired-looking sockets, and her sharp (slightly crooked) nose. Ada wasn't naive, she'd heard stories, she'd heard the soldiers home on leave, standing around town, lighting cigarettes and boasting of their conquests. 'What's a bloke to do when it's offered on a plate?' They were a long way from home. Who would ever know?

* * *

'Did you know?' she asked Beatrice.

'No.'

'Will you write and ask your husband?'

'Ask him?'

'If he knows who this woman is. What was she to Jim? Do they all use prostitutes?' she said, closing her eyes as the word came out of her mouth.

Beatrice felt cold. She said nothing.

'If you don't write to him,' said Ada, 'I will.'

*   *   *

Lizzie couldn't sleep. She could hear the wind outside. She could see Tom in the trenches. A crunching of snow. Did he need a scarf? Or did he have his own French girl to keep him warm? Was he with her now? Rest and recuperation. That's what Jonathan had said. Perhaps he was in a small hotel. Like the one they had stayed in on their honeymoon, two shy youngsters, who had never spent a night away from home, locked nervously together in Room 17.

*   *   *

Madge didn't go to bed. The windows were rattling. She took her limp eiderdown and wrapped herself in it, lying on the sofa. The clock ticked loudly, so she got up and wrapped a cushion round it. Looking at the empty grate, she could see another fire burning and a girl with pliant hands was rubbing Frank's back, while he babbled on about their stinking bouillabaisse. Who had told him about bouillabaisse anyway? When had he eaten fish broth? Where? Who with? And why had he been so anxious to get back to the front? He wasn't well enough. He wasn't ready for it. His mind was somewhere else. It was melting.

*   *   *

Beatrice had already written to Jonathan. As soon as she'd seen the name in Jim's battered wallet, she'd written to ask him what to do. Can I tell her? Can't you break your promise? It would be better for her. Surely you can see that? But Jonathan hadn't replied and lying in bed she could hear his voice saying, *You must never tell, you must always keep your promise.*

* * *

The women watched the sky. The clouds were thin and grey.

'She must know something,' said Ada.

'Why must she?' said Lizzie. 'Do you think she's heard from Jonathan?'

'Probably. Captains send letters all the time. They've nothing else to do.'

'Do you think she'd tell us?' said Madge. 'About those Frenchwomen?'

'No,' said Ada. 'She'd keep her mouth shut.'

'Why?' said Lizzie.

'Because captains and sergeants encourage it,' said Ada. 'Don't look so shocked, because that's what I've heard. The men need to—well, you know . . . The army pay the women a wage. Every trench has its brothel.'

'I don't believe you,' said Lizzie.

'It's true all right,' said Madge. 'And I've a feeling my Frank would know his way there in the dark.'

'Like my Jim.'

'But not my Tom,' said Lizzie. 'He wouldn't.'

'He would,' they said in unison.

'You might as well face it,' said Madge. 'He'd be in there like a shot. They all would.'

* * *

It snowed for a week. The ground turned to stone and the reservoir had shards of ice floating on the surface like broken stepping stones.

Lizzie received a postcard from Tom. The women studied it, the picture, a row of khaki-clad soldiers on parade shouting, *'Are we downhearted? No! No! No!'* The words on the back. *Thanks for your letters. Hello, Martha. Hello, Harry. Hope you're being good for your mam. Cold here. Everything white. See you all soon, I hope. Your loving husband, Tom x.*

'He must be cold,' said Lizzie.

'He doesn't say much,' said Madge.

'Your loving husband?' said Ada. 'Why does he have to remind you?'

'He doesn't. Does he?'

'Looks like it.'

'Don't be cruel,' said Madge.

* * *

'What do we know about Beatrice?' said Ada.

'She's American,' said Lizzie.

'She's a good-looking American,' said Madge. 'And don't look at me like that, because you can't say that she isn't.'

'She used to sell postcards,' said Lizzie.

'And she ate out all the time,' said Ada. 'Funny. My niece works at Bradshaw's in town selling cards and paper and such, and all she has for her dinner is a bit of bread and dripping and she's happy with it.'

'But she isn't an American,' said Lizzie, biting the edge of her fingernail. 'Americans are different.'

'And don't we know it,' said Ada. 'She got married in a town hall. Who on earth would want to do that?'

'She might have been married before,' said Madge.

'Now, there's a thought.' Ada could picture Beatrice with a string of husbands, and all of them still living.

'She met Jonathan when he bought some of her cards,' said Lizzie. 'I remember that. I thought it was romantic.'

'It was quick,' said Ada. 'That's what it was.'

'But I do like Jonathan,' said Madge. 'I've always liked him.'

'Why are we talking about Beatrice?' said Lizzie. 'It's Tom I'm bothered about. Tom and those French girls.'

'But she might know about it,' said Madge. 'I'll bet Jonathan tells her everything.'

'Then let's ask her,' said Lizzie. 'It's eating me up. I want to know. We should just go over there and ask her.'

'No,' said Ada. 'We'll wait a while. That's what we'll do. We'll dig around and wait.'

* * *

Beatrice liked knitting. The feel of the wool through her fingers. The way it turned into something else. When she was knitting she had to concentrate, so it was hard to think of anything. She'd knitted as a child, scarves for her and Elijah, a pair of gloves that hadn't quite worked, the fingers were too thin, and they wouldn't go in, however hard you pushed.

'We should give ourselves a name,' said Lizzie. 'We could be The Anglezarke Army, or The Warrior Ladies, what do you think?'

Madge rolled her eyes. 'We don't need a name,' she said. 'How many times have I said this? Why do we need a name?'

'Was it cold in New York?' said Ada, looking up from her muffler. 'When you were selling your postcards, did you ever freeze?'

Beatrice stopped. 'We closed the open stall in the winter,' she said. 'We went inside, though there were never many visitors after fall.'

'You closed the stall?' said Ada. 'Was it yours to close?'

'Of course not. I just worked behind the counter, but I liked the work all right, I liked meeting people from all walks of life.'

'Like Jonathan,' said Ada.

'Yes,' said Madge. 'You were lucky there.'

'Was it a very short engagement?' said Lizzie.

'Long enough.'

'So you went and booked the town hall?' said Madge.

'That's right,' she nodded. 'You see, Jonathan had to get back here to work, we didn't have time for anything grander.'

'What was it like?' said Lizzie.

'The town hall? We had a lovely big room. We filled it with hothouse flowers and a friend of ours played the piano. It was a very special day.'

'So, why not a church?' said Ada.

'It would have taken too long,' Beatrice told her. 'Like I said, we just didn't have the time.'

Lizzie thought about her own wedding day. The

showers of rice and rain. Her father's arm trembling as he walked her up the aisle.

'Did your family get to meet him?' Lizzie asked.

'I don't have much of a family. No one to speak of. Haven't I told you this already? My father died in a house fire. My brother went to Chicago.'

'That's right,' said Madge, nodding. 'So he did.'

The snow began to fall. The windows were clogged with it. Beatrice talked with dry lips about her father's collections of birds. She didn't mind. They didn't seem real any more.

'The house was full of them. Beaks, claws, feathers. Their dusty eyes were everywhere.'

Lizzie shivered. She could almost see them. They were cocking their heads and screaming at her, like the rooks at the top of the farm. She started crying—it seemed she was always crying these days. She was thinking of Tom, his shotgun over his shoulder, bringing home a pheasant. The fields were full of them.

'It doesn't seem the same without Jonathan,' said Ada. 'This house. Does it feel too big without him?'

'It feels empty in the mornings,' said Beatrice. 'All that hustle and bustle, and all that English tea.'

'China,' said Madge. 'The tea comes from China.'

'Or Ceylon,' said Lizzie. 'It sometimes comes from there.'

'Don't you drink tea in America?' said Madge. 'What do you drink if you don't drink tea?'

'I like coffee,' said Beatrice. 'Good, strong coffee.'

'Well,' said Ada. 'You might speak English and have the same coloured skin and everything, but it's the little things that turn you into a foreigner.'

* * *

The snow kept falling. Beatrice waited for her letter, but even if he'd written, the postman was trapped at the top of the lane.

'Have you heard from him yet?' said Ada.

Beatrice shook her head.

'Did he ever mention the name Solange?'

'I've never heard that name before.'

'Name? So you knew it was a name?'

'A place,' she said. 'I thought it was a place.'

'Did he tell you anything else? Did he say anything about the brothel?'

'Brothel? No, of course not. He never mentioned such a thing.'

'I just want to know,' said Ada. 'I don't want you to put my mind at rest, it's too late for that; I'd rather know the truth.'

'Sure you do, and of course I understand,' said Beatrice, 'but perhaps it isn't what you think at all? This woman could be anyone. She could be someone's mother, a nurse, anyone.'

'A mother?' said Ada. 'Don't make me laugh.'

A few days later, the postman appeared, his face burnt crimson, his shoulders bent tight against the wind. Beatrice opened the letters in order. A bank statement. A postcard from Jeffrey. The letter from Jonathan. A coal bill.

Jeffrey had been injured. He was writing from a field hospital in Normandy. *'It's my right arm, so a nurse is writing this! I am cheerful, and not in any pain. The cold is worse than anything. The nurses keep our spirits up. Best wishes to you all, and hope to see you soon, from Jeffrey.'*

She felt sick. She opened Jonathan's letter. That handwriting. It made her stomach lurch.

My Dearest Beatrice,

I had no idea what was contained in Jim's effects, but I do know this. Just days before he died, I made a solemn promise not to tell a soul about Solange Devaux, especially not to Ada, and although I had already broken the promise by talking to you, I renewed it there and then, and there is no way on earth I would like any of it divulged, and especially not *to* Ada!

What good will come of it? You must simply deny all knowledge. I urge you. You are in England and far away. Surely denial is an easy thing to do? We must respect the wishes of the dead. Perhaps it's all we can do, and all they have left?

I will write again when I can.

Your Jonathan

So that was that. She folded the letter and put it with the rest, and then she changed her mind and slipped it into the drawer containing her underwear, beneath a pile of oyster-coloured camisoles.

* * *

Ada was in the shop when the postman appeared. He was panting and bitter cold. His fingers were bent. She pushed a cup of tea in front of him. A broken Bourbon biscuit.

'Just a coal bill? Is this all you have for me? Still,

I've had my telegram, so things can't get any worse.'

'That's true enough,' he said.

'What about Mrs Crane?'

'What about her? I don't deliver telegrams,' he said. 'I never touch those.'

'Did she get anything from France?'

He scratched his head. The tea had warmed him through. 'She did,' he told her, licking crumbs from his fingers. 'A letter, and a postcard from Jeffrey Woodhouse. I didn't recognise the hand. A nurse wrote it. He's injured. It's his right arm.'

'And the letter?'

'I can't see through paper,' he grinned. 'Though there's many a time I'd like to.'

'It was definitely from France?'

'Yes,' he said. 'That letter was as French as they come.'

*　　*　　*

Late in the afternoon, Ada changed into her best grey dress and dabbed her neck and wrists with rose water. She packed a basket of things from the shop. A tin of sliced pears and a fruit cake. She found two bottles of lilac wine. A small bar of chocolate.

'You can't take all that,' said Madge. 'It's like stealing from yourself. All those luxuries. Whatever are you doing?'

'I have a plan,' said Ada, tapping the side of her nose. 'Trust me.'

'Since when did you turn into a woman with plans?'

'Do you think she'll like pears? I could change

them into peaches.'

'So, you're a magician now as well?'

'I'll stick with the pears. Everyone likes pears. Even Americans.'

'All this is for her?'

'No. It's for all of us,' she said.

The snowflakes were the size of sixpences as Madge watched Ada go, her basket under her arm and her blue scarf trailing. Beatrice hesitated as she opened the door, she was more than a little surprised to see Ada standing on her own, but she managed to smile. It was seven o'clock, she'd been sewing, and a needle was still pressed between her fingers.

'I thought we'd treat ourselves,' said Ada, holding up her basket.

'You have snow on your eyelashes,' laughed Beatrice. 'You'd better come inside.'

She felt awkward. 'All these lovely things. What about the others?'

'I did ask,' said Ada sitting down. 'But they're busy.'

Beatrice poured the wine. It smelled like summer, and with the strange light from the snow, and the small lick of a fire, Ada looked like Nancy, and the talk made her think of the old times. The wine was sweet and thick and she could hear her voice slurring as they talked about Morecambe, how it seemed far away, a lifetime away, that grey-coloured tide, ear-shaped shells, and the Sand Pilot's landlord sipping whisky from his hip flask, doing card tricks for the children, before they fell asleep.

Ada refilled her glass. 'Do you have any pictures?' she asked.

'Of Morecambe? There's one just there, on the fireplace.'

'Of your old life. Where you came from. America?'

She shook her head. 'I brought nothing with me. Only my wardrobe. The basic essentials. You know, I did have pictures, but not many, and most of them were lost when I moved from Illinois.'

'In the house fire?'

'Yes, in the house fire.'

Ada stared down into her glass. 'I have some pictures of Jim. Thank goodness. Mind you, he looked self-conscious standing there in his uniform. Now they're all I have left. And I wonder how long it'll take before I need them, because I can't remember his face.'

'You'll remember.'

'And what about you? Do you have photographs of Jonathan?'

'Yes. He looks proud—kind of haughty. I'm not that fond of the pictures.'

'Do you keep them with his letters?'

'I have one framed in the bedroom. The rest are with his letters, yes.' She nodded towards the cabinet. 'It's like a collection,' she said. 'Letters, photographs, postcards.'

'Yes,' said Ada. 'We're all collectors now.'

The fire looked hazy. The snow was filling up the windows, and the wine was making her sleepy, hungry for the pears, and the chocolate.

'It's like a blizzard out there,' said Ada. 'I've never seen so much snow.'

Beatrice yawned. 'Shall we eat something?' she said. 'I have some boiled ham. We could have sandwiches, and then I could open the pears.'

'Yes,' said Ada. 'Let's do that.'

While Beatrice was in the kitchen cutting bread, Ada walked around the room, touching things. The candlesticks. An empty blue vase. The small smooth handles on the cabinet. She could feel her heart humming.

'Sandwiches.' Beatrice appeared with a tray. 'I'm starving. It's the wine. The wine always gives me an appetite, however much I've eaten.'

'Yes, I know what you mean,' said Ada.

After they'd eaten Beatrice opened the other bottle of wine. Her head was swimming. She looked towards the window. It was a slab of cold white and the glass was swollen.

'I can't imagine Jonathan fighting in this weather,' she said. 'How can he can see what's in front of his face?'

'Is it snowing in France?' said Ada. 'What did he say in his letter?'

Beatrice stifled another yawn. 'Nothing much. He didn't mention the weather.'

'Still, it must be cold.'

Beatrice held up her glass. She was giggling. 'This wine,' she said. 'Isn't this the wine that's supposed to give you such good dreams?'

'So they say. I don't dream very often, and I'm grateful for it.'

'I do like dreams,' said Beatrice. 'But only if they're pleasant.'

Ada rolled her eyes. 'I really should be going.'

The snow was so thick that the door wouldn't open.

'Stay here,' said Beatrice. 'There's plenty of room, and I'd like you to stay. Really. Just go ahead, find a bed upstairs and sleep.'

'All right, but we might as well finish this last bottle. It's not ten o'clock.'

'It isn't? I feel like I've been up all night. Not ten o'clock? Gee, are you sure?'

Beatrice was drunk and she soon fell asleep, her hands underneath her head, pressed tight together, praying under her ear. Ada was wide awake.

'Beatrice?' she tried. Then louder. *'Beatrice?'*

Nothing. Then an incoherent muttering. Ada stopped. Listened. The words didn't make sense; she was just talking in her sleep.

Ada went straight to the cabinet. She opened the drawer. Underneath a few tatty copies of *Woman's Weekly*, she found a scarf, a bottle of cologne and an old coffee tin. The letters were inside. She read them. There was nothing about the Frenchwoman. The prostitute. She looked quickly at the dates. She closed the drawer carefully as Beatrice stirred a little in her sleep.

She went upstairs. Hadn't Beatrice told her? Find a bed. Sleep here tonight. The walls were full of shadows and she could hear the snow sliding. A slow dripping sound.

She stopped in the doorway of what appeared to be Beatrice's bedroom. It was such a big room. You could walk right around the bed. There were screens decorated with scallop shells and a painting of a woman lying underneath some leafy trees. All these beautiful things to look at. Two large wardrobes. A dressing table. A set of six drawers.

She sat on the edge of the mattress. She pressed her face against the eiderdown. It smelled of soap flakes and stale salty skin. She walked to the head of the bed, pushing her hand into the pillows. Which was hers? His? All those days and nights she'd walked past this house. Jonathan and his father inside. Looking for their shadows. A voice. Would he see her? See how she'd pinned up her hair. The scarf she had borrowed. Practising a smile. Her best Sunday shoes.

The room was bright with moonlight and snow. She walked slowly. The floorboards didn't creak. There was a thick red rug to pad her feet as she instinctively chose the small drawer on the left. She put her hand inside and felt the cool shine of the silk, the rough-edged lace, and now her fingers smelled of lavender as she prised them underneath. It was easy. She waited a moment. Dug inside. Deep. She felt the rough edge of an envelope. Then a small paper package. She had found it.

FLYING

Brooklyn, New York
Winter, 1913

Towards the end of November, when the wind began to whip across the Atlantic and awnings were weighted down with sandbags, there were whisperings among the Coney crowd. Wiping off their greasepaint, drinking beer at Feltman's, sweeping the pier, frying onions, keeping warm, whatever it was they were doing, the words were always the same. *The angel is flying away.* Eli the elephant keeper took bets that she'd be gone before the start of next year. Others said spring. A few of the dancers who'd had enough of the scratchy costumes and shoes that made their ankles ache, said, 'Why should she wait? Why would anyone wait? She could be gone by the end of the week.'

The truth was, Beatrice Lyle had thought about leaving, but she still hadn't made up her mind.

'Just pack your bags and get out of here,' said Magda. 'You can't help who you fall in love with, an American, Englishman, or a man from darkest Africa. You have to follow your heart.'

'I've heard England is a wonderful place,' said Marta. 'It's genteel and dignified. The people are very polite.'

'I heard uptight,' said Magda. 'But who knows until you get there?'

Beatrice shrugged. It seemed so far away. What if it didn't work out? She'd known Jonathan Crane for just a month or so, but she had seen him every day.

'Every day, and you still get on with him?' said Magda. 'Some people would call that a miracle.'

'Or do you argue?' said Marta, her eyes flashing. 'Do you fight like cat and dog?'

'We argued once over a pair of theatre tickets,' said Beatrice. 'He wanted the stalls and I preferred the balcony.'

'Theatre tickets?' said Magda with a shrug. 'Tsk. Theatre tickets are nothing.'

'But do you really love him?' said Marta. 'Can you think of your life without him?'

'It's hard,' said Beatrice. 'I know I'd feel empty. Kind of lonely. I really can't explain.'

'So there you have it,' said Marta. 'You need

him.'

'I don't know,' said Beatrice. 'It would be easy to run after him, but what if I want to come back?'

'You could save up for a ticket,' said Magda. 'We'll still be here, collecting up the hoops.'

'We'd welcome you back with open arms,' said Marta. 'We'd never forget you. We'd be waiting here, like family.'

* * *

Night after night Beatrice thought of nothing else, lying alone in her room watching the shadows rippling over the walls, hearing the woman next door talking to her cat, and then the clopping horse going off to work, the blue in the sky, brightening, darkening to grey, and one less day to think about it.

'What's there to think about?' said Jonathan.

'I'll have nothing over there.'

'You'll have me. Won't I be enough?'

'Truthfully? I don't know. How do I know?'

'You love me?' he asked.

'Yes, but I'm used to being busy—working, and then spending time with friends.'

'There are women in the village. You'll make friends. Hell, I'll be your friend.'

'It's such a huge change. England.'

'We speak the same language,' he said. 'Well, almost.'

'And I like my job.'

He smiled and scratched his head. 'Well, that's something I can't say you'll be keeping. I don't think Anglezarke village is ready for the Angel of Brooklyn, and I don't think they ever will be.'

She never stopped thinking. Walking through the Bone Yard, eating lunch, listening to the wind whistling through the tracks. She thought about England, making her way along the cold hard stretch of dirty beach, the tide spewing all the season's debris, the candy-bar wrappers, cigar butts, paper cups. It was as if the sea had had too much of it. Shivering in her wings with the half-smile she used (she thought the angel was looking too serious these days), she thought about keeping house again. It reminded her of Normal. She thought about the scrubbing, chopping, sweeping. She pictured Joanna, panting at the stove, her arms spattered with angry red burns, her fingernails black with grate polish. And then there had been Mrs Oh, standing at the door, grinning, smelling of soap crystals, her tight blue-black hair damp with steam. Did England have its own Mrs Ohs?

* * *

'So, what's the worst thing that can happen?' said Nancy. They were sitting outside Franny's. The air was sharp and they were the only ones braving it. 'So hey, you might only get to Breezy Point before you change your mind, but you can always come straight back. You have money. All that money you saved from the book.'

'It's for my brother,' she said. 'In case anything happens. I want him to find me.'

'Find you? But does he know where you are? Where you might be going?'

'I'll write to him again.' She looked into her wine glass. Did people drink wine in England? Did they sit chewing the fat, looking at the ocean? The birds above their heads were screaming. They looked like silver missiles. 'I'll leave word. He might turn up one day.'

'I'll keep my fingers crossed for you.'

'Me too. So, what do you think of Jonathan?' Beatrice asked.

'I think he's a sweetheart, even for an Englishman. I know he'll be good to you. Believe me, I've watched him very closely, and observed him from afar. He passed my test with flying colours, though there were times when I wished he would fail.'

Beatrice sighed. The waves were clapping at the wall. 'I still don't know.'

But then, suddenly, she did. The day began with a dark streak of sky, and most of the sideshows were closed. The hot-food stalls were doing brisk business, warming people through with their twists of fried potatoes and tubs of steaming chowder. Jonathan had travelled to Port Washington. He was meeting a man who had something to do with his father's insurance business. He'd be gone for a couple of days. Beatrice was glad to have the time for herself.

'More thinking time?' smiled the tattooist. She was sitting in his ink-filled parlour, staring at the walls full of wide-mouthed snakes, mermaids and blue-edged angels, drinking hot black coffee and breathing in the steam.

'Sometimes I want to run away,' she told him. 'And sometimes, I don't.'

'What would you be running from?'

'I don't know. My wings?'

The tattooist poured himself more coffee. His

fingertips were stained pink and orange and blue. On the back of his hand, a swallow spread its wings from knuckle to knuckle.

'Your job isn't something you should be ashamed of,' he said. 'It's not something to run from. What you do, it isn't bad. It's merely—unusual.'

'I could only do it in Coney. And I keep thinking. I might be nothing without it.'

'I'll tell you this,' he said, 'I'm from Glasgow, and it's not so different there. On Saturday nights you'd think you were in the back end of Coney. We drink and brawl and sing with the best of them. Or the worst, whichever way you look at it. But, you know, if you have the right person by your side, it doesn't matter where you are in the world, you'll still feel at home.'

'And do you?'

'I feel more at home here than I ever did in Scotland.'

'Why?'

'I just fitted right in. No question. I felt accepted. Welcomed. But if I hadn't? I'd be working my way back over there and knocking on my ma's front door.'

'Did you fall in love?' she asked.

'I fell in love all right,' he said. 'But it wasn't with a woman. It was with Coney Island, New York, this fat stinking corner of America.'

She walked slowly down the boardwalk. Sometimes, it was hard to think that New York, and Coney, were only pieces of America. What about the rest of it? Why couldn't Jonathan bring his business over here? Didn't people in Brooklyn need some insurance? He would have his business and she would have hers.

Locked in her thoughts she didn't hear the commotion at first. The sound was ahead of her, but instead of voices, she heard the hungry gulls, screeching and crowing, circling the shoreline.

She began walking faster. The air was cold and there was a crowd up ahead. People were running in all directions, waving their arms. Mr Yip appeared.

'What is it?' she asked. 'What happened?'

'A woman,' he told her. 'She just jumped from the back of the ferry when it was landing at the pier. Smashed the back of her head. Now she's floating, dead, and they can't fish her out.'

'Who is it?' She could feel her voice shaking, feel her hands tightening into fists.

Mr Yip shrugged. 'I looked quickly into the water, but I've never seen her before,' he said. 'No one from your booth. A tourist probably. Who knows? It's a bleak time to visit, that's for sure.'

She felt calmer as she walked towards the milling crowd. When she reached them, she stopped. She could hear people saying, 'Her dress is caught up in the ferry.' 'We need a swimmer. A good strong swimmer.' 'Hell no, we need a lifeguard. What are we waiting for? Someone go fetch a cop.' She wanted to walk away. She wanted to tell the people to go home, to go back to their business, because the cops were there already, and what use were they staring down at someone's tragedy? But like most human beings, she was drawn to it. Standing at the back she could see nothing through the shoulders. A woman was crying. A man was saying, 'It's the jumping season. Heck, I've lived here seven years and we have two jumps a year from this ferry, it's really nothing to write home about, unless of course they live to tell the tale, and it's a strange way to end it, because it's not a guarantee. It's not like jumping from a building.'

Beatrice felt sick. She could feel the bile rising in her throat. In front of her some men had been pushed towards the side, and there was a gap, and a sharp acrid smell of burning coal.

'They're bringing her out,' said a man.

'Let's go back,' said his friend. 'Christ almighty, haven't we seen enough?'

The police were telling the crowd to move away. To give them more space. Someone had brought a stretcher and a blanket. Suddenly there was water running over their boots, and there she was, lying flat and heavy with oily salt water, her dress ripped to her waist, her leg black, her eyes still open. People covered their mouths and looked away. She was heavy. It was hard to get her up and onto the stretcher. They weren't fast enough with the blanket, and Beatrice saw her face. Then she started running.

* * *

At first she made no sense. Her skirt was full of vomit. She kept rubbing her hands over her face, through her hair, pulling at it.

'Tell me,' said Nancy. 'Is it Jonathan?'

Beatrice bent over, she was retching again. She was pummelling her feet. Whimpering.

'Has he left her?' said Celina. 'I'll kill him.'

Beatrice whimpered even louder. Eventually, she spoke.

'It was me. I killed someone,' she said.

'What?'

'You heard. It was all because of me. I killed her.'

'What are you talking about?' said Nancy, handing her a glass of water. 'You wouldn't hurt a fly.'

She was crying, bent at the waist. The water spilled across the floor and the glass cracked.

'Now look what you've done,' said Celina.

'So tell me, who's dead?' said Nancy. 'Who is it?'

Beatrice looked up. Her face was white, but her red-rimmed eyes were dark and it looked like someone had punched her. She took a few deep breaths.

'I don't know. They were dragging her from the water and then I saw her face, and I knew straight away why she'd done it.'

'You mean the suicide this morning?' said Celina. 'I heard about that.'

'It was her. The woman. The one who came to look at me. Do you remember her?'

'Oh, I remember,' said Celina. 'The wife.'

'She said I was killing her.'

Nancy stroked her face. 'Don't blame yourself, honey. It wasn't you. Not really. Look, who knows what she was thinking. People kill themselves for a hundred different reasons.'

'She's right,' said Celina. 'Maybe she couldn't pay her meat bill, or something.'

Nancy glared at her.

'No,' said Beatrice. 'It really was me. I know it was, for sure. The wings. The angel. The pictures. I didn't think I was causing all this pain. I should have known.'

'Don't let her ruin everything,' said Nancy. 'Come on, Celina's right. Perhaps she was unhinged?'

‘I can’t do this any more,’ she said. ‘Her husband came to see me. He sat on that chair and he fell in love with the image. Or he thought he was in love. He took the image home with him. It broke his wife’s heart and now she’s dead.’

‘Would you like a glass of brandy?’ said Celina. ‘That’s what I’ll do. I’ll go and find some brandy.’

*   *   *

She sat with Mr Cooper. He’d been crying. He couldn’t bear to see her so upset.

‘You’re too good for this business,’ he said, blowing his nose and sniffing into his handkerchief. ‘Didn’t I always say that? Perhaps I pushed you into it. I don’t know. I never meant to make you feel this bad.’

‘I need to go,’ she told him.

‘Yes, go. You must go. If that’s what you want, I won’t try and stop you. I’ll be happy for you. I’ll be waving you off at the dockside, with those long paper streamers, and I’ll miss you.’

‘What about your business?’

‘It’s almost December. The season’s done and dusted. I’ll find another angel for next year. She won’t be the real thing, but she’ll just have to do.’

‘Do you think I killed her?’ she asked.

He looked at her. He couldn’t lie. ‘I don’t know what to think,’ he shrugged. ‘I don’t know what to think at all.’

*   *   *

Soft with brandy, she went home where the room had a chill to it, and a bleak kind of light fell in squares across the furniture. Since meeting Jonathan she'd abandoned the blindfold, but now she wanted it back. It fitted tight around her head and kept out all the light. It was the only thing that would do. After looking in drawers, cupboards and underneath the bed, she had to make do with her pillow. She slept for hours, but it felt like a week. She woke up crying. They'd been watching her. The men on the chair. They had bulging eyes. They were laughing. Pointing. They were dressed in filthy clothes and she could hear someone crying, like a cat. When Billy opened the drape, they were all there, the wives, the girlfriends, they were weeping, hungry-looking children clinging at their skirts, but then one of them turned and she had something in her hand. What was it? A slingshot? A pistol? The women were going to kill her. She could see it in their eyes. She could feel it.

* * *

The *Brooklyn Daily Eagle* told them what was missing. The woman's name was Mrs Susan Ethel Wingate. She was twenty-nine years old. She jumped from the ferry at 11.05 a.m. Her husband, Mr Thornton Wingate of Queens, was distraught, but not surprised when the police informed him of the incident. He'd found a note that morning. It said, *'I just can't stand it anymore.'* When police asked him what this note might have meant, he said, 'Life. It was all too much for her. She was a fragile thing. Always was. But she was my wife, a mother, and I don't know how we'll cope without her.' Mrs Wingate left two small children, aged three and eighteen months. The children were staying with relatives.

* * *

'Why did you ever want to do it?' Jonathan asked. They were sitting on the empty beach, wrapped in blankets. A bottle of red wine had been sunk into the sand. In front of them a pile of papers were weighted down with stones.

'I had nothing else, no one else, and I was good at it,' she said. 'It didn't feel wrong.'

'You looked beautiful,' he told her. 'You were breathtaking, and I can't condemn you for it, because if it wasn't for the angel, perhaps I never would have seen you again. And yes, it was something that we'd heard about and something we wanted to see. Red-blooded Englishmen,' he smiled. 'Looking for the risqué part of Coney. We were there. We saw. What else can I say?'

'That the rest is history? You could always say that.'

'But is it?' he said. 'Do you really want to hang up your wings and follow me to England?'

She nodded. 'I'm more than sure,' she said.

'Then we'll say goodbye to the angel part of Brooklyn. If you want to be my wife, then you'll have to let it go. Every single part of it. You mustn't take anything with you. Not a postcard. A picture. A feather.'

'I don't want to,' she said. 'I want a new life. I've brought all the cards and pictures. We'll burn them all.'

'One last look?' he smiled, picking out a postcard from the pile. 'Can I?'

'You can,' she said. 'But I've seen enough to last

me a lifetime.'

*   *   *

The room smelled of flowers. It was full of them. The town hall had never seen so many winter blooms. They were a gift from Mr Cooper and his flower-store neighbours.

'But it's December,' said Beatrice, 'they must have cost you a fortune.'

'Church or no church, you have to have flowers at a wedding.'

They had a week to organise everything. Nancy and Marnie had taken her shopping and they'd seen a dress in a Brooklyn store window that stayed in their heads all day. It had been a perfect fit. Fifty seed-pearl buttons and a lace-covered yoke.

'Do I look like a bride in it?' she whispered.

'Sure you do,' said Nancy. 'It's white, and fancy, and it has a little train at the back, you look beautiful.'

'But do I look . . . ?'

'New? Virginal? Yes,' she smiled. 'You look as new as they come.'

Marnie made the cake, and after the ceremony they sat on the steps at the back of the town hall, and ate it with the champagne that Celina had brought in an ice bucket. The winter sun was shining.

'I'm a married woman,' said Beatrice, showing off her ring.

'You look married,' said Celina.

'Yes,' said Nancy. 'You'll soon be baking pies, and knitting socks, and everything.'

'Is it compulsory?'

'I told you,' said Celina. 'What did I say? You could have set up home with me, and you wouldn't have had to do a darn thing. We'd eat out all the time. I'd knit my own socks.'

'I want to knit socks,' said Beatrice. 'I want to do everything.'

* * *

While Jonathan was packing, Beatrice Crane spent her last day in America taking postcards and pictures of herself from Nancy and slipping them between the thin empty pages of a notebook.

'It's vanity,' she said.

Nancy handed her another one. 'Vanity, nothing,' she said. 'This angel was your life.'

'My old life.'

'Still. I'd want to take her with me.'

Beatrice nodded. She sat on her trunk with the lid pressed down, pulling at her lip. 'It's just a long stretch of water,' she said. 'How different can it be?'

'You'll write?'

'I'll write so often, England will run out of ink.'

'And then what?'

'I'll use pencils of course. Hundreds and hundreds of pencils.'

* * *

Leaning over the ice-cold rail it was like she was looking down on herself and it was her hand that was waving up to someone else. They were all there, Mr Cooper and Violet Murphy, Nancy,

Marnie, Celina. Marta and Magda were waving yellow streamers and causing a small stir of their own. Her arm was aching, and she was grateful when the ship began to move at last, and the people she had loved were merely dots, and all that was left was an outline.

ASHES

Anglezarke, England
December, 1916

The world was still white when Beatrice woke up, curled on her sofa, shivering. Her head was thumping and the empty bottles of wine stood on the hearth like two glass skittles. She could feel her hands shaking. She was parched and holding onto the sink, running a glass of water, when she first heard the banging on the door. She grimaced. The banging in her head was bad enough, and the cold; she could feel it round her ankles. If only she'd banked up the fire. Sitting at the kitchen table, she was too tired to answer the knocking. They'd come back, they'd have to. But when the banging moved to the back door, she suddenly felt scared. She swallowed. Was that the telegram boy? Was he telling her that Jonathan was dead?

She pushed herself up and groaned. The room was moving; the pans on the hooks, the jars of rice and flour, and all the willow-patterned plates were going round in circles. Still the banging continued.

A shot of cold air brought her round. The door was wedged in snow, and it wasn't the telegram boy, it was only Ada.

'But I thought you were here,' said Beatrice, rubbing her head. 'I thought you were sleeping upstairs.'

Ada was wearing black. She looked like a crow standing in the snow. Her eyes, usually so wide and pale, were like shining chips of jet.

'Well, she's not,' said a voice behind her.

Ada, Madge and Lizzie walked into the kitchen, stepping carefully. They had ice on their boots. Beatrice backed towards the warmth of the stove, she was rubbing her hands and smiling through her confusion.

'I've such a bad head,' she said. 'I'm a mess. I've just this minute woken and I must look something awful.'

The women said nothing as they stood around the table. Lizzie was rubbing her forehead. Madge had her arms folded. Suddenly, Ada was reaching deep into a pocket, pulling something out, skimming a package over the table.

'So, now we know who you are,' she said, breaking the silence. 'Who you really are.'

She didn't have to open it. Beatrice, her heart pounding, knew exactly what it was, and she could feel the floor tipping, gaping, and all her life pouring through the holes.

'It seems like such a long time ago,' she said, trying to keep herself together, putting water into the kettle. 'It was a different time. A different place altogether.'

'But you have nothing on,' said Lizzie, sitting down. 'Nothing on at all.'

'They're just pictures,' Beatrice swallowed, not wanting to turn round and face them. She looked through the window but the snow made her eyes ache. 'Some might call it art.'

Ada laughed. 'Art? Is that your excuse?'

'I don't need an excuse,' she said. She felt weary and her head was throbbing, but she busied herself making tea. 'Some might say they've seen more flesh in a gallery.'

'A gallery? I've been to a gallery,' said Ada. 'And there might be some flesh now and then, but those pictures are different, and they're not something you'd pass around through grubby fingers for a cheap kind of thrill.'

Beatrice spilled the tea leaves. 'I've seen worse.'

'Worse? Worse? Just listen to yourself,' said Ada. 'Is this what you Americans get up to? Has your dirty captain husband been passing them around?'

'Of course not. Never.' She shook her head, shocked. 'He doesn't even know.'

'Know what?' said Ada. 'That he went and married a whore? That you took off all your clothes and stood bold as brass in front of a camera? Shameless.'

'Poor Jonathan,' said Madge.

'No, I mean he doesn't know that I brought the pictures to England. He thinks I burned them all.'

'Jonathan knows about the pictures?' said Lizzie. She looked pale, and grateful for the cup of tea that Beatrice pushed in front of her. 'I don't believe it. I don't.'

Ada shook her head. 'What did I tell you about captains? They're all at it.'

'At what?' said Beatrice.

'What do you think?'

Beatrice sat down. She could see the first picture on the pile. *The Angel Would Like You to Stay.* It looked so familiar and she could feel the weight of those wings on her shoulders, and now she didn't know whether to smile, or to cry. She looked away, tired of pretending. It was snowing again.

'It's how we met,' she said at last, and suddenly she didn't care if they knew.

'You sold him those dirty pictures?' said Lizzie. 'Those were the postcards?'

'Yes. No.'

'What?' said Ada. 'Yes? No? Which is it?'

Beatrice shook her aching head. She could see the bottle of aspirin standing on the cupboard, but she couldn't move to get it.

'Go on, tell us,' said Madge.

'Yes,' said Ada. 'I'd like to know how a respectable young man goes to America and comes back with a whore.'

Lizzie flinched.

'I'm not a whore,' Beatrice whispered. 'Of course I'm not.'

'She's not,' said Lizzie, looking relieved. 'See. I told you. I knew she couldn't be that.'

Ada shook her head. 'How do we know? You're a liar. How do we know that you're not the same as that Frenchwoman I found in Jim's wallet?'

'She wasn't a whore,' said Beatrice.

'So, who was she?'

'I can't tell you. I promised.'

'More lies,' said Madge.

'No, it's in the letter,' Lizzie blurted. Then she blushed. 'We read the letter. It said she made a promise. They both did.'

'I don't care about promises,' said Ada. 'I want to know about the whore my husband was lying with before the Germans got him. Is that so much to ask?'

Beatrice licked her lips. Her teaspoon was rattling. When she looked down at her hands she was surprised to see them looking so still. It felt like they were jumping.

'He didn't lie with her,' she said. 'None of them did.'

'So, enlighten us,' said Madge.

Beatrice looked around the kitchen. The jars of rice and flour. The empty marmalade pot. Everything the same. She looked at the women and took a deep breath. They were only women. That's all they were. She spoke carefully, and slowly. It was becoming hard to think straight.

'You took the letter and read it, so you know I made a solemn promise, and I won't break that promise, but still, I want to say that Solange Devaux was a good woman, and she did not take advantage of your husbands.'

'What about you?' said Ada.

'What about me?'

'Did you take advantage?'

She shook her head in bewilderment. 'Of course not. However could you think it?'

Ada snorted. 'Because we've seen the pictures,' she said, banging down her hand and making Lizzie jump. 'They're here on the table. We have proof.'

Suddenly, Beatrice felt stronger. She took a deep breath. 'Just because I posed for some photographs once upon a time, it doesn't mean to say that I prostituted myself.'

'Listen to her,' said Ada. 'All airs and graces, and a fancy way of talking, when underneath those clothes she's nothing but a trollop.'

Lizzie began crying, softly into her hand. 'You're beautiful, so beautiful, and they're all in love with you, aren't they? My Tom. He could never take his eyes off you.'

'That isn't true.' Beatrice reached towards her. 'No.'

'And you never tell lies,' said Ada. 'Do you?'

Beatrice shook her head. 'I don't. These pictures belong to me,' she told them. 'They're private. I never meant for you to see them. For anyone here to see them.'

'So, who has seen them?' said Madge.

Beatrice shrugged. 'I don't know. Lots of people.'

'Who?' Lizzie looked like she was going to be sick.

'Customers in America. People who came to the stall.'

'I can't believe it,' Lizzie moaned. 'How could you do such a thing, Beatrice? All those eyes on you? It just isn't right.'

'But who's to say it isn't right?' said Beatrice. She felt cold. She wanted to snatch up the pictures and stuff them into the packet because they were hers and they meant something to her.

'Well, of course it isn't right,' said Madge. 'What decent Christian woman would want to take off all her clothes and parade around in a pair of angel wings pretending that she's holy.'

'Not holy,' said Beatrice. 'I never meant to look holy.'

'It's a sin,' Lizzie breathed.

'It's a picture,' said Beatrice. 'That's all they are, they're pictures.'

'Just tell me,' said Lizzie, her wet chin quivering.

'With your hand on your heart, did you touch my Tom?'

'No. Of course not. Never. I didn't touch any of them. I promise you. On Jonathan's life, I promise you.'

'Then we should go,' said Lizzie, getting up. 'I believe her.'

'You just *want* to believe her,' said Madge.

'Look, I am truly sorry if the pictures offended you,' said Beatrice. 'You were never meant to find them.'

Ada reddened. 'I came across them by mistake,' she said. 'And I'm bloody glad I did.'

'So, there you have it,' said Beatrice quietly.

Madge moved in closer to where Beatrice was sitting. She'd been thinking about Frank. His talk of floating angels and the twins. Had he seen these pictures? Had he touched them?

'So, there we have what?' said Ada. 'A liar? A traitor? Who do you think you are? Flouncing around. Ruining our lives. Look what you did to poor Mary's mother. You broke her heart, and at her own daughter's funeral; you gave her the shock of her life, how could you?'

'It wasn't like that,' said Beatrice.

'It was,' said Ada. 'I saw it. I was there.'

'Then I'm sorry.'

'Did you hear that?' said Ada. 'If she's saying sorry, she must have done something to be sorry about.'

'No. I didn't mean—' She rubbed the back of her neck. All these words. All this talking; it was never going to make any difference. She wanted them to go.

'Mean what?' said Madge. 'What didn't you

mean?'

'Anything,' said Beatrice.

There was a sharp gust of wind and the door blew open, suddenly filling the room with an icy blast of air.

'You always looked so pure,' said Madge, shivering. 'But you're dirty. Filthy dirty.'

Lizzie had her eyes closed. She could feel the snow flying through the kitchen; all at once she could see Tom, her Tom, and he was laughing at her, and perhaps they were right about Beatrice?

'Look,' said Beatrice, walking towards the open door. 'Let me close this and we'll have some more tea, and I'll tell you how it was. About my life in New York. About my life before New York. You'll know everything, and it won't seem so bad after that.'

But now Lizzie was on her feet, the blood had drained from her face, she could still see Tom, and now his trousers had dropped around his ankles, his hands were on Beatrice's perfect-looking breasts; they were all over her.

'They were right,' Lizzie said, walking across the room, suddenly finding a voice. 'You don't belong here. This is Jonathan Crane's house, and you don't belong. Get out!' She gave Beatrice a push and her bare feet went sliding onto the ice as Lizzie slammed the door behind her. Standing with her back to it, she looked exhilarated. Exhausted. The women were breathing heavily. They were panting, open-mouthed. The kitchen was silent after that.

*   *   *

Sitting at the table they watched the clock, the black hands shuddering towards the next number. The package was still on the table. The teapot was warm.

'She'll be knocking in a minute,' said Madge.

'We'll have to let her in,' said Lizzie.

'I suppose so,' said Madge.

'She'll be freezing,' said Lizzie, calm now, and worried. 'She didn't have a coat, or her boots.'

'She'll have run off somewhere,' said Ada. 'She'll be sitting with Lionel, drinking his tea and telling more lies.'

Lizzie looked relieved. 'Do you think so?'

'Oh yes,' said Ada. 'Definitely.'

For half an hour they sat at the table and waited. Ada started humming. They didn't know what else to do.

'I don't feel right,' said Lizzie. 'My head hurts.'

'She'll be packing her things tomorrow,' said Ada. 'She can't stay here.'

'Not now,' said Madge. 'Not now we've seen what she is.'

Eventually Ada opened the back door. The wind caught her off guard, the air was white, dizzying, and so thick it was hard to see your hand in front of your face. Taking a step back, she wiped her eyes and peered into the ice. Silence. She opened her mouth, she was going to call out, but the snow tasted bitter on her tongue and her voice was lost in the fug of it. Through the shifting white she could just make out the wide clumping shape of the house on the opposite corner, and the tall crooked trees. Already numb with cold, she took a step down and stopped as the air suddenly cleared and the wind tugged the mound at the bottom of the steps, revealing a hand, a piece of blue sleeve and a startling red bloom. Ada closed her eyes to it. She felt faint. Perhaps the snow was playing tricks? The harsh light. The cold. But Lizzie had come up behind her crying out, 'No! Oh my God, just look at her.'

Madge was there. She was gripping hard on the doorframe.

'She must have fallen on the ice. Hit her head.'

'But I pushed her,' Lizzie trembled.

'No, Lizzie,' said Ada, watching a new fall of snow wrapping up the fingers. 'Poor Mrs Crane must have slipped.'

* * *

The women tidied up the kitchen and left the back door open. They took the package. The letters. They went out the front way, checking that no one else was about. Arm in arm, they looked towards the sky. It was snowing again. It was dropping thick and fast. It was treacherous.

'Look at it,' said Ada, pulling up her collar. 'It's coming down in feathers.'

* * *

That night they burned the package. They sat and watched the flames licking around the wings, her face, her small outstretched hands, until there was nothing in the grate, but a fine grey powder that was still warm when Ada swept it up, into her pan, throwing it out into the yard, where the wind quickly took it.

ACKNOWLEDGEMENTS

I would like to thank Mum, Simon and Emily. Jon Glover. My agent David Miller. All the team at Chatto, with special thanks to Poppy Hampson and Alison Samuel.

And to my dad, the late Harry Jenkins, who taught me that all things were possible.